BEAUTIFUL ROSE

ELIXIR BILLIONAIRES

VIKKI JAY

Copyright © 2021 by Vikki Jay

All rights reserved.

No part of this book may be reproduced in any form or by any electronic or mechanical means, including information storage and retrieval systems, without written permission from the author, except for the use of brief quotations in a book review.

This is a work of fiction. The names, characters, incidents and places are product of the author's imagination. Any resemblance to actual people, places or events is purely coincidental.

❦ Created with Vellum

For my love,
I couldn't have done it without you, babe.

AUTHOR'S NOTE

Dear Reader,

This book was previously published as a duet, Beautiful Rose and Loving Rose. But now, you can enjoy the complete love story of Zander and Rose without any interruption.

-Happy Reading.

1

ROSE

My fingers run across the ergonomic keyboard as I touch-type the latest code while shifting my gaze between the two monitors. On one black screen, the chemical elements get attached and removed in the large cyclic organic compound. On the other screen, I glance through the report that summarizes the effects of the potential drugs developed by these modifications.

A knock on my door startles me, and I jump in my seat. Oscar Hawthorne, chief of staff at Elixir Inc. and my boss and friend, peers at me.

Oscar takes a few steps into my office. "I thought you were off today, Rose. Aren't you working over the weekend for the live release of your code? Is someone from your team supporting you?"

Heat climbs up my neck, and I rub it through the thick flannel collar of my shirt as Oscar hammers me with questions. My gaze jumps from his perfect face to the cursor blinking on the computer screen.

"You know, I...work best alone." I hate giving him the same bland response every time and busy myself with adjusting the perfectly aligned monitor to hide the humiliation that is likely palpable on my face.

A moment passes, but I don't look up. I'd hate to see the disappointment on his face.

"What are you working on?" He perches on the chair to my left. Placing his beloved silver Zippo lighter on the table, Oscar peers at the monitor.

Scooting to the edge of my seat, I turn the screen, ensuring he has a better view.

"I've developed a program that simulates chemical synthesis and generates results on the side effects and drug efficiency. It's using the top three international drug databases to map the information." I glance sideways to see if he's following the discussion.

A proud smile lights his face. "That's amazing, Rose!"

Giving my computer screen one last look, he settles back in his chair.

"Did you reconsider the promotion?"

"I… I can't take it, Oscar. I'm happy being a data scientist. The new position you're offering involves having direct reports beneath me. That requires a lot of…interaction."

Glancing up, I notice his gaze glued on me, most likely wondering what twenty-six-year-old engineer denies a promotion because it involves talking to people. But he surprises me.

"We can always redefine a role more suited to you."

"It would be unfair to other employees who can"—I sweep my hand to the side—"do much more." And by much more, I mean not hiding behind computer screens during discussions, their blood not running cold at the mention of presentations, or them not quaking in their shoes whenever someone calls their name in a meeting.

Thankfully, Kristy sashays into my office, looking pretty as always in her teal A-line dress and stilettos and putting a halt to the uncomfortable discussion.

"Didn't I tell you he'd love it?"

"Why do you get to see everything first, even though I'm the boss?" Oscar leans back in his chair before crossing his arms over his chest.

"You might be the boss, but I'm the roomie. The best friend."

He shakes his head before getting up. "We have a lunch reservation at Giovanni's. If you're both late, I won't wait for thirty fucking minutes like last time."

Kristy makes a funny face behind Oscar's back before following him out of my office.

LUCKILY, today we managed to reach Giovanni's, one of the most famous Italian restaurants in Cherrywood, on time.

"So, what's new with the management?" Kristy asks Oscar as the waiter brings our drinks. "Is Zander Teager's trip confirmed?" I settle back in my chair at the reserved corner table in the back of the restaurant.

Oscar lightly nods, his gaze focused on reading the label of his soda can.

"You don't have to be so tight lipped. It's not like his travel is a secret."

I bite my lip, trying to hide the creeping smile. If Kristy wants something, even a small piece of information, she'll get it, no matter how.

Oscar shakes his head. "I don't like gossip, Kristy. You know that."

"What's the gossip here? I'm just curious. None of the Teagers have visited Cherrywood since any of us joined." She turns in her seat toward me. "You tell me, Rosie. Aren't you curious?"

Their gazes rivet on me as I take a while to answer and then hesitantly nod. "Has Mr. Teager ever been to Cherrywood?" I ask.

"Yeah. When the Teagers first purchased the office property, all three of them drove down to Cherrywood. That was when I joined the group." Oscar pauses before taking a sip from his soda can. "Since we're on the subject, I wanted to run something by you, Rose." He rakes his hand through his neatly trimmed beard, something he often does when he's uncertain, and that only escalates my anxiety. "Zander has requested a meeting with senior managers. I'd like you to be there."

"But—"

Before I get a chance to decline the offer, Oscar interrupts me. "I know it's outside your comfort zone and also your job description, but I'd really like Zander to know we have you here." He tilts his head to the side, waiting for my answer.

When I don't reply immediately, Kristy's hand lightly presses on mine under the table. I glance up at her, and she gives me an encouraging smile. Something she's continuously been doing since we were kids.

"Forget it—" Oscar starts to backpedal.

"I'll be there." I try hard to ignore the quivering in my stomach and focus on the proud faces of my friends.

The waiter brings our pizza, and I welcome the distraction

I'm pulling a slice of the warm cheesy bread when Oscar says, "Zander will know what an important asset you are to his company, Rose. I'm proud to have you on my team."

This is something he tells me a few times a week. I don't know what I'd have done without these friends and this life in Cherrywood. They have accepted me with all my flaws, and I never want to lose the stability I've finally found in my life.

. . .

AFTER A QUIET HOUR POST LUNCH, Lily from Kristy's team asks if I can look at her latest code.

I skim through it as she's perched on a chair next to me. Her tapping fingers on the table break my concentration every once in a while.

When I finally lean back in my comfy office chair, she asks, "What do you think?"

I meet her excited gaze as she bounces on her seat. "You ran it through our testing software successfully. Why are you asking me to recheck?"

Hearing my words, her eyes widen in surprise.

Was I too blunt?

I'm about to apologize when she says, "You catch bugs that our software never flags. Oscar has specifically asked us that no code goes in live release without being reviewed by you."

"Oh." This is news.

"We all call you the bug detector." Her shoulders bunch a tiny bit, and her lips part in an amused smile.

Bug detector. That doesn't sound too bad.

"So, you don't mind when I find an error in your work?"

"No, I like it. I learn a lot from your feedback."

"Oh. Okay." I wipe my hands on my jeans before fixing my glasses. My heart calms knowing people don't take me as a know-it-all, contrary to what I sometimes think. Although after over three years, I still can't believe my colleagues want my opinion on their work.

The rest of the day goes by fast. I do a few more code reviews and update a presentation for one of my team members.

Finally, my cell phone buzzes with the reminder that it's time to leave for the day.

After turning it off, I follow my daily routine. I power off the computer and check the water level in the moisture sensor of my small bowstring hemp plant. After closing the windows, I give my office a once-over and quickly clean the table using a moist paper towel.

At last, I place my wireless headphones around my neck and my backpack over my shoulders before turning off the light.

I amble toward Kristy's office, and my gaze lands on a picture of the Teagers on the cover of an international magazine.

Oscar's words revisit me. *"I just want Zander to know we have you here."*

I look again at our CEO, a small smile on his lips that leaves a dimple on his left cheek.

Do I want him to know I'm here?

Do I want anyone to know I'm here?

2

ZANDER

I enter the hotel room in this small town of Cherrywood. Looking around at the beige walls that I'll call home for the next few days, I sigh at the sterility of it all. Collapsing onto the mattress, I call my brothers.

Zach picks up after a few rings, and I can barely hear his greeting over the loud background noise.

"Where are you?" I almost yell into the phone so they can hear me.

"I decided to take baby brother clubbing. He needs to learn to have some fun," Zach drawls. "Although I must say, St. Peppers has lost some of its shine since Zander Teager, the sexiest bachelor, has been away."

"It's only been a few hours since I've been out of St. Peppers. Or are you just upset that you've been dethroned from the sexiest-bachelor-in-town title by your big brother?" My body shakes as I suppress the burgeoning laughter, knowing my brother doesn't take jokes, especially those at the expense of his image, too well.

"Grow up, bro. I'm happy those magazines are no longer following me with a camera on my face."

I don't believe him for a minute but still let his comment slide.

The phone is pulled away from Zach, and I hear my youngest brother's stutter. "How's-s Cherrywood-d? S-same or any different?"

"So far, things don't look too different."

"You ready to drop t-the big news-s tomorrow?" Zane asks.

They must have stepped out of the busy club, as the background noises fade significantly.

"Yes. Let's see how it goes."

I end the call, knowing my brothers deserve an occasional fun night.

After an early dinner, I amble toward the grand terrace attached to my hotel room. I place a glass of whiskey on the circular glass table and my laptop on the gray couch before walking toward the railing.

How will my staff in this whimsical town react after hearing the big news? Maybe it's not the best idea to break the news of firing employees on the day they meet the CEO for the first time. A cell phone ringing interrupts my musing.

"Tell me you haven't already fallen in love with my town."

A deep chuckle leaves me at hearing Oscar's excitement. Cherrywood is partly Oscar's town. Established by his great-great-great or some of those grandfathers, a major portion of the business in this town is controlled by Hawthorne Estate.

"That depends on how tomorrow goes. Are we all set?"

"Yes, we meet at eight and don't be late." That smartass ribs me.

"Isn't this something you should be telling your team? They're the ones meeting the CEO for the first time," I comment while walking back to my drink.

"As you say, Mr. CEO. Have a good night's sleep. We have a long day tomorrow."

With a smile on my face, I flop down on the couch and

take a sip of the single malt whiskey. I fire up my laptop and go through some of the emails as the light night air hits my face.

After coming inside my room, I place the empty glass on my nightstand and change into sweatpants before getting under the covers. Quiet nights alone are usually my time to reflect upon life, my day, and ponder about what's waiting for us in the future. So many thoughts and memories flash across my mind. My brothers and me working in our company headquarters at St. Peppers in those early days. We three driving down to Cherrywood, scouting locations for our research division.

Four years ago, when we started Elixir, no one had imagined that we'd someday be the largest growing pharmaceutical company in the country. A year after we opened our main office in St. Peppers, we were able to setup our research division in this small town. But none of that success was handed to us on a silver plate. We have worked hard for every dime. We were boys who had seen too much too soon.

As they do every night, my thoughts drift to those early dark days. I try to bring them back to now, when things are simpler, safer. But I know it won't be easy. Tomorrow is the anniversary of the day when, years ago, our lives changed in ways we never imagined. It's also the death anniversary of the woman who taught me an early childhood lesson: this world is a savage place and it preys on the weak.

And I have taken a vow to never be in that helpless position ever again.

As soon as I hit the pavement for my run, I'm greeted by the beautiful morning. Mixed hues of red, orange, and gold paint the sky as the sun eagerly rises from the mountains. It'll be a heavenly experience to go cycling on these rough terrains. My favorite workout garage band buzzes in my ears as my feet hit the ground on the way back to the hotel. I tell myself I should visit Cherrywood more often. Not to my liking, this is only my second trip in this town. The first was before the office was even up and running.

I look around as the small town slowly wakes up. Smoke rises from the chimneys, shops open and the line outside the local cafe continues to grow. Everything mundane yet a bit magical.

Giving a final glance at my surroundings, I enter the hotel building and return to my room. After taking a quick shower, I open the closet and my hands, due to some reason, halt for a beat at the tie rack before I pull out the cherry-colored tie.

Finally, I'm all ready and out of the hotel. I open the door of the white rental SUV and stop dead in my tracks. My eyes focus on the ornament hanging in the rearview mirror. Small pink roses made from something soft, like velvet, are woven in a circular ring. My legs shake, and I tighten my grip on the door to avoid falling as memories flash through my mind.

"Aren't they pretty, my boy?"
"They are, Mommy! Beautiful. Just like you. Rose is my favorite flower because it's named after you." The kid who looks like me runs around the garden filled with rose bushes.

"Fuck." I squeeze my eyes, trying to push the mental images away.

"Get ahold of yourself, Zander." My voice quivers.

I shake my head, fighting through the haze of nightmares, and pull that shitty shiny thing and throw it out of the car without even noticing where it lands. Once I get inside, I fix the mirror displaced by my jerky movements and take a deep breath.

Fuck. It's already seven forty-five. I hate being late.

With a hammering heart, I start the engine, program the address on the GPS, and drive toward the company office. I speed on the way, and a few minutes past eight, I'm in front of the building reception. I give a nod to the receptionist, who stands as she watches me marching toward the opening elevator door.

When the elevator car reaches the fifth floor, I find two men punching the call buttons with full force. When I step out, they look up expectantly before their hopeful expressions die.

Okay. I hadn't hoped for flowers or anything, but I was expecting my staff to greet me with at least a smile.

"Zander, you're here." Oscar joins me and the other two men in the lobby. He introduces me to the two interns before leading me to his office. "Sorry, we're little distracted," he explains.

"What's the matter?"

"We're unable to find Rose, our lead data scientist. She should be somewhere in the building."

Unexpected panic seizes my brain upon hearing her name. *Rose.*

What the fuck?

Is nature playing some sick joke on me? Every year on this day, I try so hard to keep myself away from this word, this name. But today, it seems there's no escape.

Unbeknownst to my state, Oscar continues, "We had a new software's live release this weekend, and she was in the office. Now we can't get ahold of her. Security confirmed that she hasn't checked out of the building."

"What can I do?" I ask, only after I'm sure my breathing

has returned to normal and I'm not going to sound like a squeaky teenager.

I try to loosen my muscles, which have bunched in the last five minutes. Even if I'm uneasy, there's no way I can ignore any of my employees, especially an assiduous one, from the way Oscar speaks.

"Look around. That's what we've been doing for the last ten minutes."

I nod and exit his office.

Releasing a heavy breath, I look around the corridor and hustle toward a row of conference rooms. I open each door and peek inside but find nothing. When I exit out of the empty coffee corner, my gaze lands on the small door labeled *Office Supplies* in a mounted gold label. I turn the knob, expecting it to be locked, but it opens with a soft squeak.

The small room is dark with only a stream of dull sunlight filtering through the small vent. I open the door wider, and it takes my eyes a few seconds to adjust before I spot the light switch. When I flip it up, there's faint swishing sound behind me.

Swiftly turning around, I find a small frame dressed in a green flannel shirt, jeans, and red Converse, bunched in an old two-seater leather couch.

Her face is turned away from me, hiding in the backrest, but then she turns on the couch, which isn't quite big enough for her to move around on.

On reflex, I take a step in her direction. Instead of falling face-first onto the floor, she lands in my arms.

Her face squishes against my neck, and I feel the press of her eyeglasses on my chin. My grip on her tightens in an attempt to support her, and she stills in my arms for a beat before struggling to get away.

I immediately let go, as she scampers until her back hits the front panel of the couch. I shift back, trying not to scare her further.

The young woman fixes her red-framed glasses before looking up at me.

Fuck.

My heart stops the moment those blue eyes meet mine—it's the deepest blue I've ever seen. Her eyes almost shine behind the red frames. There's something in her gaze that sucks all the air out of my lungs, and I'm struggling to breathe. Her gaze drops the next second, and only then am I able to take in the next breath.

What the heck was that?

"You must be—" I chew the insides of my cheek. How can I finish the sentence without panicking and also not coming off as a weirdo? "—who I'm looking for."

A *V* forms on her forehead as she furrows her brows.

At the very second, a redhead accompanying Oscar rushes into the cramped space. "Rosie. Thank god we found you. Are you all right?" I get up and make way for the new arrival as she fusses over the woman I found sleeping on the couch.

Standing by the door, Oscar calls someone, letting them know we've found the missing woman. But my gaze doesn't waver from the two girls as the redhead leads the couch girl out of the room.

My gaze remains on her as she passes by me. And then when she glances at me over her shoulder, her eyes meet mine and the odd spark hits me again.

Judging by the way her eyes widen and the *V* on her forehead deepens, I know she felt it too.

3

ZANDER

The two women from before enter the conference room, and they couldn't be any more different from each other.

I watch as the redhead glides into the room. There's a wide smile on her face as her long legs, covered in a tight gray pants suit, slide onto a chair across from me on the other side of the table. The way she sits tall, shoulders pushed back, leaves no doubt that she carries herself with great self-esteem.

And then there's couch girl, who's unlike any girl I've seen. She takes the chair next to her friend and places a laptop in front of her on the table. And immediately opens the flap before pulling on the sleeves of her flannel shirt, which is buttoned up all the way to the collar. The loose-hanging fabric eats up her frame, and it's hard to make out anything about her. But it's her face, her innocent, devoid of any makeup face. She can't be more than twenty-five, which surprises me. This is a senior management meeting, after all.

Her continuous fidgeting makes it obvious that she wants to be anywhere but here. I glimpse a hint of pink on her cheeks, a shade I've never seen before.

Unlike every eye in the room, which is fixed on me, hers are focused on the laptop screen. Her shoulders are slouched forward, like she just wants to be invisible.

"Zander, meet Kristy Asher, one of our senior managers, and Rosemary Marlin, our tech wizard. Rose holds a PhD in computer science, and all of our software goes through her keen eyes before a live release. I've requested her to join us in this meeting." Oscar's warm voice is filled with pride as he makes the introductions.

My nod is returned by Kristy's enthusiastic smile but goes unacknowledged by the couch girl.

The door to the conference room opens softly, and after giving Oscar a gentle nod, two guys pull a small food cart inside. They arrange coffee, bagels, and pastries on a side table.

Upon my request, Oscar has arranged breakfast for the group. "Everyone, please dig in," I say. "I must admit, those cinnamon rolls are quite addictive."

The managers chuckle at my remark, and in groups of two, they amble toward the breakfast table.

"Zander, can you give me a few minutes? I need to have a word with Rose." Oscar is already up from his chair, and couch girl's wide eyes trace his movements before she vacates her seat in a rush and follows him out of the conference room. Oscar closes the glass door behind him, effectively preventing anyone from hearing their conversation.

Uneasiness and anxiety thrum in my chest as I watch Oscar talking to her. His shoulders are bent forward, his stance friendly. Unlike in the room, she meets his gaze and shakes her head to whatever he's saying.

My control snaps when he places a hand on her shoulder.

I close the door behind me and join them outside. "Is everything all right?" His hand on her shoulder drops.

"Yeah," Oscar replies.

A weird relief hits me when I see that he's not irritated by my interruption; instead, concerned.

"Unlike you, Rose isn't a fan of cinnamon rolls." He smiles, but the girl's face remains impassive. "Are you sure I can't order something else for you?"

The extent of Oscar's concern for this woman's breakfast confuses me, but we've been friends for a long time for me to know that he doesn't do things without a reason.

"I saw a café down the street," I chime in. "We can place an order for you, Dr. Marlin."

With her eyes glued to the floor, she whispers, "Please, you don't… have to call me doctor, and please don't bother. It's all right. I…prefer a very…um, precise breakfast anyways."

I watch as her fingers tug the cuffs of her shirt, her knuckles turning white. Her almost scared reaction surprises me, but the nervous lilt in her voice does something funny to my chest. I'm almost tempted to rub it away.

"That's no problem, Ms. Marlin." My words come out overly tender.

I search for the café on my phone and place a call. When I ask the female barista about a special breakfast order, she readily agrees.

"We can deliver the breakfast in thirty minutes to your office, sir. We have smoothies, oatmeal with soy milk, French baguette sandwiches—what are you looking for exactly?"

"Can you please give me a second?"

I repeat some of those breakfast specials to the couch girl.

"I'd like a simple omelet. Um, half onion and half tomato. And, um…cooked in two teaspoons of butter," she replies, startling me once more with her words.

She runs her sweaty palms over the denim of her jeans.

"Can you, um… please also ask for five strawberries, and…five blueberries, and…five raspberries." Her shoulders slouch further. "Can you please also tell them not to make the omelet any other way? That's all. Thank you." The entire time she recites her, as stated, *precise* order, her gaze doesn't move an inch from the floor.

I explain her order to the barista, who says, "Sir, I'm sorry, but the kitchen doesn't have blueberries today. Can I replace them with five extra strawberries?"

"Give me a second." I put my palm over the microphone and turn to the enigmatic couch girl. "Is it okay if they replace blueberries with strawberries? Or something else?"

I watch as her eyebrows furrow. The simple change of fruits somehow affects her immensely, which in turn surges my curiosity for her several folds.

I quietly take a few steps away from Oscar and the couch girl, before whispering into the phone, "Can you arrange the fruits as requested? Please add whatever extra expenses you incur to the bill."

I hang up and after we return to the conference room, the meeting starts slowly.

After some presentations, it's Kristy's turn to show the progress report of her team.

"One of our biggest accomplishments this fiscal year is the software we released this weekend. The entire development and production were led by Rose."

Hearing Kristy's words, I glance toward couch girl, but her entire focus is on her laptop. This isn't the first time someone has pointed out her name and how she single-handedly implemented some of our most critical projects. Oddly enough, all of her work is presented by other people.

"These new changes put us in a very strong position among our competitors," Kristy continues.

When she mentions the couch girl for a second time, I can't resist myself from asking, "Ms. Marlin, would you like to add something, as this project is your brainchild?"

Her hand on the mouse jars upon hearing my voice.

There's a weird silence in the room, which stretches for several more minutes until she replies.

"There isn't...much to add. The slides...um, contain everything."

After her quick, throaty reply, the meeting progresses as before.

Every time her name comes up, I glance in her direction and some other times, like now, my eyes automatically find her.

What is this weird effect she is having on me?

As much as I'm haunted by her name, there's something mystical about her.

Or am I just shit crazy this morning?

"And now Zander has a big announcement," Oscar says, breaking my weird chain of thoughts.

I get up from my chair. Straightening my jacket, I address the group. "First of all, I'm very proud of the work you all have put in over the years. I apologize for not visiting sooner, but I promise I'll be seeing you more often."

My gaze falls on couch girl, who's still buried behind her laptop.

"Regarding the news, as you all are aware, we're soon opening our third office of Elixir. This comes with restructuring of staff both at St. Peppers and Cherrywood. Some of the employees will have to relocate to the new location. There might be an option to move back in the future, but when, we don't know."

As expected, there are some pale faces, and I notice couch girl's fingers stopping over the keypad of her laptop.

"There's no need to panic," I assure the group. "The reorganization won't be in management, so you've nothing to worry about, but we'll have to let some of your junior associates go. I must also add, as the overall headcount is lower in Cherrywood, there will be fewer changes here."

"How many?" Kristy asks.

"I don't have the exact numbers yet, but I want to rearrange the staff and funds with minimal disruption to everyone and also not hamper our current production and research. As I've learned now, Ms. Asher, you and Ms. Marlin have the largest team, so I'd like to discuss first with you ladies." I try hard to keep my gaze fixed on Kristy.

Oscar looks at me in confusion and mumbles, "This was not planned."

I avoid his gaze, not knowing how to reply. I don't particularly like keeping him in the dark. But I hadn't planned on meeting couch girl today. I hadn't planned on feeling this weird pull toward her.

I now wait for a response from her. She can no longer avoid me. I saw something in her eyes when they met mine for a second. It was a pure, rare innocence. I'd like to know if it was real or fake.

Can someone even fake such innocence?

"Is there…an alternative?" she asks in that same delicate voice, her gaze fixed on the table. A smile breaks on my face just hearing her voice.

I fucking smile.

"Not to my knowledge. Do you have any ideas?" My full attention is on her and her fingers clutching the armrest of her chair. I wonder if it's my presence that's scaring her or if she's always this timid.

"What if the employees bring external funding, um… maybe in collaboration with the university? This might… give them an option…to choose if they want to move immediately or not." Couch girl continues staring at the table as if it's the most interesting thing known to her.

When no one responds to her suggestion, she looks up hesitantly, but not at me. Her gaze searches Oscar.

The uneasy feeling settles again in my chest as I watch her

familiarity with my friend. There's no doubt she trusts him, and he nods for her to proceed.

"We receive regular inquiries from professors…for collaborations." She tugs once again on the cuffs of her shirt, and I'm guessing it's a nervous habit. "Due to…lack of policy, um…we decline such offers."

I'm not fully on board with her unconventional idea, but I want to hear more. I'm not sure if it's because I consider the idea great or if it's my desire to know more about this skittish girl who appears to be completely ill at ease in this meeting room.

"Can you give some numbers on this, Ms. Marlin?" I ask.

"It's…hard to say at the moment. I…need to do…some analysis."

Her voice is getting stronger word by word, but she's still looking at the stupid table. For a brief second of insanity *I wish I was that table.*

I quickly shake my head to clear the crazy thought.

"That's no problem. Can you prepare the data? I would like to discuss further, possibly tomorrow morning, if that's all right with you."

She gingerly nods as the meeting ends.

My heart warms with a foreign feeling of anticipation for the next day.

As everyone leaves the conference room, I notice I've an unopened text. It's from the café, alerting me that couch girl's breakfast order was delivered to reception.

"Ms. Marlin, shall we pick up your breakfast? It's at the reception desk."

Her wide blue eyes meet mine, but before she can reply, Oscar intervenes. "Why don't we let Rose pick up her breakfast *alone*? I'd like to have a word with you, Zander."

My jaw tenses upon the unwanted interruption. I swallow the unexpected irritation down and give him what I hope is a friendly smile. "I just want to make sure Ms. Marlin gets her promised blueberries."

"Of course you do. But it's urgent, Zander."

Urgent, my foot.

4

ZANDER

"What the hell was that?" I twist the knot of my tie as we step inside Oscar's office.

He closes the door and runs his palm over his face. There's a hint of rare nervousness in his stance, and there should be. I'm the fucking CEO for fuck's sake.

"Zander, listen." Oscar curses under his breath before pulling on his hair. "The coincidence just slipped my mind or else I would've made sure she wasn't in the office today."

"I have no idea what you're talking about." I stand before him *too* casually, hands in my pockets as if I really have no clue.

"I know how attached you are to your past." He looks at me pointedly.

After too much whiskey, mixed with fatigue, I spoke too much that night two years ago when I shared bits and pieces of my past with him.

"That girl out there"—he cocks his head toward the door—"is not your normal girl, which you might have already noticed. She's special."

My fists clench hearing that word, *special*.

My father's words spoken years ago resonate through me

as we watched the woman we both loved dancing in the rain. *"Your mother is something special."*

Very early in my childhood, I learned that every special thing in life comes with a price. My brothers and I have paid heavily for a handful of special moments.

I take a few controlled breaths, hating how much that woman can affect me after all these years, even from her grave.

"I don't know what that word means anymore. Maybe special is just an absurdity we don't know what else to call." As soon as the words leave my mouth, I look away, not liking the pity in his eyes, and plop myself down on one of the leather chairs.

"There is nothing absurd about that girl, Zander." Oscar grabs his neck as if undecided on what more to say. "Rose is the first person we hired on our tech team. She came here for an interview three years ago. At the age of twenty-three, she had a PhD and graduated summa cum laude."

A small smile plays on his lips.

"Dressed in sneakers, jeans, and a checked flannel shirt, she looked so young and was overly fidgety. I thought she had entered the wrong room. We were also holding interviews for part-time desk jobs. But then she gave me her file. Her grades and her research articles were immaculate. There was also a recommendation letter from her professor."

From his bookshelf, Oscar grabs a red folder and passes it to me. The first page is the letter. It reads:

TO WHOM IT MAY CONCERN

Rosemary Marlin is a genius.
When you hire her, you'll get so much more than what you ask for.
Don't bother interviewing her.

I return his smile as he continues. "So, I asked her only

one thing. Why was she here, in Cherrywood of all places in the world? She replied, 'My friend is interviewing for another position, and if she wants that job, I want this one.'"

A chuckle escapes me as Oscar grins.

"She said *wants the job,* not *gets the job.* Soon, I realized why. Kristy and Rose are the best. For the next six months, it was just me and them. We spent a lot of time together, and I got to know them better."

A foreign wishful voice whispers in my ear. *If only I'd visited sooner.*

He's about to say more when there's a knock.

Kristy pokes her head through the half-open door. "Oscar, do you have a minute?"

I welcome the interruption and get up from the chair. "Please come in, Ms. Asher. We're almost done." I look over my shoulder and tell Oscar, "I'll see you in a bit."

I jump into the descending elevator car on my way to thank the barista in the café for arranging the unconventional breakfast order, while the recipient of that said breakfast invades my thoughts.

WHEN I STEP BACK into the building, the soft, velvety voice that is slowly taking up residence in some hidden corner of my brain gets my attention. I open the door closest to me and swiftly enter what looks like a janitor's closet. My nose crinkles when I breathe in the strong bleach smell, but my attention returns to the two girls who have, by some miracle, just stopped outside this door.

"Kristy, do we really have to leave?" couch girl asks.

I notice her voice is no longer quivering. She's clearly more comfortable around her friend.

"Of course. You haven't been home in two nights. Why are you even complaining?" Kristy puts her hand on her hips, staring at her friend. "And by the way, why weren't you home last night? Wasn't your work supposed to be done by Sunday evening?"

"Yeah, but... I ran into a bug. By the time I was done with the fix, it was already six in the morning."

Kristy frowns and doesn't look very happy with the answer. "Why didn't you call me, Rosie? I was so worried when I couldn't find you this morning. Your phone was off."

"I… I'm sorry. I didn't…think about it."

I watch through the peephole, couch girl looking at Kristy with apologetic eyes. A moment passes before Kristy links her arms with her friend.

"It's okay. It's a good thing Oscar gave you the day off. You need some rest."

Jesus, how long was I gone? Oscar already had the time to send her packing.

"And why do *you* get a day off?" Couch girl raises an eyebrow at Kristy. The tease in her voice surprises me.

Is she the same girl who was stammering in the conference room?

"I don't. I'll be working from home and making sure that *you* get some rest."

"But I need to research for tomorrow's meeting with the CEO."

I kick myself inwardly. She's been in the office for the past three days and deserves some time off. But in my own excitement, I forgot about it. I also hate the fact that she's calling me the CEO. It feels…impersonal.

Is she intentionally avoiding my name like I'm avoiding hers?

I wonder how it'll be to hear my name from her lips.

The nagging ache in my heart is back.

Fuck, this girl is doing crazy things to me.

Kristy growls. "Inconsiderate! That's what he is. If Zander Teager thinks he can boss us around, he's definitely got it all wrong."

Kristy is scary! I wonder how my timid couch girl is friends with her. *My? Jesus!*

"I think he can, and he *is* the boss." A beautiful giggle escapes her, and it's the most melodious sound.

"Traitor! You're taking his side instead of mine?" There's a hint of teasing in Kristy's voice and

I wonder if it's usual for them to tease each other or if this is something exclusive for me.

"Huh?" A deep frown etches on couch girl's face.

"Don't you *huh* me. You think I didn't notice how he was staring at you or how your cheeks turned pink every time he said something to you."

My heart thumps loudly in my chest. If it's their usual banter, I don't want to hear any more.

"*Ship!*"

Did she just curse politely? I suppress my chuckle at her over-the-top manners.

"No shit. Care to explain what I'm missing?"

"It's…nothing." The nervousness in her voice is back.

"I hope it's not." Kristy raises an eyebrow at her.

"Why do you say that?" Couch girl tilts her head to the side before fixing her red glasses.

"He might be gay, you know. I read an interview where one of his brothers mentioned that Zander Teager is probably gay."

What the hell? Fuck Zach and his stupid jokes.

"*Crab*. You mean I'm attracted to a gay guy?"

I'm still reeling from the surprise that this woman can't say the word *crap* out loud, and then realization hits. Did she just say *attracted to*?

"Did you say *attracted to*?" Kristy puts my thoughts into words.

I peep through the crack in the door. The girls have now crossed the lobby and are standing outside the elevator. My face is plastered to the wooden door as I struggle to hear couch girl's next words. It's only because there's an echo in the big, empty lobby that I manage to catch bits and pieces.

"I don't know, Kristy; it doesn't matter. I'll never be able to talk to him. And if he knows... forget it." Her shoulders slump in defeat and the deep heaviness in her voice surprises me.

What does she mean by *if he knows?*

All these feelings, this confusion, has turned my stomach into knots. Any good that walk did is now gone. I glance at her one more time as the elevator door opens before them. When she steps into the car, I get out of the closet and trudge in the other direction to take the stairs up the building. I'm only half paying attention when I collide with someone on my way.

5

ROSE

A holler captures our attention, and Kristy presses the button to stop the elevator door from closing. We step out to see what just happened.

The mail boy yells at Zander as he disappears behind the door leading to the stairs up the building. There are mail strewn on the shiny floor.

My legs go weak, and my hands turn clammy with sweat.

How long has he been here? Did he hear us?

"Crab!"

Kristy stares in the same direction, most likely thinking the same thing.

"Do you…think he heard us?" I ask, not even sure if I want an answer.

"I don't think so," she replies in a hesitant voice, playing with the strap of her handbag.

"Oh my god. What if he did?" Sweat beads collect over my forehead, and black spots threaten to cloud my vision.

"Don't panic, Rosie. I don't think he heard us. Even if he did, it doesn't matter."

"What…do you mean?"

Didn't I just say I was attracted to him?

Fishing amazing, Rose!

I rub the back of my neck to ease the heaviness kicking in.

"He's our boss, Kristy. Not just boss, but really like the boss of all bosses in the company." My hands tremble. I take a few deep breaths, trying to compose myself before I turn into a bundle of nerves and pass out.

Kristy puts her hand over my shoulders and presses on the bunched muscles, knowing it calms my anxiety. She guides me back inside the elevator and peers at me in the mirrored door.

"It'll be all right. You know, he was eyeing you throughout the meeting. And the way you were avoiding him, he was obviously making you uncomfortable."

"That's not news," I mumble.

I'm uncomfortable around most people, especially when I meet them for the first time. It's something I might always struggle with. Even my therapist confirmed that on my last visit to her.

Most days, I don't really mind. I'm already proud that it's been a few years since I've last taken an antidepressant, or a *happy pill*, as my therapist used to call it.

It could be because of this new life I've carved out in this town or the supportive new people who came into my life here. But I think a major part of my progress is owed to one thing that's been consistently good in my life—my friend Kristy.

Since the day Kristy decided we were supposed to be best friends, she has held my hand and kept to her promise of never leaving me, unlike everyone else.

"What has you thinking so hard?" She peeks over the sunglasses she just put on as we step out of the elevator and into the underground parking lot.

I shake my head and get in the passenger seat. I glance toward my friend as she steers the car. I'm reminded of the moment we walked into the conference room and I caught Zander staring our way.

I thought he was checking Kristy out. Guys do that all the time, and I'm all too happy for the lack of attention. My sneakers and flannel shirts hold no competition to her fitted suits and pencil skirts. But to my surprise he was observing me.

Giddiness that he was looking at me, *me* and not Kristy, is foreign.

We make quick work of getting home, and the second we do, I unlock the door of our two-bedroom rented home and park myself on the breakfast bar in our open kitchen.

Kristy opens the refrigerator and grabs a bottle of iced tea. After pouring the drink into two glasses, she passes one to me.

"Do you want to know more about him?" She gazes at me above the glass of cold liquid.

"What do you mean?" I look away, feeling uncomfortable under her probing gaze.

My heart beats rapidly as I wipe the condensation on the cold glass. I quickly swipe my smart watch screen to check my rapid heartbeat, but Kristy's words halt my fingers.

"We could Google him, you know."

I look up to find her hands clasped on the table as she watches my every move.

"Google? Don't we already know about him?"

Though this is our first face-to-face meeting with Zander Teager, we've seen him and his brothers on numerous business magazine covers, some of which hang in the office corridor. In the annual mandatory online safety training, Zander always talks for the first five minutes about the company's policies and his vision in a pre-recorded video.

"Not in *that* way." Kristy gives me a conspiratorial smile before dashing into her room and returning with her iPad.

"What are you doing?" I try to peek over her shoulder, but

she shifts the screen away from me.

"Impatient, are we?" She raises one eyebrow at me.

"No...not at all." I sit back, but not before reminding her, "You don't have the day off."

"I know, spoilsport."

She finally turns the iPad toward me, and on the small screen are the three Teagers sitting on a couch. The video is around three years old, and Zander looks younger than he did today. There's a striking resemblance between him and his brothers. Tall. Sculpted shoulders covered in expensive suits. Long fingers. Sun-kissed skin as if they'd recently spent time on a beach.

The interviewer is an attractive blonde girl, bouncing in her seat. She asks numerous questions about the company.

With excitement shining in his eyes, Zander explains how they came up with an idea of a non-traditional pharmaceutical company, Elixir Inc., which, along with drug development, focuses heavily on researching new technologies. Four years ago, when they opened the first office in their hometown of St. Peppers, they had no idea it'd be so successful that a year later they'd be opening another office in the state.

I know quite a lot about the company but not so much about the owner, so I tune out most of the conversation and instead admire the handsome man on the screen.

The way his hands move as he explains about Elixir. The way his eyes sparkle when he talks about their early days. I take everything in. Then the interviewer moves to their personal lives.

"Tell us more about your family," she asks the three men.

"You are looking at my family." Zander gives her a lopsided grin, showing his left dimple.

The girl smiles, her cheeks turning pink.

Ouch. I run my tongue over the inside of my cheek where I've just bitten accidentally. I don't really like her getting all chummy with Zander.

"Of course, but what about your parents?"

Zander's gaze darts from the blonde to his brothers as he runs his fingers through his hair. He blinks rapidly for a second as if clearing out a fearful memory. It's ephemeral, but my own experiences have made me more observant. It also might be because my gaze hasn't moved from him for a second.

Zander tries to act nonchalant, shrugging his shoulders. "Our parents passed away when we were very young. We spent some time in foster care before Ashcroft Miller took us in."

Oh my!

I look at Kristy and her worried gaze is fixed on me. But the interviewer appears satisfied with the answer.

After finishing the hour-long interview, I prepare myself an avocado and grilled cheese sandwich and bring it to my room while Kristy is up to her ears in online meetings.

I fall onto the bed and think back to the unusual day, or one stranger in particular. My gaze scoots up to the Wolverine collage on the wall. When I heard Zander's soul-spearing baritone voice in the small closet, it somehow reminded me of Wolverine.

I grin at the comparison.

My mind replays the moment Zander's eyes met mine for the first time. On such rare occasions, I'm thankful for my photographic memory. I can still feel the unexplained heat and warmth coursing through my body.

I get up from the bed and walk toward the photo frame hanging proud on the wall. It's a cheap black wooden frame that holds a shabby collage of superhero images from newspaper clippings. But it's one of the most cherished memories of my otherwise frigid childhood. I waited seven months to find a perfect picture of Wolverine, which now sits in the center of the collage.

I remember the day Kristy's mom, Sophia, brought me

comics for the first time. She asked me to choose one out of the three colorful illustrated books. There were superheroes fighting against the bad despite their twisted past, and I believed in those stories. I still do.

Two of the three books were of masked superheroes in a spider and bat mask, but my childhood brain was fascinated by the man who had claws on his hands—claws sharp enough to even cut metal. A thought appeared in my then-immature mind. If only I had such claws, I might have avoided all my nightmares.

I now understand that it was not my most intelligent thought.

But isn't life about getting hopes from wherever you can?

For me, it was those colorful rough pages and the tiny letters written in white bubbled spaces.

They told me my life wasn't over just yet. There were things beyond what I'd seen, what I'd suffered. There was a life beyond mine, waiting for me. I soon became a huge Wolverine fan, and the giant comic book collection under my bed is a testament to that.

After tracing my fingers along the cold glass over the shiny metal claws one last time, I amble to my study table.

I put together a presentation about upcoming grant applications and the professors interested in collaboration. I add each of my team members who would fit well in these new roles.

My hands falter as I draft an email to Kristy and Oscar, attaching the slides so they can appoint someone to present this to Zander. The feeling of relief I usually feel when I'm out of any social situation is not as strong today. Maybe—

Stupid, stupid Rose. What the hell are you thinking?

I'll possibly end up having a panic attack before I even walk into that conference room, knowing I have to speak to not just anyone but my attractive, Wolverine-voiced CEO.

My senses return and I hit send.

6

ROSE

I'm reviewing the code of one of our interns when I hear Kristy's angry voice before she marches into my room with Oscar following her. "Oscar, you listen to me!"

"Hold on, Kris. I'm not forcing her to do anything." Oscar turns to me, clearly irritated with my best friend.

"W-what's happening?" I ask as Kristy shoots daggers at our boss and friend.

"It's about the presentation you sent yesterday." Oscar stands at the other side of the table.

"Is something not right?" I fix my glasses and scour for the email in the sent folder.

"No, the presentation is good." He gives me a tight smile before rubbing the back of his neck. "It's just... I've always tried to make sure you feel comfortable here, Rose. You know that right?"

I'm surprised by the sudden change of discussion but nod in confirmation. "Um, yeah, and I...really appreciate it. But you are...scaring me at this moment. Did I do...something?"

Before he can reply, Kristy saunters toward us and stands behind me. "Did you hear? You're scaring her," she yells, and I almost feel for Oscar.

"God, Kristy. You're scaring *me*." He shakes his head before turning my way. "Zander has requested that you present the slides to him."

"But…" I grab the edge of the table.

Oscar takes the chair on my left and speaks softly, "I know."

I glance at him and he smiles—the same kind smile with which he encourages me whenever I feel I'm falling short.

"I tried to tell Zander about you. I—"

"You told…him…about me." My voice wobbles, and this time, for different reasons.

I don't want Zander to know.

"No, he didn't," Kristy replies on his behalf, and I fall back in my chair, filled with an unexpected relief.

"But like I said before, I do want Zander to know what an asset we have in you here." Oscar lightly pats my hand. "But no pressure. Say no, and I'll talk Zander out if it."

Does Oscar even have that kind of power? Zander is the CEO after all.

When I don't reply immediately, he says, "It doesn't have to be a formal presentation. Just show him your findings in *your* office. Use *your* computer." He nods at my PC.

Before I can think more about his idea, there's a knock on the door, and we all turn to find Zander leaning against the doorframe.

"Good morning, Ms. Marlin."

He smiles and my eyes fix on his dimpled left cheek. It somehow looks different in real life.

"Good… good… morning."

"If it's all right, I'd like to discuss the project proposals with *you*. It'd be better than going back and forth with a third person in the middle."

I glance between Kristy and Oscar before giving him a nod. "Um… okay."

"Very well." Zander walks inside as Oscar leaves with an uncooperative Kristy.

Before I have time to prepare myself for this unexpected endeavor, Zander slides into the chair just vacated by Oscar.

I'm immediately hit by a woodsy scent. Generally, strong smells give me nausea and a headache, especially the kind that some men prefer to wear—smelling like a walking perfumery. But this smell is fresh. It's subtle and nice, like… a forest.

"I hope you got some rest yesterday." He slides forward in the chair, getting a good view of the monitor, and I'm momentarily distracted by his hands on the table.

He has beautiful hands.

Clean, long fingers. A light dusting of hair on the back.

I'm sure they smell nice too.

"Ms. Marlin?" His hands open and close, as he most likely caught me gawking.

My heart skips a beat, and I try to busy myself with opening the slides.

"Yeah…yeah."

My right hand holds the mouse in a firm grip, almost breaking the plastic. The familiar unease settles in my gut, today mixed with a foreign warm, feverish feeling. My face is hot, my palms clammy. It feels as if all the air is sucked out of my lungs, and I'm unable to breathe. The last thing I want is to pass out in front of Zander.

"Are you okay? Do you need a minute?"

His words are a reality check for me.

What was I thinking?

As if I'd ever have a chance with anyone, let alone someone like Zander. I don't even have the courage to sit with him alone in my office, a place where I'm at my best.

My eyes sting, but I push back the tears. It takes all my will to not keen. My mouth is dry, and with trembling hands, I pick up a glass of water from the table.

What do I do now?

What I *want* to do is run and hide someplace far away.

"You know, when I'm nervous, I take deep breaths," he says in a soft voice. It's so different from his Wolverine voice from yesterday.

I peek at him through wet lashes, and he watches me closely. I'm sure he's guessed by now what a dork I am.

But he surprises me.

"Ms. Marlin, it's perfectly okay to feel nervous when discussing the future of your team, your staff." He pauses, giving me time to absorb his words. "I understand how you're feeling."

Oh, trust me, you don't.

Thank goodness. He thinks team-restructuring is the reason for my nervousness. I clear my throat and look at the presentation, trying to pull his attention away from me and back to my work.

"Um, I did research on the grant applications and contacted some professors. I think…we can avoid major reorganization in tech."

"Really?" His eyebrows shoot up in surprise. "Are you sure?"

The anxiousness in my chest slowly subsides as I walk him through the data I collected last night.

"But this comes with a salary dip. Do you have some stats on the pay cuts?" He rubs his hand across his five o'clock shadow, and my breath catches at the prosaic act.

I pull my gaze away from his chiseled face and bring it back to the computer, then I open the graph where I have some rough estimates on the net salary per position.

"Please note, this is not…comprehensive. I have used, um publicly available tax numbers for…rough calculations."

"You think employees would still be interested?"

"I…think so. At least, this way you can give people some time…to wrap their head around the news." I clear my throat when his eyebrows furrow as he glances at the slides hesitantly. "Some people...are not so good...with surprises, you know."

I feel his gaze lingering on me as I close the presentation.

After a few moments of weird silence, he says, "That was very good work, Ms. Marlin. I'll discuss with Oscar how your initiative can be implemented—Wow, is that Wolverine?"

My head jerks up at him in surprise as he points to my screen.

Crab. I've closed the presentation and there he is—my favorite superhero with his claws drawn and ready to attack.

"Yeah," I reply sheepishly.

So much embarrassment for one day. *Way to go, Rose.*

In the past hour, I've not only demonstrated that I'm extremely paranoid but also a superhero junkie.

"Are you a fan?" he asks in an excited throaty voice.

I nod, shifting nervously in my seat.

"Me too. I liked the movies, but they aren't up to par with the comic books."

"Huh?" My mouth falls open, and I have to remember to close it before a fly becomes my midmorning snack.

"I mean, they skipped a lot of details in the movies," Zander explains as if *I* don't know.

I can't help but simply stare at him. Is he one of those rare people who shares my enthusiasm for Wolverine comics? *Not movies, but comics!*

"Have you read the comics?" I don't think I heard him right.

"Of course. I didn't like how the relationship between Sabretooth and Wolverine was modified in the movie." His forehead puckers in irritation.

"You *have* read the comics," I squeal in excitement and end up laughing like a fool. There are very few things that can ease my anxiety, and Wolverine talk tops that small list.

"Of course. I can recall quite a few instances where I've been referred to as a Wolverine junkie."

I look at him for the first time without fear or nervousness, and he's grinning from ear to ear. I'm sure my face mirrors his expression.

I'm about to tell him that Kristy calls me by the same name when there are three brisk knocks on the door.

Kristy and Oscar look at us in confusion.

Oscar's brows furrow, while Kristy raises an eyebrow and their piercing gazes zoom in on my wide smile. Realization suddenly hits me—I'm smiling and laughing with my boss, who I've met just yesterday and is an almost *stranger*.

Zander gets up and straightens his jacket. "It was very nice talking to you, Ms. Marlin. Keep up the good work."

I'm momentarily amazed at how swiftly he switched from superhero groupie to serious CEO.

As the men leave the room, Zander looks at me over his left shoulder, and my stomach does a strange flip-flop when I see his dimpled left cheek.

7

ROSE

"This legit looks empty," Kristy says at the absence of the usual line at Steamy Beans, the café opposite our office building.

"It's because we're an hour early." I drag myself to the counter in a huff.

It's not that I have a problem getting up at six in the morning. In fact, my first morning alarm is set for six. But I do need two hours to get all my tasks done. Brush, floss, twenty minutes of stretching, shower, breakfast, and I'm ready at eight. But at six thirty this morning, while I was just setting up my yoga mat, Kristy stormed into my room announcing that we'd be leaving in thirty minutes.

"Why are you so grumpy? I'm making a new habit today." She points to the book in her open handbag on healthy habits, which ironically, I gifted her last month on her birthday.

What was I thinking?

"I'm grumpy because I had to rush through my morning schedule and skip my stretching and hair wash." I run a hand through my small ponytail. "My hair feels oily."

"Your hair looks good." Kristy pulls my hand away. "Don't

you see? Today, we can sit and enjoy our coffee in the café? It's empty."

"You left home early to…sit in a café?" I'm seriously confused. "Wasn't the habit about starting work early?"

"The habit was to *reach* work early." She points in the direction of the office building. "We are almost there."

Before I can call her out, she turns to the smiling barista and places our order of two latte macchiatos and a blueberry muffin for herself. Thank God, I had time to get my breakfast right.

When we grab a corner table, I sit across from her, facing the chalkboard wall as she takes a chair facing the door.

As the time passes, the café starts to buzz with the usual morning sounds, voices of people placing their breakfast orders, the front door continuously opening and shutting.

"Are you seriously not going to talk about yesterday?"

This is the third time she's asked me this question since she caught me smiling with Zander.

"I told you already. I showed Zander my findings and he was pleased."

Remembering our meeting, a warm sensation fills my chest and flows everywhere through my body until it settles into my fingertips and toes.

"He looked more than pleased." She wiggles her eyebrows, probing me to say more. But when I don't take the bait, she looks me in the eye, straight-faced. "You were smiling at him —*with* him."

"I know. Believe me, I'm equally surprised." I fix my glasses and rub my forehead, trying to find the next words. "Toward the end, it became easier…talking to him. I wasn't as anxious as always. It was…different with him."

I'm distracted when a shadow appears behind me, my nose tickling as it takes in the woodsy scent with a hint of vanilla.

"Hello, Ms. Asher." Zander appears in my full sight. "I

hear the coffee's good here." He tips his take-away cup in Kristy's direction.

"Hello, Mr. Teager," Kristy replies in an overly chirpy tone. "You heard right."

Turning to me, he says, "It's nice seeing you again, Ms. Marlin."

His lips curl and a beautiful smile lights up his face. My eyes transfix on that dimple for a second before giving him a nod and hiding away from his mysterious, warm gaze.

"I hear our girl left you speechless yesterday."

My eyes widen at Kristy's unnecessary remark. *Why does she have to say that?*

I grab my coffee mug and bring it closer to my lips, just so I don't have to speak.

"Rose is a woman of few words," she continues. "You might have noticed that."

What's up with her?

Usually, she jumps into discussion whenever there's a chance I might become the center of attention. But today, not to my liking, she continues to babble about me.

"Yes. I'm finding out that everyone here has an outstanding work ethic."

"And to that note"—Kristy glances at her watch and then at me—"I gotta run to a meeting. I can leave Rose to your company if you like."

W-what's happening?

By the time I stand, grabbing my half-empty coffee mug, Kristy has already exited the café.

"Ms. Marlin, do you mind?" Zander slips into Kristy's empty chair.

Why is everyone so fast?

I've hardly had time to place my cup back on the table and he's already comfortable in the chair.

"Um…"

"Just one cup?" He tilts his head to the side. "Until you finish yours." He smiles, and something warm fill my insides.

I pull on my shirt cuffs and nod, looking away. The nervous hammering in my heart is familiar, but today, it's beating to a foreign beat.

I sit back, and in nervousness, gulp the remaining coffee.

"Would you like a refill?" He cocks his head toward my now-empty cup.

Crab.

"N-no if that's okay with you. Actually, I already had my one morning cup." My hands hide under the table as I rub them over the denim of my jeans. "I…get anxious when I have too much caffeine."

And isn't that the understatement of the century?

"Excuse me." Zander takes out his phone from his breast pocket. "Hello. I'm near the building. Can you postpone?"

My eyes widen. *Is he postponing a meeting because of me?*

Looking right back at me with a very serious face, he speaks into the phone, "Sixty minutes? Thanks."

The call ends.

I shiver under his piercing gaze. "You didn't…have to do that."

"I'm asking for your sixty minutes, Ms. Marlin. I promise, not a second more."

I nod, surprised to see he's concerned about my time more than his.

"You were telling me about your coffee habits. So, only one cup, huh? You have good caffeine restraint, then. Most days, by the time I reach work, I'm on my third cup."

"Three is too much. You can have anxiety and…insomnia." The words are out of my mouth before I realize. I snap my lips together as he considers me with that piercing gaze. "I'm…sorry. I'm normally not so…opinionated. In fact, I'm never opinionated, and…definitely not so verbose."

I clamp my mouth and eyes shut. I always have a hard

time speaking, but with him, words are rolling out of my mouth like someone has possessed my tongue.

When I open my eyes, I find Zander staring at me. As our eyes meet, the now-familiar feverish feeling is back.

"You have a beautiful voice, and I like you verbose."

The way his words are spiking my body temperature, I'll certainly have to use the cold compress in my office.

I look away, not sure what to do. When I peek a glance at him, he's staring at my hands on the table, which are busy tugging on the cuffs of my shirt. My grip on the fabric tightens.

He clears his throat, pulling my attention back to his face.

"You did great work yesterday. I'm really impressed."

"Thanks." My heart swells at his approval.

When I look away this time, it's not because of the usual nervousness where I want to run away and hide from everything, but it's a weird flutter in my heart that makes me almost dizzy, and something inside me wants this to continue.

Zander clears his throat once more.

I'm too distracted—with him, with the way I feel around him, with my newly found flutter.

"If you don't mind, I'm curious about something," he says, breaking the weird silence.

And here it comes.

My stupid brain tells me he's about to ask all the usual questions.

Why are you so weird?

Why do you look so frightened?

But I hold onto my dazed feeling for just another second and nod.

"You work on live code release alone?"

His question catches me off guard. I'd hoped he would ask something other than the usual.

I still for a second, letting the relief sink in.

Maybe he doesn't find me weird after all, a small voice in my head whispers.

He looks at me patiently, his brown eyes soft, so different from all the pictures of him I've seen over the years.

I don't have time to frame a reply to his unexpected question, so I give him my honest thoughts. "I think... I enjoy the feeling of working under pressure and stress."

"Did you just say you like to work under stress?" One of his perfectly shaped eyebrows arch, and a playful smile appears on his lips.

Crab, so much for speaking my mind.

"I-I mean, it reminds me of my hackathon days...at the university."

"Aha, got it. You're an adrenaline junkie."

"What?" My eyes pop out, and I gulp so loud that I'm sure he heard it. "No. Not at all. I'm not an adrenaline junkie. In fact, I'm everything minus an adrenaline junkie." I'm just blabbering now.

"Relax, Ms. Marlin, I know what you mean." His lips curl into a smile, and I swoon over the dimple that appears on his left cheek once again.

How can someone be so dashing?

His skin is bright, and the light stubble of facial hair makes him look like a model from a fashion magazine cover. He has a beautiful face—square jaw, pointy nose, full lips, captivating brown eyes, and long lashes.

He's wearing a charcoal gray suit and a cherry-colored tie. The deep red fabric peeking between the lapels of his jacket steals my heart.

It's the color of the flower that has given me its name.

My very first happy memory.

He rakes his hand through his hair—his perfect hair. Obsidian black, no strand out of place. *How would it be to run my fingers through it?*

W-what was that thought?

Sweet Sugar.

"Does your mind wander a lot, Ms. Marlin, or am I that boring?" Zander smirks, interrupting me from making a mental canvas of him.

Ship. How am I not quivering in my seat while brazenly eyeing my boss? Okay, I'm quivering, but not in the usual way.

Why does he give me a weird sense of comfort?

"Is it rare?" he asks, and I realize I've spoken the last words out loud.

I lower my gaze. What do I say to this?

"Sorry, I didn't mean to be intrusive," Zander whispers. "You are…"

My mouth dries as I wait for his words.

How will he finish this sentence? I try hard to silence the voice in my head, which thinks the worst of everything.

"Beguiling." His grip on the coffee cup tightens as if he doesn't like his words. But when our eyes meet, a slow smile builds on his lips. "If it doesn't offend you, I have a request to make."

Hearing his hesitant voice, my hands falter where I'm circling the rim of the coffee cup with my index finger.

"Yeah?" I don't know where he's going, but I'm curious.

"I'd like to know you better. After all, we do share a mutual love for Wolverine." His smile wavers a little when he adds, "We could be good friends, don't you think?"

"Um…I don't know…what to say?"

"I'm a decent man, Ms. Marlin."

"I'm sure you are, Mr. Teager."

"If we're to be friends, you might want to call me by my name."

"Ah, yes. I guess you should too."

8

ZANDER

*F*uck.

Looking at this beautiful girl sitting across from me, I reminisce on yesterday morning, something I've done quite a lot the past twenty-four hours.

While she was busy explaining her findings and analysis, I couldn't help but notice the subtle things she did unknowingly. Like the way she brought the tip of her tongue between her lips to wet them. *Damn.* She looked so sexy. The way she tweaked her nose after adjusting her glasses—adorable.

My brain is soon going to exert itself, failing to connect the person I see to the name I know.

Her low coughing interrupts my trail of thoughts.

Shit. She asked me about her name. I've just offered her a friendship, and I can't lie to her face. What a shitty friend would I be?

I run both my hands through my hair before meeting her expecting gaze.

"You mentioned you aren't comfortable around people. Does it also extend to things?"

Her gaze drops from mine to the table between us. Her folded hands on the wooden surface lightly shake before her fingers start tugging on the cuffs of her shirt. Embarrassment evident on her red cheeks and I realize she's taken my comment personally.

I try hard to keep some semblance of sanity in my next words.

"Small things, which many might not even notice, can sometimes be a trigger for some in ways we can't imagine." My words have trouble finding a voice. The top button of my collar feels like a vise around my neck.

But I have her complete attention, her entire body still. There's a flicker of understanding in her wide eyes, which persuades me to whisper in a throaty voice, "I'm uncomfortable with your name. I…don't think I'll ever be able to say it out loud."

I regret the words upon seeing her flinch and her body crumbling onto the chair. I watch as she swallows hard and closes her eyes.

"It's okay." Her dejected voice cuts me deep.

"It's not okay. In no fucking way," I say through gritted teeth.

This week. Her name. Her smile. The way my heart beats upon seeing her. It's all a fucking disaster.

"The offer of friendship still stands, if you can live with…" I don't know how to finish the sentence.

Minutes pass by, but she says nothing. I'm thankful for the sound in the café, as her silence is killing me.

"How will a friendship even work when my name brings out all the nightmares you are trying to forget?"

It's the first time her voice hasn't trembled while speaking to me. Like that's the one thing she believes wholeheartedly.

Her words rattle my core. I just mentioned a trigger, but she couldn't have explained my reaction to her name any better.

What are your nightmares, couch girl?

"Because I'm here, talking to you, hoping hard that you're

not completely weirded out by me and would still consider my friendship."

"Oh." She looks at me in surprise for a second before she's flustered again, pulling on those flannel cuffs.

"I know we've only met yesterday, but trust me, couch girl—"

"Couch girl?" She does a double take. Some of the lost color returns to her face, telling me she isn't offended by the nickname.

"Yes, the mysterious girl I found sleeping on the office couch."

Her lips make an adorable *O*.

"That's the name I'm using when I'm thinking about you," I admit. "But of course, I have the copyright on that."

When I give her a small smile, she blushes a beautiful shade of pink, and my heart soars in delight. I release a deep breath of relief, knowing that a major part of the crisis is averted.

"You can't call me that…there." She tilts her head toward the office building. "Everyone will think I'm some crazy couch lady."

I bring my attention back to her face from her fingers, which are lightly tapping on the empty coffee cup.

"Don't worry, I won't let anyone think of you as crazy, Ms. Marlin." An inspiration hits me as I push my chair back. "Would you like to share a piece of pie with me to celebrate our new friendship, *Marr*?"

Her eyes widen at my swift use of her new nickname. "S-s-sure. They make, um…very good custard pie here."

"One custard pie coming right up."

As I walk to the counter, my chest inflates. Given all the weirdness, I'm so damn happy with how this morning is turning out with my new friend.

Sweet and cute couch girl. *Marr*.

I return with a piece of pie and two forks. When I place

the small plate between us, using her fork she divides it into two halves. She even pulls her piece a little more toward her, creating a small gap.

I cock an eyebrow at her, but she just ducks her head.

I let her actions slide. If she's cool with my weirdness, I'm cool with hers.

As we enjoy the pie, I ask more about her.

She starts hesitantly, telling me about her recent projects, then swiftly moves to her colleagues until she's raving about the town.

Finally, I have to interrupt her. "So Marr, in the past thirty minutes, I've learned about almost everything except you. I'm more interested in knowing *you*." I point the tiny fork to her, but my simple words have an undesirable effect. Her blushing pink face pales, slowly turning white. "Hey, I'm only asking little details that friends know about each other. Like, maybe your age. Or your phone number."

"Oh." She slowly relaxes back in her chair and whispers, "I'm twenty-six."

"I'm thirty-two."

"I know." Her eyes widen before she plays with her cuffs. "I mean...I didn't *know* know, but I *assumed*. You are the CEO...you should be thirty-one...thirty-two."

My lips curl into a smile as her face reddens and her hands move animatedly. I take pity on her before she faints.

"I understand what you mean."

Did cute Ms. Marlin look me up?

"And what about that phone number?"

"I heard you postponed the conference call this morning," Oscar states as the waiter picks up our empty dishes.

"And?" I wave for the young man to bring another round of drinks.

"I heard you were with Rose."

"Don't tell me you have your little birds spying on me."

Why the hell am I at dinner with this killjoy?

"No spying, boss." He smirks for a moment before his lips flatten and his eyes fix on me. "There are things you don't know about her."

"And you're going to share those *things* with me?" I cross my arms over my chest.

"Don't you see what I'm trying to tell you?" He sits tall in the cushioned leather chair of the five-star restaurant.

"Not at all. I've no clue what you are trying to do." I narrow my eyes on him in irritation.

"I'm trying to tell you to stay away from her. She's not someone you play around with, Zander." Oscar presses his lips together.

"And how many women have you seen me playing around with?"

The joke about me being gay didn't start overnight. I'm no saint, but I'm also not a player. Relationships are something I never considered for myself. I have had some hookups here and there during college, and occasionally, someone would hit on me during a business meeting. But after a casual fuck, I would always go back to my room. I've never slept with a woman in the literal sense.

"That's not what I mean. She isn't your usual girl, Zander." Oscar scrapes a hand through his hair as if nervous about something. "She has already seen too much pain for one life. You getting closer to her this week and then leaving to not return for another three years isn't something she needs in her life right now."

Our dear waiter chooses this moment to bring our drinks. When he retreats, Oscar sips his single malt Irish whiskey as if he didn't just drop a bomb minutes ago.

"Are you really going to just sit there and not explain more?" I ask.

"It's not my story to tell."

"But you already started." When he doesn't budge, I lean back in my chair, trying to act nonchalant. "I've decided to prolong my stay in Cherrywood."

That gets his attention. "What do you mean by prolong?"

"Exactly as it sounds. I want to put Marr's plan of collaboration with the university into action."

"Marr? Jesus. So now you're her BFF?" His hands make the air quotes while saying that ridiculous word.

"That's the hope." I smirk, but he doesn't take the bait. Instead, he sits there like a fucking stone. I sigh. "Look, Oscar, I like her. She's cute. Weird but funny. She agreed to be my friend today."

"Are you in high school?" His grip on the glass tightens, and I realize I can't force the words out of him.

"Tell me about her," I plead instead of bossing him.

After staring at me for a few seconds, he shakes his head and releases a heavy breath.

"I don't know the whole story. Rose is very tight-lipped when it comes to her personal life." He pauses, obviously uncomfortable with the discussion. "I'm fucking betraying her trust, but you seem to be hell-bent on this friendship thing." He grabs his drink from the table and gulps back the remaining liquid. "I just want to give you an idea of her."

My heart beats a little faster, as if already knowing Oscar's words are going to affect me hard.

"It was the first Christmas after the girls joined the team. The office was closed, and I'd just dropped by to pick up some papers. To my surprise, I found Rose working. That day, she told me about her family, or lack of it. She grew up in some sort of…home. I don't think she knows who her parents are. I have no idea if she was abandoned at the time of her birth or later, but she didn't speak till very late in her childhood. Kristy's mother was her music therapist. That's how the girls met."

Bile rises in the back of my throat.

"You know the feeling of abandonment, Zander, but can you imagine picturing your parents and siblings every single day, knowing they're out there living a life without you?"

My fists clench on the table. Heavy, nonsensical words like fucking *coincidences* and *destiny* run in my ears.

As if he hasn't already said enough, stroking his chin, Oscar continues, "She suffers from social anxiety disorder—was diagnosed in her early teens. But with medication and support, she handles it well. She's a fucking treasure for the company, Zander, but she's nervous about new things and *people*."

He raises an eyebrow at me, accusing me of being a nerve-racking stranger. "And that's why I'm protective of her. I'm concerned about you bulldozing into her life—going on coffee dates when she doesn't even like sitting in crowded places." Oscar falls back in his chair, his mouth pressed into a hard line.

I hate his familiarity with Marr and the fact that he's rubbing it in my face. "She's not yours to protect, man."

"But she's *yours*, Mr. BFF?"

My hands tremble as I hold the cell phone, indecisive on whether or not to call her. I'm still trying to get my head around the information Oscar gave me this evening.

I was curious about Marr before, but now I feel something…stronger. Maybe it's sympathy, or maybe understanding.

I always believed women take advantage of people, situations, and fucking everything. But there's this one, breaking all my beliefs with her gullible eyes and feathery voice. And then there's her name: *Rose*. The word I've dreaded and hated my whole life.

I decide to send her a text.

Me: Hello, couch girl.

Couch girl: Zander, you sent me a text.

My lips curl into a smile. Her immediate reply with my name does something funny to my heart. I rub my warm chest while reading her text again.

Me: Yeah :) What are you doing?

A few minutes later, my phone chimes, announcing a new text message. She sent me a photo!

The focal point of the picture is her computer, where some code is running on a black screen. But it's the glimpse of her room that makes me do a double take.

Her computer table is facing a window, partly hidden with soft blue curtains. The wall is painted pastel pink. There's a chaise, which looks super comfy with dozens of throw pillows. On one side of the window is a wall shelf with miniature decorative items. Moon-shaped string lights hang from the shelf.

Everything looks so homey, and *so not Marr*. I've been to her office. The only non-work-related item there is a plant. There are no photographs or postcards. Not even colorful post-its.

I look again at the picture and get a glimpse of a black-and-white poster.

What could it be?

My first instinct says Wolverine, but then maybe some actor or singer? I can't fathom the idea of some half-naked actor's or rock star's poster hanging in her bedroom. This girl is driving me crazy. It appears she has so many layers. Every time I feel like I know her more, she reveals something new.

Me: Wow.

Couch girl: Yes, it's amazing. Would you like to see it in person?

Holy shit. Is she inviting me to her place? Unfamiliar exhilaration fills my bones and muscles. *Is she the same girl from this morning?*

Me: Yeah. Sure.

Couch girl: Great, I can email you the details later tonight. In short, it's an algorithm that uses AI for synthetic drug development and the prediction of effectiveness and side effects of the compounds developed.

Ah, the code running on her PC. My excitement deflates, but the smile stays on my lips. *That's the Marr I know.*

Me: That's brilliant. But for a moment, I thought you were inviting me over.

I see the three dots appearing and disappearing on my screen as she types and deletes multiple times before finally sending me an emoji.

Couch girl: :\

I let her off the hook.

Me: Don't forget to send me the details of the code.

Couch girl: I don't forget anything. :)

Me: I'll keep that in mind Ms. Marlin for the day I need your superpowers.

Couch girl: LOL You are funny.

Me: I'd really like you to tell that to my brothers. They think I'm too uptight.

Couch girl: Really? You don't look uptight to me.

I lie on the bed, my stupid hands shaking as I type.

Me: Then how do I look to you?

Again, there's a period of her typing and deleting. I'm almost tempted to change gears, but thankfully, her new message arrives.

Couch girl: You appear prudent. Judicious. Levelheaded.

Me: Your adjectives made my head hurt. Now I know you see me as an eighty-year-old businessman. :(

Couch girl: Crab! I didn't mean it like that. :P

My lips curl up as I read her weird, one-of-a-kind cursing.

. . .

LATER THAT NIGHT, before placing my phone on the nightstand, I open the messenger app and read her texts one more time. When I get into bed, there's a smile on my face.

I close my eyes, waiting for the darkness to engulf me. For the pain of the rose thorns as they cut my skin. But something flashes in the middle of the red and black. Blue eyes, making me sit upright on my bed. For the first time in the past two decades, my haunted nights are invaded by something new, something not from my jaded past. My heart races and I'm drenched in sweat, but for the first time, I'm not scared to lie back again.

What are you doing to me, couch girl?

9

ROSE

After returning to my office with a lunch of veggie delight salad and an iced tea, I power on my computer. Before perching back in my office seat, I check the water level in the moisture sensor of my small bowstring hemp plant.

When I unlock my PC, there's an unopened email in my inbox from Zander.

The tea almost slips from my grip as I see his name.

I place the cold bottle on the table and wipe the spilled drops.

Something tickles inside me as I read his email.

From: Zander Teager
Subject: New Project
To: Rosemary Marlin

Dear Miss Marlin,
I read the report about your latest project. I'm very impressed and would like to discuss more. Would you meet me in my office at 4 today?
Waiting for your response.

Zander Teager
CEO, Elixir Inc.

I chew on my lips, mulling over how to reply. My eyes focus on his words *waiting for your response*.

You weren't so nervous last night while texting him. Don't make it a bigger deal than it is. He's your boss and he's just curious about your work.

I spend a few more minutes giving myself a pep talk before my trembling fingers type him a response.

From: Rosemary Marlin
Subject: New Project
To: Zander Teager

Dear Mr. Teager,
I'll see you at 4.

Rosemary Marlin
Lead Data Scientist, Elixir Inc.

At four, I stand outside the corner office that has a new gold nameplate with Zander's name written on it.

I knock softly.

When the door doesn't open, I knock again.

I try to turn the knob, but it's locked.

Did he forget our meeting?

The foreign tingling in my heart is immediately replaced by a familiar feeling of embarrassment. I peek around. *Did anyone see me lurking outside the CEO's office?*

I'm about to leave when a tall frame looms over me.

Turning around, I find Zander standing with his hands full, holding a paper bag and two coffee mugs from Steamy Beans.

"I'm so sorry. I didn't realize there would be such a long line."

He looks out of breath, as if he rushed his way back to the office.

My heart does a weird, happy dance when he gives me his lopsided grin, reveling in the knowledge that his dimple is exclusively for me.

"No…worries. I was afraid, um…that you forgot."

"You are hard to forget, couch girl."

His curious gaze holds me captive, and I can't look away. His brown eyes shine as afternoon sun rays fall on his face, filtering through the floor-to-ceiling windows in the lobby. The five o'clock shadow on his face makes him look impossibly handsome.

Why the hell is he wasting his precious time with me? The voice in my head whispers, and I try my best to ignore it.

Our locked gazes break when the printer in the adjoining copy room whirrs and I look away.

"Marr, can you take out the keys?" He cocks his head toward the right pocket of his jacket.

I blink rapidly. *He…wants me to…put my hands…inside his jacket?* I look nervously at him and then to his pocket and then back at his face. My cheeks flush at his simple request, and I tug on my sleeves.

"Or can you hold this?" He brings the paper bag forward, and I grab it eagerly.

Anything to get that door open.

"Come in." Zander leads me inside his office after unlocking the door.

"I didn't know about this room," I murmur, looking around at the high-definition projector screen, brown leather couch, slick desk, and the sleek silver laptop resting on top of it.

"Yeah, I declared it as my own on my first visit to Cherrywood when we purchased the building." He smirks, sinking gracefully into the leather chair.

While I sit with a thousand butterflies fluttering in my stomach, Zander leans forward and opens the paper bag.

How does he do it?

Make a mundane activity of unpacking dessert some sort of sensual act. Watching his long fingers meticulously unwrap the two slices of pie, my face warms.

"I got us each a custard pie. I didn't know what else you liked," he says, catching my gaze.

"Thank you," I reply, torn between the desire to look at his face and the anxiety forcing me to look anywhere but at him.

After passing me a coffee mug and a piece of pie with a plastic fork on the side, Zander places a few paper napkins between us.

"You wanted…to discuss something?" I ask, taking a sip of the latte macchiato.

He nods before wiping his mouth. "I'm very interested in the project. I'd like to know more. What's the current state? Do you need some support from us? How much time does your team need to make it ready for alpha release?"

I place my coffee back on the table and rub my hands on my jeans, unable to decide which question to answer first. "Um Zander, I mean Mr. Teager—"

"Marr, I thought we settled on the name issue yesterday." His honey-sweet voice makes my heart stop.

When I don't reply immediately, he raises an eyebrow, an amused smile on his lips.

"Yeah, yeah." I fix my glasses and run my tongue over my dry lips. "The thing is, there is no team…working on this. I started it, um…as a side project."

His eyes flare in surprise. "When do you work on it?"

"Mostly weekends and some evenings…when I don't have much to do."

Great. Why don't I just plaster on my forehead that I've no life outside of work?

My cheeks warm with embarrassment.

"You should never be embarrassed about loving your work." He gives me a kind, encouraging smile. "So, show me where are you with this project."

"I-I don't have my laptop with me. I can get it." I put the fork down and am about to stand when Zander interrupts me.

"Is the project data on the company server or your personal computer?"

"Everything is on the server." It's Elixir's policy to safeguard against any data loss.

"Then use my laptop." He turns the said device toward me, taking me by surprise.

"A-are you sure?"

"Of course."

When I make no move, Zander gets up and stands behind me. Leaning forward, he fires up his laptop, and I inhale his earthy smell up close.

It's intoxicating.

"It's connected to the screen." He turns his head in the direction of the projector.

Before straightening back, he gives me a smile. His face is so close to mine that I worry he can hear the wild thumping of my heart.

I login to the server with trembling fingers, and twice, I enter the wrong password. It's a good thing Zander is back in his seat and can't see my clumsy movements.

Taking heavy breaths, I try to compose myself while searching for the data.

When I have what I need, I pull my gaze away from the laptop to find Zander peering at me with a pleasant smile.

"Ready?" he asks.

. . .

"I DON'T KNOW what to say, Marr. When you said it was a side project, I didn't expect this level of perfection and complexity. If it's okay with you, I want this idea to be pitched to our sales and marketing team. That's Zach's department."

Holy crab. Why didn't I think of that? But he surprises me again.

"I'll ask Kristy to prepare the presentation and arrange for a meeting with Zach's team." He's already opened a blank email, ready to write Kristy.

"You don't want me to present?" I blurt, putting my foot in my mouth.

Zander's eyebrows shoot up, and this time, it's his turn to hesitate. "I…thought you didn't like giving presentations. Did I understand wrong?"

I shake my head in embarrassment. *Why did I dig my own grave?*

"Doesn't it bother you that…" I don't finish the sentence, because I don't know what to include and what to skip. There's a huge list of things that one can find annoying in me.

"Does it bother you that it took me three reads to fully understand your email?" he asks, and I'm startled by his strange question. "Didn't Einstein say something about not judging a fish for its tree climbing abilities?"

Even through the tension, my lips curl into a smile.

"What?" He inquires with a bemused smile of his own.

"I never took you for a guy quoting Einstein."

"I can be mysterious, couch girl." He winks at me, and that tingling is back in my heart.

MY PHONE VIBRATES, reminding me it's time to go home.

I quickly check Kristy's calendar online and see that she's not in a meeting. Then why isn't she here already?

I leave my office in hopes to find her with Oscar, but my steps come to a halt outside the office of the HR manager, Brenda.

"Do you think Zander Teager is gay?" Brenda asks someone.

"Nah, I think his brother meant it as a joke."

I don't recognize the other person's voice.

"Uh-huh. But he's not seen with many women. With those looks and that bod, girls should be falling head over heels for him. Do you think he's single?"

I barely hear Brenda over the rustling of plastic.

Are they discussing Zander over a bag of chips?

My stomach hardens at the thought. *How do people think they have the right to discuss and dissect someone else's life?*

"I hope so. As long as he's single, I still have my chance with him." The other girl laughs.

"Same here," Brenda replies before they both start giggling.

I don't like the thought of Zander with Brenda, or whoever the other person is. I turn around, ready to stomp back into my office, forgetting Kristy.

But two steps in and I hit a wall. A warm wall.

I feel the heat of Zander's hands through my flannel as he grabs my shoulders.

"I-I'm sorry." I gaze up at him, lightheaded.

Why does it have to be him?

"Where are you going in such hurry?" he asks, composed as ever while I'm brimming with foreign irritation and weird jitters.

"I'm...looking for Kristy," I reply, creating a good distance between us.

"I saw her outside your office." He tilts his head behind him.

Of course she'd be there now.

"Thank you," I whisper before making a run for my office.

"How was your day? Anything special happen?" Kristy asks as I place the paper bag containing our dinner on the kitchen counter.

"Why do you ask?" As I remember my meeting with Zander earlier in the day, my insides tingle and the warm feverish feeling returns, heating my face.

"I got an email from Zander about your fabulous work. He says he wants me to pitch it to the sales team." She arches an eyebrow at me.

"Um, okay." Avoiding eye contact, I slide onto a barstool next to her and open my salad box.

"Um, okay? This is all you're telling me?" She turns toward me, forcing me to do the same. "You met with him today?" Her eyes gleam with excitement.

I gently nod, trying to not make a big deal out of it.

"And?"

"He asked me to give him details on the project." I shrug, pushing my fork into the mozzarella ball.

"But no one knows about this project except Oscar and me." Kristy's full attention is still on me.

"I told him in a text." I look at her under my eyelashes as she does a double take. "I mean, he texted me first, asking what I was doing. So, I sent him a picture of the code."

"You guys are texting?" Her mouth hangs open, her eyes as wide as saucers.

"Yeah, he took my number in the café. When *you* left me alone with him!" I try to put some blame on her plate.

"Hold on, this is my chance to be pissed off. You cannot hijack my moment like this." She gives me an irritated look for a few more seconds before her lips curl into a wide smile. Her hands clasp together above her chest. "Holy shit. Zander Teager, the reputable bachelor, is crushing on you."

My pulse speeds up, my head becoming light. But then I remember his face when he told me how he can't say my name.

Stupid, Rose.

"I...don't think that's true, Kris. I think, I just confuse him."

"You leave the job of interpretation to me. Just tell me everything, and I mean *everything* that happened between you and him so far."

My words have no effect on her excitement.

"Nothing happened—"

"Everything!"

I shake my head in defeat. It's better to cave in than sit here the whole night, so I explain everything to her.

"HOLY CRAP. He said he finds you beguiling."

My pulse quickens in false hope at her words.

"I think, I just confuse him," I tell her again.

"What does that mean?" Kristy's brows furrow.

"He can't say my name, Kris. Don't you think that's weird?" I don't tell her that this adds his name to the long list of people who find something wrong with me, something inadequate.

"What do you think it means if a guy says he can't say your name, but you as a person beguile him?"

I jump at Kristy's voice.

Ship. She's on the phone, most likely asking Oscar's opinion.

Why did she include him in this? He's friends with Zander.

I thump my head against the table.

"Uh-huh." She peers at me, but her face gives nothing away. "So, if you are really, really interested in me, you'd say I beguile you."

Her eyes sparkle in delight, skyrocketing my pulse.

What are they discussing?

"So, what's the deal with Zander? Why can't he say Rosie's name? It's such a pretty name."

Whoa, she didn't just ask him that!

I elbow her, but she gives me the stink eye before rubbing her side and going back to listening whatever Oscar has to say.

"Yeah. They are *texting* now." The way she stretches her lips, giving an extra emphasis on the word *texting*, it appears like she means something else with the word. "Hold on, I'm putting you on speaker."

I shake my head, torn between curiosity and nervousness.

"Hey, Rose. How's it going?"

"G-good."

"You gave Zander your phone number?" There's no hiding the surprise in Oscar's words.

"Mm… yeah. I mean, he asked so—"

"You don't need to explain anything to me, Rose. I'm just curious. I know how cautious you are about sharing your number."

Oscar waits for a few moments, but when I don't say anything, he finally breaks the silence.

"Zander is a great guy to be friends with. If the name thing bothers you so much, ask him. I'm sure he has a valid reason. But don't let anyone railroad you into doing something you don't like."

Oscar ends the call, leaving me with mixed emotions and feeling more confused than before.

Later that night, I receive a new text.

Zander: Just so you know, I'm certainly not gay and very much single. Good night, couch girl.

10

ZANDER

My two-day trip to Cherrywood has stretched into a week. But what an exhilarating week it's been. Every morning when I step inside the office building, I feel the giddiness of a five-year-old on his first day of school.

When you do something for so long, even if it's as exciting as running a company, you don't realize when it becomes a part of your routine and its buzz fades out. Since starting Elixir, I've been laser focused. The only thought on my mind as soon as I enter the office door is the company's growth and success. How can I be better in this business? How can I not fail the people who count on me?

But this week, I've thought and been excited about ridiculous things like Wolverine.

Me: I see you have a new wallpaper.

Marr's cell phone vibrates on the glass table, and she picks it up before everyone in the conference room is disturbed. I notice her as she reads my text, and then her gaze meets mine. She immediately looks away, turning her head slightly to the side as if making sure no one is watching.

I lean back in my chair and briefly glance at Oscar, who's presenting the quarterly progress report to the group.

My phone stirs in my hand.

Couch girl: It's an exclusive. I had an illustrator design it for me.

Me: I didn't know your obsession ran so deep, couch girl. Are you campaigning for the biggest Wolverine fan?

I've just hit send and there's a short giggle in between Oscar's words.

All eyes turn to Marr as she starts to cough. I notice her transition as she almost cowers in her chair and hides behind her laptop screen, her face turning pale.

Everyone's attention is quickly pulled back when Oscar starts to talk about some sales numbers in a high-pitched voice, and I wonder if his increased enthusiasm is for Marr's benefit.

When I look in her direction again, I find Kristy staring at me, eyebrow arched. I give her my sweet smile, not wanting to be in her bad books.

Me: You have a beautiful laugh. I love knowing that I did something to make you smile. But next time, I'll make sure I don't do such a thing in a room full of people.

Some tension leaves my body when I watch the beautiful pink reappearing on her face.

"W-when are you r-returning?" Zane asks as I press the keycard to the sensor and open the door to my hotel room.

This part of my day, coming back to an empty, stale room, is no fun. Although, I'd be returning to my empty apartment in St. Peppers too, but that's usually after spending a fun evening with my brothers. Other days, when I want a break from things, I'd cook something and have them over. It might sound strange to many, but cooking has always been therapeutic for me.

"I don't know." I open the fridge and fetch a water bottle.

"Is th-there a problem?"

"No. It's just…" I try to find the right response for my brother. "I like it here. I feel different." My grip on the plastic bottle tightens.

"You s-sound different. But d-don't leave me alone w-with Zach for t-too long." He chuckles.

"Don't worry. I'll most likely return at the end of this week," I tell Zane before ending the call.

The thought of leaving Cherrywood bums me out.

This is fucking crazy. I yank at my tie in irritation.

What the hell am I thinking?

I'm acting like a five-year-old in Disneyland, not wanting to return home. I have a life in St. Peppers. A business to run.

My topmost priority at this moment should be getting everything ready for the third site.

Instead of picking up the menu and ordering dinner from room service as I do every other evening, I decide to go out.

My hotel is located in the heart of Cherrywood, and I start my hunt for a good meal that'll cheer me up on foot.

I stop outside a fine dining restaurant. Although I was looking for something casual, now the thought of sitting in a crowded place doesn't interest me too much. I step in and a waitress greets me.

"Would you like a table, sir?"

"Yes, please. Just for one."

"Sure. We have a place here." She points to a setting between a large dinner party and a teenage birthday celebration. "Or there is also a small, more private table in the back." The young blonde girl gives me a kind smile.

I shrug. "I'm looking for some quiet tonight."

"Sure. Please follow me."

We walk beyond the celebrations until she takes me to the end of the big restaurant and—holy fuck, there's Marr and Kristy.

"Hello, ladies," I greet them, barely holding back my excitement as my mood makes a one-eighty shift.

"Zander, what are you doing here?" Kristy asks, and my eyes quickly scan their table—some barely touched appetizers and drinks that are still full. Looks like they've just started.

Thank fuck.

"I decided to skip the usual room service," I tell Kristy as I smile at Marr, who gives me a shy smile of her own.

"Sir, would you like me to add a placing for you here?" the patient waitress asks.

"Oh no. I wouldn't want to impose." Inside, I'm frantically wishing against my words.

"Are you kidding? It's no imposition." Kristy is already picking up her drink and the bread basket, making a place for me at their table.

I look hesitantly at Marr and she nods.

"So, how are you liking Cherrywood?" Kristy asks after I've settled in.

"Much more than expected. I wasn't prepared to be so amazed." My gaze lands on Marr, who shies away while sipping her cocktail.

The waitress hands us three menus, and I place an order for whiskey and braised lamb. After returning the leather-bound book, I peer at Marr, her eyebrows furrowed as she mulls over the choices.

Next time, when she turns the page, her eyes meet mine over the menu covering half her face.

I think it's on reflex—her gaze lowers, but then seconds later, she looks up again. There's a twinkle in her blue eyes as she adjusts her glasses. She turns to the waitress and places her order before smiling my way.

Our drinks arrive—a whiskey for me and a round of refills for the ladies.

"What are you drinking?" I look in amusement at their glasses filled with colorful liquids.

"I'm a cosmo girl." Kristy raises her glass to me. "And Rose will drink any cocktail as long as it has a trace of iced tea in it. What is it today?" She tilts her head toward her friend.

"Um, it's a gunpowder gimlet," Marr mumbles with a touch of embarrassment.

"Even your drink sounds like a superhero." I raise an eyebrow, suppressing my smile.

Kristy snorts upon hearing my remark. "That's so true." She composes herself before asking, "What does an evening in St. Peppers look like?"

From the corner of my eye, I see Marr sliding forward in her chair, leaning in to listen.

"Mostly hanging out with my brothers."

"You three are quite close," Kristy remarks.

I nod. "Relationships are very important to me. Be it with my brothers or…friends."

Marr leans back, hiding her huge grin behind that cocktail glass. But it slips upon hearing my next words.

"That's why they're continuously asking when I'm coming back."

"Oh, I didn't know you were already planning to return." Kristy looks between Marr and me.

Does she know there's something—whatever that is—going on between us?

"My trip was originally meant to be two days. Nobody expected me to be out of St. Peppers for a week."

"I hope we'll see more of you, Zander." Kristy smiles.

"You will certainly see much more of me. This town and its people are growing on me."

. . .

Later in the night, I send Marr a text.

Me: I was serious when I said I'd be visiting more often.

Her response is immediate.

Couch girl: I'm glad to hear that.

Couch girl: I was surprised to hear about you leaving.

My hands tingle as I type a response. I press my lips tight, holding back the wide smile from making an appearance. My heart fucking bursts with joy knowing she isn't unaffected by my return.

Me: I'm surprised at how much I don't want to leave. Your cute town is growing on me. Some people more than others.

As usual, when her fingers type, I see the consequential three dots.

Couch girl: Some of those people would be happy to see you more often.

11

ROSE

My phone buzzes on the table as I bite on the sandwich I have for lunch.

Zander: Did I tell you about Pippi?

Me: What's a Pippi?

Zander: Pippi is the one keeping me awake at night.

I look at my phone. The crazy thing about texts is that you don't know if they're meant as a joke or said in earnest.

Is Pippi a *lady friend* or… something else. And how do I feel about the former? Thankfully, Zander clarifies before my brain goes into overdrive.

Zander: Pippi is my neighbor's obnoxious new parrot, who is still on a different time zone. That stupid bird starts squawking before sunrise and goes on and on…

Reading his words, my lips twist in a smile.

Me: LOL I can't believe it's so bad.

Zander: Don't make fun of me. I'm operating on very little sleep.

Me: How much coffee have you had already?

Zander: Don't you even start on the coffee.

Me: You are grumpy!

Zander: Pippi is to blame.

. . .

A FEW DAYS LATER, while I'm sitting in the passenger seat as Kristy drives us to work, my phone vibrates along with a tweet sound, which I've assigned to Zander.

Zander: Pippi is gone.

I giggle, and Kristy arches an eyebrow at me.

Me: I hope you had nothing to do with it.

Zander: Not at all. I think Pippi's owner was equally pissed by him.

Me: I'm glad to hear your nights will no longer be painful.

Zander: Amen to that!

Zander: Did you have a pet while growing up?

My smile drops as I read his text. I chew on my lips, debating how to respond. He doesn't know the kind of childhood I had.

Me: I grew up in an orphanage. We weren't really allowed to have pets.

I type but then hesitate. Should I hit send, or reply with a simple no? That would be much easier and possibly less awkward. But then Kristy makes a sharp turn, and my wavering thumb presses on the send button.

Taking me by surprise, his reply is immediate.

Zander: I don't know if you're aware, but I was in foster care for some time before moving in with Ashcroft. Was your home good?

I read his message a few more times, not sure if he's deliberately trying to make light of my unconventional childhood or if it really doesn't matter to him.

Me: It was good for the most part.

Zander: Hmm. That's good.

I try to pull the topic of our discussion away from sappy childhood memories.

Me: But if I had a pet, I'd have killed it in a week. Or maybe myself in the stress of keeping it alive.

Zander: LOL You need a low maintenance pet, couch girl.

TWO DAYS LATER, I receive a delivery from the local pet store. In a state of daze, I bring in the glass bowl where a goldfish is swimming, perfectly unaware that it has just been assigned to the most paranoid person.

Me: You sent me a fish!

Zander: They delivered already? Great.

Me: Zander, I can't take care of a fish! I've never had a fish.

Zander: Calm down, couch girl. Did they give you something else?

Me: Yes, the delivery guy gave me a package.

Zander: Open it. I asked them to prepare a starter's guide for you. Don't worry, this is the easiest pet to have.

I look at…*my first pet*, a pretty golden fish, laid back with not a care in the world.

My hands frantically open the cardboard box, and I find some food and a binder. I flip through it, and the top of the first page reads *First Five Days with Your New Friend*.

My gaze falls back on the fellow floating in the water. I guess I can give it a try, if this little guy is up for it.

Me: What should I name him?

Zander: What are you thinking?

Me: LOGAN.

Zander: I didn't expect anything less from you, Wolverine junkie. ;) Enjoy your new friend.

With a new-filled excitement, I bring the fishbowl to my room and place it on the nightstand.

"Please don't die on me, Logan," I murmur.

"Why am I in this meeting?" I ask Kristy as we walk toward the teleconference room.

"I really don't know. Maybe because it's your idea," she mumbles, biting her phone between her teeth as she fixes her hair.

"But I've initiated several projects in the past and…I've never had to sit in a sales and marketing meeting." My eyebrows furrow in confusion, wondering what am I doing in a S&M department meeting.

"I don't know what to say, Rose." She stands before me with a perfect top bun. "The invitation came from St. Peppers. Maybe Zander asked for you."

"Zander? Is he going to be in this meeting?" I stop just outside the door.

We've talked so much over the past few weeks but only in texts, and that's… simpler, easier. In those texts, he doesn't feel like my boss, but rather a friend I'm slowly developing a crush on.

"Yes. Is that a problem?" Kristy takes a few steps back to me.

I shake my head. Suddenly, my feet feel as if they have heavy weight tied to them—possibly the weight of the storm rolling in my stomach as I enter the room.

We are thankfully some of the first people here, and I quickly grab the empty chair at the far end, beyond the scope of the camera. Kristy raises an eyebrow at me but thankfully doesn't say anything.

The meeting starts and six people appear on the projector screen. Sitting in the middle is Zander, and on his one side is Zach Teager. I guess the rest are the team members of S&M.

Zach is about to say something when Zander asks, "Is Ms. Marlin not in the meeting?"

Oscar glances my way. My panic-laden eyes meet his for a second before I look down at my laptop. "She is here and listening," he confirms.

Zander doesn't look pleased with the answer, but he doesn't argue further. Throughout the meeting, his gaze wanders.

Is he searching for me?

Zander: Why couldn't I see you in today's meeting?

Me: I don't know. Why was I even there? Was it a mistake?

Zander: No. You were there because I wanted to see you.

My breath hitches at his unexpected and direct response.

Me: Oh. But wouldn't it have been easier to video call me instead of asking me to attend a video conference?

My phone rings. *Holy moly, he's fast.*

But I'm in no state for a video call. I'm sitting in my pajamas and pigtails, ready to get into bed. I end the call.

Zander: What?

Me: We can talk some other time. I'm not ready at the moment.

Zander: Not ready for what? A call? Just pick up, Marr.

I ignore his call again. But when my phone rings for the third time, I know there's no way I can ignore him tonight.

"Hello," I mutter, embarrassed at being caught in such a state.

"Hello." He smiles, and my eyes widen at the sight of Zander, who's sitting on what looks like a balcony.

Does he know how impossibly handsome he looks under the yellow LED light?

The top button of his shirt is undone, and his tie sits loose around his neck.

"How…are you?" My voice shivers.

"Good. I just wanted to see you," he says, giving me that killer smile and dimpled cheek.

"I look crazy." I peer away from his piercing gaze.

How did I land here? Looking like a dork in pigtails ready

for a hair wash tomorrow with an oily night cream on my face, while he's all set for a photoshoot.

"You look cute. Pigtails suit you." Zander smirks.

My heartbeat accelerates at his comment. "Don't make fun of me." I tug on my braided hair. "I wasn't expecting a late-night video call from my boss."

"I'm your friend. Oscar is your boss," he states with a shrug. As if there is any truth in that technicality. Zander changes the subject. "How's Logan?"

I turn my camera to the fishbowl beside my bed and bring it closer to my new roomie. "Alive, so far. I just wish he had some lips." I glance at Logan's expressionless face. "This way I could know if he's happy and smiling. Right now, I have no clue."

Zander bursts into laughter. "You're funny."

My heart feels lighter knowing I said something to get that laugh out of him.

"Lips or no lips, he looks happy, couch girl."

"Why are we here?" Kristy asks, and by here, she means sitting on our living room's vintage rug with pizza from Giovanni's and iced tea.

"I need to ask you something," I reply as she takes a bite of her pizza slice.

"About Zander?" She's wearing a gray T-shirt with a cute coffee mug and *I love coffee* written in perky letters.

I nod, sipping the cold iced tea, hoping it'll cool down some of the anxiety rolling in my stomach.

"He wants Logan back?" Her eyes bug out at me, and a giggle slips from my mouth in the middle of my nervousness.

"No, Logan is safe here. It's…" My words falter as my grip

around the glass tightens before I place it on the floor. "I'm…"

"What's the matter?" She places her hand on my knee and squeezes.

"I'm confused." My hands pull on the cuffs of my flannel nightshirt. "You know Zander and I, we've been texting for a while."

She nods. "Yeah, Rose. I know he likes you."

"You…think so?" My heart stumbles over its next few beats.

"The way he's organizing unnecessary video calls, sending all those fish—"

"It's just one fish," I correct.

"You know what I mean. But what's the problem?" She gives me a pointed look.

"Of late, the language of his texts is… different."

"You guys are sexting?" she yells so loud, I jump in my seat, my back hitting the couch.

"No! God, no. Most likely…it's nothing and I'm just imagining things." That's my biggest fear and also the reason why I need Kristy's advice.

"Tell me what he said, and I'll decide if it's nothing or not."

With great trepidation and my heart hammering against my rib cage, I tell her how, two days back, Zander put me in a mushy daze while he commented on my sleeping habit.

"If you were my girlfriend, Marr, you'd have to be in bed at nine to continue your routine of sleeping at twelve. I'd need three hours to have my way with you."

And when I asked him nervously what he meant by having his way, he simply replied, *"I'll talk to you for at least three hours about our day before I let you sleep. You are a very easy person to talk to."*

I know guys flirt often, though not many have flirted with me. But with Zander, I don't know. Is this even flirting?

I have no clue whether the ginormous texting spree that has been going on without a break for over a month now has changed my relationship with the man who became my friend over an empty cup of coffee or if it's just my confused, hallucinating brain.

"I'm stumped," I tell Kristy, who's hanging on my every word.

"I can't say I'm surprised. Mighty Zander Teager, *enamored* of our Rose." Her gaze doesn't leave me as she leans back, taking support of the love seat.

Her words make my heart race, which is its usual state these days.

"You think…so?" I wish so badly for Kristy's words to be true.

The feverish feeling I have around Zander is like his personal electricity directed toward me. I feel it every time there's even a reference to him. It's only recently that I've realized this feverish feeling isn't bad. It makes me warm like hot cocoa in winter.

"He's totally into you. Did you not see how upset he was when our camera didn't work on the last conference call?"

I chuckle while remembering the day. He was so restless throughout the whole meeting.

"When he met us in the café that morning, I wasn't sure if his attraction was because of your genius freaky mind or your sweet shyness." She taps the tip of my nose with her finger.

"Only you can call me a freak and sweet in the same sentence." I pout, and it's her turn to giggle. I remove the empty pizza box and lie back on the rug next to her, my gaze following the concentric circular design on the ceiling of our living room.

"Do you really think it's possible, me and Zander? As much as I want it to be true, I'm scared. He doesn't know…" I can't finish the sentence, the familiar cold engulfing me.

"No, Rosie. Don't go there. Zander is lucky to have grabbed your attention." My best friend grasps my hands tightly, willing me to believe in her words.

I know she's right. I should be happy for these unfamiliar sensations and feelings. For so long, I thought my life would be just me, my work, my comic books… basically *only me*. But now Zander is knocking on the closed doors of my heart, urging me to open them. The question is: am I prepared to find out what's inside and ready to take a chance?

Can I risk the stability I finally have in my life?

"What are you thinking?" Kristy turns to her side, facing me.

"This looks like a gamble."

"Love always is."

Oh my. Are we really talking about the big L-word?

Before I can mull or hyperventilate more, Kristy distracts me.

"You really like him, don't you?"

I'm sure she has no problem reading the fear on my face, but she presses my hand lightly and smiles.

After several minutes of silence, she playfully nudges my shoulder. "Maybe next time when he's flirting with you, you simply play along before he makes a U-turn."

"I don't think I can do that." I nervously rub my forehead.

She pulls my hand away. "You don't have to go all gaga over him. Just play up some of your cute charm."

I don't dismiss her idea this time. Not because I'm going to act on it immediately, but because it's tough to argue with Kristy. Instead, I ask, "What do you think happens next?"

"You guys will probably move beyond the virtual world and go on… real dates."

Dates? Sweet sugar! Am I up for it?

12

ZANDER

"Did you hear about the upcoming party?" My phone is tucked between my shoulder and ear as I open the door to my apartment.

"Yeah. I read the email," Marr mumbles.

"Are you excited?" After grabbing a beer from the fridge, I open the balcony door and flop onto the recliner.

"Everybody is." The disinterest is clear in her voice. This crazy girl.

"Marr, I'm not asking about your whole town. Are *you* excited?"

"I… I'm not really a party person. Also, crowds…make me nervous," she mutters the expected response.

The upcoming party is Elixir's first annual meet in Cherrywood. It's the first time staff from St. Peppers will drive down to Cherrywood. Seeing Marr's lack of interest in presenting even her best work and the way she has either bailed or managed to hide in all the conference calls I've arranged over the past month, I know parties aren't her thing.

I take a swig of beer before asking, "I meant, are you excited to see me?" My voice comes out raspier than usual.

"Um..." She hesitates before whispering, "I'll be...if you'll be."

The beer bottle stays on my mouth for a beat longer.

Holy fuck. Did I hear right, or are the soft and breathy words my imagination?

When did you become so courageous, couch girl?

"I'll be thrilled to see you." I can barely contain the excitement bubbling inside me. "It's been so long hearing your voice, listening to your laughs." Her rare audacity fuels my suppressed attraction, emboldening me to say the things I'm trying to bury inside. "I'm eager to see you in person again, walk with you through the streets of Cherrywood, meet your still-alive-and-kicking Logan, and admire your one-of-a-kind superhero collage."

She stills, and I can only hear her heavy breathing.

Fuck. Did I take things too far, too quickly?

"Marr, say something." I can't fucking hide the trembling in my voice.

"I... I'd also like...all that," she whispers before ending the call.

It's a day before we drive down to Cherrywood. I'm in my office looking at the list of awardees for this year's function. Marr's name is written next to the innovation award.

This list is supposed to be a surprise, and for the past fifteen minutes, I'm trying to imagine her face when her name is announced in a room full of people and she's asked to collect the prize on stage.

In none of the several imaginations I've crafted so far, is she happy and excited. Instead, her face is pale, scared, nervous. She's tugging on her cuffs and focusing on something like her canvas shoes. In one of my wildest thoughts, I even imagine her bolting out of the party hall. I have to tell her.

She picks up the call, and her beautiful face fills my phone screen. "Hello."

"Hello to you too. How are you?"

"I'm good. Same as I was four hours ago." She giggles and my heart soars into overdrive hearing her laughter and seeing her this comfortable with me.

"I'm very pleased to hear that my concern amuses you, Ms. Marlin."

She blushes deep red. "Your concern *pleases* me."

Every day we talk, it feels like we're taking a tiny step closer, but often, my deepest fear confronts me. She has *that* name.

How can I trust someone who is called *that?*

Why the hell am I putting myself in the way of hurt?

But then I see her. A girl who purchased a high-precision scale just to ensure she's feeding her fish the recommended amount and not even a tiny bit more or less, and I chastise myself for thinking about hurt and her in the same sentence.

"Zander?" she calls my name, and as always, it sounds different coming from her mouth.

"Yes, sorry. I have to tell you something."

I watch as she chews on her lips, her hands adjusting her glasses before she brings them down. I'm sure she's tugging on her cuffs. She's not so different from me, always thinking the worst. "What... is it?"

"You have won the innovation award this year."

"Oh."

My heart squeezes watching her shoulders slump in relief and not delight. She is much more apprehensive than me.

"That's a...good thing, I guess."

"It's a very good thing. You were unanimously selected. Everyone in St. Peppers is in awe of your recent project. No one can believe you single-handedly executed it."

"It's…no big deal." She looks away, embarrassed by the attention.

"The awards will be given out during the party," I say carefully.

Her blue eyes widen as they meet mine. They're filled with nervousness and fear.

"I'll be on the stage, Marr. There's nothing to worry about. It's a small group of people. People you know. You don't even have to give a speech or anything."

I watch closely as her face pales and her eyes close.

I'm so thankful to Oscar for filling me on Marr's anxiety issues, otherwise I'd never understand her response. I watch her chest move up and down as she breathes heavily. I wait patiently and a few minutes later, her eyes open.

"I… I'm sorry."

"You don't have to be sorry. You told me social activities aren't your thing. I understand."

A light color stains her face, and she gives me a weak smile. I didn't realize her panic was contagious. My spiking heartbeat slowly settles as more color appears on her face and her breathing calms.

THE PAST TWO months have been surreal.

Marr—her hesitant smile; her breathy voice. Even her cuff tugging hovers on my mind throughout the day. A weird mix of calm and excitement fills my heart every time I speak to her. But I also regret not visiting Cherrywood sooner.

I've really taken a shine to this cute town, with all its streets lined with Cherry trees and the blue-roofed houses. So have my brothers. As we arrive in Cherrywood, Zach and Zane are instantly on board with the idea of biking on its captivating hilly trails. But that's for another day. Today, my only focus is on Marr.

As I pull out the charcoal gray suit and the cherry red tie hanging in the hotel suite closet and place it carefully on the bed, a smile tugs on my lips. They're the same clothes I wore on my first day to the Cherrywood office two months back. The day I met Marr. This tie has recently become my favorite, and so far, has been a lucky charm. All the meetings I attended wearing it were overly successful.

After getting dressed up, I come downstairs and find the event manager, Nikita. Damn, she's done an awesome job. The hall is bathed in soft purple lighting. In the sitting area, the round tables are covered with silky soft white linen and hold elegant light centerpieces that give an illusion of flickering candle flame.

The bar on the side is up and running, bartenders checking everything for the last time.

My inspection is cut short by Vanessa's interruption.

"Hello, handsome. Where are you hiding these days?"

Her voice makes me want to cry for help, but I can't let her ruin my mood today. Vanessa Hilbert is the daughter of Mathew Hilbert, one of our major shareholders and a respected man in the business community. As Mathew is also a close pal of Ashcroft, our association with the Hilbert family extends beyond business.

There was a time when we three brothers were quite close to Vanessa. But in recent years, after she opened one of the top fashion houses in the state, something changed, and her behavior grew erratic. Every now and then, she would pass by the office, flirt with me, and behave indiscreetly. In the beginning, I worried for her. I even tried to talk to her, but she simply flirted in response, and I finally gave up.

"Zander Teager, I'm talking to you," she screeches.

"Hi, Vanessa. How are you doing?"

"Now, good. It's very good to see you." Her hands grab my forearms before sliding up my chest. Her touch feels like several snakes crawling up my body.

"Great." I take a step back, attempting to put some distance between us.

"Hi, beautiful." Zach saunters toward us.

"Hello, handsome." Vanessa's hands shift from my arms to Zach's. She doesn't even bother using a different opening line.

"Nikita is looking for you." Zach raises his chin in my direction, giving me an out from Vanessa. On a normal day, I would hate Zach's playboy attitude, but today, I have more important things on my mind.

"Thanks." I wink at him and leave. Zach can handle Vanessa for a day.

I'M PACING in the hall, waiting impatiently for my couch girl. So far, I've made several unsuccessful visits to the entrance hoping to find her, only to return empty-handed.

The hall is slowly filling with people dressed in fancy party clothes. Some have even mustered the courage to get on the purple-lit dance floor. The party theme is "dance till you drop." I wonder if I can get Marr on the dance floor with me. Deep in my thoughts, I notice Oscar walking in, followed by Kristy and *her*.

Our eyes meet, and she gives me her exquisite shy smile. My mouth dries at the sight of her, and my heart does that weird thumping it always does whenever she's around. I give her a once-over, and damn, she looks breathtaking.

Her usual ponytail-tied hair is loose, and the soft curls rest just above her shoulders. The billowy flannel shirt and jeans ensemble is replaced by an elegant dress.

Does she know my tie matches the cherry color of her dress?

The high waistline flaunts her perfect figure. When she turns to hang her brown leather jacket, I get a good look of her curvy legs covered in black stockings. But it's her charcoal gray ankle boots that suck all the fucking air out of my lungs.

As she moves a strand of hair behind her ear, I see small pearl drop earrings. Pearls suit my couch girl. She has a tinge of makeup, which only adds to her natural beauty. One look at her pink lips, and I'm dying to get a taste.

She looks at me again and instinctively licks her bottom lip in nervousness, I guess. But fuck, what it does to me. The flick of her tongue seems to have a direct connection with my already raging cock. I adjust my jacket, ensuring I'm not sporting a hard-on to a room full of people.

I give her a smile, and she smiles back. So much has changed between us since my last visit. We've outgrown our friendship to something more, without mentioning it explicitly. As I take a step toward her, someone grabs my hand from behind.

What. The. Hell?

"What do you want, Vanessa?" I turn around as she climbs my body like a fucking viper.

"I saw you searching for me," she slurs as her glassy eyes roll.

"I wasn't searching for you." I pull her tipsy body away. My girl is waiting for me, and I have no interest in wasting my time on drunken women.

"You don't have to lie to me, Zander Teager." Vanessa giggles, batting her eyelashes at me seductively, and it distracts me for a second.

"What's going on, Vanessa? Is everything all right?" Why is she coming on to me, and so brazenly? I've never given her any indication that I'm interested in anything beyond friendship. And I always thought she and Zach had something going on.

For a fleeting moment, her gaze turns downward and her shoulders curl over her chest, but she soon recovers and pats my tie.

"Everything is peachy. If you're so worried about me, why don't you get me a drink? We can talk more about us."

"I think you've had enough for tonight. And there is no us; there was never an us. If I ever gave you any indication otherwise, I'm sorry. But I'm not interested." I yank away from Vanessa and march to get my girl.

13

ROSE

As I enter the reception hall, my eyes search for Zander. And it doesn't take me long to find him near the bar staring right at me.

I'd thought the warm feeling his presence brings would have disappeared by now, but boy was I wrong. It feels like the temperature in the room has increased several degrees. His beseeching eyes hold me captive and take my breath away. Someone walks through our line of held gaze, breaking our trance.

I recognize his tie, and a smile forms on my lips. Yesterday, Kristy insisted we go to the mall to shop for the party. My dress collection is quite scarce, with parties being a rarity in my world. I also knew I couldn't show up in my flannel shirt and canvas shoes. So, even though the idea of shopping didn't stir my blood, I joined my friend.

When I saw the full sleeve red dress smushed between a shimmery backless green and a floral peach, his cherry tie came to my mind. Although the dress, with all its ruffles and layers, isn't my usual style, the color drew me in.

I'm about to take a step toward Zander after leaving my jacket at the coat check station when a woman grabs his hand from behind and my heart stops. All the confidence I'd gathered after hours and hours of pep talk ebbs away, leaving me panicky and nervous.

The same old me.

She looks like a supermodel. Her hourglass figure draped in a green cocktail dress is exactly how someone would imagine Zander's girlfriend. In high stiletto heels, she's as tall as him.

And here I thought my new boots were cool.

Her hands curl around Zander's arm in a tight grip as she whispers in his ear, giving him a sexy smile. I can't see his face, but I can see hers and it's clear they're intimate.

Stupid Rose. What the hell was I thinking?

I misinterpreted his friendly behavior for something more. Remembering all the times I flirted back with Zander in the past few days, my chest cringes with shame. I turn around, hoping to run away from this place before bursting into unstoppable tears. But a clearing of a throat interrupts my escape plan.

"Marr."

Why does he have to talk to me now?

"Hi," I reply without looking at him.

"I was waiting for you." He guides me to a secluded corner with a warm hand on my back, burning my skin though the soft fabric.

Liar. "Sorry."

"Don't be. It's not that I didn't enjoy waiting for you; I just wanted to see you sooner."

"It doesn't…look that way," I say under my breath.

He chuckles. "Someone's feisty."

I peek under the hair falling over my forehead to admonish him, but as always, his dimpled smile gets to me. His kind and warm eyes hold the same affection that I've felt in his voice over the past few weeks.

"She is a friend, Marr. Acquaintance is maybe a better

word. Vanessa is the daughter of Mathew Hilbert, one of our board members. We've known each other for a long time. She likes to throw herself at men, but I have never encouraged her." He then asks, "Wouldn't you know by now if I was with someone?"

"I don't know." I shrug, but his words slowly bring my confidence back. Maybe the past few weeks weren't my imagination.

He takes a step closer to me and asks in a serious voice, "Marr, who am I?"

"Zander Teager, the CEO of Elixir. Did you forget?" I try to lighten the mood. I like playful Zander more than this broody man.

"Smart mouth." He chuckles. "But I'm serious. What do you say we are? Friends?"

"Yes," I reply, though I was hoping we were more than that.

"So, I'm your friend, like Oscar?" He cocks his head to the side.

"No. I mean, I—what do you want me to say?" I whisper, looking away from him.

"I want you to say what you feel, Marr," he replies oh so gently.

I glance up at him. "Why don't *you* tell me what you feel?"

"Me? I feel many things. I'm not sure you're ready to hear them all, but I hope—I really hope—I'm more than a friend to you. I hope you feel the same way as I do."

His whispered words create a thousand butterflies in my stomach. By the end of his sentence, I'm a buzzing, shaking mess of heat.

"What is it…that you…really feel?" My words come out as a stutter as I come close to hyperventilating.

"So you want *me* to do all the talking." He raises an eyebrow and winks at me. "Not here. Someday when you're with me, completely willing and mine, I'll not only tell you but show you what I feel. But today, I'll say that when you walked into this hall, wearing those boots and that beautiful dress, damn, you made my heart stop. I had to remember to breathe. You take my breath away every time you're around. Ever since I got back to this cute little town, I've been dying to see these gorgeous blue eyes hidden behind the red glasses."

Wow. I didn't know someone could describe feelings so beautifully. It almost feels like a poem. His wonderful words make my heart flutter, dreaming about the possibilities of what he hasn't said and enjoying what he has.

With my heart being in an entirely different world, I whisper, "I also liked the boots."

"Yes, you look ravishing."

"Zander!" My eyes widen at his brazen remark.

He finds me ravishing.

He chuckles. "What? I'm just trying to clear the air. I don't want you friend zoning me again."

"I didn't friend zone you," I reply in haste.

"Oh, really? You just said we're friends."

"But I meant like…close friends."

"Like you and Oscar?"

What's his deal with Oscar?

"No. Like me and no one. You're…special," I whisper under my breath. I'm not sure if he heard me.

But he did. "Thank you. So much effort to hear special from your smart mouth."

"And…" I drawl.

"*Yeesss.*" He stretches that yes, making it sound sexy and seductive like he does on our phone calls. "And what Marr?"

"I like your tie. I was hoping you'd wear it today." I tug on the sleeves of my dress.

His eyes blaze at my admission. "Why, couch girl, I'm glad my attire meets your approval. And I love your dress."

I get lost in his soul piercing gaze. I don't know how long

we stand in that corner, staring at each other. Maybe five seconds, five minutes… maybe ten.

A strange, hoarse voice breaks our moment, and Zander's lips pull up in an affectionate smile.

I turn around to find Zane Teager standing behind me, looking at us with a bemused smile.

"Zand-der, who's your fr-riend? Introd-duce me."

It didn't go unnoticed by me how Zane framed his sentences in a few words.

Zane is tall, even a few inches taller than Zander. Contrary to Zander's serious features, Zane has a soft and compassionate face. I've seen the three brothers on the internet several times now, but the online pictures do no justice to their stunning features. I have no doubt their birth parents were beyond beautiful.

"Marr, this is my brother Zane, and Zane, this is Dr. Marlin. She is a lead data scientist here in Cherrywood."

"Nice t-to meet you, Marr. Due to some r-reason my brother can't s-stop smiling since you w-walked in." Zane's lips curl up as he bumps his shoulder with Zander's.

I enjoy watching them. Over the weeks, I have heard so much about Zach and Zane from Zander, it feels like I already know them. Maybe it's the reason I don't feel my usual uneasiness around him.

"Nice to meet you too. I've heard a lot about you."

Zane's eyebrows rise in surprise. "I mus-st confess, I haven't hear-rd much about you. My br-rother kept you a secret."

The smile on my face drops hearing his words.

Doesn't Zander want anyone to know about me? About us?

But immediately, Zander clears his throat and gives me his soft dimpled smile. Slaying the monsters of my insecurities, he says to his brother, "I wanted to introduce you and Zach to Marr in person this evening."

As always, his words make my heart flutter in delight, giving me jitters of happiness.

We walk further into the room to Kristy and Oscar when there's an announcement on the stage. Zander is introducing Kristy to Zane while the event organizer addresses the crowd. After delivering the welcome note, she invites Zander on stage.

Giving me a discreet smile, he makes his way through the crowd. His stride is confident and controlled. I briefly pull my gaze away from him to notice the admiring eyes of men and women fixated on him as he takes the mic and starts to speak.

"Hello, everyone. Thank you for joining us on this wonderful evening. Four years ago, my brothers and I came up with the idea of Elixir Inc. It was our dream to revolutionize the world of pharmaceuticals. Little did we know, we would be opening our second office a year later in this charming town. Over these years, several people joined us in our journey. And it's their hard work, *your* hard work, that has turned our dream into a reality."

Everyone bursts into applause as Zander finishes his speech.

My clapping hands pause when I feel someone new beside me and find Zach Teager standing next to me. I'm seized by startling numbness when I realize I'm surrounded by Zander's brothers, Kristy, and Oscar.

Familiar people. Friends or future friends.

"What's up with him today? If he smiles any more, he might get stretch marks," Zach drawls, breaking my reverie.

My lips twitch up in a smile. The middle Teager is notoriously famous for his sense of humor.

"Zach, meet Ms-s. Marlin and Ms. As-sher," Zane introduces us to Zach. "You might have already s-seen them in the conference calls in the past month." As we are shaking hands, he adds, "Mar-rr is a very good fr-riend of Zander's."

A look passes between the two brothers, but only for a second before Zach smiles. "It's nice to meet you, ladies." He cocks an eyebrow toward me. "So, Ms. Marlin, you are our tech genius in Cherrywood. My sales and marketing team is smitten by your work."

I shy away from his inquisitive gaze, but Kristy replies on my behalf.

"Rose is certainly a tech genius. We are so proud to have her with us."

Before our discussions run further, Zander starts announcing the awards.

A middle-aged manager with salt-and-pepper hair from human resources receives the outstanding leadership award. A woman around my age dressed in a gray skater dress steps onto the stage to collect a customer service award. There's no mistaking the pink in her cheeks as she takes the trophy from Zander.

Who wouldn't fall for that face, and more importantly, the person behind it?

Zander looks at me, and I know it's my turn. I have tried to prepare myself as best I can for tonight. My phone is flooded with Zander's texts telling me how everything will be all right. I think at some point he was more nervous than me, which was both scary and gratifying.

"This year, we have a special category for one person who has impressed us all by her innovative ideas and admirable work ethics. I am very happy to present, for the first time, the innovation award to Dr. Marlin," Zander declares, his eyes never leaving mine.

As he announces my name, Kristy squeals beside me. I didn't tell her about the award, because ideally, it's supposed to be a surprise, and also, I didn't think it was such a big deal.

Kristy throws her arms around me. "Congratulations, Rosie." Next, Oscar shakes my hand. I hadn't expected to feel such pleasure at seeing the proud smile on his face. He briefly touches his shoulder with mine in some form of light hug.

After Zach and Zane have wished me congratulations, Kristy whispers in my ear, "You'll be all right?" Her head cocks toward the stage.

I look at Zander, waiting patiently for me with a glass trophy in his hand.

"I'll be fine," I whisper, putting one hand over my chest, attempting to slow my heart rate.

Kristy glances at me and then at the stage before she gives my shoulders a gentle squeeze and a kind smile touches her lips.

I climb the two steps, and Zander is already by my side when I'm on the raised podium. His eyes shine with excitement, which sends a warmth through my body, warding off the nervous cold.

He gives me his lopsided, dimpled grin, and for a second, I forget that I'm in a room full of people staring at me.

He holds my gaze captive in his, not letting me look anywhere but at him as he hands me the award. My ears briefly register the claps and flashes of cameras. When I'm about to turn around, Zander's palm presses on my damp hand under the glass trophy.

He doesn't want me to look away.

"This was the last award," he whispers. For a brief second, his gaze leaves mine and he glances at someone behind me.

Then I hear the woman from before, addressing the crowd and asking everyone to join the dance floor. While the crowd's attention is elsewhere, Zander and I get down off the stage.

Kristy, Oscar, and Zander's brothers join us, and Kristy immediately pulls me in for another hug.

I can feel the woodsy vanilla scent around me as light conversation about the party and office starts to flow.

Zander's hand brushes against mine in the bunched group, and a shudder runs down my body. He held my hand before on the stage, but my brain was in a nervous daze then. This time, I register *everything.*

His long warm fingers touching mine. His cold watch hitting my wrist.

My head jerks up to him. There is a hint of confusion in his gaze as it bores deep into mine, but then he grabs my hand and intertwines our fingers together. I look down at our joined hands. My pink painted nails from this morning press against his sun-kissed skin.

Hard and soft mixing together.

14

ROSE

"You gotta be kidding me. Really? Her Zander, really?"

Vanessa's shrill words get everyone's attention. Her eyes burn with rage and hatred as they fix on me before her gaze slides lower, and a spiteful smile plays on her lips. She raises our held hands up in the air for everyone to see.

That's when I know this isn't going to end well.

Zander takes a step forward, and my limp arm falls down. "What the hell, Vanessa?" he hisses.

"You tell me, Zander. What are you doing with this girl? She was the one on stage, right?"

"Not-t-t here, Vanes-s-sa." Zane stands beside her, somehow not scared to approach even though she's swaying with anger.

"No, Zane. You stay out of this. This is between me and Zander." Some of her perfectly pinned-up hair falls on her forehead as she shakes her head.

"There's nothing between you and me, Vanessa. What the fuck are you talking about?" Zander's eyebrows squish together as he rubs his forehead with his fingers.

As if she hasn't even heard his words, Vanessa's voice turns down a notch with a hint of seduction, which I absolutely hate. "Zander, this is what you like? *A fucking mouse?* You could have told me that you're into those kinks…"

Utter humiliation fills me. I never thought someone would interpret me and Zander together in this way.

I'm still in shock when Kristy grabs my hand and almost drags me toward the door. Her face is fuming. I wish I could have expressions like her for once, but I'm just stunned and anxious as several pairs of eyes focus on us—on me.

But Vanessa has other plans. She tugs on my free arm, pulling me away from Kristy. "Not so fast, missy. You aren't going anywhere."

In the tug of war between the two girls, I lose my balance, but Zander catches me by my waist.

"Leave her be, Vanessa." His deep growl vibrates through my body as his hands dig into my hips.

Vanessa lets go and stands in front of me, her hands crossed over her chest as she scowls. My eyesight blurs, and it feels like everyone is moving in closer, surrounding us like sharks ready to feed and I am the prey.

"What the hell is going on?" Zach asks, eyebrows raised in confusion.

But before anyone can respond, Zane moves in front of me, effectively shielding me from Vanessa's view. "You're t-too drunk, Vanes-ssa. Let me t-take you to your hot-tel room."

"No, Zane." Vanessa pushes past him and points her finger at Zander, red nail polish on display—almost the same color as *our* red, my and Zander's. "Just tell me what's going on between you two."

At her insistence, Zander's grip on my waist tightens almost painfully. I turn, grimacing, and he releases me with a jerk. I try to remember in all my video calls or meetings if I've ever seen Zander this tense and agitated, but I can't remember one instance.

"What does it look like?" he asks, glaring at Vanessa.

I don't like the way Zander's mouth twists as his words are spoken quietly, laced with a controlled anger. His death stare slides away from Vanessa and toward me, and the coldness turns to confusion.

I hate it.

I wish, just once, someone would accept me publicly. But maybe that's too much to ask.

My eyes well with tears, and a million emotions feed my tumultuous heart. I drop my gaze and my shoulder's slump. Any high I had from earlier—after seeing Zander—is gone. I'm barely holding in a sob when he speaks again.

"Marr and I are together. And if you have no more questions, I would really like to get the hell out of here."

My heart sputters with muted joy as my mind sorts through the implication of his words. He doesn't give me time to process them before he retakes my hand and leads me away from everyone.

Once outside, he releases his tight grip and runs his hand through his unruly hair in frustration. "This was not how I had planned this evening." He takes my hand again, his touch much more gentle than before.

My breathing grows heavier, and as much as my hands want to tug on my sleeves, they also want to stay clasped in Zander's warmth.

"What I said inside—"

Zander's words are interrupted by Kristy's stormy arrival. "Rosie, are you okay?" Her eyes scan us, standing close, hands held together. "I was worried. I'll…come back later," she mutters.

"Kristy, wait. I have to make sure everything is back to normal inside." Zander nods toward the entrance through which she appeared. "You stay with Marr." He squeezes my hand before whispering, "I'll be back soon."

I nod lightly and he heads back inside.

"I had no idea things were going *so* well between you

two." Kristy briefly shakes her head in disbelief. Or is it hurt? I'm not sure. She has never looked at me like this. "I knew you guys were talking, but I didn't know you guys were together."

"Kris—"

"Why didn't you tell me?"

Oh my God. I betrayed my best friend.

"Kristy, I...didn't know. We never...talked about it?" My throat chokes and I feel more upset than before.

"About you being the girlfriend of the hottest bachelor?"

Her question throws me for a loop.

Is this how everyone is thinking about me and Zander? The diffident me and the Adonis him.

This evening turned out so unexpectedly. I had only wished to have a nice time with him like a normal girl.

He said we were *together*. A word I've nervously imagined while lying on my bed, lights out, covers pulled up to my head, scared to even dream it in broad daylight. But every time Zander whispered the word in my dream, he wasn't so...frustrated. In my dreams, he was delighted.

But tonight, he said my dream word to shut Vanessa up.

Kristy's hands grab mine, stopping me from harshly pulling on the cuffs of my new dress. "I want to be angry with you. But when you do that"—she cocks her head to my fidgeting fingers—"I can't be."

"I'm so...sorry." All the confusion and the stress of not only the past hour but the entire day of prepping myself up exhausts me. A tear rolls down my cheek. "I never wanted to...hide anything from you. But there wasn't anything to hide. You know that, right?"

"What are you saying?" Her thumb gently wipes my cheek.

"Zander said...that...to shut Vanessa up," I whisper between hiccups.

"I don't think so, Rose. I think he likes you." She grabs my shoulders, squeezing them gently.

"But why? Do you really think someone can be attracted to me? And do you really think someone can stay attracted to me after knowing everything?" My voice trembles.

She gives me a tight smile, and I look away from her pity-laced face.

"You won't know until you take a chance. Maybe Zander is your happily ever after."

Traitorous tears roll down my cheeks. "I can never have a happily ever after. No matter how much I want it, how much I pray for it. All my ever afters are tarnished by my ever befores."

"You can't mean that." I hate the tears pooling in her eyes, but there's no missing the hesitancy in her voice. Even when she denies my words, she knows there's truth in them.

"Believe me, Kristy, I am happy. My life isn't exactly what someone would want for themselves, but I've got no complaints." I press on her cold hands, which are still holding mine. "However, there are certain things I can't dream of. My past has ruined every possibility of some things in my future."

She throws her arms around me, and I can feel her tears as her body shakes in tandem with mine.

In between hiccups, I mutter, "I like him so much. I have never…felt like this before." My voice shivers as I confess my feelings. "I feel alone…every time we end a call, and my heart does a weird fluttering when he texts me. This all…scares me…so much."

She pulls back. "Then tell him."

Before we can argue more, heavy footsteps approach us. I know it's Zander; I can feel it. My heart has started doing that fluttery thing it does every time he's around.

Zander stands beside me, and I hide away from his gaze. I

don't want to remember the moment he was compelled to make the absurd declaration.

"Shall I take you both home?" he asks.

"Why don't you and Rose talk? I'll let the guys know we're leaving," Kristy replies.

What? No. No, Kristy. Don't do this to me. Don't leave me alone with him. Not now.

"I…should come with you."

"No. You stay here and *talk*." She squeezes my shoulders before scrambling inside.

"Marr?" Zander's voice is soft and calm. "How are you?" He grabs my hand, and I shiver under his touch. The tears I'm trying to send back roll down my cheek.

When he tips my chin back with his finger, I peer up at him. A soft smile touches his lips.

"Okay." My heart clenches when his thumb wipes my tears, and he even rights my glasses.

"About what I said inside—"

"It's okay. You don't need to explain. I understand." I shake my head, and his hand falls from my face.

"What do you understand?" he urges, confusion laced in his eyes.

"That…that it just came out…of your mouth."

"I didn't blurt out some random stuff, couch girl. I hadn't planned on making such a huge declaration, but…"

My heart no longer flutters, but there are raging storms inside me that make me tremble. "I don't understand. What… are you…saying, Zander?"

"I like you, Marr. I thought I made that clear with my insistent calls and copious texts." I feel his gentle hand on my wrist as he pulls on my butterfly charm bracelet with his index finger. It's just a whisper of a touch.

My breathing stops. "B-but you don't know me."

"I know you enough to know I like you."

"Zander—"

"I know we missed some big steps in between. It'd have been better if we had gone on some dates and I'd dazzled you a bit more."

Did he just say dazzle me more? Doesn't he know he's already swept me off my feet?

"Why are you doing this?" My muscles twitch as something between excitement and nervousness fills my heart.

"Because I mean what I said inside." He tugs on his tie.

His hesitation is palpable, and his fingers on the cherry knot around his neck feel like they are saying much more to my crazy brain.

"I like you, Marr. Very much." He pauses once more.

His words and nervousness befuddle me. He looks equally confused as me, but his speech somehow doesn't falter as mine does.

"And though I didn't plan to say it this way, and definitely not in a room full of a hundred people, I really want to see where this can lead us." He waves his hands between us. "I have never felt like this before. I'm still not sure what *this* is, but I don't want to stop or go back to being just friends." Zander rakes his hand through his perfect hair and looks at me with wild eyes before his gaze softens. "But I also can't demand feelings, so I would like to know—what do you want?"

My pulse goes into rapid beats. "Why would you…even want me?" I whisper.

His eyes widen in surprise. "Why would I not? You are smart, intelligent, funny in your own way. You are so different from others. With you, I never pretend. Being with you is like being in a bubble of happiness, and I want to stay in that bubble. I—"

"Stop. Please. Stop." I jerk away, causing his finger to slip from my bracelet. Taking a step back from him and his affection, I stumble and fall on the ground outside the hall.

Incessant tears run down my face. There is only so much

I can take. Things that are offered to me today will be robbed from me in the blink of an eye, and it'll be no one's fault. Just my poor luck, as always.

"Marr! Are you okay?" Zander crouches next to me but keeps his hands to himself.

After hearing his words, after hearing how he feels about me, I just want to embrace his affection, be in that bubble with him.

"Are you hurt?" He's close enough for me to feel his heat but he's not touching me. The night sky is dark, but there's enough light from inside the hall that I can make out his face and expression. "Can I help you up?" There is so much sincerity in his voice.

He knows me. He understands me. With him, I don't feel like I'm different. I can say all my insecurities to Zander without being judged. Can I give *this* a chance?

"Yes," I mutter.

He holds my hand, his touch sending jolts of electricity throughout my body. Our fingers intertwine like before. I look at our connected hands and then at him. He gives me a smile and then pulls me up.

"Yes," I whisper again.

"Sorry?"

"Yes, I want it." There's momentary confusion in his eyes before his lips curl into a smile. My eyes rivet to his dimpled cheek. "But there is something you need to know."

"Anything you say or tell won't change how I feel about you." He looks around and asks, "Do you want to talk here?"

"Can we go someplace...*private*?" My heart pounds against my rib cage. A part of my brain screams at me to run in the opposite direction, but I try to ignore the voice tonight that has governed every decision in my life.

"Sure. Come with me."

We walk hand in hand, his stride confident and positive of our future together.

Me? I'm a shivering mess with a haunted past.

We enter through the hotel's back entrance and take the elevator to the third floor. When we step into the lobby, he turns to me. "I have a suite here. But before we go in, Marr, I want to tell you whatever you're going to say will not change how I feel about you."

"Please. Let's go inside." I can't look at Zander anymore. I never imagined I'd open up about my past to a stranger like this, but I need to do it before I cower and back out.

With my head held low and my hand captive in his, I enter the room. I take a few steps inside and stand under the center light. He nods toward the couch, but I hold my ground. His grip on my hand loosens, and he takes a seat, looking at me in confusion.

My body trembles. The heat of Zander's attraction isn't enough to stop the tremors that keep me awake at night.

He brushes his hand lightly against my arm, and a startled cry leaves me. My mind has already transported to places I hate.

Stunned by my response, he blinks rapidly. When he tries to speak, I shake my head. I just want to get my story out without any interruption. All the energy and warmth that was around us moments ago is no longer there. I know he expects me to narrate some sob story, but my wounds are sharp and deep. They draw people around me into a dark abyss.

I peer away from his concerned gaze and drag the zipper of my dress down.

"M-Marr, what's going on?" He jumps from his chair and stands before me. Grabbing my hands, he stops me from lowering the straps. His grip tightens almost painfully as his knuckles turn white. "Why are you…" He swallows and I watch his Adam's apple bob. "Why are you taking off your clothes?"

"Please let me do this," I whisper. Tears of shame fill my eyes and spill down my cheeks.

His pained face turns white, and he stammers, "This is crazy. I have no idea what you're trying to tell me, but no, not like this."

I haven't even started, and he's already hurting. I can feel his hands shaking over mine. My heart crushes thinking about the pain I'm causing him. This is what he gets for liking me—pain and heartbreak. My brain again screams to leave this room, this town, and run far away from him. But my greedy heart whispers repeatedly to take a chance.

Take a chance.

"Please." I listen to my heart and jerk away from him. My action causes him to lose his balance, and he stumbles a step back. Taking the opportunity, I lower my sleeves, pulling my dress down until the heavy fabric rests on my waist.

Zander turns his back to me. "Marr, I don't understand what you're trying to tell me. But not like this, please."

My feelings for him move to a whole new level. Even when I'm vulnerable, he is protecting me and my tarnished dignity. I pray to all the forces of nature who have led me this far and brought him into my life. Please let him be the one. *My happily ever after.*

I move to where he's standing and turn so that he can see my back. He can see that I'm not who he thinks.

15

ZANDER

"Please take a look," she whispers.

I'm beyond confused and having a hard time understanding how we got here. When she said she wanted to tell me something, I didn't know what to expect.

But right now, I'm shit scared to look at her or whatever she is trying to show me. Her trembling, cold body, and her vacant stare reminds me of myself in those nightmare-laden nights. She is physically here, but her mind is lost in a world of horrors.

"Marr, put on your clothes." I grab a blanket from the bed and am about to put it on her shoulders when I see them.

"Fuck."

Her entire back is marred with scars. Not small crisscrosses but long, deep marks, making her skin uneven. There's barely any of her light skin visible as the dark recesses cover her back. They appear to be stretched with time. Unconsciously, my index finger traces one of her scars just below the shoulder blade, and she squeals at my touch.

"Shit. Shit, Marr."

She picks the blanket I just dropped on the floor and covers herself before turning toward me.

My eyes glimpse her black bra, and I pull on the two corners of the blanket, covering her front. When I squeeze her in a hug, she flinches at the sudden contact, and her entire body tenses. But I don't let go. My mind is running a race. My thoughts are incoherent. I'm not sure what to think. I hold her tight, hoping her touch will give me some answers.

Time passes, and her body slowly relaxes in my grip as I lead her to the couch. She hasn't spoken a word, and now I'm dreading if she thinks she has already shared enough.

I turn to her, giving her the space she needs, and whisper in a hushed voice, "Help me understand, Marr. For the past half hour, my mind has been racing, and now I'm scared of my own thoughts. I can no longer sit in this mental train dreading what happened to you. Please stop this frenzy for me."

"What are your worst thoughts?" Her eyes shine with tears, but her voice is steady.

Her tears are not of sorrow, but it's the pain of opening herself, being vulnerable in front of me. *She doesn't know how much I respect her in this fucking moment.*

"No, we are not playing the guessing game. You're going to tell me everything that you planned to when you asked me to talk in private. You'll tell me every-fucking-thing you planned to tell me."

She swallows, glancing nervously up at me, indecision clear in her shiny blue eyes.

"Oscar told me you underwent treatment for social anxiety disorder," I say. She blinks rapidly, her eyes large and lost. "I twisted his arm. I wanted to know more, anything, about you."

"I grew up in Kindred Hearts Orphanage. Nobody knows about my parents," she says and again goes quiet, maybe giving me a chance to absorb her words. But her words make no fucking sense.

"I know it's hard, but you'll have to give me more than that, baby," I whisper softly. I'm still as a stone, my head buried between my hands with elbows resting on my thighs. I don't want to cause any disturbance, and break her trance.

"A lady who worked at Kindred Hearts found me in a dilapidated house…in a gruesome state. My back had wounds"—her hands reach behind her back over the blanket—"filled with blood and pus. I was…barely breathing. Doctors said I might have been in that state for several days as my wounds were severely infected." The couch moves as she shivers, reciting the horrid events.

While she catches her breath, my breathing has stopped.

"I stayed in the hospital for several months. Forensics roughly estimated the scars to be three or four years old. My age was also an approximate guess. So, who—" Her words come out raspy, like her throat is having difficulty forming sentences. "Whoever had me, had me for a few years. That means I couldn't have been more than a few weeks old before I…I was…in the possession of—"

"W-who took you?" My hands grip the corner of the couch as my brain tries to comprehend her words, my body taut with fear, anger, and frustration.

She shakes her head, her eyes not meeting mine. "Don't know. After the crime was reported by Kindred Hearts staff, police searched the area, but they couldn't find anyone. Most likely someone dumped me there."

"Your parents?"

She shakes her head again. "I had only three memories when they brought me to the hospital. Pain, immense pain, seeping through my bones. Sleep—I was always sleeping. Doctors believed I was mostly sedated."

"What's the third thing?"

"Roses." For the first time, there's a faint lightness in her voice. "I only remembered the smell of roses. Wherever I was, there were roses."

Can this be any more fucked up?

I clear my throat, my heart running a mile a minute. "H-how do you know that?"

"I was in the hospital, and one day, a nurse brought red roses for me. Before that day, I had never spoken a word or reacted to anything. But I pointed to the bouquet and smiled. She asked me if I liked roses and that was my first word: *rose*. So, they started calling me Rose, and I got the name."

"No one came to find you?" My throat struggles to form sentences, but I also need to know her story.

She shakes her head in denial once more. "No. There was no report of a missing child. My case stayed open for a long time." Her hands twist around the edges of the blanket. "When I moved to Cherrywood, I requested they close it."

I gaze ahead and run both my hands through my hair. "You don't want to meet your parents?"

"I don't have parents, Zander. The people who brought me into this world forgot about me long ago. I don't want to be a burden on anyone. I don't want to be… unwanted, again." There's not even a pinch of hatred in her voice. She says it as a matter of fact. How can she not hate those who should have protected her but failed horribly? But before I ask her that, I need to know more.

"What happened to you all those years?"

She takes a deep breath, as if praying to some heavenly force for courage. "Not sure. I have burn marks of something sharp. My skin was torn and loose. The charity trust of the hospital donated for some grafting surgeries. Doctors believe someone kept me on a bed of hot metal or something."

"Fucking hell!" My razor thin control snaps as I burn with rage.

I rise to my feet and start pacing back and forth. How can someone do this to a child? My own demons crawl from the dark. I grab a decorative blue stone kept on the dresser and throw it hard to the wall. The full-length mirror shatters with a loud noise, and there are shards of glass everywhere. But it does nothing to lessen the rage burning inside me. I feel like there's a shortage of air in the room and I'm suffocating.

So many questions—how, why, who—run through my mind. But I ask something else. "Were you...were you violated?" I stammer.

She looks at me in understanding. Her tear-stained face and hollow eyes will haunt me forever. Holding my gaze, she replies, "No. This was a surprise to everyone. There were no signs of rape."

"Fuck. Fuck."

My brain fills with varied sentences, starting from *I'm sorry*, but the words don't seem like enough. I look at her. Still draped in the blanket, she looks so small and tiny.

My precious, brave girl.

"Marr, I..."

"It's all right." An angelic smile pulls on her lips for my benefit.

"Nothing you told me is all right. It's all fucked up." I breathe heavily through my nose and try to calm the raging storm inside me.

Moments later, I ease back on the couch beside her and pull her to me, still covered in the blanket. I want to hold her, take her pain away. But I don't think I'm strong enough for both of us.

My phone vibrates in my jacket. Marr shifts away from me, pulling on the blanket and covering herself as her gaze fixes on the coffee table. I'm reminded for a second of our first meeting in the conference room—that day, I chalked her off as someone too nervous, too timid. But right now, I'm awestruck by her grit.

How did she reach from that hell to here?

My phone vibrates again with Kristy's name flashing on the screen.

"Zander, is Rose still with you?" Kristy's panic-laden voice greets me.

"Yes. We are in my suite upstairs."

"Okay." She hesitates before asking, "Is everything all right?"

"Yeah."

I end the call and turn to Marr. "That was Kristy."

She nods in response.

"Marr." I press on her hands, which are holding the soft plush blanket. "I-I don't know what else to say, but it means a lot that you shared your past with me." I know these words aren't enough, but I'm struggling with my own feelings. "Kristy is waiting for you." I tug a soft curl behind her ear, and my eyes register the pearl earring. "Feel free to use the bathroom. I'll be right outside. Take your time." I squeeze her hands once again, and before standing, I place a kiss on her forehead.

My heart constricts at the sight of a tear that rolls down her cheek when my lips touch her warm forehead.

Ten minutes later, she reappears out of my suite. Her dress and hair are as perfect as before, but her blue eyes are no longer sparkling. She looks exhausted, and I don't blame her.

Like before, I clasp her hand in mine, and her wide eyes meet mine in surprise. But I don't let go. She stares at our conjoined hands as the descending elevator takes us to the ground floor and we find Kristy and Oscar in the foyer.

"Shall I take you both home?" I ask Kristy for the second time this evening, my hand still grasping Marr's cold fingers.

"I will drop Rose and Kristy off. We drove together." Oscar looks between Marr and me before tilting his head toward the parking area.

I hesitantly look at Marr. Her gaze is fixed on the floor, and her shoulders droop low. I don't want to leave her, but I also need time to process all that she told me.

"I can text you later," Oscar adds when he notices the indecision on my face. For a second, I wonder how much he knows about Marr's past. He wasn't too pleased with me getting closer to her in the beginning. I'm still staring at him, lost in my thoughts, when Marr gently squeezes my hand.

"Oscar can drop us."

I glance hesitantly at all three of them before giving Oscar a gentle nod. I press on Marr's hand firmly before letting go.

She clumps toward the parking lot, and my heart squeezes with the feeling that I'm letting go of something precious.

16

ZANDER

I watch as Oscar's car leaves the parking lot. When the red taillights disappear in the dark night, I turn to the hotel building where a few guests are still celebrating. But the party that had me excited for weeks has lost all its appeal and is now just a boisterous room to me. I call my driver, Greg.

When he arrives with my car, I get into the rear seat. "To a bar."

He turns and looks at me over his shoulder. "Any particular one, Mr. Teager?"

I shake my head. "No. Just someplace quiet." My head meets the padded headrest as I close my eyes.

Marr's back, her wet puffy face, her words… God, her words. Something dark claws around my throat, and I loosen my tie.

Time ticks by, but I'm too lost in my thoughts to notice it.

"Mr. Teager, we're here," Greg announces, and I open my groggy eyes, looking out of the car window. Neon red block letters shine, forming the word *Rendezvous*.

I step inside the bar with a single aim: to dunk all the uneasiness that's gripping my chest in booze. There have been a handful of moments so far in life when I wanted to forget everything over a bottle of Scotch, but today is the worst of all. I perch on one of the barstools.

"What can I get you?" the bartender asks.

"Scotch. Neat."

I grab the faceted glass and take a sip of the amber liquid. My mind wanders to my girl. Feelings of anguish that gathered around me when Marr recited about her childhood still aren't gone. I remember her raw voice, her corded neck muscles, her clenched fists holding the blanket, shielding her from the cold and dark that engulfed us in that room.

Someone taps on my hand covering the now-empty glass, and I look up to find the bartender glancing my way, an eyebrow raised.

"Girl trouble?" she asks as I point for her to refill my glass. "You look pretty damn worked up."

"You mean fucked up." I shoot the liquid back, not giving a shit that it's intended to be savored.

She fills my glass again when I ask her to keep them coming.

"That girl must be something. You have a pretty face over there, and by the look of you, you seem loaded too. If I didn't have a five-year-old hunk at home, I'd so be hitting on you."

"Yeah, she is something. She's everything."

"Wanna talk about her? The bar is pretty much empty." The bartender nods toward the neighboring vacant barstools.

I shake my head. "No."

"Come on, man. It's only you and me here. Your story can compensate for all the tips I'm missing tonight."

I point for another refill when she doesn't do it on her own.

"Don't down this one like the others," she mutters, filling my glass and placing a bottle of Johnnie next to me. "I want to hear the complete story before you pass out on my table."

"If I pass out, call my driver. He's outside." I'm so gonna pass out. I already feel lightheaded.

"Okay. I promise you'll be in your bed tonight. Now, I guess I deserve a story in return." She bats her eyelashes at me.

"You are in the wrong profession, persistent woman," I slur. *Shit. How much did I drink already?*

"Maybe, but I do just fine." She places a glass of water in front of me, which I ignore, of course.

When she turns to attend to the two old fellas at the other end of the bar, a hand grabs my shoulder.

"What the—" I try to get up from the stool but stumble. I hold the bar just in time to prevent falling on the floor.

"Fuck. Zander, you're wasted," Zach states as he and Zane glare down at me.

"What the hell are you two doing here?" I rub my forehead to ward off the growing headache. I just wanted to be alone with a bottle of Scotch. Instead, I got the persistent bartender and now my brothers breathing down my neck.

Can't a man have a moment of peace?

"Part-t-ty's over. We could-dn't find you, s-s-so I called Greg." Zane plops down on a barstool beside me.

"What the fuck is going on, man? Since when do you keep secrets from us? First a secret girlfriend, now a secret bar visit." Zach slams his hand on the bar, making my empty glass jerk.

The bartender rushes to us, removing the glass along with the bottle of Johnnie Walker before giving us the stink eye. But Zach doesn't waver. His fist remains clenched, and his lips pinched tight. He shakes his head and mutters, "It's like we don't know you anymore."

I hate the expression resembling betrayal on my brothers' faces.

"She isn't my girlfriend, or wasn't until this evening."

"We'll need a little more than that, Zander." Zach crosses his arms over his chest and looks down at me.

I know he isn't knowingly trying to overpower me. It's a defense mechanism we developed as teenagers for every time we felt the need to protect ourselves from someone or something.

"Can you please sit?" I nudge the next barstool closer to him with my foot.

Zach shakes his head before settling down and ordering a drink. Taking a large swig of his beer, he inquires, "Are you going to say something or what?"

I look at my brothers once again and then tell them everything from the moment I caught Marr falling from the couch the first morning till tonight when I walked out of the hotel suite with her.

I watch as everyone, including the bartender, an additional audience to my story, throws back a few shots. They all flinch when I tell them about the scars on her back and the incidences that led her to having those wounds. Fuck, I flinched myself while narrating the story.

"You like a girl named Rose? Fuck, Zander. Why didn't you say anything?" Zach looks at me in confusion.

"I wanted to know what it was first, for myself." I look away from his perplexed stare. Is it so weird that I like someone named *that*?

"And you d-d-do now?" Zane raises an eyebrow, his demeanor much cooler than Zach's.

"I know that I like her." As I say the words, a strange thrill unfurls inside me.

"She is different. You need to be sure before this goes any further." This is something I never thought I would hear from Zach. He's never been the caring one, especially when it comes to the feelings of a woman.

"What, man? Stop fucking staring at me like that. You do

not mess with girls like her. I might act like..." He pauses, trying to find the right word.

"An asshole," I supply, causing Zane to chuckle.

"Yes, and I don't regret it. But you cannot be an asshole here, Zander. She has suffered a lot."

"Give it t-time. Who knows, maybe sh-she won't like him for long." Zane chuckles.

"Fuck man, it stings." I snicker, rubbing my forehead. Talking to my brothers about her is liberating. My heavy chest unclenches.

"Does this mean one of the hottest bachelors in the country is no longer on the market?" Zach playfully shoves me forward.

"It appears so." My adrenaline spikes just saying those words. Hope builds inside me. Maybe she and I, two broken souls, can rescue each other after all.

"I'll drink to that." Zach waves his hand to the bartender, who instead of making our drinks, scowls at me.

"You left her?" she mutters in disbelief.

"What?" I have no idea what she's getting at, but her voice hurts my head. Maybe I should've skipped that last drink.

"She told you about her, and you said, *Okay, thanks. But now you need to leave with your friend*." Her glare could've burned me right here, the bar providing enough tinder for her cause.

"I did not," I sputter. "I just needed some time to get my shit together." I glance toward my brothers, but their blank faces are no help.

I look at the bartender, who throws her cleaning rag toward me. My reflexes being at their worst, the cold cloth hits my face.

"Call the girl," she comments begrudgingly.

"Isn't it better to go in person?" I ask my new friend. She appears to be having the best advice right now.

"You're too wasted to go anywhere but your bed. Call her now and then visit her tomorrow morning."

I hop off the barstool and drop several hundred-dollar bills on the counter. I certainly owe this woman.

"I'll be outside," I tell my brothers before making a beeline to the door.

With trembling fingers, I dial Marr's number. It rings twice before she picks up.

"Hi." Her soft voice sounds like heaven.

"Hey. Reach home safely?" *God, could I sound any lamer?*

"Yeah. We've been home for some time now." Her voice sounds guarded as she waits for me to say something, to explain where we stand after tonight. The bartender chick was right; I did leave her hanging.

"So, the general consensus is that we're together."

She takes a sharp breath, making my complete body shudder. "Are you sure?" Her voice is almost a whisper.

"I told you, nothing you say will change my mind."

"Oh." I picture the O formed by her puckered lips and her eyebrows knit together. "You didn't say much," she finally murmurs.

"It was a lot of information, Marr, and unexpected." I pinch the bridge of my nose. "I'm sorry. Not only for now." I don't know what else to say. What can you tell someone who has suffered so much? Sorry seems so *scant*.

"It's okay, Zander." Her concluding tone makes me change the topic.

"You looked beautiful tonight."

"Thanks, but you already told me that." Thank God for her tiny giggle.

"Earlier, I told that to my friend. Now, I'm telling my girl that she looked breathtaking. Fucking cute and adorably sexy." I take a chance, my chest light and warm for the first time this evening. How does she do that? Lighten up my mood like that. A moment with her is like the best thing that has ever happened to me.

"Zander!" The mix of surprise and delight in her voice tells me she's not offended by my comment.

"What?" I grin, too happy to care for anything else in the world.

"You can't say things like that." Her breathy voice makes me crazy. I want to jump inside the phone and hold her tight in my arms and do so much more.

"Why not? It's under my rights as your boyfriend to say all the sweet and sexy things to you and..." I pause dramatically.

"And?" Her hoarse voice is making me crazy.

"Curious, Ms. Marlin?"

"Um, no," she whispers. I can imagine her fixing her glasses, wetting that plump bottom lip nervously.

"Really? Not curious at all?" I chuckle. "But I think I'll deliver the rest of my thoughts about my rights face-to-face." My lips curl into a shit-eating grin.

She hums before asking, "Zander, are you all right? You sound different."

"I had a few drinks. But tonight, it's you, couch girl, that has me zonked out." I hear her breath hitch and press the phone closer to my ears. Her breathing travels directly to my groin. Before my inebriated mind schemes something for which she isn't ready yet, I rush out, "I gotta go now, but I'll talk to you tomorrow. Sleep tight and dream of me."

She laughs softly and it's music to my ears. "Good night, Zander."

Before the line goes dead, an idea forming in my mind manages to find voice. "Marr, won't you give your boyfriend a goodnight kiss?"

The call disconnects, but not before I hear her gasp.

Life is going to change, and it's going to be fun with my

couch girl. I walk inside the bar with the biggest grin on my face.

"Hey, man, you look like a fucking whacko. Stop smiling. You're scaring us off," Zach hollers from the bar.

"Zander, get-t up. Get-t up, man."

"What the hell?" If not for the panic in Zane's voice, I wouldn't have bothered to reply after the events of last night.

"Zander, it's serious." Zach shakes my shoulders, waking me up from the beautiful dream.

"What's going on?" I sit upright on the bed. As I try to stand, everything around me spins.

Shit. I drank too much last night. I hold the headboard for support and rub my throbbing head.

"Th-this is no t-time for a hangover." Zane hands me a glass of water and two pills.

I gulp them without question.

Zach hands me my iPad. "Open your email." While logging into the company server, I try to recall any major projects, but fuck, my head has nothing but pain. *What the hell happened in the last ten hours?*

I open my official email account—thirty emails, and all under the same subject line.

I'm fucked.

"Non-Fraternization Policy at Elixir Inc." I somehow read the typed letters despite my blurring eyes.

Holy Fuck. How the hell did I miss this?

"Who?"

"Vanessa." Zach spits out her name.

It fucking makes sense.

I rub my head, remembering when we were discussing company policies in her father's dining hall. Mathew Hilbert brought up the subject of a non-fraternization policy, stating that it might be a good idea to keep it, at least in the early days. I'd planned to remove it later at some point, but that point never came and it just slipped my mind. Vanessa was right there, sitting across from us with her mother, aware of everything.

"When?" It seems one-word sentences are all I can manage at this point.

"After your gigantic romantic gesture, she devised her horrendous plan. Everyone received the fucking email. She even mailed the investors and stakeholders." Zach's words are filled with hate, as he explains what happened in the world while I was fucking asleep.

"Everyone?"

Zane nods. "I s-saw it at t-two in the morning. Already talked to Beas-st and Mat-thew."

I have no clue when Zane sleeps. He's the first to act when a crisis like this arises. I'm sure he already has a fix for the situation. Calling Mathew Hilbert was definitely a step in the right direction, but I have no idea how Beast will react.

As if reading my mind, Zane adds, "Beast isn't pleased-d, especially when there's a girl involved-d."

"Shit. I need to talk to him." All this new information is just increasing my dizziness. I grab the table next to me for support.

"Yeah, you do. But everything is under control." Zach grabs a chair and slides it behind me. I gladly accept and flop down on it. "Don't get anxious, Zander. Zane has issued an email stating that the non-fraternization policy has been annulled since last week. We have the official changed policy signed by the board," Zach explains. "It's a no-brainer to guess the reasons for the change, considering Vanessa's email. But at least we are legally safe. Plus, Zane has removed the security footage from the party where you heroically announced your relationship with Marr."

Hearing her name brings back memories of the day

before. I had planned to visit her first thing in the morning, but fuck, she might have already seen the email.

"IT just now removed all t-t-the unopened copies-s-s of the email from our s-s-servers. But if Marr already read..." Zane doesn't finish.

I know he's done all he could. "It's okay. But how did you manage to remove footage?" I ask warily. I don't want him to get involved in such stuff.

"Don't worry. I didn't do anyt-t-thing. I called Luke. He had-d-d a *talk* with the hotel manager," Zane explains, but I have a good idea what he means by talk.

Of course, it's Lukas Spencer, Zane's closest friend, to the rescue. As always, my jaw tightens hearing his name. Knowing that Zane sought him out to clean up my mess gives an immeasurable boost to my headache. I try to hold on to the fact that at least my brother wasn't directly involved in all the *talking*, so that's a relief.

"What's next?" It looks like they have everything under control, and I'm grateful for that, as my fucking head is useless this morning.

Zach hands me my phone. "Call Beast and then Marr."

17

ROSE

When I get up this morning, I have a big smile on my face. I don't remember the dream, but it was about Zander and his sensual voice from last night. As I brush my teeth, I remember his words: *fucking cute and adorably sexy.* As much as the words scare me, they also give me a sparky, warm feeling.

His late-night words took away the sting of the previous incidences. Vanessa's outburst and me sharing the most shunned part of my life.

Before his phone call, I googled Vanessa and Zander's name together but came up empty-handed. It quieted my insecurities, especially the voice in my head that repeatedly questions me. *What is Zander doing with me?*

Lost in my thoughts of the pivotal night, I have no idea when Kristy entered my room. She stares at my reflection, and when I meet her gaze in the mirror, I see the weirdo she sees. Toothpaste foam drools from one side of my mouth.

Crab.

She smiles, but a moment later, her smile falters. "Rosie, as much as I want you to carry on with the hallmark movie running in your brain, there's something we need to see. I just received a text from Oscar about some updated company policies. Let's see what's happening in the actual world, *lover girl*."

Lover girl!

I wash my face in record time and meet Kristy in our open space kitchen. She logs in to the office server while I prepare coffee. Adding sugar, I take a whiff of the warm smell when she curses. "Fuck."

I peer toward her laptop screen, and my eyes widen at the subject of the opened email. *Non-Fraternization Policy.*

The spoon slips from my fingers and falls onto the wooden counter, leaving coffee splatters on the surface.

"Rose, calm down. Take deep breaths." Kristy holds my hand, and that's when I notice my fingers are shaking like dry leaves in the wind.

I'm jolted from my seat at the ringing of my cell phone. Zander's face appears on the screen. Weeks back, I downloaded one of his pictures from the internet and added it to his number on my phone.

"Hell-Hello." With all the trembling, I have a hard time forming words.

"Marr. Are you okay?" Hearing his silvery voice, my breathing starts to pacify.

"Y-Yes."

"I guess you've already seen the email." He releases a deep sigh. "I'm so sorry. I should have been more careful."

"Will I lose my job?" I ask.

Kristy cleans the counter with the kitchen rag next to me. The swiping motion distracts me, lulling my anxiety.

"Hell no. I'll never let that happen."

"Okay. We haven't read the entire email yet."

"Then don't read it. Can I come over?" he asks hesitantly, and then adds, "This is not how I'd planned this morning.

But I really need to see you and tell you everything that's happening in person." I can feel the frustration in his voice.

"Can you hold for a moment? I need to check with Kristy." It's the first time I'm inviting a boy home. I'm not sure what the protocol is and if we have some unspoken rule about not having guys over.

"Of course, he can come over," Kristy answers before I can ask her.

As I place the phone back to my ear, Zander replies, "I heard her. Message me your address, and I'll be there soon."

It's been an hour since Zander's call. I showered and got dressed in my black jeans and checkered white-and-black flannel shirt. When the bell rings, I nervously open the door. And there he is, dressed impeccably as always. Today, he's wearing a navy-blue striped suit, mauve shirt, and a purple tie. But there are some new tired lines under his eyes.

"Hi," I whisper.

"Hello, Marr," he replies with a smile, and some of those worry lines disappear. Taking my hand, he tugs me closer. Caught off guard, I stumble toward him before he steadies me with his hands around my waist.

I try to pull back, muttering a soft, "I'm sorry." But he doesn't let me go.

My face is only inches away from his broad chest, and I get the first close whiff of the woodsy vanilla scent, which is another of those things that remind me of Zander these days.

"Don't be." His amused voice is thick and warm.

We stand at the doorstep with his hand on my waist, gazing into each other's eyes until Kristy's holler breaks our trance. "Is that Zander at the door?"

I step back so he can come inside.

Before I can go far, he grabs my hand and intertwines our fingers. I don't protest. Since last night, I've come to realize that I like Zander's touch. His touch makes me feel safe—safe like I have never felt.

"Hey, Kristy. How are you?" Zander waves to my friend lying on the recliner as we both enter the living room together.

"Hey, boss. We were hoping you could enlighten us on what the hell is going on. But let's sit first." As we move to the living area, she sits upright and asks, "Would you like coffee or something?"

Zander settles on the couch and pulls me next to him. "I forgot to mention that Zach and Zane would like to come over with breakfast." He glances at me for confirmation, and I look at Kristy. I'm still confused about the rules of my one-day-old boyfriend and his brothers coming over.

"What? Will you ask my permission for *everything* you do with him?" She squints, her eyes shining with mischief.

"No," I murmur, my cheeks flaming at her question.

Zander puts his arms around my shoulders and pulls me close before looking down at me with his breathtaking smile. He then says, unexpectedly, looking between me and Kristy, "I never noticed you both have identical eye color."

I giggle as Kristy laughs at his off-tangent remark. "That's because you were too busy checking my friend out."

He peers my way once more and arches an eyebrow before turning to Kristy. My insides tingle under his attention.

"My brothers aren't too pleased with me. They think if I'd handled things better last night, we wouldn't have such a mess on our hands right now."

My best friend snickers. "They didn't like your grand Romeo move?"

"No, they aren't really Shakespeare fans," Zander

comments back and smiles at me when I giggle. "But they want to personally assure you before leaving that everything is handled, and you don't need to worry about anything."

My heart skips a beat at the sweet gesture of his brothers. I smile back at him until I realize what he just said. My eyebrows furrow in confusion. "You're leaving?" It hasn't been more than twelve hours since we decided to take it a step further in our relationship and he's leaving already?

"No, Marr. I can't go so soon. Can I now?" He smiles his oh so affectionate smile. I can't believe this handsome man is here for me, even after knowing my truth.

"Okay, boss, tell us what's going on, and then I'll leave you lovebirds alone." Kristy slides from the recliner and sits on the ottoman closer to the couch where I'm huddled with Zander.

"Vanessa is no wallflower. I've known her for many years now," Zander says. He hasn't released my hand since we walked into the house; it's as if he's worried I'm gonna run away.

No chance, mister.

I interrupt him. "Were you and her…ever?"

"No, Marr. Never." He runs his hand through his hair, peeking at me under his lashes. "She tried to get close to me in the past, but when I didn't return the gesture, she brushed it off with a laugh. That's why I was surprised when she came on to me so strong last night." His grip on me tightens. "Vanessa has no affection for me. I think when she saw you and me together, she somehow took it as a personal offense." He looks between Kristy and me before asking, "You believe me, right?"

I reply to Kristy's raised eyebrow with a subtle nod. Over the weeks I've known Zander, he's given me no reasons to doubt him. But I'm not surprised like him. Even if they weren't together before, why would Vanessa not hit on him? Zander is the complete package.

"Yeah, we believe you," Kristy replies. "But we weren't aware she was involved with Elixir Inc. directly."

"She isn't. We have a long association with the Hilberts. Mathew, Vanessa's father, is not only one of our first investors but also a close friend of Beast." He stretches his long legs under the coffee table.

"Beast?" My ears perk at the weird name.

"That's what we call Ashcroft." Zander chuckles.

"You call Ashcroft Miller, your guardian, Beast? Why?" I ask, thrown for a loop at the weird nickname.

He cracks up at my confused open mouth and wide eyes. "You'll know when you see him."

Sweet Sugar.

Are we already talking about meeting family members? Guess so. His brothers are on their way to my place and Kristy, my only family, is busy bantering with him.

"Vanessa supports Mathew in his business, and that's how she's aware of the internal company business and policies. But there's nothing to worry about. You just need to know that the non-fraternization policy has not been in effect since last Friday." His thumb gently strokes my hand when he feels me stiffening. "So apart from some internal office gossip, everything will stay the same."

"I'm going to work tomorrow with a bag of popcorn." Kristy wiggles her eyebrow at us.

The wide smile that grows on Zander's face is reassuring, and I lose myself in it. Everything will be all right. I repeat the words in my head, over and over again.

After another thirty minutes, I answer the doorbell for the second time this morning and find Zach scowling at Zane.

"Would you have minded *too much* if we had one bagel on the way?" Zach's serious eyes peer at me.

"Um…no," I reply to his strange question with confusion.

"Did you hear? No one cares about *one* bagel." Zach angrily points one finger at Zane.

"S-s-sorry, Marr. Someone's cranky, as it's past his br-reakfast time." Zane smiles, handing me the bags from Hawthorne Bakery.

"You can't stay hungry for fifteen minutes?" Zander asks his brother when we meet him in the living room.

Kristy helps me in getting the plates from the kitchen, smiling at the annoyed, yet amusing Zach Teager.

The three brothers fill our modest living room. Dressed in impeccable suits on a Sunday morning, they look perfectly out of place in our boho decor.

After wolfing down one bagel, two cupcakes, and half a croissant, Zach surprises me with his question. "Are you sure about this one?" He cocks his head toward Zander sitting beside me. "He can be grumpy at times."

"What are you talking about? I'm a sweetheart." Zander throws a bread piece at his brother before turning my way. "Don't listen to him." He smiles, showing me his perfect white teeth, and my breathing stops.

He is so beautiful.

There is no other way to describe him.

"You're a guy who calls himself a sweetheart," Zach comments. Sipping his coffee, his grumpy mood is forgotten.

"I am to her," Zander mutters before pushing a half-bitten blueberry cupcake into his mouth.

My Sweetheart.

Holy Moly.

Zander's brothers share stories and jokes about the office and their life in St. Peppers. I feel like I've known them for years and not just since last night. They treat me like I'm one of them, a part of their family.

I look around and wonder *can this be my family? Zander and me, with my best friend and his brothers?*

Watching everyone interact gives me hope—hope for a new life filled with love. Love, which was always out of reach, always two steps ahead no matter how hard I ran. I know it's silly to think about such things so early in our relationship.

But when does the heart follow logic?

18

ZANDER

I knock on the door of the conference room, and Marr lifts her head from where it's buried behind the laptop screen. She's in a brainstorming session with Kristy and her team. Every pair of eyes turns from the projector toward me, but my attention is only on my girlfriend.

"Are we all set for tomorrow?" I ask from the doorstep.

She nods and then looks away. For some strange reason, she's still shy around me in the office. I don't understand why. It's not like our relationship is a secret.

I step into the conference room, and everyone starts shuffling in their seats, turning my way.

I'm just checking on my girl, people.

Nevertheless, I praise my hardworking staff, toiling away on a Friday evening. "Great work, everyone. Keep it up."

I reach to Marr as she slouches lower in her chair. Her coyness amuses me greatly.

"I'll pick you up at twelve?" I ask in a hushed voice but still loud enough for everyone to hear.

She nods, looking at her laptop screen.

"Got a date, boss?" Kristy, sitting opposite Marr, grins at me.

"Sure do," I reply with a grin of my own behind my blushing couch girl.

Everyone smiles, but Marr stays buried behind the black screen. The pink in her cheeks is the only indication that she's not appalled by my Don Juan move.

"WHAT DO YOU SAY?" I put the car into park and point toward the sign.

"Pegasus Gallop Farms? What are we going to do here?" Marr clutches on the cuffs of her shirt, and I know the tugging will start any minute.

As much as I want our first date to be memorable, I'm also perceptive toward her anxiety issues. I wanted to take her outdoors, near nature someplace so we could talk in the quiet. So far, apart from the dinner where I basically invited myself to her and Kristy's table, we haven't been out. Our paltry time together has been through texts and calls.

"Horseback riding." I get out of the car and wait for her to step out.

It takes a while before her door opens, and one after the other, the red canvas shoes softly land on the ground.

"Zander, I have never ridden a horse before. I… I can't do it." Her eyes nervously move from the green racecourse to the open fields.

I hold her hands in mine before she rips that cuff off.

"Marr, the guide will take us to the hills. He's picked his most docile horse for you." I tip her chin up with my finger. "It's a smooth ride. I'm told you can see the whole town from the top." I point my finger toward the top alpine meadows.

"How…do you know all this? I had no idea we had a horse farm in Cherrywood." Her breathy voice and skittish manners, standing here like a deer in headlights, makes me want to fold her in my arms until she melts against me.

But one step at a time.

"I've been working on this date for a week now," I confess, trying to tell her how important she, and this day, is to me.

"A week?" She licks her lips, and I'm about to forget my resolve of one step at a time before Bill joins us.

"Are you ready for the ride, miss?" he asks Marr.

When I booked the *Date in the Hills* package with Bill, I told him my girlfriend scares easily.

Marr gingerly nods her head as we shake hands with Bill. He leads us to the stables, and I grab Marr's hand.

I turn her to me. "You can still say no. We can watch the horses grazing on the meadows. There's no pressure."

"Were you really…planning for a week?" She blinks those big blue eyes rapidly.

I nod. "I wanted our first date to be memorable."

She looks between the two horses Bill's leading out and then back me.

"If I don't like—"

"You just say the word."

"How are you feeling?" I look at Marr as she walks beside me on the jet-black mare.

"It feels…different. I can feel her…move." She looks from the horse to me.

"But not bad, right?" I grin when she shakes her head.

Bill leads us to the brow of the hill, where a lunch basket is waiting for us. He lays a white picnic blanket on the ground and leaves us to return in a few hours.

"What do you think?" I ask Marr while passing her a glass of iced tea.

I'm hoping her answer to this question is *amazing*, but she replies in her own sweet style.

"You took me for date in the hills, on a horse, and had lunch delivered from Giovanni's. I think I'm becoming a fan of dates." She eyes the insulated food box from her favorite Italian restaurant.

"Does this mean that my attempt at making you forget all your previous dates was successful?" I smirk, but I'm only half joking. I want her to think about no other man but me.

Way to go, Zander! With this attitude, you're going to scare her away.

The pink in her cheeks spreads beyond her neck and the collared T-shirt.

"How many dates do you think I've been on?" Her fingers play with the edges of the picnic blanket, and I cock an eyebrow at her.

What are you saying, couch girl?

Before I can start the guessing game, she turns and gazes ahead. From this far and at this height, Cherrywood is nothing but a doll village.

"I thought dates usually take place in crowded restaurants."

"Dates can be anywhere you like." I sit upright and move closer to her.

"You seem to have a lot of practice." She looks my way, biting her lip in suspicion.

Does she know how alluring she looks right now?

"I am aware of the art of dating." I grab her hand resting between us and bring it closer to my lips. "Doesn't mean I'm a practitioner of the art." I glance at her before placing a kiss on her palm. Her hand shivers under the touch of my lips. Her blue eyes gleam behind the red frames in the daylight. Watching her face reflecting my own excitement, I kiss her thumb, then her index finger and the next, until I reach her pinkie. I bite it softly, and her wide eyes close while a soft moan escapes her lips.

Her sun-kissed face, her slightly mussed hair by the wind, and the heavy rising and falling of her chest makes me forget every resolve. Since I met this girl, she has made me crazy. Crazy with fear, worry, nervousness, and passion.

What the hell was I thinking bringing her to such a secluded place?

I bring her face closer and lean down, covering her lips with mine.

First thing I notice is that she tastes divine.

But it takes me a second to register that she has gone rigid under my touch. My hands on her face feel her cold skin, and her wide eyes are filled with panic. But my body hasn't received the memo yet, and my rock-solid cock throbs in sync with my heart.

"Marr—"

"C-can we…leave? P-please?" She stands up, straightening her shirt and already collecting the empty iced tea bottles.

Nothing makes a dick go limp like your girlfriend wanting to bolt on the first date without eating dessert.

I pack everything back after making a call to Bill.

Half-eaten pasta, untouched cannolis, extra iced tea, and fresh strawberries in the lunch basket are going to haunt me the rest of the day.

19

ROSE

I open the passenger door, thankful that the drive to my home is finally over. I'm about to step out when Zander lightly touches my arm.

"Marr," he calls my name and pauses.

For the first time since we left the farm, I peer at him and immediately look away to the dashboard.

I ruined our day.

Something he'd been planning for a week for me, for us.

When he calls my name again, I shake my head, pleading with him to not say anything. I can't take any more of his sweet and kind words trying to make light of my freak-out.

"I need to feed Logan," I blurt the dumb excuse and make a run to the house.

Tears I've been holding for an hour stream down my cheeks as I shut the main door. My feet are heavy as I plod toward my room.

"Rosie!" Kristy calls out from the couch, where she's lying with a phone to her ear.

She swiftly ends the call with whoever is on the other side before running to me.

"Are you okay?"

I shake my head and fall on the floor next to the kitchen island.

"Careful!" She holds my head, which almost hits the wall. "Are you hurt?"

Her hands roam over my arms and shoulders.

"I-I messed up, Kris," I mutter in between sobs.

"What do you mean?"

"Zander kissed me and I...froze."

"You were uncomfortable?" She looks at me carefully, her fingers on my shoulders tightening.

"Not in the way you think," I quickly reply, clearing the suspicion on her face about Zander. "I didn't know how to react."

My eyes well up again, and she wipes my face with her fingers. After guiding me to the couch, she pours me a glass of water.

"Tell me what happened exactly."

I gulp down the cold liquid before putting the incidences of the day into words.

"He took you to the Pegasus Gallop Farms?" When I nod, Kristy murmurs, "The hilltop is referred to as the most romantic place in Cherrywood."

Her words don't surprise me. Zander would never choose anything less than the best.

He only went wrong in the selection of his girlfriend.

His imperfect girlfriend.

"You think it was too soon?" Kristy's fingers gently knead my neck muscles, trying to calm me down.

"I...don't know. I just thought I would mess it up." My fingers dig into my forehead as I whisper, "And I did."

"What did Zander say when he dropped you off?"

"I didn't let him speak. I made a run for the house. I can't face him, Kristy, not after what happened."

"What are you saying? You just froze when he was kissing you. It's no big deal."

"It was not…just a…kiss. It felt like he was bottling me inside him. He was holding me tight. His touch…" I shiver at the memories of the foreign sensations.

She looks at me with wide eyes, and my cheeks inflame in mixed embarrassment.

"He asked if this date made me forget all my previous dates. I feel like I'm cheating him, Kris. He is so…strong, powerful, and experienced, and I'm…*me*."

Her hand stops me from tugging on the cuffs of my flannel shirt.

"You are cheating no one. He knows about you, about everything that's important."

She tries to make me believe in her words, like always, and maybe any other day, I would. But today, it's different.

I saw Zander's face. I saw his face when he realized what a dork I am. He took me on a date, to one of the best places, yet I freaked out.

There's only so much a man can take, even I know this. He'll soon realize how much work I am, if not today, then certainly later.

And once again, I'll be left alone.

Before stepping out of my office, I poke my head out. When I see no one is in the corridor, I grab my empty water bottles and make a run for the coffee corner. I make sure that I dispose of them in the recycle bin at a time when this area is least busy. Yet, I hear some faint noises from inside.

I pause at the doorstep, making sure it isn't Zander.

I've tried my best to keep my distance from him. I'm now waiting for him to stop calling and texting me and just realize that he's wasting his time with me.

The voices in the coffee corner aren't Zander's, but they're no better.

"Is it true that Rose and Zander Teager are an item?" It's an unfamiliar female voice.

"I can't believe it myself, but Zander said it in front of a room full of people." I'm unable to recognize even this voice as the person starts the water, most liking filling a glass for themself. "You've worked with Rose. How is she?"

Crab!

My breath hitches at the question. In general, I try so hard to avoid other people's opinion about me. I don't know how their views and thoughts will affect me. But today, I can't make myself turn around and hide back in my office.

"She's nice. A little weird, but nice. Though I always thought she would end up with some geek like her."

There's a large slurping sound before the other person speaks. "I know! Zander Teager, the sexiest bachelor, fell for the office geek. This sounds like a Cinderella story."

I take a covert step forward, and a glance from the side tells me it's Brenda and another of her colleagues from HR.

I turn around with the empty bottles in my hand and the words *sexiest bachelor* ringing in my ear.

How does Zander not see the disparity between us that is so evident to everyone else? How does he not see that I don't fit beside him in his perfect world?

20

ZANDER

It's been a week since the disastrous date. Disastrous not only because of what happened on the date but also what followed. Marr is holding back on our calls and texts like never before. If I thought she was shy in the office before, she's fucking scared of me now. Whenever she sees me in the office corridor or coming her way, she bolts in the other direction. It's a fucking mess, and I'm the only one to blame.

I've tried everything short of kidnapping her in an attempt to make her talk, but nothing seems to be working. Not knowing what else to do, I decided to take some external help.

I'm sitting in a restaurant with Kristy, desperate for an olive branch on how to get my couch girl back.

"How did the meeting go?" I ask. Kristy is working with Zach on our new office location.

"Everything went well. Zach has arranged a conference call on Monday to discuss more with you," she replies.

I nod, having almost no desire to convolute this meeting with office conversations. I have more pressing things to discuss.

"Zander, what's the matter? You asked me to come alone and not say a word to Rose." Kristy repeats my sentence from this morning. "Everything all right between you two?"

I'm quiet for few moments. I don't know how to voice to my girlfriend's best friend that her friend is giving me the cold shoulder because I tried to kiss her on a date. In my mind, it's a genuine problem, but when trying to put it into words, I feel like a pervert.

"I don't know how to start, Kristy."

"Did something happen between you two?" Her gaze fixated on me is more curious than surprised, and I wonder if she's already aware of the proceedings of my perfectly planned, horribly executed first date.

"I fucked up big time." I run my hands through my hair, hesitating for a second before realizing I don't have too many options. "We were having fun on our date until I pounced on her, and now she wants nothing to do with me."

"What do you mean by pounced on her?" Kristy leans back in her chair, her blue eyes never leaving me.

I'm once again stuck by the resemblance between her eyes and Marr's. How did I never notice it before? Possibly because I was too busy observing my couch girl and her idiosyncrasies.

"Hello." Kristy waves her hand in front of me. "I asked you a question."

Grabbing my neck in frustration, I rehash the disastrous date.

"I think I'm losing her." My voice sounds pathetic, even to my own ears.

Kristy chews on her bottom lip. I watch as she struggles with something, tugging on her golden bracelet before meeting my eyes.

"I'm putting a hell of a lot of trust in you." She pauses, waiting for my nod. "Rose never really had any close relationships, Zander. You kind of know that."

I nod again, not understanding her words, but hope and anxiety slowly builds inside me.

"You are the first man in her life," she continues. "Her first boyfriend."

Holy fuck.

I gulp back something heavy that's clogged in my throat. I'd imagined Marr to not be very experienced, but…I'm her first boyfriend?

The thought never even occurred to me.

Of course she's scared. Who wouldn't be when your boyfriend jumps on you on your first fucking date?

But the real question is, will she ever want me back?

Kristy slurps loudly around the straw of her cocktail. "Whenever you're back to earth and ready to talk, I might have a plan."

The next evening, I park outside Marr's place. After grabbing the bouquet of white lilies and purple orchids from the passenger seat, I trot to the foyer and ring the doorbell.

She opens the door and does a double take when she sees me.

"Zander. W-what are you…doing here?"

But all the air is sucked out of my lungs. I'm dumbstruck by this sexy version of my girlfriend. Her regular collared shirt is replaced by a pink top, the sensuous V-neck teasing me with a hint of her cleavage. Her jeans are replaced by pink shorts reaching mid-thigh. For the first time, I get a good look at her bare, toned legs.

Hell, I've been imagining her legs for a month, but standing on the doorstep, she's beyond my imagination.

"I thought you were the pizza guy," she whispers, shifting her weight from one leg to the other.

I thrust the bouquet into her arms and grab her hand.

"So, this is how you dress for the pizza guy?" I tug her gently toward me.

She shakes her head and drops her gaze to the floor.

"I'm just toying with you, couch girl. Aren't you going to invite me in?"

"Y-yes...please come in." She hesitates, clearly uncomfortable with me showing up out of the blue at her doorstep, but today, I'm not going easy on her. I'm following Kristy's plan to the letter.

Speaking of Kristy, I find her in the living room as expected, tying the straps of her high heels. Dressed in a short black dress, I'm not sure if she's going out on a fake dinner or a real one.

"Hello, boss. I didn't know you were coming over." She stays in her role of the ignorant friend.

"I had a canceled meeting, so I thought I'd have dinner with my two favorite ladies."

"I'm sorry to disappoint you, but I have a meeting of my own. I'm sure your most favorite lady will appreciate the offer, though." She collects her purse from the table and her jacket from the coat rack before sauntering out the door.

"I didn't know Kristy was seeing someone." I take a seat on the couch as Marr sits across from me on the loveseat.

"What do you mean? She's having dinner with some colleagues." Marr furrows her eyebrow in confusion.

I let it go. If tonight goes as expected, we'll have ample opportunities to discuss Kristy's love life.

Fifteen minutes later, Marr's pizza arrives.

She sits back on the loveseat, supporting her plate on her lap.

I can't look away from her face. Her beautiful, relaxed face. She has no idea how incredible she looks, sitting in their bohemian living room. Her normally tied ponytail is replaced by a bun, a few strands falling on her delicate shoulders.

Immediately, images of that black hair hiding her face just after I released her from my hold fill my brain. I shake my head, willing them away. I'll fix this. Even if I have to beg her the whole night.

We eat in a pleasant silence. I realized much earlier that Marr doesn't like to talk while eating. A remnant of her disciplined upbringing, I suppose.

After we're done, I take the dishes to the kitchen and start the water to rinse them.

"No, you don't have to do that." She follows me and tries to pull me away from the sink.

"I know I don't have to, but I want to." I voice the most repeated tagline in dating.

Marr glances at me in uncertainty. I'm sure she didn't expect me to stick around after dinner.

But when she sees that I've already lathered up the sponge, she gives in. "Let me help you, then."

We work in unison. I wash the dishes while she dries them with a kitchen towel and places them in their designated place. The entire act is so domestic that I should be running for the hills. But somehow, I'm enjoying it so much that I wish we had some more stuff to clean.

When we're done, she passes me a towel. Before she can drop the end still in her grip, I gently tug on the soft linen. Her hands land on my chest, and her hold on me tightens as she tries to balance herself.

My breath stills, as I worry that I've just made another wrong move.

"What...happened?" she stammers, her gaze not wavering from my chest.

"Do you resent my touch, Marr?"

My unexpected question gets her attention, and she looks up.

God, how breathtaking she looks. Her blue eyes behind those glasses, all confused, trying to figure out the meaning behind my words. Her cheeks are scarlet, shaming the pink of her T-shirt.

"What are you saying?"

"Since last week, you've been avoiding me like I have cooties. And don't say you haven't. But today, I want to know why?"

She remains quiet, her eyes no longer on me but focused on something interesting she's found on my tie.

"If you want our relationship to be platonic, which involves talking on the phone, random dinners, and nothing more, I'll accept it. I like you Marr, a lot. I'm dying to have any part of your life that you want to share with me." My grip tightens on her waist. "It's been weeks since we declared to a room full of people that we're together, yet you're not comfortable with a kiss from me. If that's something you don't want in our relationship, please tell me. But if that's something you fear, then talk to me."

She flinches in my arms as frustration seeps through my words.

"I'm sorry. I don't want to sound angry." I ease my grip on her waist, and thankfully she doesn't step back but remains glued in place. She doesn't say a word, so I keep going. "I'm confused as hell, couch girl. Seeing you like this, so damn sexy—you can't even imagine all things I want to do to you. But I'm scared shitless to even hold your hand, dreading you'll bolt like last week. I have no idea what to do."

She slowly rests her head on my chest. It's the first time she's initiated a touch, and my heart soars with happiness. I'm also apprehensive that doing anything would scare her away. And that's when I feel the wetness on my skin—her tears soaking my shirt. Her body shudders as she sobs.

"Fuck, Marr." I crush her in my arms. "I'm sorry. Leave it. It's not important." She sniffles against me, and even though I'm terrified to know her response, I ask, "Do you want me to leave?" Leaving her like this is the last thing I want to do, but I don't even know if she wants me to stay.

"No, don't go, please," she whispers, shaking her head as her hands tighten on the lapels of my jacket.

Thank heavens.

"I'm scared." Her soft voice is barely audible above my thumping heart.

"Of me?" I hold my breath. After the night Marr showed me her scars, we never talked about it. I never had the courage to bring it up, but now I fear that incident has turned her off men.

"Not you," she whispers.

I don't say a word, giving her a moment to gather her thoughts.

"I've never been close to anyone other than Kristy. I-I don't know…how to open up to someone. And believe me, it's not that I don't want to share things with you." Her breathing picks up, and she gulps loudly. "I I'm not like other girls, Zander."

"You're perfect for me." I tuck a strand of hair behind her ear as I've wanted to do since I stepped inside her house.

"I never had a boyfriend." Her head drops low. She has no idea what those words do to me, but I don't interrupt her. I silently stroke her back, begging her to continue.

"You are so…handsome and—"

"You think I'm handsome?" I can't help the words, and the small smile that pulls up my lips.

"Everyone thinks so. I overheard Brenda from HR saying…"

"What did you hear, couch girl?"

"That you're on some list of sexy bachelors. Nobody believes we're together, Zander, because nobody thinks we fit together."

My insides vibrate at those soft words. I peer down at her

pretty face, scarlet as she attempts to hide away from my gaze. Tightening my grip on her, I whisper, "All I care about is if *you* find me sexy, Marr."

"You've seen me, Zander, and you know about me. I'm me and you're you. You're the man of every girl's dreams."

"I have no clue what you're saying. I just want to be the man of *your* dreams." I tip her chin up. "Since that Monday morning when you fell from the couch and into my arms, not a single day has passed that I haven't thought of you. There hasn't been a day that I've seen something blue and your blue eyes haven't flashed before me, hidden behind red glasses."

"Really?" she squeaks.

"Damn fucking true." I loosen my grip on her and look down at her smiling face. *This is my Marr.*

"Hey, beautiful." I smile back at her.

"Hi," she coos, and damn her face, her voice, makes me hard at once. The air around us is no longer tense; it's charged with a deep intensity.

Her cheeks are red, eyes heavy, hair all messed up, and she stares at me in anticipation. Her tongue glides over her dry lower lip, and the sight of it forces me to cross all borders of hesitation as my lips find hers.

I suck her lower lip. Only when her hands tighten their grip on my arms do I realize what I'm doing. I open my eyes without breaking contact and find hers squeezed tight. I know she wants this, but I'll never force her. Not after last time. Not after knowing about her.

I pull back a little, breaking our kiss, but I'm still close enough to feel her breath on my skin.

She whimpers in response, confirming that she wants this as much as I do. But I still say, "Marr, if you want me to stop, tell me *now*." My self-control is pushed to its limits as I say the words.

She opens her eyes, and her hands go around my neck, pulling me closer. It's all the encouragement I need, but her words take me over the edge. "Please don't stop."

21

ROSE

"Please don't stop."

As the words leave my mouth, Zander's soft eyes light up with passion. His grip on my face tightens, and his gaze flicks up to my lips before they lock with mine again. His touch is unlike anything I've ever experienced. His soft hands cradling my face makes me feel wanted, protected, and... loved. Everything I've never felt in my life.

"No more tears, couch girl." His lips press against my cheek, capturing a tear that has managed to escape. "You've had enough things to cry about. From today, no fears, and definitely no tears."

His foreign words of concern break the dam of my emotions, and everything comes crashing down. I hide my sobbing face in his hard chest.

"Shh, Marr." He strokes my back with his long fingers. Bending his knees, he lifts me off the ground.

"Zander!" I squeak.

"Shh." His hands settle under my behind. My hands automatically lock around his neck and my legs around his waist, hugging him like a koala. He walks into the living room, carrying me as if I weigh nothing.

Holding me in his arms, Zander takes a seat on the couch. I try to move away from his lap, but his firm hold prevents my move.

"We were in the middle of something," he whispers before relocking his lips with mine and continuing his magic, taking me someplace far away, where things aren't scary.

He sucks and nibbles on my lips, his warm breath mixing with mine. Without hesitation, Zander pushes his tongue into my mouth, swiping my teeth before rolling it over my tongue. For one second, I think about how I didn't brush my teeth after dinner. But in the next second, that thought is wiped away by his intoxicating touch.

My tongue hesitantly enters his mouth, and he sucks on it hard before biting and sending a jolt between my thighs. A loud moan escapes me, and his hips jerk forward in response. That's when I feel him, big and hard.

Am I prepared for *it* tonight?

He places his forehead on my cheek and whispers in a husky voice, "Feel what you do to me." When I tremble at the feel of his warm breath on my skin, he adds, "Don't worry, we'll ignore the little soldier today."

"He doesn't feel little," I murmur back.

Zander chuckles before his voice gets serious. "I'll never do anything without your permission, you know that right?"

"Yes." I don't need to think twice before answering. I trust him completely.

"That's what's important. And believe me, in the future, you will be glad he isn't small." He winks, making my entire body tingle with that dimple, which is so close to me today. "For now, let's give him some room. Why don't you get your laptop, and we'll watch a movie? Meanwhile, I'll try to bring the little guy down."

I've never heard anyone talk about their private parts in the third person. I look down at his pants and notice the huge bulge. God! I can't take my eyes off him. I'm trying to make out how big the little soldier really is when Zander puts his finger under my chin and lifts my face.

Ship. How long was I staring at his penis?

"If you keep looking at him like that, you'll only be encouraging him. Unless you want to play with him tonight?" He raises one eyebrow, grinning with his perfect white teeth on full display.

"No. No playtime tonight," I reply in a hurry.

"That's what I thought. Now go get your laptop." He playfully smacks my behind before pushing me off the couch.

When I enter my room, I take a deep breath before jumping on the bed. I press my face in the mattress which muffles my squeals.

My heart pounds as I glance at myself in the mirror. Red hot cheeks, wild eyes, ruffled hair, and a huge smile. The girl in the mirror doesn't look like me. Before I can think more, I hear Zander moving some furniture in the living room.

I grab my laptop and bounce toward the living room.

I place the laptop on the coffee table and hand Zander my super soft, plush fleece blanket. "It gets cold at night."

He finds a classic on Netflix and gets rid of his jacket and shoes. His tie hangs loose, with the top two buttons of his shirt undone. Zander looks so different in my living room. In the office, he has this bossy and commanding demeanor, but here, he looks so young and laid back, but no less appealing.

"Come here," he beckons to me, and I sit beside him and throw the blanket over us. He looks at me, perplexed, before pulling me snug under his arm. I relax close to his pounding heart and toasty body. No longer scared of the proximity, I bury my nose in his chest and take a whiff of the Zander-vanilla smell.

When he sees what I'm doing, he chuckles. I hide my face in his chest, and he hugs me tight. But I can feel his body shaking with suppressed laughter.

. . .

Somewhere in the middle of the movie, the heroine and hero get into an argument, and she starts calling him silly nicknames. I can't hold back my giggle at *yummy bums.*

"Don't get any ideas," Zander growls against my ear before biting my earlobe.

His touch makes the butterflies in my stomach go wild. My breathy voice comes out shaky as I say, "Don't worry. I think your name is unusual enough."

He stiffens at my lighthearted remark, and his deep voice transforms into something edgy. "You don't like my name?"

"No…I like it, very much," I reply in haste. "Actually, it suits you," I assure him, patting lightly on his chest.

He looks down at me, his soft gaze still a tinge wild. "Zander means protector, and I'll always protect what's mine. My family, my brothers, and you, Marr."

My heart hammers loud and fast against my constricting chest. He doesn't know what his words mean to me. How much I want him to protect me? How much I've wanted someone to look after me, keep me safe? I swallow my emotions and bury myself deeper under his arm, in his warmth. Maybe I can finally have my happy and safe place.

A sensual scene plays on the screen, and Zander pulls me into his lap. His hands are on my waist, sliding to my stomach. Pausing every so often, he gives me time to get used to his touch. But nothing could have prepared my pounding heart when he nuzzles my shoulders. My skin burns as his fingers rest on my bare belly under the cotton T-shirt. He continues the playful assault of his lips, adding his tongue and licking my neck.

I groan, leaning back into his chest, unsure whether to focus on his hands or his mouth. Using his teeth, he drags the neck of my T-shirt over my shoulder, exposing me to his urgent tongue.

"Zander," I moan as an unknown feeling engulfs me, making me delirious.

"Relax," he whispers in my ear.

What is he saying? How can I relax when he's doing all that?

My hands slide up to grip his strong biceps, anything to ground me. But he gives me no chance. His exploring hand ascends my body. When I realize where his hand is going, I feel scared and shy at the same time. No one has touched me like this.

"Zander."

His hand is hovering over my right breast when he asks, "Do you want me to stop?"

I don't want him to stop. I want to experience everything with this man I'm deeply falling for.

"No. It's just...I-I haven't…I've never—"

"Hush, Marr. We're in this together. We'll learn about each other together." And just like that, his hand settles on my breast. His soft fingers gently graze the edges of my bra under the T-shirt. "It's sexy. Tell me the color."

"P-pink," I stammer.

He chuckles, his lips pressing on my shoulders. "Pink seems to be your color tonight."

"I like…pink," I confess, my head resting on his broad shoulder.

"I like you *in* pink," he says, pulling the lacy bra cup under my breasts.

I freeze, feeling too exposed.

"I just want to feel you. Nothing more." His breath caresses my skin, his touch reverent. "Is this pink too?" he asks, pinching my pebbled nipple.

Sweet Sugar! Do people talk like this?

"Tell me." He pinches hard. "Or should I check for myself?"

"They are pink," I rush. Thankfully, it's dark. The only light is coming from the laptop screen, the forgotten movie still running.

"I'm already in love with them," he says, giving my breast

another squeeze. "God, you are fucking soft, beyond anything I imagined. Like cream and butter."

He imagined me, us, like this?

His hands move behind me, and he swiftly unclasps my bra, faster than I've ever managed to. Grabbing the hem of my T-shirt, he drags it up in an attempt to remove it.

"Zander!"

"I want to touch you, feel your skin, and give you a taste of me. Nothing more, I promise," he whispers reassuringly before removing my T-shirt and my already hanging bra. I try to cover my exposed chest with my arms, but his hands beat me to it, and he takes ahold of my breasts from behind again.

"No hiding from me, sweetheart." His mouth moves lower on my back as he gives me a long lick from one shoulder to another, and I squirm under the touch of his hot lips.

His hands glide slowly from my sternum toward my stomach, and I shiver as his index finger makes circles over my belly button. His exploring hands travel further down, moving past the waistband of my shorts and skating over my panties. My brain's in a crazy mixed state of fear and excitement.

I suck in a breath as his fingers gently pat my mound and send every nerve signal from my brain to the part of my body which, till today, was only acquainted with me.

"Is this also pink?" he asks, tugging my panties between his fingers. When I just hum, he whispers, biting my earlobe. "Is that a yes?"

"Hmm." That's all I can manage, and my inability to speak amuses him greatly.

After making several circles on the cotton covering my sex, he moves lower and sighs. "So wet, Marr."

His fingers gently brush over the cotton, trying to collect the moisture. The friction ignites something unknown in me, and I moan. After bringing his hand close to his face, Zander inhales.

Ship! Did he just smell my...

"Your scent is breathtaking." He groans.

Oh, my. He did.

His hand returns to the inside of my shorts, over my panties, and this time he rubs harshly. The action pushes the cotton into my wet folds, and all my nerve endings fire in response. I arch my back, and my hands go around his neck, my head resting on the hollow of his right shoulder. I pull him closer as he starts to make fast circles over my sex.

"Ah," I cry.

"So responsive, Marr. I'm not even touching you." His hoarse voice is foreign to me.

"Zander!"

"Yes couch girl, let it go. I can't believe you can get off so easily. Fucking hell."

When he pinches my cotton-covered clit, something unknown loosens within me. I scream so loud that he has to put his free hand on my mouth.

I burst into tears from this unfamiliar sensation of freedom.

"Holy shit, Marr. Did I hurt you?" He turns me in his lap and peers at me with worry-filled eyes.

"No, not at all. But I-I can't seem to stop." I wipe the tears rolling down my face.

He holds me in his arms as I bury my face in his chest, holding on to him like he might disappear and this night will turn into nothing but a dream.

Several minutes pass until Zander caresses my back and asks warily, "Do you want to talk about it? Didn't you enjoy it?"

I hate myself for making him feel this way. "I...liked it. Very much. My head...was light, and it reminded me of the only time I had too much wine," I try to explain.

I can feel his smile on my hair. "It feels good, right?"

"Yes. But I can't stop my tears." I look at his handsome face. Is he disappointed?

"It's okay, Marr. Sometimes good and bad emotions come together. It's normal."

I know it's not normal to cry while making love, but Zander would never let me feel any different.

"It was...it was..." I try to put the feeling into words.

He chuckles. "An orgasm, baby."

"My first orgasm," I whisper, knowing my teary face has a hundred-watt smile.

An identical smile lights his face. "Yes, your first orgasm. There are several more you're going to get, but not tonight."

Surprisingly, his words make me sad. Now I know what all the fuss is over, and we haven't even done it yet.

He helps me put my T-shirt back on and pulls me to his chest. "Thank you, Marr," he says against my hair.

"You're thanking me?" I ask incredulously.

He tips my chin up with a finger and lazily places his lips over mine. "Thank you for sharing this intimate moment with me."

"*Thanks* to you too," I whisper, my beaming face telling him, for sure, how much I'm thankful.

"You are very welcome." He smiles and gives me a swift kiss. "But I need to make some adjustments."

I don't understand until he gets up and tugs on his pants. I realize we didn't do anything to ease him, but I'm not sure what the protocol is in this situation.

"Um, do you want…me to…" I try to ask, not knowing what exactly I'm asking.

"Have you given a blow job before?" He cocks his head to the side and raises an eyebrow.

"No," I reply hastily, which causes a dimpled smile to pull on his lips.

"I think we've had enough adventure for the day, babe."

He must have caught my drooping lips, because suddenly he tips my chin up with his fingers. "I don't want to overwhelm you, Marr. Don't worry about me. Today is just the beginning. I'll definitely ask you to return the favor one day." He leaves the last sentence hanging in the air as a warning before sauntering toward the kitchen.

My heart thumps too loud. I'm not sure if it's from the excitement or fear of his declaration.

He returns with two cans of soda and hands me one. His eyes never leave mine as he sips the drink. The movement of his neck as the liquid flows down seems unreasonably erotic.

Placing the can next to the laptop on the table, he asks, "Can I stay the night?" There's a hint of hesitancy in his voice, as if I'd deny his request.

"I'd love for you to stay the night." I stand and my hands naturally curl around his strong waist. My head rests over its favorite place tonight: his warm, pounding heart.

22

ZANDER

I stand awestruck in Marr's bedroom, which is straight out of some glossy interior decor magazine and a complete one-eighty from the bohemian living room.

It screams color, light, life. Everything from the pink pillows, baby blue curtains, and the zillion string lights is swanky and chic. I take in the room, perusing the several knick-knacks.

"What do you think?" She shifts on her feet, nervously looking around like she's trying to see her place through my eyes.

"It's beautiful. But I honestly didn't expect your room to be this…gossamer. I expected superhero posters, but not this." I glance toward her bed, which thankfully is queen-size, and notice a handful of photographs hanging from the string lights.

"I know, but…it's my safe and happy place." She smiles, fixing her glasses and making light of a serious thought.

I place my finger under her chin, and her hesitant blue eyes land on me. "What's the real reason, couch girl?"

Her eyes close briefly before she takes a deep, cleansing

breath. "Sometimes, I just…wish I could…rewind time. Live those…lost years of my life."

Her wistful words force me to imagine Marr as a young girl, alone, trying to find herself. I pull her closer to my racing heart. "Thank you. And I'm not only talking about the room." I want to tell her how much this whole evening means to me.

She blushes a beautiful shade of pink, which I've seen plenty of times in the past. But today, somehow it looks different. More *mine.*

I place a kiss on her forehead and plant my butt on the corner of her bed. "Is there something else I should know, apart from your obsession of glittery, pink things?"

"One more thing." Raising her index finger, she dashes to her dresser and returns with a wooden box. "Don't make fun of me. I'm just making you aware of all my quirks."

I bite back my smile at her words. She is certainly the quirkiest person I know. Starting from those flannel shirts all the way up to her precise breakfast. I'm curious to know what else I should add to that list.

With a wide smile, she opens the latch, and a shock of panic zips through my heart. The box contains different accessories like bracelets, earrings, and other girly stuff. But the distinct feature in each of them is a *rose*. I clutch the bedsheets, attempting to think of anything other than the darkness.

Unbeknownst to my feelings, Marr picks a silver bracelet and swiftly ties it around her wrist. "This one is my favorite."

I can't look at anything other than the metallic rose. I stare at it and wait for the dreadful cold to engulf me and take away all my happiness.

"I'm sorry, Zander."

She stares at me with big apologetic eyes before quickly untying the terrifying bracelet, placing it back into the box and sitting beside me. She closes the dreadful box with a loud thud, trying to shut away my monsters. But they're already out.

"I'm so sorry. I didn't realize..." After taking a deep breath as if mustering some courage, she asks, "We have different memories with the flower, right?"

I'm dumbfounded how this girl, who everyone thinks doesn't understand emotions well, is not only perceptive about my fears—which, by the way, I thought I hid well—but is also careful enough to replace the dreadful word with *flower*.

I nod in response.

"Will you share it with me?" I hate the hesitant lilt in her tone.

When I pull her back into my arms, she rests her head on my chest. I'm surprised how my anxiety subsides at her simple touch.

"Of course, but not today. I want this day to be a happy memory for both of us."

Completely satisfied by my answer, she walks to her dresser with the box and returns with a Polaroid. "Then let's capture it."

She gingerly sits on my lap, and I completely pull her down, urging her to rest her head over my wild, rabid heart.

When the photo ejects with a whirl, she shyly hands it to me.

In the picture, I'm looking at her as she concentrates on holding the camera right. My attention is fixed on the shy smile on her face. I look like a guy who can't keep my eyes off her for a minute.

Someone unconditionally in love with her.

"I hope we can make more memories like this." Her voice sounds dreamy as she clips the picture on the row of string lights above her bed.

"This is just a start, Marr. We will certainly make lots of such memories."

She walks back to me and perches softly beside me. "Will you tell me more about you? You don't have to share anything you're not comfortable with." She quickly adds that last part.

"Sure, but you too will have to spill some beans." I grab her hand and love the pink that rises on her cheeks. Since I have her approval, I can't stop touching her any way that I can.

"I've been very forthcoming, Mr. Teager. I showed you my room, my accessories box." Her voice drops as she realizes that maybe the latter wasn't the best idea.

"Marr, I'm a sucker for you and everything about you. The box just triggered some not-so-good memories. But that's nothing. I can bear a million crappy memories to learn a happy memory of yours." I push away a wild strand of hair from her forehead and watch as her eyes turn misty.

"Wow, Zander. That... might be the nicest thing... someone's ever said to me," she whispers before placing an innocent peck on my cheek. My skin burns where her soft lips make contact.

We get into the bed, and Marr rests her head over my outstretched arm as she listens to silly stories of Zach and Zane.

I'm still talking when her eyes close and she drifts to sleep.

I admire the most innocent and beautiful girl in the world and thank all the heavenly stars for landing her in my arms. I place a tender goodnight kiss on her perfect heart-shaped lips. When that's not enough, I taste her full lips with a swipe of my tongue. She stirs in her sleep, and I quickly pull back.

MY EYES OPEN, and I'm puzzled with the new surroundings before the memories of last night flood in. The place next to me is empty and cold. Of course Marr is an early riser.

My lips curl into a smile at knowing another of her quirks. Getting up, I stretch my arms above my head, working the kinks out of my muscles. A queen-sized bed isn't the best for me, that's a given.

My gaze lands on the string lights still turned on, and I zoom in on the recent additions to Marr's collection. Our pic from last night, with my beautiful girl on my lap. Next to it is another picture of me, lost in sleep with disheveled hair under Marr's pink comforter. A sense of happiness fills my heart upon seeing it. *Am I smiling in my sleep?* A rarity for sure.

While walking toward the attached bathroom, I notice Logan in his fishbowl on her computer table. I knock the glass gently with my finger. "You be good, Logan. Don't bother my girl too much."

After using her bathroom, I tiptoe in the kitchen. The smell of cooked eggs fills the small space as Marr prepares breakfast with complete focus. Quietly, I stand behind her and place my hands around her waist.

Unexpectedly, she shrieks upon my touch.

The glass bowl filled with beaten eggs slips from her hands and lands on the floor with a crashing sound.

"Fuck, Marr. It's me." I turn her in my arms to find her panicked face, her eyes shut, and hands tightly clasped over her chest. "Marr. Open your eyes. Please." My hands rest gingerly on her shoulders.

I die a thousand deaths watching tears run down her cheeks. Her face is white with fear and anxiety. "I-I am... so sorry." Her voice trembles in sync with her entire body.

"No, baby. I am sorry." I remove the burning pan from the heat, turn the stove off, and lead her to the barstool. After fetching a glass of water and placing it between her trembling hands, I gently rub her back. Minutes later, her breathing returns to normal. "I am so sorry, Marr."

"Don't say that." Tears roll down her cheeks. "Now you

see... what it's like to be with me. I can't... even be surprised without... freaking out." Her insecurities rear their ugly head.

I squeeze her shoulder. "It can happen to anyone, couch girl. You were lost in your thoughts, and I startled you." My words have no effect on her as tears continue to flow. I know I can't erase all her insecurities in one day. I'll just have to be patient. Cradling her face, I make her look at me instead of her feet. "It's all good. We still have enough breakfast." I point to two plates topped with food.

"I was making you another plate. I thought"—she gives me a weak smile—"maybe you eat more... as you are so... big."

"You haven't seen big. Not yet." I playfully wiggle my eyebrows at her. When she blushes, I take that as a green signal and add, "But that's gonna change tonight."

"What do you mean?" she squeaks, trying to mask her amusement and failing badly. The previous incident is forgotten for a second.

"We're going out after breakfast, and you're spending the night with me. Not like last night, where after I give you a mind blowing orgasm, you sleep on me."

"Zander! I *did not* sleep on you." She puts her arms around my neck, her tear-stained cheeks scarlet with memories of last night.

"Yes, you did." I kiss her lips and wink at her. "Now, feed your hungry boyfriend some breakfast."

She looks at the mess on the floor indecisively.

"Why don't you set the table. We'll clean up later."

After devouring the breakfast of a Spanish omelet, a bowl of mixed berries, and a cup of coffee, I tell Marr to take a shower and get ready while I clean the kitchen.

When I'm satisfied with my handiwork on the floor, I fetch a change of clothes from my car.

Marr is already in the living room dressed in a deep green

shirt and tight jeans. Damn, this woman has a killer body. Like all her other shirts, today's is collared with full sleeves, but it's not as billowy as usual. I get an eyeful of her delicious curves, still fresh in my memory from last night.

I place my clothes on the coffee table, and this time, I announce myself before getting close to her. "Hey, beautiful." I hold her from behind, kissing her soft, nice-smelling hair. Now that I know she likes me and my touch, I'm having a hard time keeping my hands off her.

"Hi." She turns around in my arms.

"Is it okay if I use your bathroom?" I nod toward my change of clothes.

"In a moment." She goes somewhere in the house and seconds later returns with a new toothbrush and a towel. "Here." She hands them to me.

I take the toothbrush but return the towel. "Don't need this. I'll use yours."

Her face beams at my crazy statement, the beautiful pink back on her cheeks.

Getting in the shower, I notice her exquisite shower gel collection. *Jesus, this girl.*

She is so paradoxical. I smell each of the seven bottles labeled with feminine words like sun, honey, cherry, wishes, and more, before deciding to go for the purple bottle labeled moonstone something.

After the quick shower, I get dressed and take a look in the mirror. My hand grazes my five o'clock shadow, which has grown a bit wild. Maybe I should add a spare razor along with the clothes in my sleepover bag. I'm eagerly looking forward to many more nights in Marr's bed.

Entering the living room, I find her in those damn killer boots and a sling purse on her shoulders. A whistle shoots through my lips. "Did I tell you that you look fucking hot in these sexy boots?" I whisper in her ear before biting her earlobe. My hands grab her waist.

She shivers and murmurs back, "On several occasions."

When she turns around, I kiss her with every intention of keeping it soft and sweet. But the way she falls into me tells me she's looking for anything but soft.

My control snaps at her reaction, and I give her my all, which she returns with equal fervor. I suck her lower lip, and she mimics my action. When I push my tongue inside her mouth, she rolls hers over it. I can't fucking believe she's responding this way.

I open my eyes and find hers shut tight, lost in the kiss. My hands move over her body. I memorize the shape of her curvy waist and her heavenly breasts as I caress her through the fabric of the blouse. I'm itching to take it off, but I know with one touch of her skin, I won't be able to stop myself. I want our first time tonight to be special. I am damn adamant on making this another happy memory for her.

I feel her nipples hardening under my thumb through the fabric. And when she rubs herself over my cock, I lose it. I jerk with a loud groan.

"Fuck, Marr. No." I pull her gently away, creating a sliver of distance between us. Gradually, I get some blood flowing to my brain instead of it all going to my cock.

"S-sorry." Her face turns beet red, a heavenly mixture of embarrassment and lust.

"No, baby. You don't know what you do to me, or maybe you do," I say, pointing to the big bulge I'm now sporting in the front of my jeans. "You responding this way is like fuel to the already scorching fire inside me. But as much as I want to do this right now, I want our first time to be special. I promised you last night that we'd have many more memorable moments."

She lowers her head in embarrassment.

"Marr. I am yours, baby. You can do anything with me. Just give me today and then we can make love anywhere, anytime. Fuck, I have wild dreams of you in my office… doing what you offered last night."

Her eyes widen in shock at my brazen words before she swallows hard.

I grin, looking at her as she smiles sheepishly.

I know she's thinking about what I just said.

"You're spending today and tonight with me. Tomorrow is a corporate holiday, so I'll bring you back home tomorrow evening. No need to pack; just inform Kristy. Where is she anyway?"

"She messaged me last night that she was spending the night with Oscar's PA, Beth."

Sure. If we're calling her date Beth.

"What are we doing today?" Marr asks, bringing my attention back from Kristy's dating life.

"I know what we'll be doing post dinner." I waggle my eyebrows suggestively. "You can decide for the day."

She looks at me open mouthed, and after gulping loudly, mutters, "Would you like to go near the lake?"

23

ROSE

It's a beautiful, sunny day with some scattered clouds. I sit in Zander's Cadillac as a woman's soulful voice filters through the speakers. I glance at the man beside me, who's smiling and humming along with the music.

This is the first time I'm seeing him out of his usual three-piece suit and tie. Even last night, he slept in his dress shirt and suit pants. But today, he's wearing a casual button-up shirt, sleeves rolled up to the elbows, and crisp blue jeans. His eyes, hidden behind his aviator glasses, and his hair not set as usual cheat his CEO image. My fingers hesitantly glide through his soft locks. I've dreamt about this since our first meeting in the café but never knew this small action could be so sensual.

"Marr?" Zander's hoarse voice halts my movements. My fingers are still lost in his obsidian bunch when he looks at me with fierce eyes. His gaze tears from the road to me before he pulls back and shifts in his seat. "You can't do that to me while I'm driving."

I have no idea what he means.

What am I doing?

He's the one who's making me a crazy bag of emotions.

After long moments of silence, I comment, "Your hair is softer than it was last night."

"Oh yeah?" He raises an eyebrow. "I might have stolen some of your ocean secret product."

"You're welcome to use it anytime." I giggle; I can't hide my smile around him.

"If this is an invitation to spend more nights in your bedroom, we need to meet Kristy's guy."

This isn't the first time Zander's insinuated that Kristy is seeing someone, but I'm not sure. Since I've known her, Kristy has never been the one to hide her dating life. But come to think of it, I haven't heard any of her recent dating stories.

"Do you think she's seeing someone?" I ask, now seriously considering the idea.

"I have a strong feeling her guy is from Elixir," Zander says casually.

"What?" I look at him in surprise. Why wouldn't she tell me?

"She has very sneakily brought up the non-fraternization policy annulment thrice in our discussions," Zander explains, raising an eyebrow. "I want to meet the guy and make sure he and I don't end up at your place on the same evening with a sleepover bag. I have no desire to have any other man hear my girl's screams of ecstasy."

"Screams of ecstasy?" My face heats at his words. He might be exaggerating, claiming last night's moans to be screams, but I'm surely not a quiet person.

"And tonight, I plan to hear them all night long. Be prepared," he says as if in a warning.

Crab. Am I prepared?

WE WALK hand in hand along the shoreline of Cherry Lake. It's a vital part of Cherrywood, giving the town not only its name but also attracting several tourists every year, especially during spring. This season, the cherry blossoms are in full bloom and the lake turns a beautiful pink.

Mountains surround the lake on three sides, and one can always spot those obnoxious seagulls flying over the shore, ready to snatch everything from your hands. I've learned my lesson about not eating a snack at the shore the hard way. But even then, I always love this place, and walking here today with Zander makes it more special.

As we traipse toward the park, the crowd thickens—kids with young parents, older couples walking hand in hand, and teenage girls giggling when they see Zander. I look at him, lost in his own world, oblivious to the effect he's having on women and girls alike.

We soon reach the park entrance, and above the iron gate is a gigantic yellow banner with red letters saying Three-Day Carnival. Fair-style tents cover the entire park.

"There's some big party going on here." Zander looks around.

I hesitate at the entrance, watching the serene park that's turned into a fiesta. This isn't a surprise, as once a month, there's usually some event going on in the park. But what gets to me is that, today, I didn't check the town's website. Zander and his words distracted me, somehow bringing my guard down, making me less paranoid. His presence and its effects are much stronger than any medication or therapy I've been subjected to.

"I guess it's because of the long weekend," I mumble, glancing around nervously.

"What is it, Marr?" He holds my cold hands and pulls me to the side, out of the way of the crowd. "We can go somewhere else."

His warm fingers gently stroke the back of my hands, comforting me, bringing my escalating heartbeat down.

"Am I so predictable?"

He smiles at my question. "I spend an unhealthy amount of time following you, thinking about you, looking at you, couch girl."

My lips pull up in a smile, and when his thumb grazes my lips and my eyes flutter close, I forget that we're in a public place, surrounded by strangers.

That has never happened to me before.

"Let's go inside." Nervous and curious to know what else Zander can make me forget, I take a step forward.

"Sure, babe. Whatever you want."

Babe.

Zander has used so many endearments in the past twenty-four hours—baby, babe, sweetheart—and every time he uses one, my heart flutters with excitement.

As we enter the park, an enchanting carnival scene welcomes us. There are colorful stalls with an assortment of games, women selling homemade baked goods, and artists with crafts.

My grip on Zander's hand tightens. I look around at the color, life, laughter—everything I want and miss in my life.

But maybe not for much longer, my heart softly murmurs.

"We can leave if this makes you anxious."

My heart tightens at Zander's concerned voice.

"It does a little… or maybe too much. But I'm also liking it. There is so much… life and happiness. Things I've always missed." My hands curl around my wrists, and I resist the need to pull on my cuffs. "It's also helpful that most people are too busy with themselves… to notice me."

Before I can dwell more, Zander pulls me in his arms and hugs me tight. I'm sure he's feeling sorry for my childhood, but I don't want to think about our past. Today is a happy day, and I want to keep it that way.

"We've found a place to spend the day, and at night, we go by your plan." I pull him by his hand.

"Why, Ms. Marlin, are you impatient for the night?"

His words make my heart jump a little. My cheeks flush and the feverish feeling flows through me like hot lava.

He raises an eyebrow. "Who would have thought after just one dose of my magic fingers, you'd be *coming* back for more. Wait till you get the real drug, baby."

"Zander!" His heated voice fills me with an unbridled excitement for that real drug.

"What? Don't tell me you don't want it."

"I'd have never guessed the CEO of Elixir could be so rowdy."

"I'll show you rowdy in a few hours," he whispers in my ear, making me shiver all over.

A loud wail of a child who just dropped his ice cream breaks our trance, and we walk further into the park.

Zander and I roam around hand in hand before settling on a bench. When I'm looking away at the acrobats performing a show, I hear a clicking sound. Zander takes another picture of me when I turn to him and then shows me his cell phone.

He made me his wallpaper.

"Rose. Rose," someone yells through the thick crowd. I turn to find Clementine Hawthorne scurrying toward us.

My muscles relax, and the corner of my mouth quirks up at the sight of one of my few friends in Cherrywood. I wave at her.

"Who is this handsome man?" She cocks an eyebrow at Zander, making me chuckle. I haven't met anyone more candid than Clem.

"This is Zander. Zander is the CEO of Elixir Inc."

The way Zander's arm rest over my shoulders, it's a no-brainer that he is more than my boss, but to make it perfectly clear, he adds, "And her boyfriend."

"Hello, boss boyfriend. Do you have any brothers even half as handsome as you?"

Zander chuckles, and I tell him, "Clementine is Oscar's youngest sister."

Zander nods. "Your brother often speaks about his family. It's nice to meet you."

"Make sure you check out my latest stuff." Clementine nods toward a tent with her name embroidered in silky thread.

We enter her stall followed by a few other customers. I'm once again reminded about Clementine's talent as an independent fashion designer. Her designs are unique and heart touching.

I peruse through the beautiful metal accessory collection and notice some interesting car mirror decorations. One that stands out is a steel butterfly with the words *"Remembering you"* engraved on its wings.

I take it with me to the cash register where Zander is picking up a small paper bag. I wonder what he bought. I pay Clem and promise her that Kristy and I will visit her soon.

"I bought you something." It's a silly gift, but I want him to have a memory of today.

"You did? What is it?" The smile that lights up his face makes me want to give him a piece of my heart along with this ornament.

I place the metal butterfly on his palm. Zander twirls it between his fingers and smiles. "It's very thoughtful, Marr. It will remind me of today, of us." He places a kiss on my lips.

I realize that Zander is one of those guys who doesn't shy away from displays of his affection. He doesn't care where we are or who's watching, and I like that about him. Whenever he's pulling me closer or placing a peck on my cheeks, I get those butterflies in my stomach that poets and writers rave about. I feel the excitement and anticipation of more instead of my usual fear of rejection. With every passing moment, I'm falling more and more for this amazing man. The affection in his eyes and the tenderness of his touch are gradually taking down the rigid walls of my insecurities and fears.

"What is it, baby?" He caresses my cheek with the back of his hand.

"Nothing." I clear my throat. *It's too soon, Rose. Don't make a bigger deal out of this than what it is.* "I just remembered my favorite car charm, which I misplaced somewhere."

"How did you lose it?" he asks in a concerned voice as we continue our walk, looking around at the festivities.

"It got misplaced while my car was with the mechanic." I shrug. "I bought it six years back in a garage sale, even before I had a car, in hope of having one someday." I smile at my own stupidity.

He smiles back. "It must have been something special. Tell me about it."

I remember the beautiful piece that I'd found while returning to my dorm room after hearing an applied physics guest lecture at a hotel outside the university's campus. I was walking down the streets of a residential area when my eyes caught the pink velvet band with several roses around it. I had thought it was a Christmas ornament. By the time the old lady from the garage sale told me what it really was, I had already decided on the purchase, car or no car.

Lost in my memories as I reminisce about those days, it takes me a while to notice Zander has stopped walking.

"Zander, what's the matter?" Turning around, I find him taking something out from the pocket of his leather jacket. "Oh my god! How? Where?" I run and cover the few steps between us. My lost charm dangles from his fingers. There's no question it's mine, because one rose is bigger than the others.

"Fuck, I can't believe this," he mutters and releases a heavy breath. "I rented a car on my first visit to Cherrywood from the Douglas garage. I guess that's where your car was for repair."

I nod. But it was months ago.

What are the odds of my car charm ending up in his rental?

"I found this in that car. Since that day, I've tried to get rid of it, but hell, it keeps coming back to me. The room service guys keep bringing it back to my hotel room, and a couple of times, I've found it in my office bag. Today, I found it in the trunk of my car. Please take it and relieve me from the guard duty of your prized possession."

I don't know what to say. I'm too stunned by the coincidence. Quickly, I slip it into my purse. "You really hate the flower, don't you?" I ask as we resume walking.

"You have no idea." He squeezes my hand tight, and I know that is all I'm going to get from him.

Before I can prod more on Zander's reaction, he deflects my attention.

"What will you have? I'm kinda hungry and the turkey sandwich looks tempting." He points to the food truck and rubs his stomach with a huge grin.

My breath hitches as I stare at his beautiful face. The afternoon sun behind his head is forging a golden aura around him. The finger under his lip as he looks at the food truck thoughtfully makes my heartbeat wild. Memories of how his fingers played with me last night revisit, and I have to close my eyes to compose myself and dismiss the burning sensation.

Photographic memory sucks.

When I open my eyes again, Zander is staring at me with a knowing expression. My cheeks burn and I look away. He tugs me closer and whispers in my ear, "If you continue looking at me like that, I'll have to throw you over my shoulder and take you behind those scanty bushes."

I suck in a breath. I know he would never be so reckless. Zander is one of the most sensible people, yet I can't control the shiver that passes through my body at his touch and his words. I close my eyes, taking everything in. I tell myself that this is real, not a dream.

"We need to move, baby, or else we'll scare that little girl away," he says in a gruff voice.

It takes me a moment to comprehend his words, and I turn in his arms to find a young girl watching us while licking her ice cream like we're a part of some show at the carnival. The confusion on her face makes me chuckle, and I drag Zander away before we really scare her.

I take a seat on one of the benches as Zander grabs us food. He places a salad bowl and lemon soda in front of me before taking a bite of his sandwich.

"A question, if you don't mind?" he asks.

I nod, biting through the soft goat cheese.

"Why a precise breakfast, but not a precise lunch and dinner?" He nods toward the salad bowl.

"Precise lunch and dinner didn't work out while I was at college." I smile.

"Explain."

I'm still getting used to the idea of someone being interested in me, in little things about me, like my lunch and dinner choices.

"We had fixed menus at Kindred Hearts. I didn't know any other way, so the first day out of the orphanage, I hung the same menus in my dorm room. But soon I learned that the university cafeteria didn't have most of the items on my menu. I thought about cooking in my room, but it turns out I'm a horrible cook. I spent a big portion of my scholarship money in the first month paying restaurants extra to deliver my special requests. I knew I had to learn to adapt. Gradually, and for one meal a week, I started experimenting with the cafeteria food."

I don't tell him how many times those days I went to bed with an empty stomach because I couldn't touch the new food. It took years before I learned to eat lunch and dinner on a whim—anything, anywhere.

"But you kept the breakfast menu?"

I nod. "I noticed that the cafeteria served similar breakfast options. I prepared a menu out of those, and some days I ate good old PB&J in my room." Looking at him, I hesitate on whether to stop here or say more. But the look of affection-filled interest on his face decides for me, and I continue. "The familiarity kept my anxiety in check, and it was also my way of keeping my childhood with me. I didn't have pictures on my dorm room wall of my parents, of trips with them, posters of rock bands…"

A sad expression etches over his handsome face.

"I'm fine," I tell him, closing the empty salad box after dropping the plastic fork and paper napkin inside.

He collects the garbage and takes it to the trash can. We walk around some more when he asks, "Not even a Wolverine poster?"

I snort. "I had the same superhero poster you saw yesterday to keep me company."

"Good. I would worry that you didn't get your Wolverine high those days."

"I don't need a Wolverine high." I playfully push against his chest. "Maybe you do."

Pulling me closer, he says in his sexy gruff voice, "I just need your high, Marr."

A paper bag rustles in his pocket as we come closer.

"What did you buy from Clem?" I remember him slipping a paper bag in his jacket.

"Something for you," he says after a beat.

"Really? Let me see." Without a second thought, I push my hand inside his jacket, but he grabs my wrist and halts my movement.

I freeze. *What did I just do?*

Glancing at me, he immediately releases my hand, which

is still clutching the paper bag. "Jesus. Don't look at me like that, couch girl. It's just a little surprise. I want to give it to you when the time is right."

Releasing the paper bag, I try to compose myself. "Sorry, I thought you didn't like me touching you."

"God, Marr, you'd run for the hills if you knew how much I want you to touch me. Touch me, kiss me, scratch me—I'm all yours, baby."

He groans at whatever expression he sees on my face. "What the hell was I thinking, bringing you to a place full of people and kids where I can't even kiss you properly? This is torture. Come on, let's get out of here."

I spot a makeshift photo booth as we approach the exit. "Picture! Please, for my string lights."

Zander closes the curtain and turns the camera on before kissing me hard. I lose track of time as his one hand wraps around my small ponytail. He pulls me closer to him by his other hand on my waist. I can feel him harden as he thrusts into my stomach, his wandering hand moving up and down my spine. My own body is hot and wet.

"Fucking kids," he whispers, pulling back, and that's when I hear some kids impatiently waiting outside.

"But our picture?"

He points to the several photographs lying on the transparent pickup slot.

When did he take them? I grab the pictures, and my face heats at the sight. My shirt is riding up as Zander's hand splays over my waist. I'm clutching his neck, pulling him close. Even though we have clothes on, these pictures are…sensual.

"Are you done?" a young boy's voice comes from outside of the tent.

"No, we were just starting, you dipshit," Zander mutters under his breath.

I quickly put the photos into my bag before anyone can

see them. We walk out of the booth and realize why the kids are impatient. It's drizzling and everyone has taken shelter in whichever place they can. I guess no one was expecting rain, as it was bright and sunny this morning.

By the time we reach the car, it's really coming down. We quickly get inside and calm our heavy breaths. I brush my hair with my fingers, trying to untangle the wet locks. I'm soon joined by Zander, who plays with the wet strands. Beads of water cover his handsome face.

I wipe some of the water drops from his cheeks. Somehow, the feel of his spiked stubble under my fingers makes me grin.

"I guess I need a shave every day," he whispers in an amused tone, stroking his beard like men do in shaving cream advertisements.

"I like it. You look hot," I whisper.

We stare into each other's eyes as the air inside the car gets warm and humid. Zander pulls my face closer to his, moving his hand from behind my head to my neck. I lean into his kiss. Surprisingly, the dampness around our bodies is sensual. He licks my lips, something he does often, like he's savoring my taste. He gently nibbles my bottom lip, and I moan into his mouth. When he drifts his tongue into my mouth, I meet him with mine. I love how he takes his time exploring my mouth. It's enticing and erotic.

He lifts me from my seat and pulls me over his lap after pushing the driver seat back.

"Zander," I whisper, my hoarse voice foreign to my own ears.

"I want to have my first experience of making out in a car with my girlfriend," he rasps in my ear and nuzzles my neck.

I love that his first experience of making out in a car is with me.

His pointed stubble tingles my neck as he whispers over my skin. "I had one of the best days of my life. Thank you."

He rubs my back, the wet shirt creating a strange friction. Until yesterday, I didn't know simple things like a rub on the back could be so arousing.

"Me too." I shiver as my head rests on his chest. And then I sneeze.

No! Not now, please!

But crab, I sneeze again.

"You cold?" he asks, raising my face as I quickly wipe any remnants of the cold from my nose and upper lips.

Zander smiles and grabs a napkin from the dashboard, wiping my face with it. "Better. Let's get you out of these wet clothes. I don't want you to be sick, especially tonight." Placing a swift kiss on my lips, he sets me back in my seat and starts the car.

The uninvited black clouds hover over the lake, and it's dark sooner than usual. Light reflections dance on the lake as heavy raindrops pop the water. A classic piece of Beethoven buzzes through the car's music system. Everything around us looks magical, like a scene cut out from a painting or a classic romance movie, including the man by my side. His one hand is on the steering wheel and the other is holding mine.

"I can never get bored of this place," I blurt. But it's true, Cherrywood has felt more like home to me than any other place.

"I'm starting to see why." His eyes gaze over Cherry Lake before his focus is back on the road.

"You know this piece?" I ask, nodding toward the stereo after a long silence.

"No, but I'm sure you do." He raises an eyebrow.

"It's Beethoven's Moonlight Sonata. It's very befitting in this weather." I look around at the rain.

"I can think of so many other things befitting this weather." He winks and I snicker in response.

"I'm noticing you have a one-track mind, Mr. Teager."

"Only for you, Ms. Marlin," he replies, increasing the volume of the music.

"Who got you this music? I'm sure you didn't select Beethoven by yourself."

"Your confidence in my music interests is humbling, sweetheart." He chuckles, making me giggle.

"So, am I wrong, or is there a hidden virtuoso inside you?"

"If there was a hidden virtuoso, Beast would have dragged him out of me. He painfully made us play piano for several months before we could give it up."

"Really?"

Zander nods. "Beast is an amazing pianist. In the past, he even gave some public performances. So, he tried to teach us, even arranged a music teacher and all. I couldn't connect with the instrument, and neither did Zach. Zane, however, took an instant liking to the flute. He found it in our music teacher's studio. He'd practice for hours and hours, making me and Zach nearly deaf. It was a surprise, as those days, he wasn't…speaking much." A pained expression dawns on his face.

I'm getting to know this look. It's the same from when I asked him to say my name in the café. And the same when I showed him my accessory box yesterday.

"What happened to Zane?" I motion toward my neck.

"He was sick as a baby, and I couldn't provide him the needed medical care." The guilt in his voice surprises me. Zander would have been a kid himself back then.

"You guys were in a home?" He'd once told me that before Ashcroft Miller adopted him and his brothers, they lived in a boys' home.

"No. We were with… some other people." He swallows hard after saying the last three words. The numbness in his voice, the fear, scares me. And now I know something happened when he was with *those other people.*

I squeeze his hand. "Someday, if you want to talk about it, I'm here to listen. But do not feel obligated. If you decide not to share, I'm still here."

He gives me a weak smile that doesn't reach his eyes.

We stop at the traffic light when he asks me, "So how did you turn into a Beethoven protégée?"

I smile coyly. "I am no protégée, but I did take piano lessons for several years from Kristy's mother. In fact, that's how I met them. She's one of the most graceful pianists."

He nods, asking me to continue.

"Kristy's mom, Sophia, is a music therapist. She worked with Kindred Hearts Orphanage. One day, I heard her play while she was working with another student. I stood outside the door listening to her for the entire hour of the class. The same evening after dinner, I went to the music room and tried to play, at which I failed, of course." I smile, remembering my silly effort. "Someone reported this to the headmistress. The next day, she called me into the music room and Sophia was waiting there. Dressed in all white, with blonde hair and pink lips, she looked like an angel. Her eyes were exactly like mine. I wondered at that moment if I would look like her when I grew up." I look at him, making sure he's following me.

He pulls the car on the side of the road and stops the ignition.

"What—" I'm silenced by his finger on my lip.

"Continue." He holds my hands in his, which tremble in hopeful nervousness.

"It was the first time I'd thought about my future. Before that, I never realized I would grow up and do something with my life." I peer at him after saying those words, and Zander, being his beautiful self, places a kiss on my palm, smiling and urging me to continue.

"Sophia asked me to sit on the bench, and when I did,

without saying a word, she directed my hands with her soft ones on the keys."

I skip the part where I shrieked after her first touch and bolted out of the room. Those early days, anything and everything scared me. After four days of convincing from the headmistress, I returned to the music room, where Sophia used a small wooden rod to direct my hands. A month later, we were able to get rid of that stick, and I had the first feel of motherly soft hands.

"Kristy is also a Beethoven protégée, I presume." He grins, breaking my chain of thoughts.

But I can't return his smile on that one. "No, she has different memories with the instrument."

"What does that mean?" he asks, confused.

"It involves her father. But that's her story to tell."

He nods and starts the car.

We go back to listening to music until he parks in his hotel's parking lot. My heartbeat picks up as we reach the entrance, and Zander pulls me closer. I'm a ball of nerves by the time we step inside the elevator. When I see his reflection in the mirror, the sensuality and heat in his eyes makes my knees weak, and my body trembles with anticipation. The elevator stops at the third floor, and his warm hand rests on my back as he leads me to his suite.

When we're inside, he crushes me into his chest and releases a heavy breath. "Finally, I can have you in my arms without those little monsters eyeing us." He places a kiss on my cheek and whispers, "You take my breath away, Marr."

My total unromantic response to his passion is a sneeze. But I know it's far from being over. I sneeze again and again and again…until I lose count. Zander releases me and grabs some tissues from the nightstand.

"God, I'm such a klutz," I mutter as I wipe my face clean.

"No, you are not. You're cute and wet, and maybe cold."

"It's just... I sneeze often when I'm cold or nervous." Another sneeze comes out of me.

"What are you now? Cold or nervous?" He lifts my chin with his finger.

"Nervous, I guess," I whisper.

"But good nervous, right?" He smiles, knowing my answer well.

"Yes."

"Don't be nervous, Marr. I won't eat you." He grins mischievously. "Or maybe I will. But I'll feed you first."

He goes to the sitting area and picks up the phone before giving me a wink. "Oh, yes, I'm going to feed you food. You need practice before we can feed you other things."

I'm frozen at the same spot with my mouth hanging open. I can't believe the sweet and caring Zander, with whom I spent the entire day, transformed into this dirty talking Romeo. I have no idea what he's saying on the phone. It's like my ears are clogged with nervous excitement. I only notice his lips moving.

Ending the call, he returns to me. "If you keep your mouth open like that, baby, I'll have to start the practice now." He lifts my lower jaw with one finger and pecks my lips. "I'm going to take a quick shower. There's something for you to wear in the closet. Bathroom is all yours after me."

God, how am I going to keep up with *this* Zander?

I open the cabinet and see a rectangular cardboard box with *Couch Girl* written on top in bold black letters. I'm not sure if I want to see what's inside. This is how Zander wishes to see me—will I also like it?

With trembling hands and a dubious mind, I take the box to bed and open it.

Every uncertainty is out the window as I take out my pink T-shirt and shorts from the previous night. I laugh but stop short when Zander walks out of the bathroom.

With only a white towel wrapped around his waist, he prowls toward me and smiles.

"You looked so breathtaking last night. It was like a new Marr—my Marr—and I want to see you always like this. Relaxed and comfortable with me." He bends and kisses me.

A kiss in which you lose track of time. A kiss that wakes up every sleeping cell in your body, that feels like a drug, soft yet demanding. There's no fight to control, just possessing each other. I put my hands on his shoulders to balance my intoxicated mind, and the first touch of his skin liberates something in me. I do the unthinkable; I bite his lower lip.

"Ooh...easy baby," he whispers.

"S-sorry."

"No need to be sorry. Just be gentle with your man." He squats before me while I'm sitting on the bed. In this position, we are eye to eye. This sexy Zander is a sight to behold, and I want to get lost in his piercing gaze and stay like this forever, but he gets up and pulls me with him.

He walks me to the bathroom. "I don't want you to get cold." He kisses my forehead before handing me a purple *Hers* bathrobe.

I take the fastest shower in human history. Under the robe, I put on the fresh pair of undergarments that I slid into my handbag along with a toothbrush this morning. When I step out of the bathroom, I find Zander looking at his phone. With his shoulders bunched forward, I see some ink on his back.

"Can I see your tattoos?"

He looks up, smiles, and turns around, giving me a good view of his back.

Holy ship!

I'm stuck in place, awestruck. With all the touching and kissing, I knew Zander was fit. But this is crazy. It looks like someone chiseled him into perfection. I wonder how much time he spends in the gym to maintain this body.

"How often do you work out?" I whisper in amazement.

"Quite a lot. Like what you see?" He smirks, looking at me over his shoulder.

"Hmm." I think I'll go brain dead. For someone who had no male attention, this much masculinity in one day feels like a drug overdose.

"Which one you like the most?" He raises an eyebrow, turning around.

Crab, he's talking about the tattoos. I was so busy crushing over his body that I forgot to pay any attention to the art.

"Can I get another look?" I ask sheepishly.

"Sure, but this time, make sure to see some art and do less of the eye-fucking."

His back is a myriad of drawings, some vibrant and colorful but some just black. It looks like a picture book, where each image has its own story. There are three boys holding hands. Then a boy is hiding behind a door. In the next, a boy is kneeling on the ground, his head toward the sky. Is he praying or crying? But what shatters my heart are the rose thorns and stems drawn on his shoulder blades. Wherever the prickles end, there is red blood. It's so vivid, and for a moment, I believe it's real blood oozing out of his skin. Below the thorns is a word in block letters.

~~ALEX~~ZANDER.

24

ZANDER

I hear her sobs as her fingers trail remnants of the most vile memories of my childhood. Her hands rest over the scars buried beneath the ink. Turning around, I find her misty blue eyes fixed on the rose thorns. "It's okay, Marr."

"No, it's not. It's...just not fair." She throws her arms around me as all her emotions unleash and she weeps into my chest.

"Why does it have to be like this?" she asks in between her heavy sobs.

I know she's thinking and wishing against reality. I've been doing the same since the night she told me her story.

Why is this so fucked up? Why can't I say the name of this girl, who in such a short time has become so important to me? Why can't I laugh and joke rather than be hysterical when she shows me her silly jewelry?

I hold her tight, mustering the courage to say words I haven't spoken out loud in a long time.

"My father died in a car accident soon after Zane was born. He was a middle-class man who sought happiness in the smaller things in life, until he met this young theater actress who only dreamt of Broadway and Hollywood." I sift through the broken memories my father has shared with me.

"After a few months of courtship, they got married and welcomed their first child before their first wedding anniversary. Middle-class life and a newborn threw all the glamorous dreams out the window. What remained were continuous arguments, petty quarrels, heavy drinking, and constant smoking." I smell the smoke, just as I do whenever I think of those days. I don't know if these sensations are real memories or just my imagination. I shake my head, clearing my thoughts as Marr clutches my forearms.

"Add another child to this shit, and the occasional drinking and smoking turned into alcoholism and drug abuse. But children don't understand; they think it's affection, even when reprimanded." *How dumb and stupid kids can be?* "After my father died, his wife did what any other twenty-eight-year-old girl who had to sustain three kids under the age of six along with her addiction would do. She moved in with a man who gave shelter to her three boys, which included a six-month-old baby, and tended to her craving. Her supplier."

"Zander." Marr pulls away from me, and I'm pained by her puffy bloodshot eyes. I hate to hurt her, but I also want to share my life, my secrets, with her. She said she would be there for me if I ever wanted to talk. And I want to take her up on that. Averting my gaze from her, I continue, about to unravel the most horrifying years of my life.

"We left our house and moved to a devil's den. The woman was always high, and a six-year-old had to fend for his baby brothers."

"Oh my god." She gasps as tears roll down her cheeks. My throat dries as I revisit my horrifying past.

"It killed me to see the woman, whom I once loved the most, decaying every day. But it was not her that changed our life. It was the demon who got three weak preys. He was a pervert, a sadist, a pedo—"

"Stop. Please stop," she cries, and I take her in my arms.

"I'm so sorry, Marr." Sweat trickles down my back.

"I don't want this. I don't want any of this. I hate this life. I hate it Zander, so much. What did… we do to deserve this? Why did people do this to us? Why did no one love us? Why did they not fight for us?" she cries, and I have no answer to her questions. "Did he—" Heavy sobs cut down her words.

"He whipped me every night, every fucking night. If I resisted, he would lock me out of the house, naked on chilly winter and sultry summer nights, but he never touched me. I was"—my mouth is suddenly dry—"too old for his taste. My age became my immunity, but not so much for the others." Tears threaten to spill from my eyes, remembering the dreadful night when I was a witness of the gruesome incident. That night changed everything for us. The next dawn was as black as the earlier night, taking away the life of the woman I loved the most *then*.

"The woman died of a drug overdose. She did one good thing; she never married the devil. One day, I got a chance and sneaked into his office, where there was the only phone in the house, and I called the police. They sent us to a boys' home, and the rest is history."

I'm relieved that it's finally over.

"The devil?"

"Died."

"The woman's name was Rose." It's not a question but a statement. I'm relieved that Marr didn't refer to her with the *M* word. She looks at me with so much agony—it's not pity but grief in her eyes. If there's someone who can understand my suffering, it's her.

Several minutes pass by without a word. We let everything sink in, every fucking fucked-up thing. I hate to see the remorse on her face. I tell her more, not wanting her to think that I have no happy memory of her name.

"Before all hell broke loose, there were some happy moments in my childhood. My father made the most beautiful garden in the country. There were... roses"—I shiver saying the dreaded word—"of every kind, every color. He became so popular that we had press at our doorstep to cover the story of the amazing roses that bloomed all year round. It was a magical place, my home."

I reminisce about those few happy days. I don't do that often, as Zach and Zane have wiped out any memory of our life before Beast. I would also love to do the same, if I didn't have these few moments with my father holding me back.

"The entire neighborhood smelled of roses. On Valentine's Day, people would stop by and my father would sell one rose for one love story." I smile. "He was a sucker for love stories. I asked him once why he didn't sell the flowers for money, at least on Valentine's Day. He said, *'You can buy anything but love in this world. Remember that, my boy. When those people share their stories, they share their love, their heart, with us. No money can compare to it.'*"

I remember my father's words. How he nipped every rose carefully and tied a ribbon around it, listening to his customers with great attention. "My father even taught me how to plant hybrid roses."

"I'm so sorry, Zander. I'm so sorry for everything you and your brothers faced. I'm... so sorry for making this much harder for you than it already is," she says, pulling me into her soft arms.

"No, Marr. You make everything beautiful. You make this hell of a life worth living. As paradoxical as it may sound, you replace those old, dark memories with newer, brighter ones. You make everything endurable. You—"

"I love you." Her admission stops me mid-sentence.

I wrench her away from my chest and peer into her eyes. "Say it again."

"I love you, Zander," she says without hesitation. "There are so few things I am certain about in this life and falling in love with you is one of them. I'm not expecting anything in return; I know I'm not an easy person—"

I don't let her finish whatever silly reasoning she's concocted in her brain and ravish her lips. "I love you, Marr. So much." I seize her lips again.

My mind becomes unfettered, and I bathe in the euphoria of passion. My hands get lost in her hair as I rub her silky strands between my fingers. I grab the back of her neck and tilt her head so that my intruding tongue has better access to her sweet mouth. She mewls against my lips as my hands descend to her shoulders and lower. I hate the feeling of the bathrobe. I want her naked. While my lips continue seducing her, I pull on her belt. Breaking our contact, I look down at the most exquisite body.

Last night, I got a glimpse of her under the low light of the laptop screen. But today in my arms, I savor her beauty. She's wearing a sea blue lace bra with a small white bow in the middle. It's swanky yet modest. It covers most of the swell of her breasts, showing only her cleavage—*a perfect tease.* I chuckle.

"What?" She looks at me, puzzled.

"You are an anomaly, Marr. What is this, some Victoria Secret's piece?" I ask, tugging on the small bow.

"Actually, it is," she says, feigning pride beneath her blushing self.

"Then let's take a look at the complete set." I take a chance and glide my hands over her soft naked stomach. But when she doesn't protest, I continue.

Holding her gaze, I tug on the elastic of her underwear, and when it hits her stomach, she gasps. Consumed by the need to see her, all of her, I carry her in my arms. After throwing the bathrobe on the couch, I place her on the middle of the bed.

Fucking hell!

A similar bow sits in the middle of the waistband of her panties. I place one knee on the bed. Hovering over her, I take in the beauty of her smooth skin shining under the glow of soft light. Her damp hair spreads out on the pillow, and her hands rest awkwardly, as if she doesn't know what to do with them. She blushes so deep that her neck and ears turn scarlet. Her legs are tightly closed, highlighting the sexy *V* of her sex.

"Zander." She rolls on her back in embarrassment, but it makes my view fucking better.

My eyes scan her toned legs and her partly covered soft butt cheeks. As I progress further up, I halt at the sight of scars marring her back. That night in the hotel room, I just had a glimpse, but now I see them clearly. Deep marks on her entire back. I bend down and kiss the one closest to her waist.

"*Crab!*" She turns around fast, looking shocked. "I'm… sorry."

"What is it?" I crouch, bringing my face closer to hers.

"Nothing. For a moment… I forgot," she whispers. "I'm sorry. I know it's not a sight you want to see."

"Marr, I want to see you—all of you. You have the most beautiful body. When I see your back, I don't see scars; I see the pain you've suffered, and it hurts me. But there is nothing I want to change in you or on your body. You are perfect just as you are."

A tear trickles down her cheek.

"No more tears, couch girl." I place a soft kiss on her lips before I get down to show her just how much I love her body.

I kiss in between her breasts, just above the white bow of her bra. She relaxes under my touch as I feather kisses around the edges. Her hands grab the sheets, clutching them tight as I increase the frequency and depth of my kisses, licking and sucking in between. When I know my lips have covered every part of her uncovered soft skin, I shift lower and kiss her stomach. She moans as I reach her belly button and continue going down further.

"Zander."

I press kisses along the waistline of her panties. The smell and anticipation of what's to come makes me nervous. I've never felt like this during sex, but with Marr, it's different. We're making love. I want to make her first experience good —not only good, but the fucking best.

I place my trembling hands on her hips and put my nose over the wet spot on her panties. She smells fucking divine.

"Zander. What… what are you doing?" She raises her head, looking down at me.

"Today, I'm gonna get the smell and taste directly from the source."

"Are… you… serious?" Her hooded eyes widen in lust and surprise.

"Why are you surprised, Marr?"

"Is it"—she crinkles her nose—"hygienic?"

I can't hold back my laughter as my forehead rests over her pelvis. Only my girl can be so fucking cute, even when we are almost naked.

"Marr, you being so innocent is only making me desperate to do all the naughty things to you." And just to show her how naughty I'm thinking, I suck the covered wet spot.

"Ship!" she cries and falls back on the bed.

I slowly drag her panties down, then throw them behind me and take in the sight of her naked sex. Glancing up, I find her face covered with both her hands, and a chuckle escapes my lips at the sight. Rising up, I slide my hands under her back and unclasp her bra. Her hands move away from her face, allowing me to remove her last item of clothing.

Marr and I look down at her naked body at the same time.

She is such a beauty. Her skin is soft and white. Her curvy body puts all skinny models to shame.

"Please don't stare."

I'm fucking proud upon listening to her breathy, hoarse voice. I haven't even touched her, yet she is so turned on.

"Why? Would you rather I do something?"

"Please don't stare, and don't talk." She hides her face behind her hands again.

I bend down and suck her nipple. Her hands drop, but her eyes remain shut tight. I blow on the wet nipple that was inside my mouth moments ago. She squirms, her soft hands clenching the sheets. Her response is making this so *hard* for me.

My dick pokes from the towel around my waist. I repeat the process of sucking, licking, and blowing on her other nipple as she moans loudly.

I travel down, littering kisses here and there until I'm fully in between her legs. I take one last look at my girl, her eyes shut, hands clenching the sheets so tight that her knuckles are white. Instead of lowering myself, I hoist her legs up and place them on my shoulders, spreading her open for me.

"Zander!" Her hands reach out to cover her sex.

"Remove your hands, Marr." When I fix her with my gaze, she reluctantly relents as I place a soft kiss over her mound.

"Don't be scared. I want to love you—every part of you. Don't hide yourself from me."

I kiss her wet lips; she's soft, just as I expected. She fusses but doesn't fight as I slowly open her more with my fingers. I place a soft kiss on her clit and then kiss her and lick her everywhere, using my mouth and tongue earnestly. I suck her clit again and again until she buckles. Her legs are trembling under my hands, and she screams my name before falling apart.

I gently place her legs back and crawl up. "Babe, are you all right?"

She hums, not making eye contact. Her shyness and modesty are my undoing.

"Look at me, Marr." I lift her chin with my finger. "I want to feel you, make love to you."

"I want that too," she whispers and gazes at me with wide eyes that are a little excited and a little scared.

I grab a condom from the night table, and she looks at the packet with hesitation.

"It's an unopened pack. I bought it last night before coming to your place."

She smiles, surprised.

Yes, I can read you, baby. I've come to realize that Marr's brain's first response is to doubt everything around her.

I remove the towel and wrap the condom over my length. Her eyes widen as she stares at my dick with apprehension.

"I won't hurt you. You know that, right?" I ask, and *thankfully*, she nods. I think I'll go mad if I can't be inside her right this second.

I lower myself between her legs and gently push my hard length inside her wet heat. The thought that I'm Marr's first boyfriend and the first one to experience her untouched body is celestial.

"It might hurt a bit." I thrust more until I am completely seated. She feels fucking tight and fucking good.

We lose ourselves in each other. No vigorous, strained moves. Just learning and getting familiar with each other's touch. My heart fills with new, raw emotions. For the first time in my life, I feel safe. I know there's no deceit or fraud in this girl's emotions, and she truly loves me.

After a while I ask, "Is it okay if I move, baby?"

"Yes, please."

I make shallow thrusts. This precious moment with her is more than sex. It's greater than anything physical I've ever experienced. Resting all my weight on my elbows, I shift my gaze to her face and am surprised to find her smiling through stray tears.

"I love you so much." My throat strains as I say the words.

"Thank you so much for being the first one to love me."

My heart cracks and melts at her open confession.

"Don't thank me, baby. I told you, we were meant to be together. I was meant to love you and I always will."

Taking her into a slow kiss, I continue making love to her, which I plan to do all night.

25

ZANDER

I wake up wrapped around Marr's soft body—her back against my chest, my hands clasping her waist, even in sleep. Her neck is stretched away from me as she whispers something on the phone. I shift, and her gaze lands on me.

"Oh, you're awake," she murmurs after ending the call. Her hair is disheveled and wild, and her eyes are heavy due to lack of sleep, courtesy of my intermittent disturbance.

"What are you doing on the phone?" I whisper back.

"I... ordered breakfast. Is it okay? It's past my breakfast time." She looks at me apologetically.

"We'll make sure to set an alarm next time." I'm aware of how important it is for Marr to stick to her schedule.

The creases on her puckered forehead loosen upon hearing my words. A shy smile curls up her lips as I pull her closer. But the navy-blue blanket wrapped around her obscures my view of her delicious body. I grab an end and try to push it lower to expose more of her beautiful skin.

"Zander!" she squeals.

"What? No hiding, Marr. Moreover, I saw you pretty good last night or you did you forget that already?"

"But... it's daytime." Her eyebrows furrow together in

confusion as she looks at the faint light filtering through the curtains.

"So? We're not a couple from the fifties who only have sex at night. We're a couple who can't wait to get each other off."

Her big blue eyes widen as her gaze wanders around, resting for a few seconds longer on my lips. She bites her own lower lip, and I'm all set to give her what she's begging me for with those lust-filled eyes. But our excitement is short lived, as we're interrupted by a knock on the door. I get up and put on my track pants, not bothering with a T-shirt. A young guy dressed in a hotel uniform rolls the food cart into the room.

I call Marr through the curtained glass door separating the living space and bed. "Would you like to have breakfast in bed or on the balcony?"

My girl, dressed in her pink shorts and T-shirt, saunters into the room. "Balcony, if that's not much of a problem."

"Not at all, ma'am. If you give me two minutes, I'll set up your breakfast table." The young man rolls his cart to the balcony, leaving us alone.

"You are proving me all wrong, babe." I place a kiss on her neck, enjoying her shiver when my lips touch her toasty skin.

"What do you mean?" She looks at me under her lashes. Her coyness, even after our night together, turns me fucking on.

"I thought yesterday was the best day of my life, but then this morning I woke up wrapped around you, and I'm wondering what I want more, to sleep with you in my arms or to wake up beside you."

"I don't care, because I'd like to have both." Her small hands stroke my chest before she kisses just above my heart.

Her simple action sends a rush of adrenaline through my body. I feel beyond loved and cherished under her shy affection. I don't think I've ever woken up this happy and rested.

Caressing her cheeks, I reply, "You speak to my heart, couch girl."

"Excuse me, sir. Your breakfast is ready. I wish you both a wonderful day." The room service guy steps away from the balcony door, giving us a glimpse of the breakfast laid out on a small table with fresh lilies and red candles. I grab some bills from my wallet and thank him for the extra effort.

We eat our meal in comfortable silence, and when I take the last sip of my coffee, I look up at the sky, which still isn't clear. Black clouds loom with the threat of more rain.

"What do you want to do today?" I ask Marr, who's curled up like a kitten in her chair.

"Dunno," she lazily replies, stretching her arms just enough to get my cock's attention. "Can we stay in?"

"And do what?" I ask in my most innocent voice.

"Talk." She pouts, looking as adorable as she is. "I love listening to you talk and learning more about you." She pauses before whispering, "Though I wish…there were more happy things." Some of that cheer evaporates from her face.

"Come here." When she takes my outstretched hand, I pull her on my lap, where she fits perfectly, resting her head on my chest. I stroke her arm up and down. She feels so good and warm nestled against me.

"It's okay, Marr. See how far we've all come?"

After a long silence she asks, "What does the name mean?" When I look at her in confusion, she explains, "The tattoo. There are a few more letters written before your name."

I take a heavy breath, not overly excited with this discussion at such an early hour. But I know how much this means to her.

"When Ashcroft Miller—Beast—took us in and legally became our guardian, I wanted to start a new life. I wanted to wipe out all the memories of my life before, or at least I hoped for that."

Her brows knit in confusion. "I don't understand."

"Zander is not my birth name." There's no way she can't feel my body tensing underneath her.

"You know, my name is also not my birth name. At least not what my parents would have thought, *if* they would have thought of any," she whispers, resting her head back on my chest. There's no missing the hint of longing in her voice.

"Do you think about them?"

She shakes her head. "I wouldn't even know where to start." Hiding her face in the crook of my neck, she murmurs, "I don't think about them, because I'm scared of my thoughts. There is no good memory that will guilt me when I curse them." Looking at me with eyes that are so sad they almost gut me, she whispers, "There's no explanation in this world that can make it right. What happened to you, me, and your brothers was wrong, Zander. It shouldn't have happened. People should have protected us, loved us, rather than leaving us in the wild among savages."

"Do you remember anything?" I ask warily.

She shakes her head, hiding her face in my chest. Her tears are hot on my chest.

"I love you, Marr, if that's any consolation." I hate to see her hurting, but I know there's nothing I can do that will make the past pain go away.

"It's not a consolation, Zander; it is my greatest treasure." Her misty eyes shine as she looks at me. "What was your birth name?"

"Alex. Alexander. My father named me after his father. Zach and Zane used to call me Xander, so I decided to keep that." I tell her about the day Zach was furious that I got to change my name, while he was stuck with lame *Jack*. Finally, we all agreed that he and Zane could change one or two letters in their names.

"It turned out quite cool." She smiles.

"Tell me more about your childhood—how you met Kristy."

"That's one of my happiest memories. One day, Sophia's daughter came along with her to the class. My piano lesson started while Kristy sat in a corner doing her homework. When the lesson finished, I stood up and was leaving, as usual, without saying a word. But Kristy called out to me, 'Aren't you going to thank my mom?'"

I stifle a laugh. I can see a young Kristy doing just that.

Marr smiles back and continues. "I had no clue how to respond. No one ever spoke to me like that. My discovery had made the staff overly cautious and wary about me. When Kristy scolded me, I simply followed her instruction, said thank you, and left the room."

She shrugs when I laugh.

"You have met Kristy, right? She wasn't very different back then. Anyway, after that, Sophia started bringing Kristy more often. We soon became friends. Kristy enjoyed the thrill of bossing me around, and I liked her company. She always treated me like everyone else, like I was *normal*."

Playing with the hem of her T-shirt, Marr says, "One day I overheard a nurse cautioning Sophia about our friendship. How Kristy was at an age when kids learn and pick up one another's habits. What good can she learn from a child like me, a freak?"

Whenever Marr shares parts of her childhood, I want to time travel and pluck her away from that loneliness. I wish I could hold her then, tell her that all will be okay.

But not all wishes are granted.

I stroke her arms, trying to relax her bunched muscles.

She looks up to see my expression and I smile, encouraging her to continue.

"For the first time in my life, I experienced the fear of losing someone. The next day, Sophia came alone, and I panicked. I shared my fear with her, and what she said to me that day changed my entire life.

"Sophia said, 'You are different, Rose, and you'll always be, no matter how hard you try. There might be times when you'll wish that your life was simpler and as normal as others. But it'll be just that—wishful thinking. Wishing things were different in the past brings us no good. Instead, you have all the power to construct your future, a future that'll be your past someday. You'll have to work twice as hard as others. You should make sure that your name speaks for you.'"

"And you did. Oscar showed me the recommendation letter from your professor."

She looks at me in surprise before glancing down at her hands. As always, she shies away from praise.

"You like Sophia?" I kiss her nose. She looks so pretty and homey sitting on my lap.

Marr nods. "I've thought about my parents only a handful of times, but whenever I did, it was Sophia's face that surfaced in my imagination. Not only because she was always so nice to me but also because of how much we look alike. A few times, upon Kristy's heavy insistence, I joined them on their family trips. People would often refer to me and Kristy as her daughters. She never corrected them, and I cherished those moments." Marr chews her lips in embarrassment, but I'm glad she had someone to look up to, like I had Beast. "Sophia and Kristy have always been welcoming to me. But still, deep in my heart, I know I'm an outsider." The sadness in her voice guts me.

"You have me, Marr. I don't know where this will lead, but here, at this very moment, I am a hundred percent committed to giving us a chance."

"Us. I also want to give us a chance." Her hopeful eyes meet mine. "I like you, Zander. A lot." Her hands move from my biceps, and she gently strokes my face. Her voice is breathy as she speaks. "If someone told me a week ago I'd be sitting like this, sharing all my thoughts with you, I would have called them crazy." She waves her hand around us. "But look at me now."

"Yes, look at you. All sweet and sexy, making your guy wonder how he ended up in this beautiful morning with you." I kiss her fingers, which are gliding over my lips. "I love you, Marr. You sharing your past means so much to me. But I want more of these moments, where we make our own beautiful memories. So beautiful that everything else of our past is forgotten."

And how much I want that to be true for both of us.

"I want the same." Her wishful words make my mind run wild, thinking about different ways to make her happy.

I nuzzle her neck, and when she sighs, I slide her bra strap further down her shoulders. I know how I can make her happy now.

"It just occurred to me that we were interrupted by breakfast."

"I guess we were." She giggles as I carry her inside. Overnight, she has mastered the style of clinging onto me like a koala bear.

I place her down on the edge of the bed and squat between her legs. Her hands rise and she ruffles my hair. The beautiful pink surges on her cheeks, which has recently become my favorite color. I love the fact that she likes my touch and also touching me, exploring me.

"What do you want to do, Marr?" My fingers glide over her lips, trailing down her chin, neck, grazing her collarbone, and further down. As my fingers roam around her breasts, she trembles. Her reaction to my touch makes my mind crazy, wondering how else I can make her delirious.

Without losing eye contact, I lean forward and bring my lips closer, sucking the peaked nipple through the cotton of her T-shirt. My one hand molds her unattended breast, kneading it in slow motion, while the other continues the journey to her waist, marveling at her heavy breathing.

When I nibble the soft flesh, she gasps—head bent backward, eyes shut tight, hands clenching the bedcovers, just enjoying the pleasure.

I pull away and her hooded eyes open, making my heart smile at the disappointment I see in them. She wants me as much as I want her.

I give her shoulders a gentle nudge, and she falls on the bed, legs hanging from the edge. Rising on my feet, I hover over her. She looks like the perfect seductress spread out on my hotel bed. I remove her glasses and place them on the nightstand. Her eyes follow my every move as I lower myself and press my lips to hers. This time, I don't lead, silently urging her to control the kiss.

A few minutes later, she does just that, sucking softly first my lower lip and then the upper. She places soft kisses all over my skin, and I once again feel the forgotten feeling of being cherished. When she hesitantly pushes her tongue into my mouth, I can no longer hold back. Our tongues roll over each other in a sensual dance.

Finding the hem of her T-shirt, I lift it over her head, only breaking the contact of our lips for a fraction of second. Her hands go around my neck as she runs her fingers through my hair. After quick work of unclasping her bra, I pluck it down her body and nuzzle the softness of her breasts and lick the valley in between. She moans and her grip on my hair tightens.

I kiss, suck, and lick her breasts before moving lower and continue worshipping every part of her body with my mouth. After running my tongue around and inside her belly button, I nip her hipbone, kissing from side to side. Finally, I drag her shorts down, taking along her lacy underwear. My mouth lowers to her sex as I run my fingers over her scant pubic hair. She squirms under my touch, and I can feel her slick arousal. Licking her folds, I nip her swollen bud and circle her clit with my thumb. Her cries are music to my ears.

"God, Marr." I increase the speed and slide one finger into her wet heat.

Her back arches as she moans. Seeing her getting off is a sight to behold. I rub her clit and thrust a second finger inside her damp center. Her cries get louder as her wetness coats my fingers.

"You are soaking wet." My hoarse comment only amplifies her noises. For a second, I'm distracted by the thought of people hearing her in the adjoining rooms, but another cry from her and I forget everything else.

Her toes curl tight, making ripples over the delicate arch of her feet, and she comes crashing down with a sharp cry. Without losing any time, I grab a condom from the nightstand, push my pants down, then wrap and position myself between her thighs. I touch her sensitive sex with my hard cock, making her aware of my intention. When I don't move, she lowers herself just a bit, urging me to take her, and I do. I slowly glide inside her, her wetness allowing me easy access. I cover her with my body, my weight resting on my elbows.

"Being inside you is my favorite place, Marr. You feel so good. I don't think I'll ever get past this feeling."

I move slowly at first and then pick up the pace.

"Fucking hell." Her moans make me wild. "See how good we fit," I tell her as I push into her, in and out, an insistent rhythm. A few more thrusts and I'm close. *God!* I want this to last forever, but with the way she's clutching my cock, I'm having a hard time holding my sanity.

At last, I give up and we both come together with a loud moan. Lying back on the bed, I hold her in my arms as she takes me to a peaceful, safe place.

I hope I'm doing the same for her.

Giving myself a few more minutes to recover from the high of her love, I get up and amble to the bathroom.

When I'm back after getting rid of the condom, Marr is exactly as I left her, spread out on the bed. I take a moment to observe her and wonder how it would be to see this sight every single day of my life.

I know we've both opened many locked doors for each other, but we're still in the murky waters of our damaged past. Anything wrong, said or done, can set us back.

As if reading my thoughts, she looks at me and states, "We promised to give us a chance. Don't think anything else."

I perch beside her as she sits up, covering herself under the sheets. Her modesty turns me on like every other thing about her. I pull her close and settle her in my arms, her back resting on my chest. Our entwined legs stretch out under the covers as she fluffs and tugs the duvet covering us both.

"How did you know what I was thinking?" I ask, pressing soft kisses on her shoulder.

"Because I was thinking the same."

I nod, massaging her shoulders, and she hums in approval. Her head falls on my shoulder, and her eyes slowly close.

"If you continue, I might fall asleep," she says in a drowsy voice.

"You sleepy?" I don't pause my pressing fingers.

"Mm-hmm. You kind of interrupted my sleep a few times last night."

26

ZANDER

The ringing of a cell phone wakes me up, and it takes me a while to realize why I'm asleep, half seated with my back resting on the headboard. I'm still getting used to Marr curled on my lap.

"Marr. Sweetheart. Someone's calling you." I shake her gently.

"Huh?" She rubs her eyes before looking around.

I point to her phone ringing on the table near the glass door.

She rises, taking the sheets away with her and leaving me buck naked on the bed. But by the time she reaches her phone, the ringing stops.

"It's Kristy. Let me call her back."

I get up and put on my sweatpants, which were lying on the floor.

"Hello, Kristy. Are you all right? Oh my god! What happened?"

I am beside her in two steps, hearing the worry in her voice.

"Kristy, where are you?" Marr bites her lips, concentrating on Kristy's words. "We're coming." She looks at me and I nod. "What are you saying? It's no problem. We'll be there in thirty minutes."

"All okay?" I ask, grabbing her hands in mine as she looks around in worry.

"I don't know. She was crying. She just told me Charlie's hurt." I can see confusion etched on her face.

"Charlie? Oscar's son?"

"Yes. I don't understand either. But she's home and we need to go, Zander." Her voice holds a touch of guilt and worry for her friend.

"Of course. Get ready. We'll leave immediately."

Marr takes a shower while I hurriedly pack my overnight bag. I'm not sure what's waiting for us at her home.

As I put on my jacket, Marr is back, dressed in yesterday's clothes, which were washed by the hotel staff this morning. She walks closer to me and pats my tie.

"Apart from yesterday, I have never… seen you in anything but suits."

"You don't like me in suits?" I ask. I know I'm good-looking, and so do the various page-three reporters who mention my looks more than our company in their social media.

"You know you're handsome, Zander. Don't fish for compliments. It was just an observation." She smiles.

"Okay, you got me. But seriously, would you prefer if I put on something casual when I'm with you?"

"No, definitely not. I like your CEO look," she says, hanging her arms around my neck. But her smile vanishes when she remembers her best friend. "Let's go. Kristy is waiting for us."

Marr remains quiet throughout the ride and jumps out of the car even before I've properly parked on her street. I walk in long strides and meet her at the door as she inserts her key into the lock.

"Kristy?"

"I'm here, Rosie." This heavy, croaky voice Kristy has is unfamiliar to me.

We both enter the living room and find Kristy sitting on the couch by the window. White crumbled tissues flood the floor. Marr steps further into the room and jumps on the couch beside her friend, while I stay rooted at the door.

"What happened?" she asks softly, and Kristy opens her watery eyes.

I never imagined Kristy like this—heartbroken.

"Kristy, do you need anything?" I ask, unsure how to help her.

"I'm sorry, Zander, that you have to see me like this." She wipes her face with her hands before glancing in my direction.

"What are you talking about? You're having a bad day; we've all been there." I look at her and Marr, who gives me a weak smile. "If you like, I can make you both some tea or get some lunch?"

"Tea sounds good," Kristy whispers.

I saunter into their kitchen. Having a good idea of where things are from the previous night, I put the water to boil and grab three cups from their cabinet. They have quite an impressive tea collection.

Plain black tea, black tea with vanilla, green tea with oranges, green tea with lemons, blueberry tea, berry cupcake tea.

What the hell is berry cupcake tea?

I sniff the sweet-smelling tea box suspiciously before putting it back in the drawer.

Once the water is boiled, I pour it into three cups and arrange them on a tray with a squeeze bottle of honey, spoons, and a box of green tea with oranges.

I place the items on the coffee table in their living room.

"Charlie was running in the backyard when he slipped

and broke his leg. He'll be in a cast for over a month," Kristy explains after taking a sip of the tea.

It's bad, but I still can't make the link between a child's broken limb and Kristy's current condition. Marr seems to be having the same thoughts.

"I'm sure he'll be fine, Kris. Charlie can be awfully naughty at times." An intimate smile breaks on Marr's face. As every other time when I see her attachment to Oscar and his family, I curse myself for not visiting Cherrywood sooner.

"Yes." Kristy smiles a genuine smile for the first time. "But it's not only that." Her voice gets a hesitant lilt. "Oscar's mother was also at the hospital, and when she saw me, it got a little out of hand."

"Really, why?" Marr fixes her glasses, as she always does whenever she's thinking about a big problem.

My own curiosity is piqued as I watch Kristy fumbling with her words.

"I gave her a pretty good reason. We were in the waiting area when Charlie and Oscar returned from the exam room. Charlie mumbled, 'Mom, can you hold me?' and that set Oscar's mother off." Kristy glances nervously between me and Marr.

Oh, boy. So, this is the elephant in the room.

A smile draws on my lips. I'm happy and surprised, but it'll be interesting to see how Marr responds to this great revelation.

"Mom? Oscar's wife is back?" Marr's brows knit together in confusion.

Okay, totally unexpected response.

"No. And he doesn't have a wife. Only an ex-wife and it's been years." Kristy stands up, almost screaming at Marr. Now that's the Kristy I know.

"Um, okay. Then who is '*Mom*'?" Marr's hands rest on the cuffs of her shirt, ready to be pulled.

"If Oscar decides to marry someone, she will be Charlie's mom, no?" Kristy doesn't sound very pleased at her friend's lack of comprehension.

"Oscar is getting... married? To someone we know?" Marr is still a few steps away from the great realization.

Kristy looks at me with exasperation, and I bite back my laugh.

"Yes, someone you know, Rosie. Someone you know very well. Maybe your best friend." She points to herself. "He's marrying me silly."

Kristy's cheeks turn pink, and in this rare moment, she seems bashful. When Marr doesn't reply, she perches back on the couch and grabs her friend's hands. "Are you upset that I didn't tell you sooner?"

"Um, no. I-I'm surprised, Kris." Marr looks from Kristy to me. "But I'm also very happy."

"But why are *you* upset?" I ask Kristy. We still haven't heard the reason for the tissues flooding the floor of their living room.

"Oscar's mom freaked out when he told her that we were together and he'd proposed to me." Kristy waves her hand, displaying a huge ring.

My gaze turns to Marr as her expression changes from confusion to excitement.

Kristy continues. "She told Oscar that he was making the same mistake again and that I could never be a good mother to Charlie; not the kind of mother he needs. She created a huge scene at the hospital, and I had to leave. But since then, Oscar isn't picking up my calls." Her voice trembles. "I'm scared I've lost everything already."

I attempt to console her. "Give him some time, Kristy. Oscar's hands are full with an enraged mother and an injured kid."

Marr puts her arm around her friend. "Zander is right, Kris. Everything will be all right."

27

ZANDER

Zach's periodic calls regarding a potential acquisition keep me occupied. I'm doing my damnedest to work with Marr's computer and my cell phone, but I know it's not enough. We need to close this deal by the end of the tomorrow, and I am unsuccessfully trying my luck at buying some more time with my girl.

I've been in Cherrywood since the party almost a month back, and I'll soon have to return to St. Peppers. But tonight seems too early. After some more futile attempts that last for another hour, I give up.

There's no point in delaying it.

I find Marr and Kristy in the living room, whispering and giggling.

"You ladies look up to no good," I say, leaning against the doorframe.

"Oh, we are definitely up to no good," Kristy replies, and I'm happy to see she is back to her buoyant self.

"As much as it hurts to do this now, I have to leave." I take a few steps into the room.

Marr plods toward me. "But I thought you packed an overnight bag."

"I did. But I need to return to St. Peppers." I pull her closer. It's been too long since I last had her in my arms, and I don't know when it will be the next time.

"Oh." She smooths her shirt, and I look down to her hands pulling at the hem.

"I hadn't planned to leave so soon, but there's a problem in an upcoming deal. I need to be there for a meeting."

Kristy gently pats my arm before leaving the room, giving us some privacy.

"I'll be back as soon as I can, couch girl," I tell her, but I know it's not going to be too soon. All my work is in St. Peppers. I've postponed and delegated a lot of things to my brothers lately, but they're now swamped. I need to figure out a permanent solution to our situation.

"Okay," Marr says, and it kills me to hear her timid voice. Over the weekend, she's been so forthcoming, but at this moment, she is again my girlfriend from the past, shy and reserved.

When her head rests on my chest for the first time this evening, I feel peace again.

"I hate to see you sad. After such a wonderful weekend, I want to see you smiling, laughing, giggling." I caress her face, stroking her silky cheeks with my thumb.

"I wish you could stay longer."

My heart tugs at the sight of her somber expression and misty eyes.

"I wish that too." I crush her against me. No one has cried for me before and a ton of emotions course through me. "I love you, Marr." I fear my time with her wasn't enough to convince her of the depths of my love. But will it ever be?

"I love you too, Zander. Remember, you're the only man I've ever said those words to." The seriousness in her tone makes me halt. I'm not only Marr's first boyfriend, but really, the first man in her life. "Don't forget this weekend. I know you don't have a good memory like me."

Her words, a lovely mix of innocence and sincerity, make me smile. "Believe me, I'm going to have a hard time forgetting anything, courtesy of the various bite marks you have placed all over my body. I don't think I can work out without a T-shirt for a week."

Her beautiful face flushes with embarrassment, most likely remembering all those moments. "Don't distract me." Her words come out breathy as she sways in my arms.

"I'm not distracting you. In fact, I'm bringing to your attention a matter of great urgency. You might want to give me a proper farewell, something girlfriend-y."

"Girlfriend-y? What's that?" Her lips curl into a genuine smile.

Before she can ask more, I drag her into her bedroom and lock the door behind us.

"We need to be quick, babe. My driver is picking up my stuff from the hotel now. He'll be here in thirty minutes."

"You're not driving yourself?" Marr comes around and puts her hand on my waist.

"No. I'll probably sleep during the ride. I've got back-to-back meetings tomorrow," I mutter while nuzzling her neck. I don't want to talk about going back.

Dammit, I don't even want to think about going back. I want to stay with her, learn more about her.

"Did your absence in St. Peppers affect the business a lot?"

"I might have to pull some loose strings when I get back but spending time here with you was worth every second, couch girl." Foreign emotion swells my heart. This ache is unknown to me. "I hate leaving when we just started. I was so looking forward to spending more time with you." I swallow hard. I've never spoken such words to anyone. As a child, I pledged to never make the mistakes of my father—foolishly loving a woman—but this girl... this girl has breached all my walls and made a beeline for my heart.

She cups my face between her delicate fingers. "Me too, Zander. But I understand that you have responsibilities." The tremor in her voice betrays the steel she's trying to put in it.

"You really understand?" I smile, already well aware of her answer.

"To be honest, I don't. I really want you to stay the night, along with all other nights." I love the raw honesty in her voice.

"Only nights? Oh, Ms. Marlin, are you using me for pleasure?"

"No." Her eyes widen. "You wicked man, I mean all days and nights."

She attempts to smack my chest, but I capture her hand before it can land anywhere over me. I bring it to my mouth, gently kissing her palm. Her eyes flutter closed when I suck on her fingers, but those blue gems, simmering with desire, open while I nibble on her soft flesh.

Her frequent moans and deep sighs take all my breath away, and once again, I curse the thought of leaving her too soon.

I lead her to the edge of the bed and unbutton her shirt before pulling it away from her soft body. I'm surprised to see a pink lace bra.

When did she change?

I rub my hands against the soft material. I'm having a hard time believing my sweet Marr has a penchant for fancy lingerie. My moving hands rub against her hard nipples, which are straining through the silky fabric. I push the material down and uncover her beautiful breasts before tugging on her nipples.

She whimpers, eyes closed, head thrown back as her hands rest on my chest, clutching my shirt tightly. I bend down and lick her skin. Her back arches further as I move my hands down to the waistband of her jeans and unbutton them. I give her a final kiss before getting down on my knees. I push the zipper down and tug her jeans lower.

She's still wearing socks, and I decide to keep them. They look cute.

Finally, she stands before me in only her undergarments and sky-blue fuzzy socks, her breasts uncovered. I undress in record time until I'm standing before her in only my boxer briefs.

"I want to try something if you're up for it," I whisper in her ear.

"W-what is it?" she stutters, seeming to be equally nervous and excited.

"Come with me." I grab her hand and lead her to the bathroom.

I had this thought while I was in her shower yesterday morning. There's an unusually big mirror above the sink.

I turn Marr to face it. Her eyes widen in surprise when she sees her reflection. Her hair's disheveled, eyes heavy with lust, face flushed, and not to mention the indecent and sensual state of her bra. I stand behind her, bringing my hands to her breasts once again and caressing her softness.

Her eyes drift close.

"No, Marr, eyes on the mirror."

She flutters her eyelids open.

I unclasp her bra and drag the fabric away. I bring my hand to the waistband of her panties, then push them down to her knees. She shuffles as the small piece of fabric lands on her feet. I bring my fingers to her mouth and she kisses them.

When I press them to her lips, I meet her questioning gaze in the mirror.

"Just suck my fingers," I whisper, and she does. She sucks my fingers in the same way I sucked hers a few minutes back.

I kiss her shoulders and bring my hand down from her

mouth to the apex of her thighs. As I move my fingers over her wetness, her breathing turns into soft moans.

I move painstakingly slow until she begs. "Please, Zander."

"What do you want, couch girl?" I feel weirdly proud as her breath hitches at my words.

"Please. Fast," she whispers and closes her eyes as if embarrassed.

"If you close your eyes, I'll stop, Marr. Don't you dare close them." My threat works and her eyes flutter open.

"I won't, but… please don't stop." She holds onto the counter for support.

I give her what she wants. I rub her clit faster with my thumb and push one finger inside her.

Her moans come short, and I continue until they turn into screams and she shatters in my arms.

When she returns to this world, I turn her around and kiss her hard, stealing her rapid breaths, trying to bottle her love in my heart.

How will I stay away from her?

My thoughts are distracted by her hesitant hands trailing the waistband of my boxers. Her fingers slowly slide inside, and she caresses my cock. Her first hesitant touch on me is everything like her.

Soft, shy, and innocent.

She brushes her fingers over my cock, almost petting me, and I groan. "Are you trying to kill me?"

"What? I've never done this before." She looks embarrassed, almost pulling away, but I cover her hand with mine and push my boxers down.

"Let me show you, then." I stroke my cock up and down. "Like this. You can apply a little more pressure." I give her hand, now grabbing my cock, a gentle squeeze. She repeats my movements, first gingerly, and then she grabs me tight and strokes me hard.

Like in everything she does, she gives me her full attention.

"Fuck, Marr. If you go…that fast, I won't last long," I groan, but she doesn't stop. My words are all the encouragement she needs, and she rolls her free hand over my balls. Her continuous pumping and rolling is my undoing.

"I'm going to—" Before I can finish my sentence, I come all over her hands.

"Oh fuck." My hands grab the sink for support, my knees going weak. I rest my head on her shoulder as she rubs the thick mess over my stomach. I know she's uncertain what to do next.

"Grab some toilet paper," I whisper in a throaty voice. Once she's back, I take it from her and wipe her hand and myself. She looks at her fingers, most likely not liking the squishy feel on them.

"You can wash it off," I tell her. But she brings her hand to her nose and takes a whiff before slowly licking her index finger.

Damn, I've never seen a hotter sight. My cock hardens all over again at her bold move.

"And?" I ask.

"It smells… different. Warm. But I couldn't get a clear taste," she says sheepishly, her face beet red.

I chuckle at her one-of-a-kind reply. "No worries. I have lots. Next time, I'll remember to give you a taste." I wink at her before pulling her into my arms. I can never get tired of her warmth. "I don't want to leave."

"I don't want you to either. But maybe I can visit you in St. Peppers."

"Would you do that?" I'm surprised, knowing Marr isn't a fan of traveling.

"I…don't know. Your sudden departure is making me emotional." She kisses my chest before asking out of the blue, "Would you like to eat something before leaving?"

"I don't think I have enough time for dinner, but can you wrap something up?" I remove my boxers and get inside her shower.

"Umm, I'm not a very good cook. I can only make omelets," she admits, her heated gaze focused over my naked body.

"If you keep looking at me like that, I'll have to just eat you."

Her eyes move back to my face, and she immediately covers herself with a bathrobe. "Shall I ask Kristy to make you a sandwich?"

"Why don't you try. I want to eat something made by your soft hands."

"You sure?"

"Absolutely," I reply before turning the shower on.

I hear the door close behind her, and this time, I pick the Misty Night body wash.

After a quick shower, I get dressed. I'm about to put on my jacket when an idea comes to mind. I go back to the shower and smell all her fancy body wash bottles until I pick one up. I'm sure my nerd has some system in place—pink on Monday, blue on Tuesday, and so on. The bottle in my hand is called Red Sun. It smells like how Marr smelled yesterday.

I leave the shower and sift through her laundry basket until I find the blue lacy bra and panties. Next, I open the closet in her room, and after a moment of hesitation, grab her accessory box. Ignoring all the flowery things, I grab the small pearl earrings she wore the first day I met her. I place all the items I collected on her bed.

Marr enters the room, her hands laden with a paper bag —holding my sandwich, I guess—a travel coffee mug, a small bottle of orange juice, and even a chocolate bar.

"I got you backup in case the sandwich turns out horrible." She drops everything onto the bed. "What's that?" Her head cocks to the collection I've assembled.

"I'm taking some of your things," I reply as if it's the most natural thing to steal your girlfriend's underwear.

"But that's dirty. Let me get you a fresh pair." She returns with fresh green lingerie.

I hold her hand as she tries to replace her underwear from my beloved collection. "I *want* them dirty—smelling of you, not detergent." My words make her think, and she blushes scarlet.

"What are you thinking, couch girl?" I can feel her rising pulse under my hand. She shakes her head before leaving for the bathroom, taking along the fresh green lingerie.

I'm all packed when she returns, but her hands now hold the pink silk underwear she was wearing moments before.

"Take these. You'll remember… our last lovemaking whenever you see them." She holds them out, looking anywhere but at me.

"I don't think I can forget any of our lovemaking, couch girl. I'm going to miss you real bad." I hug her tight in my arms.

Timing fucking sucks.

"Zander! I'm sorry to interrupt, but your driver is here," Kristy hollers from the living room.

I sling the bag over my shoulder before grabbing Marr's hand and leading her to the living room. "He's almost an hour late," I state.

"He was on time. I asked him to grab dinner at the diner across the street and be back in forty-five minutes. I thought you two would like some more time." The sincerity in Kristy's voice gratifies me.

"Thank you, Kristy." I pull her in for a hug before whispering in her ear. "Thank you for everything."

"Don't mention it. I'm thrilled to see Rose so happy."

My heart swells with pride at her words.

I walk out the door with Marr and find Greg waiting for me. I hand him my overnight bag before turning toward my beautiful girl. "I know I've said it already, but I'm gonna miss you."

"Me too, Zander." Her throat chokes, killing me inside.

If I see tears in her eyes, it'll be my undoing. I kiss her hard before getting into the car. I don't look back as the car springs forward.

It feels as if I am leaving a huge part of my heart behind.

28

ROSE

My eyes sting as I watch the receding headlights of Zander's car. A foreign sensation of loss hits me so hard that it aches. I can't remember ever feeling like this in the past.

Trying to keep the increasing thickness growing in my throat at bay, I return to the living room and find Kristy waiting for me with a bottle of wine. She is in a well-deserved celebration mood. I'm so happy for her and Oscar.

But before I can join her, I hear my cell phone ringing in my room. I look at her indecisively and she laughs. "You guys have it bad. Pick up before he comes back."

I bolt into my room and grab the phone from the side table. Breathlessly, I stammer, "H-hi."

"Hi." How is it possible that just hearing one word from his raspy voice makes me miss him more? "I'm not even off your street and I'm missing you already." Zander sighs, making me believe I'm not the only crazy one. The way my heart aches, it feels like we've been apart for days and not just a few minutes.

"Me too," I whisper, and my voice cracks. "I love you... so

much." While saying the words to a phone instead of his face, they somehow feel less powerful.

"You're killing me, couch girl." He groans while I unsuccessfully try to bite back a sob. "I'm coming back. Please don't cry." I hear him say something to the driver.

"No, no. Please," I interrupt his commands.

"Are you sure? I can return, stay the night, and leave for St. Peppers early tomorrow morning."

"No." I shake my head vigorously which he, of course, can't see, so I try to explain to him with words. "It's just… I'm not used to all these…feelings."

He's quiet for a while before I hear a tinge of familiar tease in Zander's voice. "Can I say something mean?"

"Sure." I smile through the tears, wondering where he's going with this.

"As much as it breaks my heart to hear you cry, I'm also over the moon to see you missing me so much." His raspy voice reminds me of all those moments in the past forty-eight hours when he was whispering in my ear. *Sometimes too soft, sometimes too hot.*

"Kristy is waiting for me. We plan to celebrate her engagement. Will you call me when you reach home?" I ask before I turn into another weeping mess, remembering the most amazing eleven-hundred-and-fifty-two-minutes of my life.

"Of course. I'll call you sooner than that. Go enjoy the evening with your friend. It's a special day for her."

"And for us," I murmur.

"Every day with you is special, Marr, even when we're apart."

My pulse quickens at the rawness of his gruff voice. A hitch escapes me, eliciting a groan out of him.

"You're making me crazy." Before I can tell him he's doing the same thing to me, Zander clears his throat. "No more being sad. Go to your friend before I change my mind and drive back."

I love his sweet warning, which is followed by a rustling of papers.

"Now, I'm going to enjoy a little car picnic with the snacks you packed for me. Love you, couch girl."

"Love you, Zander." In the past two days, I've said these three words so many times. Words I've rarely said in the past. These powerful and meaningful words come out so easily with him.

I enter the kitchen and find Kristy taking out a pizza from the oven.

"I thought I would get dinner ready by the time you and your boyfriend finished your monkey business."

"We were just talking." My face heats as I remember all the non-talking business we've recently conducted.

She hums, telling me she's not buying it.

When we settle on our vintage living room rug, Kristy hands me a glass of wine. We click our pale blue glasses. "To us and our love lives."

"To us and our love lives," I repeat before sipping one of the best wines I've ever tasted. "It's a good one."

"I kind of stole it from Oscar before the accident happened." Kristy pulls off a piece of pizza, the melted cheese trailing on the cardboard box.

"Wow. You and Oscar? I still can't wrap my head around this news. How did I... never know?" I'm not overly astute on such matters, but it's Kristy; I should have had some inkling. We see Oscar every day. I remember all the times I've seen them bickering. "I really am happy for you, Kris."

"And I'm happy for you. I'm sure the handsome, sexy bachelor won't be a bachelor for long." She hits my shoulder playfully.

I try to keep my racing heartbeat in check. "It's...too soon for all that, but we admitted our feelings to each other."

"I'm so glad to see you this happy, Rosie. When I told Mom about Oscar and Zander, I think she had a small heart attack." Kristy chuckles before sipping the delectable wine.

"Really? What did you tell Sophia about Zander?" I hold my breath in anticipation.

"Just that he's our boss and one of the hottest bachelors." Kristy grins. "Mom asked me to mail her pictures of both of them."

She rests her wineglass on the rug and some of the excitement drains from her voice.

"Can you imagine that she's managed to survive in this world of technology without any electronic device other than her nineties cell phone, which doesn't even have internet access?"

I don't know how to reply to Kristy's question. Sophia's technology abhorrence has never been clear to me.

"Sometimes I wonder how different our lives would be if Dad were still with us. How he'd have reacted when I told him about Oscar."

Her question prompts me to think about my own father; something I seldom do. Maybe he'd have the talk with Zander, sitting in some big study in a big chair near a fireplace with a glass of Scotch.

My odd trail of thoughts is broken when Kristy throws her phone in my face with a Pinterest board on display.

The vintage wedding.

Her inspiration.

She raves for two hours about her opulent wedding plans. But toward the end, her eyes start to get heavy. It's comical to see her trailing off, dozing for few seconds until she startles and continues rambling. Finally, I have to force her to go to bed with a promise that I'll listen to all her plans tomorrow.

I place a glass of water by my nightstand and change into my blue T-shirt and matching bottoms. With my phone in hand, I jump onto the bed. There are three texts from Zander waiting for me.

Zander: You weren't lying about not knowing how to cook, couch girl.

Below the text is a picture of a soggy sandwich.

Crab! It had too much mustard.

Zander: But I finished it.

And in the next picture, he's wolfing down that last bite. His hands are messy, and I can see the hint of a yellow stain on his white shirt.

Several minutes later, there's another text.

Zander: Call me when you can.

I press the green button adjacent to his name, and he picks up after two rings.

"Hey," Zander coos in a sleepy voice.

"Were you asleep?" I get under the covers and tuck the comforter under me from the sides.

"I think so." I hear the rustling of fabric as he most likely sits upright. "I worked a bit on tomorrow's meeting, and then I transferred your pictures from the carnival to my iPad. This way, I could see you on a larger frame. I don't remember when I fell asleep while watching you. What were you doing?"

The thought of him looking at my pictures makes my heart soar with its wings spread open. I lick my dry lips before replying, "Kristy and I celebrated her engagement with wine and pizza. Then she told me her grand plans for the wedding."

He chuckles. "I'm happy for her and Oscar."

"Yes, me too, and also for Charlie. I am sorry about the sandwich, though."

"It's no problem, couch girl. You're lucky I know my way around the kitchen."

"Really?" I can't imagine Zander in a kitchen. Actually, it's hard to imagine his tall, broad form covered in impeccable suits doing anything other than boardroom meetings.

"Why, Ms. Marlin, you sound surprised," he says in his sultry voice, which I've recently been hearing a lot of.

"Actually, I am. It's hard to imagine you doing anything other than the CEO stuff."

"CEO stuff?" He laughs his beautiful laugh. "You know very well there is nothing like CEO stuff." After composing himself, he says, "But it's true; I am a pretty good cook. So much so that I once considered being a chef."

"I can't believe it. You're just toying with me."

"Why can't you believe it?" he asks in disbelief, and I smile, hearing him so worked up. "I told you that I looked after my brothers, which obviously included cooking for them. That was one thing I enjoyed. Later, by the time I could afford someone else to cook for me, I was addicted to my own exemplary culinary skills."

I let the memory of a young Zander taking care of his brother's slide and focus on his not-so-modest comment. "When am I getting a taste of your exceptional skills?"

"I can't wait to give you a taste, couch girl."

I close my eyes at the sound of his rustic voice. He for sure isn't only talking about food.

29

ROSE

It's been a few weeks since Zander left and Kristy got engaged. Hearing Kristy's grand wedding plans, I was expecting a date at least six months ahead. But to everyone's surprise, Kristy and Oscar decided to marry after a mere two months.

Though I don't blame them.

Why would you not want to spend every moment of your life with the person you love?

I'm getting firsthand experience of distance and separation and it's hard, really hard.

When the news of their engagement was finally out, it took everyone by surprise. Sophia visited us last week to have a formal meeting with Oscar and his family.

Oscar's sister, Clementine, is doing the dresses for the bride and bridesmaids, which is where we're heading now. However, since this morning, I haven't been able to stay as enthusiastic as before.

"Rose?" Kristy calls my name before shaking her head in exasperation as we wait for the light to turn green.

Has she been calling me for long?

"What?" I avoid her questioning stare. I don't want to bother her with my silly issues.

"What is it? You're making me nervous." She cocks her head to my hands, which are almost tearing the cuff off my red-and-black checkered shirt.

"It's nothing." I halt my aggressive move, but she keeps staring at me, even after the lights have turned green. A car honks behind us, and I say, "Okay, okay. I'll tell you. Just drive."

She starts the ignition. "Spit it out before I stop again."

"Zach called me. He and Zane invited me to St. Peppers for Zander's birthday next week as a surprise," I finally blurt.

"Anxious about the travel?" she asks in understanding.

"Yeah, but that's not all." I clutch the cold door handle too tight under my sweaty palms.

"What else, then?" Kristy glances my way once before looking back to the road.

"I-I'm not sure. Everything is going so... fast." My throat dries as the unwelcome insecurities claw at me again. As ever, they try to rob any sliver of happiness that has come my way. I hate the words coming out of my mouth. "His brothers calling me like I'm a part of their family—it's scary."

Her sympathetic eyes meet my anxious gaze. "Rose, it's okay. Everybody gets cold feet when going from casual to serious in a relationship. It's normal to have second thoughts."

"I'm not really having second thoughts about Zander. I just fear..."

"What?" She pulls up at the corner of a street.

"Why did you stop? We're not there yet." I look around at the other cars on the road.

"It's okay. I want to finish our talk first."

My friend, always looking out for me, even when she has her own wedding to plan. Maybe I'm not that unlucky after all. I look away, not meeting her inquiring gaze. "I fear, eventually, he'll find something in me that he hates."

There. I said it.

"Rose, why would you say that?" She grabs my hands, making me look at her. "Did Zander say something?" Kristy asks hesitantly. I hate her doubting Zander, and I hate myself more for making her do so.

"No, never. It's all me. I know I'm not thinking straight." I chew on my lower lip. "But it's…my first relationship. I fear… I'll do something wrong and lose him." My voice cracks.

Crab, I don't want to cry on the way to shop for my best friend's wedding dress. "I'm sorry."

She smiles and puts her hand on my shoulders. Rubbing my back, she tries to calm my nerves as always. "I'll confess something but promise you won't be mad."

"Um, what is it?" I'm surprised by the sudden change of topic.

"No. First, promise." A tiny smile pulls on her face, abating some of my anxiety.

"I promise," I reply, turning toward her in my seat.

"Zander and I talked before he came to our house the first night." She pushes the red curls away from her face and squints my way.

"What?" My stomach tenses at the thought of what they might have discussed about me, and why Zander felt the need to talk to someone else. "W-what did you… talk about?"

You, you idiot, my brain screams.

"We talked about Zander's fear of losing you."

My mouth opens and closes in disbelief.

"He said the exact same thing," Kristy repeats, confirming I heard her right. She tilts her head to the side and a pleasant smile covers her lips. "He feared he might do something that'll lead you to hate him."

"Really? He said that?" I'm having a hard time imagining Zander being unsure of himself. *Uncertainty is for people like me, not him.*

But she nods. "He loves you, Rose. I can see it in his eyes. I could see it that day." She rests her hand over mine, which is clutching my bag too tight. "Don't be afraid of doing something wrong. Zander will always find something cute in those mistakes. Remember the sandwich? It's a crime to feed your boyfriend that piece of crap."

I snort, which is followed by her laughter.

As always, she's taken away my fears and rolled them into hope.

We're quiet for the rest of the drive, until we reach the small store and find Clementine lying on the floor, her legs propped up on the wall and a notebook on her chest as she sleeps.

"Someone's gonna rob you someday." Kristy opens the unbolted door and throws a tissue she just balled up at Clem, who sits upright lazily, not a care in the world.

"Hello, sis-in-law," Clementine drawls. "To be honest, I'd love for someone to come inside, even if for robbing." She gets up and grabs three soda cans from her mini fridge.

I snicker at her one-of-a-kind joke. Looking around at her store, I notice all her mannequins are dressed in silk gowns this time. I take a seat on one of the colorful chairs as Clementine dumps the contents scattered on the table to the beige carpet.

"There's an exhibition in Italy next week—*Dress in Silk*," Clem explains when she notices Kristy inspecting the dresses up close.

"Will your work be presented?" I ask, following Kristy's moves as her hands glide over the soft fabric.

"No, it's only for the local Italian fashion houses. I just got excited with the idea of being part of such an event in the future."

She waves her hand, making light of it, but even I, a fashion illiterate, can see this isn't just some random stuff done in excitement. There has to be more than ten pieces, and each is beautiful in its own way.

"One day, you are gonna get your chance, Clem." Kristy squeezes her soon-to-be sister-in-law's shoulder before perching next to me.

"I think so too." Clem beams, and I'm once again reminded of her super optimistic attitude.

I often wish I could be someone like Clem, not thinking about the worst but focusing on the good that's happening and believing in it.

"But today is about you, our bride-to-be." Clem grins and points to the dresses hanging on the side rack. "I've selected some designs based on your description. Why don't you try them on, and we can discuss what you like and what not?"

As Kristy inspects the dresses, Clem turns to me. "How's your handsome boss boyfriend?"

"He's good," I reply sheepishly, which only makes her grin wider.

"Oh, I think he's more than good. That face, that bod— you hit the jackpot with him, Rose."

Hearing her flat-out talk about Zander sparks something in between excitement and jealousy within me. I'm reminded of our last lovemaking session and our reflection in the mirror, his eyes fixed on me.

I did hit the jackpot.

"Wow, that's Zander," Kristy says as she walks toward us, carrying two gowns she's selected from the rack. "The camera does love him."

While I was revisiting my memories, Clem Googled one of Zander's pictures, and there he is looking breathtaking as always, dressed to perfection and holding a champagne flute. Black suit, white shirt, and a black bow tie. His gaze is looking straight at the camera, his head tilted to the side and a ghost of a smile on his handsome face. The proud dimple is on display.

My heart does a flip looking at him. His strength, his virility, is like an aphrodisiac, and I feel my palms and body sweating.

"I can't believe you get to be in bed with this guy. I would pay to sleep with him." Clementine fake swoons, and my face gets hotter than ever.

Guess I'm not the only one affected by him.

But she's not exaggerating. He looks so sensual in this picture. I can't believe *this* guy is the one who took my underwear—my *dirty* underwear—to remember me by.

"Okay, girls, bring your focus back to work. You'll get enough time to eye fuck Zander at my wedding." Kristy emerges from the changing area marked by a wooden partition, wearing a champagne-colored gown.

I'm too happy when Clem's attention is drawn away from my man as she shakes her head, almost pulling the dress off Kristy and sending her back to try on a new design.

Four hours later, we're back home. Kristy went for a traditional white floor-length ball gown.

Meanwhile, I called Zach and confirmed my trip to St. Peppers for Zander's birthday. The plan is that they'll somehow keep him busy in the office till midnight, and that's when we'll surprise him. Everything sounds great, and I can't wait to see Zander's expression when he finds me in his office. Suddenly, I remember his words about how he wants me to…

God, what am I thinking? I can't do that. Can I?

30

ZANDER

What a day.

It's about midnight and the work seems to only be increasing. The only consolation is that I am not working alone. I stretch my legs under the table and check the time on my Patek Philippe. It's only three minutes to midnight. The beautiful black Swiss wristwatch with white and red needles was a gift from my brothers on my last birthday. I wonder what this year's gift will be.

My office door flings open, and Zach and Zane step inside, mischievous grins on their faces.

I cock my head to the side. "What's up with the smiles?"

"Nothing, just that it's midnight. Time for your birthday gift." Zach chuckles.

"I was just wondering what's gonna beat this bad boy." I smirk, raising my wrist over my head and showing them the watch.

"I'm not sure you can wear what we have in mind." Zach's laughter fills my office. "Or maybe you can."

Zane's lips curl into a smile as his friend Lukas Spencer walks into my office and pats Zach's shoulder. "You bastard."

"Lukas, what are you doing here?" My excitement slumps upon seeing him here this late.

"Just delivering your present." He winks and nods toward the door through which he just entered.

What's going on?

But then Marr staggers into my office, knocking my socks off. No words come out of my mouth. For a few moments, I simply stare at those blue eyes that have been part of my dreams every night lately.

"Happy birthday," she murmurs.

Was her voice always this intoxicatingly smoky?

She looks around nervously as our audience blatantly stares at us.

Fuck them.

"Marr." I cover the few steps between us and crush her soft body against me. My heart beats fast, ready to burst out of my body.

God, how I've missed this feeling.

"You're here." I kiss her, inhaling her skin. She smells like herself and whichever luxurious body wash she picked for the day. I can't believe it. She's here, on my birthday! Before I can ask her all the hows and whys, Zach clears his throat.

"What?" I growl.

What the hell are they still doing here?

He laughs and says, "Happy birthday, bro."

"Thanks." *Now leave.*

"Happy Birt-t-thday." Zane shoulder hugs me, while Marr is safely tucked under my other arm. "I'm very happy to s-s-see you, Marr." He nods at Marr, who gives him a shy smile.

"Happy Birthday, Zander." Lukas comes forward. I pull my hand out, but he smacks it and hugs me, giving a wide smile to my girl. "You're a lucky guy."

"Thanks, Lukas."

I still can't believe he showed up with Marr on my birthday; I can't believe my brothers kept it under wraps. This is without a doubt the best birthday surprise they've given me.

"Zander, we'll leave so you can enjoy your present." Zach winks at Marr, who blushes scarlet while Zane and Lukas snicker like ladies. "But remember, we're meeting for dinner tomorrow, so do all the enjoying before that."

"Don't mind my brother, couch girl. He sometimes forgets his manners."

"Don't let him fool you, Marr. I never had any manners," Zach hollers as he walks out of my office, followed by Lukas and Zane.

At last, I'm alone with my girl.

I close the door and turn to find her fixed in her spot. I reach her in two large steps and capture her face in my hands. I kiss her without restraint, drinking in her scent and devouring her soft lips, which taste of some fruity lipstick. I grab her waist, and she clutches my forearms, returning everything with equal intensity.

When we pull back for a breath, I touch her forehead with mine.

"I've been wanting to do that since you walked into my office." I take a step back and gaze at her from head to toe.

She looks amazing in her stylish black dress. I know how hard it is for Marr to come out of her comfort zone. She most likely gave herself hours of pep talk before putting on this off-the-shoulder dress and leather jacket.

"You look beautiful, couch girl." My voice thickens with emotion as I crush her to my chest.

What did I do to deserve this happiness? But now that I have her in my arms, I'm not going to lose her. Feeling her melt into my arms like this, I can't imagine a life without her.

"Hey." I rub her back once more before gazing into her tired eyes. Marr is a punctual sleeper, and it's already beyond her bedtime. Plus, she doesn't enjoy traveling. "You're tired."

She jerks upright. "No, I'm not." I smile. "It's okay, Marr. I'm tired too. Come on, let's go home."

She shifts on her feet as her apprehensive gaze moves from me to my chair.

"What is it, couch girl?"

"I... I want to... to give you..." she stammers as her wild gaze locks on everything but me in my office. But now I've learned to read Marr's quirks. This time, she's nervous, but it's not a bad nervous. Whatever turned her into this jittery mess is something cute and innocent.

"You want to give me what?" I lean back against my desk, following her every move.

"Your birthday present," she whispers, still not meeting my eye.

I look at the small bag in her arms as she makes no effort to open it. "You can give it to me at home."

"No, I can't give *that*... at home." Her whole body trembles and as much as I'm curious about what's making her this delirious, I'm concerned for her.

"Marr, what is it? You're scaring me." I gently caress her cheeks with my thumb.

"I just... You once..." I hold her face in my hands. I've never seen Marr so fidgety, not even during our first love-making. I don't say a word; I just try to calm her with my touch and she continues. "Not once but twice, you said if I ever..." Her voice breaks and she swallows. "You would like... in your office."

And then it hits me.

"Marr." *Did she just propose to give me head here?* I'm in awe of this girl. "No, Marr. Not today."

"Why?" She looks close to passing out.

"None of our firsts will be in such an uncomfortable place and time."

"But I thought..."

"Shh." I put my finger on her lips and those beautiful eyes

fill with tears as she's unable to hold back her emotion. "It's a fantasy, like many others I have with you." She responds to my smile with a hesitant, teary smile of her own. "But we have a lifetime to fulfill them."

A promise of a lifetime comes so easily with her.

"Now let me take you home."

PARKING MY CAR, I consider the beautiful girl sleeping in the passenger seat. The drive from the office to my apartment isn't far, but as soon as she laid her head against the headrest, she dozed off.

"Hey." I squeeze her bare shoulder. She took her jacket off, and I love the feel of her naked skin under my hand.

"Hmm?" She shifts in the seat and opens her eyes. Her gaze jumps around in panic before she registers the unknown surroundings. "I'm sorry. I fell asleep."

"We reached my place." We get out of the car, and I lead Marr into the elevator. Her enthusiastic face mirrors my excitement, sleep long forgotten. "You are the first girl inside my place, you know that?" I stroke her neck with the back of my hand.

She trembles under my touch when I lean down to kiss her soft skin. But the elevator ding interrupts us. I place a chaste kiss on her neck anyway before picking up her travel bag. She carries her laptop case as I unlock the door.

"Home sweet home." I flip on the lights.

She takes in the living room, and my gaze follows hers. The apartment looks so bare and unlived-in. There's nothing soft or warm. If I would've known about her arrival, I would have at least bought some flowers.

Marr runs her hands over my work chair as she strolls in the office area of the living room. This is the most used corner of the house. The living room has doors connecting to the bedrooms. The master bedroom belongs to me, and the other two are often used by my brothers when they stay the night.

She cocks her head to the side with a twinkle in her eye. "And people say it's difficult to find an apartment in cities. They don't know rich bachelors have procured all the big fancy ones."

"Smart mouth." I spank her behind.

"Ouch!" So few people know Marr can be a tease. This side of her is so rare, and I love whenever she reveals it to me. I rub her behind, and she asks seriously, "It's nice, but isn't it a little big for you?"

"It is. Half of the apartment is unused. But when you're in business, you have to maintain a reputation for people to take you seriously. Big apartments are part of it, or so I'm told."

"Same as dressing in suits." She grins.

"I've a feeling either you hate my suits or you're obsessed with them." I pull her into my arms and cup her face with my hands. I'm overwhelmed with the feeling of seeing her here at my place on my birthday. I push my nose in her hair, then lower it to her exposed shoulders. "What is it, Marr? Tell me." I nip her collarbone.

"Neither of the two." Her voice shakes as my mouth moves from her shoulder up toward her neck.

"I. Don't. Believe. You." I place wet kisses all over her skin.

"I…"

"You what?" I pull away from her just enough to look at her face. Her blue eyes, hidden behind the contrasting red frames, darken with desire. I narrow my gaze, willing her to tell me.

"I… searched for your pictures… online." She hides her face in my chest. Her demureness gets me *every fucking time*. It's an act of foreplay I wasn't familiar with—or maybe it's just her. "And I didn't find a single picture of you in anything other than suits."

I smile at her admission. Before I can chaff her further, her stomach growls and she giggles.

"Sorry," she says

"Let's discuss your stalking habits later, Ms. Marlin." I pull her into the open kitchen area. "What will you have?" Grabbing her by the waist, I place her on one of the high barstools. "I learned you missed dinner tonight."

"How do you know?" She clutches my forearms. We're like moths to the flame of our love. We both can't resist it.

I remember she asked me a question. It's too easy to forget everything around her. I drag myself away from her. She needs to eat.

"Zane messaged me and said that Lukas drove you from Cherrywood this evening. I don't think you made a dinner stop. What shall I make?" I ask, taking off my jacket.

Her eyes follow my movements. She's as attracted to me as I am to her. "Anything you can cook fast. Something light."

I look into the breadbasket and find a baguette. "Panini?" I raise an eyebrow. I know Marr is crazy for Italian.

"Excellent." The reaction I was hoping for. "Lukas is your childhood friend?" When I don't reply immediately, she adds, "He said so while we were driving."

I cut the bread with more force than necessary before I glance her way. "You didn't feel nervous with him."

It's not a question; I saw it in the office. Marr even waved goodbye when he left. He won my girl at their first meeting, something even I couldn't do.

"Isn't he closer in age to you than Zach and Zane?" Marr asks.

"Lukas is two years older than me. We were in the same foster home until Beast adopted us. We went with Beast, and he went to the military some time later. He came back a few years ago and joined a security firm with some other friends," I state and add the tidbit of information that irks me the most. "But during all those years, he kept in contact with Zane."

"You didn't know about it? Is that the only reason you don't like Lukas?" As usual, no rubbish, and she hits the bullseye.

"He and I, we have a difference of opinion on several matters." I grab the back of my neck with agitation.

Sensing my discomfort, Marr concludes the discussion "Okay. When will the food be ready?" she asks and slides down the chair as if we were talking about food all long.

"Two more minutes, miss." I give her a playful salute, happy with the change of discussion.

After checking on the bread in the griller, I join her in the living room. I place the two glasses of red wine on the table while Marr is busy searching for something in her bag. Minutes later, when I'm back with two pesto turkey paninis, she's sitting on the couch with a wineglass in her hand and one small box wrapped in golden paper beside her.

"My gift?"

"Yeah." She nods nervously as I place the plates on the table.

"Other than the one you're going to give me after dinner that you were so keen to give me in my office?" My crude words catch her off guard, and she chokes on the wine. I rub her back, chuckling all along as she coughs deep. She glances at me with her wide eyes and gaping mouth.

"What? Don't look at me like that. You were really offering to—" I flinch as she smacks my chest, but I soon burst into laughter. "Tell me, Marr." My voice turns a note lower, and I whisper, "Would you have done it, blown me, if I'd have agreed?"

Her face turns all shades of red before she replies with a shy smile, "Guess you'll never know."

"Oh, baby, I'm so gonna regret this every minute of my life." I thump my head back into the couch and groan. Images of Marr dressed in her black dress crouching under my office table with my dick in her mouth is a vision I can never wipe from my head.

Fucking morals.

"Where did you go?" She strokes my fast-paced heart.

"To my imagination. You would run away if you knew what I was thinking." I look down—her head resting on me, her chin tucked on my chest.

"Tell me," she whispers.

I shake my head and look up at the ceiling. "No one has turned me on as you do, couch girl. Your one look is enough to ignite a fire in me, and I burn like dry timber."

I return my gaze to her and notice the forgotten dinner on the table.

"God, you make me forget everything. Eat." I sit upright, taking her along with me.

She takes a bite of the bread. "Wow, you really can cook." Surprise is evident in her voice.

I laugh at her reaction. "This isn't cooking. This is just some fix-up."

"I love your *fix-up*." Her twitching lips tell me she's not at all talking about food.

"Keep going baby and before you know it, I'll throw you over my shoulder and take you to bed. I will spend all night showing you my *fix-up*."

She looks at me for few minutes, eyes wide, lips parted, just asking me to do all that, until she shakes her head. "No. You still have to open your gift. I hope you like it."

"There's nothing you can give me or do for me that I won't like," I reply, kissing her nose.

Before we lose track of the conversation again, I pick up the small box from the table. It fits perfectly in my palm. I glance her way to find her nervously fidgeting in her seat.

I tug on the black silk ribbon and tear the wrapping paper to reveal a small wooden box before flipping the small golden latch open. Inside is a red resin cubic ornament tied to a chain. I place it in my palm and bring it closer to Marr.

"Explain." I know it's a thoughtful gift. I can imagine Marr thinking about it for several nights.

She covers the small cube with her hands, keeping just a small opening on the top. I peek through it and see the cube glowing in a cherry red color—*our color.*

"It's florescent," I comment, mesmerized. There's a metal piece inside, shining brightly. I get off the couch to turn off the lights in the room. When I turn around, Marr has placed the cube on the coffee table, and the metal piece resembles a sound wave, floating inside the red resin.

"What's that?"

"Me," she whispers.

"More, please." I don't know why, but there's a nervous energy around us. I don't know the meaning of her gift yet, but the exotic red thing glowing in the dark feels like a landmark in our relationship.

"I 3D printed the red florescent resin around a sound wave made of titanium metal."

"Titanium?" I know everything she does has a meaning, and I'm dying to decipher her gift. I'm eager to see it the same way she does.

"I don't want us to break," she replies. Her eyes are fixed on the red light source.

"What does the sound wave say?"

She opens her cell phone and hits the play button.

Her sweet sound vibrates from the speaker. "I love you, Zander. Yours and only yours, Rose."

"Marr, how did you do it?" My voice trembles with emotion.

"I converted my voice into a sound wave and then had it replicated in titanium. I wanted to give you a happy memory of my name." She picks it up from the table with the small metal chain attached to it. "You can hang it in your car."

The gravity of her words and the meaning of her gift hit me. She has created a piece of her, her name, in hope to wipe away the haunted memories of my past. I look at her in awe. If anyone has the power to do that, it's her.

"You don't have to keep it." She misunderstands my lack of words. She doesn't know her gift, her love, her concern, has left me speechless.

"I love it, couch girl. I love you. I will always keep it close, *Rose*." I shiver but don't feel the usual fear. For the first time in years, the word doesn't sit heavy in my mouth. Instead, it feels liberating.

"Zander. You don't have to—"

I capture her remaining words in my mouth. I was right, this gift is indeed monumental. This isn't just any souvenir; this is my girl telling me I can share her happy memories, and I'll die trying.

I grab her waist and deposit her on my lap. All my emotions are in overdrive, and only she has the power to soothe me. I caress her face.

"You're always so soft." I lean in to taste her lips again.

We lose ourselves in the kiss as our hands roam over each other's body, touching our souls, remembering what belongs to us.

I draw from her lips and kiss her shoulders. Sucking her buttery skin, I descend lower. Her exposed, flawless skin has been teasing me since I first saw her tonight. Her hands grip my hair, and her fingers graze my scalp.

My mouth roams over her chest as I tug her dress a tad lower to reveal her cleavage and kiss her there. "I like this dress. I can kiss you everywhere so easily." I demonstrate, pressing some more wet kisses on her exposed skin.

Marr shivers at my admission as I nudge her dress further down and find the black strapless bra.

"This is sexy," I rasp, gazing into her wild blue eyes. Holding her gaze, I graze my teeth over her tits and then bite down hard. Her shriek morphs into a moan as I suck her through the fabric.

I run my fingers over the black elastic fabric once more before dragging it down. Taking her breasts in my hand, I suck on them. She tastes fucking amazing.

How did I manage to stay away from her these past few weeks?

She squirms, and I doubt she's aware how she's slowly rubbing herself on me.

I continue sucking her as my hands trail lower from her waist to her thighs, finally slipping under her dress. I reach the corner of her panties and slip my fingers inside the silky fabric. They glide over the light dusting of moist hair and then over her wet folds.

I slide her on the couch and kneel on the floor before her. Nudging her legs apart with my shoulders, I kiss her inner thighs, going higher and higher while my fingers continue stroking her wet lips.

My mouth reaches its destination. I throw one last glance toward my girl—her head resting back on the couch arm, eyes closed, one hand over her breasts, trying to cover them, dress bunched around her waist and black silk panties on display. I lower my face to her sex and inhale deeply. Her scent is intoxicating. Pushing the material to the side, I put my mouth on her folds.

"Zander," she cries out.

I glide my tongue inside her wet heat. I thrust my tongue in and out, fucking her with my mouth. She responds to my passion with heavy moans, her incoherent blubbering driving me wild.

I latch on to her clit, and she grabs my hair, tugging on it hard. She thrashes in my arms, crushing my head in between her legs until she slumps limp on the couch with a long moan.

"That was some birthday gift," I whisper and wipe my mouth with the back of my hand before getting on the couch next to her. She looks at me coyly. As always, her shyness returns, and she fixes her clothes.

I pull her into my arms as a myriad of emotions hits me. Marr settles beside me, her cheeks pressed against my chest. We stay entwined with each other until I hear her soft breathing slowly getting heavy with sleep. I kiss my dozing girl's forehead.

As the entire night flashes before my eyes, the question nagging me since my return from Cherrywood has found its answer.

I can't imagine a life without my girl. A smile creeps onto my lips as I think about her sleeping like this, in my arms, for all the days of my life. Placing another kiss on her forehead, I carry her to my bedroom. A thought of her dressed in white while I cross over a threshold with her in my arms crawls in my mind, and my hardening cock agrees.

I chuckle.

Calm down, Zander. You've still to ask, and she has still to say yes.

The night light casts a purple glow on her face when I place her on the bed. I gently get her out of the dress. After taking off my own clothes, I slide in beside her.

I pull her closer to me, her back against my chest, my face resting on the crook of her neck as I inhale her scent and fall asleep.

31

ROSE

The smell of something sweet wakes me up. I look around and my gaze land on a picture on the nightstand of me and Zander from the carnival. A smile curls up on my face. He has a picture of me, of us, in his bedroom. Warmth fills in my chest at the sweet revelation.

I get up from the bed and enter his grand en suite bathroom. It's as posh as the rest of his apartment. After taking a pee, I glance at my reflection in the mirror. *Crab!* I look like a raccoon. Another reason why I'm not a fan of makeup. I run back to the room and return with my toiletries bag.

After cleaning my face of any makeup with my natural wipes, I'm about to put on my striped pink top when I notice Zander's navy blue T-shirt. I take it down from the hook and bring it closer to my nose. It smells of him—warm, vanilla, woodsy. At the last minute, I decide to switch the pink with the blue.

The cotton of his T-shirt feels soft against my skin and reaches just below my hips. I decide to forgo pants, knowing it might bring the simmering heat into his eyes, which I've missed so badly in the past few weeks.

When I return to his room, the sweet smell hits me again

and leads me to the kitchen. I've only experienced this smell in bakeries, and my heart stops at the most amazing sight.

Zander, with a black apron tied on his front, is mixing something in an enormous glass bowl. There's a fresh batch of cookies on the cooling rack.

I've never seen a man cook in a house. In restaurants, yes. But never in his own kitchen, and never so skillfully.

"You can really cook *and bake*?" I squeak in surprise.

He glances up at me with a broad smile. "Good morning to you too."

The cookies look too tempting to resist, and I grab one. "They're warm."

"They're just out of the oven," he replies with a funny look on his face.

"These are delicious. They look almost store bought." I turn the perfectly round cookie in my hand before hopping on the chair as he churns something with a wooden ladle. "I've never baked."

His hands stop and he looks at me. "What about at Christmas?"

"What about it?" I take a bite and the warm chocolate chips melt in my mouth.

"They didn't let you bake cookies at Kindred Hearts on Christmas."

"Kindred Hearts isn't a home, Zander. It's an orphanage for special needs children. They couldn't risk bringing us into the kitchen, close to sharp objects and heat."

When he looks at me, his face holds a familiar expression of sorrow and pain, which I don't like. After a beat, he drops the spoon and retrieves a big box from the overhead cabinet. Placing it next to me, he nods toward it. I open the box to find it filled to the brim with baking accessories.

I've never seen half of these things.

I take out a colorful packet stuck on the side and peek inside it to find heart-shaped cookie cutters in varying shades of pink. I burst out laughing. "I could have never imagined something like this in your kitchen. They don't really go with your image."

"Zach," Zander replies, shaking his head.

Oh! The mischievous Teager boy.

"He gifted me these for Christmas a few years back." Zander pulls me into his arms and takes the cookie cutters from my hand before placing them on the counter. He puts something around my neck, and I notice it's another black apron that reaches far below my knees. He adjusts the tie, then circles his arms around my waist.

Not taking his eyes off my face, he expertly ties the apron behind me. His hands drift lower from my back to my behind.

"I didn't know you in my T-shirt would be such a tempting sight," he says while kneading my soft flesh.

"The...cookies are...tempting, not me." I arch my back, loving the feel of his gentle hands on my skin.

"I've tasted you, couch girl. No cookie in the world tastes as good as you." He places a trail of kisses on my neck and shoulders, making me all warm and fluttery.

But before he can put me under his spell once more, the oven dings.

"As always, you make me forget everything, Ms. Marlin."

Right back at you, mister, my brain silently comments.

"Does that mean I get to bake?" I ask while Zander opens the oven door.

He nods, placing the second batch of cookies on the counter before passing me the cookie dough. "Now get started."

Zander shows me how to mix the sugar and butter, followed by something called folding the flour. What a strange expression!

Finally, I lay scoops of cookie mix on the baking paper and place the tray into the hot oven.

After baking, we sit for breakfast, and I'm again reminded of Zander's marvelous culinary skills. He perfectly arranges today's breakfast of granola with yogurt. Unlike me, where I just dump store-bought cereal into a bowl, he prepares everything from scratch.

I sit there, admiring his gorgeous hands working as he adds oats, nuts, seeds, and honey into the large pan.

As always, I wonder what he's doing with me. Before my insecurities rear their ugly head, I focus back on this lovely morning. When he places the fruits next to my breakfast, I swoon at the sight of my perfect fruit mix for the day.

Even though I might not know *why* he loves me, I know *how* he loves me.

He loves me unconditionally, making all my silly wishes and needs come true. Like the five blueberries, three strawberries, and half pear peeled and cut into cubes. I have no idea if he had them already or if he arranged them somehow this morning, but they're here on the table.

After breakfast, we shower together—another first.

I've lost count of how many firsts I've accomplished in this a short time with Zander. In the shower, he pampers me like I'm the most precious thing to him, and when we're back in the bedroom, he makes love to me again. I never knew lovemaking could be this addictive. Around Zander, I can't believe it's me, the nervous, awkward girl. He awakens something inside me that makes me confident and comfortable.

With him, I feel *safe,* and that's another first.

32

ZANDER

"It's a surprise." I watch as Marr chews her bottom lip while looking out the car window. Her eyebrows knit together, and I know what's coming. She's not good with surprises, and who could blame her? But I want to keep this a secret. I have not a whit of doubt that she'll fall in love with the place immediately.

"Any clues?" she asks hesitantly.

"No clues, but you are free to guess." I purse my lips, trying to hide the smile emerging on my face.

"Zander!" She throws her hands up in exasperation.

"What?" I state in a calming voice. "You know I'll only do things that make you happy." I only need fifteen more minutes. "Just guess. It'll be fun."

She wrinkles her nose, not liking the guessing game. But when I flash another smile in her direction, she shakes her head.

"You could take me to an Italian restaurant, but we already had lunch," she mutters halfheartedly. "You could take me dress shopping for Kristy's breakfast party, but I never asked you to do that. You could—"

"You want to go shopping with me?" I cock my head in

her direction, suddenly curious and contemplating if I should change my plan.

Her uninterested face pinkens, and she glances out the window and mumbles, "Clementine is making bridesmaid dresses, so I'm covered for the wedding day. But I need one more dress for the breakfast party the next day." Turning in her seat just a tiny bit so she can face me again, she asks, "How was the dress I bought for your birthday? You liked it, right?"

A deep chuckle leaves me. "Why do I have a feeling that the sexy black dress isn't really an option? Did Kristy ask you to buy something new?"

Marr huffs and folds her hands over her chest. "You know us too well, Zander. That's not good. Don't you know that a girl shouldn't be so predictable to her boyfriend?"

"Don't worry, couch girl. You're unpredictable enough for me. I never saw you coming all the way to St. Peppers on my birthday." That earns me her triumphant grin. "But tell me, why is Kristy not helping you? Usually, she does all these things with you."

I watch as her smile falters. "Kristy won't be… as accessible to me as she is now. She'll be busy with her new family." Marr's shoulders hit the seat again, and she looks up to the roof. "I also need to post an ad for a roommate." Her head slumps back on the headrest as her eyes close.

"You're searching for a roommate?" I can understand her anxiety now. She's never lived with anyone other than Kristy, not since she left Kindred Hearts.

"The house is too big for one person, Zander," she replies without emotion.

"How do you feel?"

She stays silent for a while and then replies while staring at the blue sedan in front of us. "I'm not thinking about it." I can see her biting her lip, meditating whether to say more or not. Thankfully, she does. "I've never lived with anyone else, let alone a stranger. What if I don't like them? What if they find me too weird? Or worse, what if I like them, but they hate me?" She hides her hands under her hips, possibly to avoid tugging on the cuffs of her shirt.

"Marr. Calm down." I internally curse at being on the highway. There's no way I can park nearby. I have a few more minutes until I can pull her into my arms. I grab her hand instead and rest it over my thigh, under my palm. "First of all, you're not weird. You are an extremely smart, intelligent, and beautiful woman. Believe in that. And you don't have to make a decision now. You can find someone for the short term and see how you feel about it."

She doesn't reply right away, but gradually, her ice-cold hand relaxes.

"That's a good idea. I'm a basket case since Kristy proposed she could help me find a roommate. I'm not thinking straight."

"That's understandable." I park the car at our destination. My enthusiasm for the surprise has dampened with this new information. "Do you want to go back home? We can discuss this roommate issue. I'm sure you'll feel better if we come up with a plan."

"No!" She jumps in her seat, her head hitting the roof of the car. I stroke where she hit herself as she continues. "You already gave me an idea. I can post an ad at the office board. It'll be easier if I can find someone familiar." She clutches my hand, taking it away from where I'm caressing her hair. "I don't want to think about this now. Please." She looks up at me, her blue eyes hesitant before she fixes her perfect glasses. "We're having... such a nice time, aren't we?"

"The best." I kiss her soft lips, reassuring her.

"Then let's keep it like this. I really want to see the surprise."

I already know that I'll do anything for this girl. But when she pouts, she makes me go crazy. I can't think, can't see anything else.

"Stop pouting, otherwise I'll have to take you home for all different reasons."

My words bring back the twinkle in her eyes, and her pout grows deeper. As much as I want to enjoy this flirty side of Marr, I know if we continue, I'll for sure drag her home. She is irresistible like this.

"Okay, let's do this. We see the surprise and then go dress shopping. There's plenty of time before we meet my brothers for dinner. By the way, Zach has changed your return flight for the day after. Any remaining shopping can be done tomorrow." I drag her out of the car before she can drive me further insane with her protests or her coyness.

"Is that…The Comic Corner?" She stops, her eyes riveted on the white vinyl banner and the red painted letters.

"The one and only." I watch as her eyebrows crinkle before she beams and throws herself into my arms. Her body trembles in excitement, and I feel ten feet tall for making her this happy. Before I can crush her against my chest, she takes a step back when we hear footsteps.

Marr's arms slowly come down from where they were locked behind my neck.

"Let's go in," she whispers as a group of teens walk past us.

I grab her hand and pull her back to me. "It's okay, Marr. I don't think people will mind you hugging or kissing your boyfriend in excitement."

Hand in hand, we enter the largest comic store in the area, and I guide her to the X-Men section. Beast used to bring us here on Sundays, but it's been years since I've last stepped foot in this store.

Marr's eyes excitedly move around, perusing one collectible after another until she stands before a twenty-inch Wolverine premium format figure. Dressed in his signature yellow and blue, the berserker lunges forward, drawing his claws with a lethal expression on his face.

"It's beautiful." My chin rests on Marr's shoulder as we stare at our fave.

"I think so too. Do you think it's a good gift?"

"You already gave me my gift, couch girl." I turn my head and whisper in her ear. "And you offered much more. I hate my morals so fucking much."

She closes her eyes, and the back of her head rests against my chest. "Will you always…tease me…about that?"

"Tease you? The second I said no to you is the most regretful moment of my life. I'm fucking serious." Our eyes meet as she looks up. Her dilated pupils mirror my own excitement, but the cock blocking teenage group interrupts us again, and Marr focuses back on the figure.

"It's not for you. It's Kristy's wedding gift."

I cough to hide the shock on my face. This girl can still surprise me, sometimes too much.

"I wasn't aware Kristy is also a fan." Fortunately, I manage to form a sensible response to her unconventional marriage gift idea.

"She isn't." Marr sighs.

I tug on her hands as they grasp the cuffs of her blue-and-green flannel shirt and pull her close to me. "Then what's the deal with the Wolverine?"

"Kristy has asked me to buy something for Charlie as their wedding gift. He's an X-Men fan."

That makes more sense. "Okay, let's buy this for the little man. Then we can find a real gift for Kristy and Oscar from us."

"From us?" she asks in surprise.

"From us," I confirm.

We're back in the car after buying the action figurine and two X-Men comics for Marr.

"Let's see what we can get them." Her fingers fly over the touchscreen keypad of her phone.

"What are you doing?" I pull my Cadillac out of the parking lot and head toward the highway.

"I'm looking at wedding gift recommendations. Zander, look, we can get them wine bottles with labels personalized for special milestones." She shows me a Pinterest page titled *Gifts for Your BFF*. The numerous heart shaped emojis tell me it's only used by teenage girls.

"That's nice, Marr. But don't you think we should gift them something that interests both of them?"

She thinks for a while and then closes her phone.

"They both like traveling. I've heard Oscar was a peripatetic, trotting around the globe with his band, and Kristy always wanted to visit Europe."

"That's great. We can gift them travel vouchers for their honeymoon. We can even make it flexible, so they decide the time depending on their convenience. What do you say?"

"Wow, Zander. That's so romantic. We can plan the destinations…or maybe not. I'd love to plan my honeymoon by myself." The casual words are out of her mouth before she can think or interpret the meaning. But then she immediately goes silent, eyes focused on her hands clasped together on her lap.

"How does such a future look, couch girl? Am I there with you in your imagination?" My heart stops, awaiting her response.

"I… I don't know, Zander," she whispers.

My palms sweat over the steering wheel as she rejects me so easily, without a second thought.

"I don't think… such a future stands for me. And about you being with me, you deserve someone… much smarter, much braver… just much *more*, than me."

My heart pounds through my chest as I find it hard to believe her fucking words. I thought we had cleared Marr's insecurities.

Boy, was I wrong.

"Do you wish for such a future with me?" My voice clogs with emotion.

"If I can even think about such a future, it's only because of you, Zander," she says, before adding hastily, "But as I said, such a future isn't for me. You don't want to be stuck with someone like me. Someone who gets panic attacks about little things like buying a dress or getting a new roommate. I can't do this to you. I...just can't." Tears roll down her cheeks, dropping onto her hands, which are clasped tightly on her lap.

I'm once again face-to-face with the knowledge that this wonderful, remarkable girl is struggling with such low self-confidence. She's somehow established herself in this world by interacting with computers, but her social life is in crumbs. She needs perpetual backing, and now I fully grasp and appreciate Kristy's place in Marr's life. I wish that someday I can be that support system for my couch girl. I also realize that I can't rush into asking her *the question*. I need to talk to Kristy and glance deeper into Marr's heart.

"A few months back, I couldn't have imagined having such a future for myself. But now, you give me hope. Hope for so much more." I take a deep breath. I want to tell her how important she is to me, but I also don't want to railroad her with my emotions. "I'll not say anything more, except that I love the future I imagine with you and would love to live it. But we'll discuss it some other day." I kiss her hand, still damp with tears. "Today, let's buy a gift for your best friend and a dress for you."

We end up buying a European holiday package for Kristy and Oscar. Upon Marr's insistence, we included a third ticket for Charlie. I'm not sure how comfortable a honeymoon with a six-year-old would be, but Marr was pretty resolute on it.

After purchasing a beautiful peach-colored dress for her, we reach Little Italy for dinner. Lukas is the first one to show up.

"Hey, guys." He sits across from us.

"Hi, Lukas," Marr replies and gives him a genuine smile—a smile she reserves for very few people. I'm still in shock that he managed to impress my girl this easily.

"Where are my brothers? I thought they were coming with you."

He points toward the door, and I find Zach and Zane talking to a guy in a blue suit with a name tag on his chest. When they notice us looking their way, Zach pats the restaurant manager on the back, and they stride toward us.

"Marr, you enjoying S-s-st. Peppers? What did you d-d-do?" Zane asks as he sits next to Lukas.

She nods. "It's nice. We went to The Comic Corner." Her bashful voice is filled with embarrassment.

"Did my darling brother tell you about his crush on Wolverine?"

I'm not egged on by Zach's comments, as Marr bursts into giggles. I owe my dumb brother for making her laugh.

"My girl can't complain. She has a much bigger crush on him." I stroke Marr's denim-clad thigh under the table as she shivers under my touch. I'm about to remove my hand when I notice her pink cheeks. My most favorite color giving me the perfect idea.

Since our talk of the future, I'm wondering how I can make her believe in our love, in our future. I'm surprised how this small gesture led me to the perfect fix for our problem. She needs assurance that I want her with all her awkwardness and panic attacks.

And I'll die trying, proving to her that I want her not just in private but everywhere, every time, forever.

I squeeze her thigh once before extending my arm behind her. I clasp her shoulder and pull her closer to me. Marr looks around, her natural response to my touch in public, before settling back. I meet the eyes of the three men sitting across from us. There's a flicker of surprise, but they recover quickly.

"We didn't know you're an X-Men junkie like him, Marr." Zach continues the conversation. "Are you a fan of the movies or comics?"

"Both." She smiles as I stroke her forearm, and I feel her relaxing against me. "But the comics more."

"That's my girl," I rasp, caressing her cheeks with my fingers.

How did I not see that Marr needs social acceptance along with love?

Someone to profess and assert his affection to her publicly.

Our food arrives, a tasting menu comprising of her favorites.

My brothers have gone all out to make this evening special for my girl. They, especially Zach, might give the impression that they don't care, but they'll die for our family if needed. In such moments, I feel blessed that we three didn't inherit the lack of a family bond from *that* woman.

33

ZANDER

"Hello, boss. I think you dialed the wrong number in Cherrywood," Kristy drawls, and the hint of a tease in her voice makes me chuckle.

"Hello, my most favorite employee. I have the right number, don't you worry." I put my aviators on after placing the empty cup on the outside table of the small family-owned café near my office.

"We all know who your most favorite employee is, Zander." She giggles before asking, "How was your birthday surprise?"

"Phenomenal! It was crazy to see Marr in my office at midnight." I don't even try to hide the excitement. "Thanks a lot."

"Why are you thanking me? It was all your brothers' doing."

"It might have been, but I'm sure Marr needed some persuading." I shake my head to the waitress offering a refill. Placing some money on the table, I get up and leave the café after waving to the owner.

"It's no problem. Your girlfriend needs a little push occasionally."

I get inside my car, which is parked on the street. "I get it, Kristy, and that's kind of the reason why I'm calling you today. I need some advice." I pause, trying to find the best way to voice my concern.

When I don't speak for several more minutes, she ribs me, "I thought you guys were beyond the *no-touching* issue. As a matter of fact, I know that for sure, as you had some of your not-so-quiet sexual adventures in our house."

"Yes, thanks to God and *you* for that." My lips pull up in a smile, remembering Marr and how she looked in her bathroom mirror.

"Then what is it?"

My chest once again tightens in anxiety. "I need your advice on something else." I loosen my tie, which unfortunately isn't cherry colored, providing me none of the much-needed hope. "I want to propose to Marr." My mouth dries after I blurt the words, more so because the phone line goes dead silent. "You there, Kristy?"

"Yes, but I'm still waiting for the part where you need my advice."

I rake my fingers through my hair. "Didn't you hear when I said I want to propose?" My anxiety morphs into agitation.

"So, you want me to do it for you?"

"No! I just…" I just what? *I just want you to tell me that Marr will say yes*, my brain screams. What the hell was I even thinking?

"You just what?"

"I don't know what I was expecting." All my enthusiasm and anxiety crumbles, and I feel like the dumbest person on the face of earth.

"It's okay, Zander." She releases a sigh. "To tell you the truth, I was expecting such a call from you, but not this soon."

My pulse quickens. "You think I'm rushing?" *Maybe I am.*

But thankfully, she replies fast. "No, definitely not. I don't think you or Rose have any doubts about each other. Do you?" I can sense the apprehension in her voice.

"Not at all. If I could, I would marry her this second." Just at the mere thought, my heart races like a horse galloping in a racecourse.

"Go easy, boss. You're famous for being sensible, not impulsive. What's gotten into you?"

I release a deep breath at her light question. "That's what your friend does to me." I lean back in my seat. The metal butterfly hanging on the rearview mirror swirls, reminding me of the carnival in Cherrywood.

"Tell me, how can I really help?"

I close my eyes and remember Marr sitting beside me in the passenger seat, teardrops falling onto her hands clasped tight over her knees.

"Do you know that Marr has memorized a list of reasons why she's not right for me?" I don't remember feeling this tense ever in my adult life. "I just can't shake this feeling that somehow her insecurities, her fears, will win and I'll lose her." My voice sounds pathetic to my own ears, but how do I not worry about her slipping away? "What should I do to make her believe in me, and more importantly, in *us*?"

"I understand your feelings, Zander. Not only because I know Rose but also because I was at the exact same place not long back. It took me ages to convince Oscar that we're right for each other. That what *we have* is right. And here we are talking about Rose. You guys have been together for only a handful of months. You'll have to give her time."

I know what she is saying makes total sense, but I don't like it. I don't want to waste years convincing Marr. Kristy's sensible words don't help my anxiety a bit.

"I know, but that's not what I want to do. What I want is for her to know that I'm here for good and I'm not going anywhere. We've lost so much time in our lives just waiting for someone to love us, hold us, be with us. I don't want to wait a fucking minute more. I don't want her to wait any longer for love."

"You don't know how happy I am for Rose, and for you." Kristy's voice quivers and she clears her heavy throat. "But—"

"My gut says I should do it, Kristy. Recently, I came face-to-face with Marr's insecurities, and I want to show her that I want her in my life, in my world."

"You have no idea how much this'll means to her." I hear a hitch in Kristy's voice as she says, "She's never had anywhere or anyone to belong to."

My heart stings at that thought just as it does every other time when I imagine my girl alone, scared. "I figured that, and that's why I don't want to delay it anymore. I want to give her all the happiness in the world."

"You already do that. You have no idea how much you've changed her. You're good for her; I have no doubt about it."

Kristy doesn't know how much Marr has changed my life.

"I'd need your help with the proposal. I don't want to make her uneasy, and as much as it kills me, I also want to give her the option of saying no."

The mere thought of her rejection is like a thousand punches rolled into one. But I need to do this. I can only hope that she says yes.

"There's no chance she's going to refuse." Kristy goes quiet for some time, thinking about my request. "Oscar and I've planned a small family breakfast for the day after the wedding. There'll be Oscar's family, my mother, and Rose. Why don't you and your brothers join us? And if you feel it's right, you can ask her there. You're welcome to invite anyone else."

I like her idea. It won't be crowded, yet everyone who matters will be there. I would love to have Beast, but he's away on a business trip. Nevertheless, he knows that I'm going to propose to Marr. I hope they can meet soon. I know he'll instantly fall in love with her.

"Are you sure? I don't want to hijack your celebration."

"Oh, please. It's a special moment, and your proposal will only make it more memorable. I'm dying to see the expression on her face."

"Me too." I imagine Marr's face, and mixed feelings of fear, nervousness, and bliss hit my heart.

34

ROSE

I stare at myself in the mirror as the hair stylist fixes the last of my curls. The reflection in the back mirror allows me to see the hairstyle better. A messy updo is what she called it. I wasn't sure if I wanted anything messy, but then she showed me a picture.

It was a *messy* but beautiful bun. What made it extraordinary were the fresh roses she had placed on the girl's hair in the photograph. In the past, I'd have asked for the same style without a second thought. Instead, I asked if she could replace the flowers with something else. Now secured in my hair is a silver hair-vine covering the major arch of the updo. Freshwater pearls shine under the light from the ceiling. My makeup is sober for an evening church wedding followed by a grand reception, but it's the maximum primping I've ever received.

Since I've been back from St. Peppers, Zander's words keep buzzing in my ears. He said I give him hope for a beautiful future that he wants to share with me. Sometimes I wonder how I got this lucky. This man, fancied by every other girl, wants a future with me. But why?

I don't doubt his love. In fact, he's the one who showed

me what love truly means. But I'm afraid to think about our future together.

Will he still love me the same when my flaws bare themselves?

Will he still love me when I struggle to interact with his quick-witted business associates or their wives while we're at some stuffy office party?

Won't he be upset if I don't *want to go* to such a party?

I'm not an expert on relationships, but I know people fall out of love for much less. And this scares the hell out of me. I don't think I'll ever be able to bear the pain of losing Zander, and more than that, see him embarrassed because of me.

"Rose, you look beautiful." Sophia looks at me in the mirror, a weird expression, possibly one of surprise, etched on her face.

"Thanks," I reply sheepishly. Sophia only arrived yesterday morning and met Oscar and his family during the pre-wedding dinner. I thought the mother of the bride would be more involved in the wedding preparations, but not always, I guess.

"You are most welcome." She pecks me on the forehead before taking my hand and leading me to the window, away from the other ladies. "If you don't mind, I'd like to meet Zander and talk to him for a while."

"Um… really?" I'm surprised by her request. So far, she hasn't asked me anything about Zander. Even when Kristy brought up Zander and his brothers multiple times, Sophia showed no interest.

She nods. "Introduce us during the reception. I can have a word with him before I leave tomorrow."

"You're leaving already?"

"Yes. I'm only a few hours' drive. Kristy can visit me anytime she wants." Sophia doesn't need to explicitly mention I'm not as welcomed as Kristy in her home. My previous excitement lessens, and the familiar feeling of loneliness revisits me. Before my mood sobers further, a tweet sound from my phone alerts me of a text, and my lips twitch into a smile.

Zander: We're at the venue. Dying to see you.

"Is that him?"

I jerk to look up at Sophia. How easily he turns my mood; his words already made me forget Sophia and whatever she was saying.

I nod to her as Zander's next message arrives.

Zander: Dying to kiss you, taste you, hug you. Meet me soon.

My face heats with anticipation.

"Don't forget to introduce us." Sophia raises her eyebrow at me as she glances at my blushing face.

STANDING at the altar behind Kristy, I look around and find Zander sitting in the third row with Zach and Zane. The three brothers stand out in the crowd of expensive suits and fancy dresses.

Zander looks breathtaking in his black tux and bow tie, his hair slicked back as if he just stepped off the screen of an old movie. He gives me a once-over, his sensual stare gazing at some parts of my body longer than others, making me delirious.

How does he do it, turn me into a hot mess by just one look?

The officiant starts the ceremony, but I have no clue what's going on. I'm totally lost in Zander and the way he's staring at me. We're pulled back to reality by the loud claps and cheers of everyone around, and I realize the ceremony is already over.

I hug Kristy, who is beaming with happiness. "I'm so happy for you, Kris."

"Thank you so much. I'm happy for you too." She squeezes me back and looks in the direction of the three Teager men.

"Wow! How do you tolerate so much hotness?" Clementine gushes, fanning her face with her hands and eliciting a giggle from every girl around us.

As everyone congratulates the bride and groom, someone shouts, "Kristy, throw the bouquet. Let's see who the next lucky one is."

I don't want to be a part of this crazy custom, but I'm crushed between Clementine and her cousins. As I make another unsuccessful attempt to get out of the crowd, there's a shout. "Here it comes!"

I stare at the purple-and-white bouquet of peonies, clematis, and wax flowers heading my way. Before I get a chance to deflect, it lands in my hands, and everyone starts cheering my name. My nervous gaze automatically drifts to Zander, who has a broad smile on his face.

"Lucky Rosie!" Kristy squeaks before hugging me and not-so-covertly winking at Zander.

After the wedding ceremony, everyone is ushered to the dinner reception venue in limos. As a part of the bridal party, I'm sharing the ride with Oscar's family rather begrudgingly. I wanted to talk to Zander, be with him. I saw him approaching me, but before we could talk, Clementine dragged me into the car. Zander seemed equally irritated as he watched me leave.

When we arrive at the reception, I'm seated next to Sophia at the center table. I can only see Zander from afar.

Finally, after an emotional round of speeches, the guests scatter, and I make a beeline to find him. At a distance, I see Zach and Zane, but there's no sign of Zander. Before I can approach them, Zander materializes before me, and without saying a word, drags me to the coat closet.

"I was getting worried that I wouldn't get you alone

today." He wraps his arms around my waist as we both stand in this faintly lit space while the wedding party is buzzing outside.

"Hi," I whisper.

"Hello, couch girl." A huge smile appears on his face. I'm sure I mirror his expression, happy that we're alone at last. After placing a quick kiss on my lips, he takes a step back and crosses his arms over his chest. He cocks his head to the side and ogles me head to toe.

"What?" I suddenly feel shy.

"Nothing. Just looking," he says with that smile girls die for. But it's just adding to my embarrassment.

"Stop it!" I take a step forward and playfully smack his chest.

"You take my breath away." He grabs my waist. "I've wanted to kiss you so bad since you walked down the aisle, but I didn't want to mess up your makeup." I feel his heavy breath on my forehead as he gently places a kiss there.

His fingers play with some loose strands. "This hairstyle looks gorgeous on you."

"It's a messy updo." I peer at his beautiful face, and his eyes crinkle as he smiles at my words.

"How did you agree to anything messy?"

As always, I'm amazed at how well he knows me. "I didn't. Not until she showed me the picture of her previous work." I turn around, giving him my back so he can see the style better.

"I love it." He pulls me closer, placing gentle kisses on my neck and making me shiver. "I've been sitting with a boner since you walked toward the altar." And to prove his point, he gently thrusts his hips forward.

"Crab!"

And what a boner it is.

He chuckles and nuzzles my neck. "I'm totally in love with your swearing."

"Only my swearing?" My words come out as a breathy whisper.

He turns me around so fast that my already dizzy head spins.

"I love your every bit. Each and everything about you makes me crazy, Marr. My heart beats so fast whenever you're around." He places my hand over his pounding heart. "And when you're far, it thrums with anxiety." I can feel my own fluttering heart beating in sync with his. "I love you so much that sometimes it's fucking painful. But I want it no other way. When you're around, everything becomes insignificant. It's only you that I want, need, and crave."

"Zander." I didn't expect an honest confession of love. I thought we were doing our usual lighthearted ribbing. But this person in front of me, with such raw emotion in his gaze and words, scares me. I close my eyes and clutch him tight. Moments like these that I get with Zander, give me hope for a wonderful future, and I don't want this feeling to end.

"Look at me, babe. Open your eyes. I'm here and I'm not going anywhere. Without you, I don't fucking exist, Marr."

When my eyes finally open, they meet his deep gaze, a little strong and a little in pain. I throw myself into his strong arms. "Zander, did something happen?"

I feel his head shaking. "Sometimes I can't bear the thought of being away from you."

I pull back just an inch. My heartbeat is wild as I glance into his eyes. "Are… you going… somewhere?" It's not normal for Zander to freak out.

"No. It's just been so long since I've seen you. I hate living so far apart." He rubs my back, sensing my anxiety.

"Me too." I hide my face in his chest and breathe his vanilla smell, trying to calm my racing heart.

"I was thinking—" He's silenced by a soft knock on the door.

"Zand-d-der?"

We look at each other, neither of us saying a word.

"I know you're t-t-there. Zach saw you s-s-sneaking in." My face heats with embarrassment. "Kris-s-sty's mom is looking for you." Zane knocks on the door once more before we hear his receding footsteps.

"Sophia wants to talk to you. Alone," I tell Zander and look for any sign of hesitation in his face. But there is none.

"I would love to meet her." He caresses my cheeks and places a kiss on my forehead. Taking a deep breath as if breathing me into him, he says, "Let's not make her wait."

35

ZANDER

A waiter holding a tray of pink champagne flutes appears as Marr and I join my brothers. I'm about to take a sip when there's a gentle pat on my shoulder. I turn to find Sophia dressed in a navy-blue suit standing behind me. I saw her earlier while she walked Kristy down the aisle.

"Hello, Zander." She offers me her hand. Her firm handshake doesn't surprise me; she is Kristy's mom, after all.

"Hello, Mrs. Asher. It's nice to finally meet you."

Sophia greets my brothers before asking Marr, "Rose, do you mind if I borrow your date for a while?"

I hand my untouched champagne to Zane and grab Marr's hand, which is pulling on the silver bracelet around her wrist.

My lips on hers force her to let go of the bottom lip between her teeth. I squeeze her hand one last time before following Sophia out of the hall.

We reach the garden where a string quartet is playing, and guests are flocking to the dance floor or the gigantic wooden bar. Sophia leads me away from all the fuss to a quiet corner. I wait for her to take a seat, and then I perch on an opposite chair. The table between us, covered in white linen with a shiny golden border, holds a photo frame with a picture of Kristy and Oscar.

"I think my daughter made a wise choice," Sophia comments, following my gaze.

"Oscar is a fine man."

"I'm not talking about Kristy."

My hand, which was straightening a fold on the tablecloth, stills. Sophia's weird statement and tight smile catches me off guard. I had an understanding that Sophia's role in Marr's life has been more of a mentor than a mother.

I give her the unvarnished truth. "I love her."

"So I've heard. Kristy is all praise for you, and I'd have to be blind to not see the way Rose's eyes twinkle whenever you're around or even mentioned."

I try to ignore the wild drumming in my chest and reply, "I feel the same way about her."

"I can see that too." She sighs, looking away as if unhappy to confirm that my feelings for Marr are not fraudulent. "I hope you know what you're getting into, Zander. Rose isn't your normal girl." Her head turns to the side, and something resembling pity settles on her face.

Does she feel sorry...*for me?* Why?

I have a hard time believing she's the same woman who is so deeply idolized by my couch girl.

"Excuse me?" My words come out with more force than I intend for them to.

"Don't get all worked up. You've known that girl for less than a year. I've known her since she was born."

"You mean found?"

Her eyes widen for a brief second before she schools her features.

"It's good to hear that you know of her past. But do you think that's enough?" Sophia leans forward, her arms resting on the table as she continues in a hushed voice. "For Rose, every day is a challenge. She fights with identity crisis on a daily basis. Even after years of therapy and surgery, she's not comfortable in her own skin and scars. She wears nothing other than those flannel shirts."

My chest clenches at her nonsense. "In case you haven't noticed, she's not wearing a flannel shirt today, though I find her equally beautiful in those. And I'm very well aware of her issues."

"Of course. That's what you are, *aware*. What about experiencing them firsthand? Today you don't mind her quirks, but what about when she can't mingle as much with your family and friends?"

"She likes my brothers and they her. That's enough for me." And so is this bullshit. I'm all ready to leave, but Sophia isn't yet done.

"What about when your brothers marry smart, socially adept girls who don't want to waste their time around Rose? People often feel that way about her. What happens when people don't let their kids play with yours because they think Rose is some kind of weirdo?"

"Stop." I never imagined my meeting with Sophia to be this caustic. "What's your problem? I thought you cared about her." I can't stop the lump rising in my throat.

Why does my Marr have such shitty relationships?

"I'm not going to take shit from anyone about her or our relationship. I don't need to explain to you or anybody else how we'll handle our future. She is a brilliant woman, and I'm lucky to have her." I roll all my anger, hope, and love into words. "If luck favors me, that smart girl will someday share a life, and even a family, with me."

I get up from my chair, no longer interested in knowing Sophia. Our small interaction is enough for me. Before I can march away, she says, "Sometimes I wonder where I went wrong."

I'm momentarily distracted as my gaze lands on her hand

resting on the table, playing with the golden band on her ring finger.

Why is she still wearing her wedding ring?

"Rose has missed a lot in her life, and most of it was due to the overprotectiveness of others, including me. She doesn't need more of that in her life. She just needs to be loved and understood."

I'm unable to comprehend this sudden shift in her behavior. For a fleeting moment, I worry about Sophia's mental wellbeing as she gets up and stands beside me.

"It was nice meeting you, Zander. I'm sure I'll see more of you."

I'm still not sure what happened in the last five minutes and how I feel about this woman, who sounds a bit crazy and a bit guilty.

Sophia is already ambling toward the main hall when I call after her, "I'm going to propose tomorrow."

She looks at me over her shoulder and smiles. "I know. You have my blessing, if that's what you're looking for."

"Zander, I can manage."

I ignore Marr's protests and carry her inside the house. When we reach the soft plush carpet by her bed, I slide her down. "I know you can manage, but I like touching you any way I can." My fingers glide over her soft cheek, and she lazily shuts her eyes. "How tired are you?"

"Not at all." Her eyes immediately open wide, making me chuckle.

"Liar. It's way past your usual bedtime. Come on."

She again protests when I lead her to the bathroom. I bring the toilet lid down and situate her there before getting on my knees.

"What are you doing?" Marr tries to pull back her leg, which is tight in my grip.

"I'm helping you get ready for bed." Unstrapping her low heels, I remove the sandals and place them just outside the bathroom door as she stays stuck in place with an open mouth.

I rummage through the cabinet under the sink until my hand grabs a pack of makeup wipes.

"Close your eyes." I remove her glasses and gently wipe her face before working on getting off her eye makeup.

"I think it's clean now," she mutters when I'm on the third time of running the wipe over her eyes.

"I'm trying to get off the fake eyelashes. What kind of super glue did they use?"

She giggles at my irritation. "There are no fakes. You'll just pluck my real ones out."

My hands halt the rubbing. "Oh, sorry." I throw the wipe into the trash before undoing the messy bun.

The gown pools at her feet when I unzip it, and Marr stands before me in nude silk undergarments, making me breathless with her shy beauty. My fingers glide over her belly button, and I watch her shiver in satisfaction.

"You were the most beautiful woman today."

"Then you didn't see the other women." She looks at me from under the bangs lying flat on her forehead.

"Why would I waste my time looking at anyone else when you're in the crowd, couch girl?" My lips press on her forehead as I try to keep my anxiety for tomorrow in check.

"You mean that?" She releases a deep breath, and her hands clutch my arms as I hold her face.

"I mean every word I say to you." My lips move from her forehead to her ears.

"Why me, Zander?" She trembles in my arms. Her eyes close as if she's scared to hear the answer to her own question.

"Because I'm a lucky bastard to have found you, to have you fall in love with me. I'm not going anywhere, Marr. I'm here for keeps."

"But I—"

My grip on her face tightens as I interrupt her with insistent kisses on her skin. "You are the most amazing woman, and you make my heart stop with just one look."

"But—" I put a finger on her lips.

"You can give a million reasons, but I'm not going anywhere."

Her breath hitches, and she offers me her hand. "Promise?"

You have no idea, baby.

I kiss her palm before placing my own hand over hers. "It's a promise of a lifetime, couch girl."

36

ROSE

I shift in my bed, and my back hits a wall—a warm wall of Zander's bare chest. My eyes open to look at the time on the bedside clock and it's seven thirty. The house is dead silent, no usual buzzing of a coffee machine or Kristy's treadmill.

This is how my mornings are going to sound from now. After Zander leaves, I'll be alone in this house. My house, which until yesterday was mine and Kristy's.

I sit upright as a feeling of nausea hits me. My chest feels heavy, and I clutch the cotton T-shirt, rubbing my chest underneath.

How am I going to live here by myself?

"Marr, what is it?" Zander's sleepy body sprouts to life, and he pulls me into his arms. "Hey, couch girl. What's the matter?"

"I… I'm alone."

"What do you mean? I'm here." He crushes me into his arms so tightly that I have trouble breathing.

"In…this…house. I'm…all alone," I stutter.

"You are not alone, Marr." Zander tucks my messed-up bed hair behind my ear and holds my face in his hands.

Looking into my eyes, he says, "You have a wonderful new housemate."

"You're staying?" Hope rises in my voice.

"No, baby. Not me." He smiles and adds, "Not yet." Before I can comprehend his added words, he continues, "But you will like her."

He pulls me out of the bed and leads to Kristy's room.

It looks the same, except all her stuff is gone, including a picture of us that was always placed on the top of her dresser. Her makeup table is empty, and her favorite pillow is gone. I purchased that *I am my own boss* pillow for her with my first scholarship money. Everything here makes me sadder.

Oblivious to my forlorn mood, Zander opens the closet.

The clothes hanging definitely aren't Kristy's.

They're way too bright and flashy, nothing like Kristy's business dresses. There's a small cardboard moving box that's overflowing with stuff hastily shoved inside. On top of it lies a photograph, placed face-first with familiar faces. Clementine, Oscar, and the rest of the Hawthorne family.

"I'm confused, Zander." I turn my gaze from the closet to him and notice that he's been looking at me the whole time, possibly gauging my reaction.

"This is Clementine's stuff. She wants to move out of her mother's house." He pauses, letting me comprehend his words.

"Oh." I can't decide straight away how I feel about this change.

"If you don't like it, she'll understand." Zander grabs my hands, which are scratching the full sleeves of my T-shirt. "Kristy asked me to put this box here so you can imagine better, but Clementine hasn't completely moved in or anything."

I pause for a long while before replying, mulling over the idea in my head. It also doesn't skip my mind what lengths

Zander went through to help find a solution to my roommate situation.

"It's okay, I guess. I knew Kristy would leave after her marriage, and…I would have to find a new housemate. For some reason, I was stalling the inevitable. But Clem isn't a stranger. I know her and she also knows…of me." I glance at him, and he nods.

"I'm also planning to stay for a few days." Zander swallows as if he's nervous about something, possibly my reaction.

I squeeze his hands, which are still holding mine, trying to reassure him and also myself.

"Thank you." But the creases on Zander's forehead don't relax. Does he think I'm going to have a meltdown? "It's good. Really good. I know Clem, and it'll be…fun." I add the last word just to pacify his worries.

Nothing new is fun.

"Okay." He releases a sharp breath and plops down on Kristy's—um, I mean, Clem's bed. Scratching his head, he tugs on his hair.

"Zander, what's the matter?" I place my hand over his to stop him from plucking his cowlick out.

Instead, he grabs my waist, pulling me close. His head rests over my stomach as I stand in front of him. I don't know why, but in this moment, he looks so vulnerable, and Zander is never vulnerable. He is strong and brave.

"You're worrying me. Is something wrong?" I try to pull away to look at his face, but his tight grip on my waist doesn't allow me to move even an inch. It's like he's worried I'll disappear if he lets go even for a moment.

"I can't lose you." His words sound muffled against my stomach.

"What do…you mean? Tell me what's wrong," I demand. His anxiety is contagious, and my own heart beats rapidly.

What happened to him?

He's been off since the wedding. The way he talked to me about love in the coatroom. The way he held me throughout the evening.

"Nothing's wrong." He pulls me down on his lap and gazes into my eyes. "I love you so much that sometimes it hurts to think what I'll do without you. I need you, baby."

I don't know what to say to his admission. My throat constricts at the emotion I see in his eyes. Nobody has needed me, *ever*.

"Zander, are you going somewhere?"

"No, I'm not. I just can't stay far from you." He smiles, but it doesn't reach his eyes.

"What happened?"

"Nothing, sweetheart. It's just—" The ringing of the doorbell interrupts him. We both turn our heads to the door. "I'll get it. You get dressed. We have to leave for Kristy and Oscar's breakfast party soon." He places a swift kiss on my lips before standing me up and walking out of the room.

When I come out of shower, I find Zander sitting on my bed, dressed in another of his fine suits. He might have taken a shower in Kristy's bathroom.

"Who was at the door?" I ask, my brain still struggling with the news of Clementine moving in. Everything is changing so fast.

"Zach and Zane. They're here to pick us up," Zander replies, playing with the ends of the peach dress I've laid on the bed to put on.

"Oh, sorry. I'll be quick." I scramble to the dresser to get my hairdryer.

"It's okay, Marr. They're early." Zander walks to me and plucks the brush from my hands. "Can I request something?"

"Mmm…sure." My voice fills with trepidation as his hesitant voice.

"Can you put on your green flannel shirt today?" he urges.

"You want me to wear my flannel and jeans?" I can't hide my surprise. "You don't like the dress?"

Why? I purchased this dress with him in St. Peppers.

"I like it very much. You look so beautiful in it." A familiar smile dawns on his face. *Thank God!*

"Then what's the matter, Zander? You're really scaring me today."

"Nothing, sweetheart." He pulls me to his chest. "I just want to remember our first meeting, and I..." He swallows deep. "I kinda have a surprise for you." He searches my face, and I'm sure he can see anxiety written all over it. "It's a happy surprise, couch girl." He plants a kiss on my temple. "Trust me."

"I was really looking forward to a surprise-free day. It's all too much," I whisper, barely holding my tears at bay.

"What is?" he whispers back.

"Everything. Everything is changing... so fast." Today, Zander has taken the role of Kristy for me. I usually discuss such fears and insecurities with her. He slowly rubs my back as I continue.

"I feel like I'll fall behind and get lost again. Kristy is gone, Clementine is moving in, and you are being strange and... weird." My voice breaks. "I feel like I'm gonna lose you too."

"You're not going to lose me, ever. From what I see, you're not falling behind but moving forward. You're not getting lost but discovering new things in life. Instead of losing Kristy, you've gained two new relationships with Oscar and Charlie. More people are entering your life. It might be scary, but you are doing so great." He gazes into my eyes, urging me to believe his words.

"You think so?" I look at him with tears blurring my vision.

He nods and smiles. "I believe so."

"Okay then. Let's check out your surprise," I mumble, walking toward my dresser to put on my green flannel.

We all sit around the giant breakfast table set in Oscar's family's lavish garden. The weather is pleasant, and the breakfast is mouthwatering, which is no surprise considering most baked goods are from the coveted Hawthorne bakery in Cherrywood.

It's a close family-and-friend gathering. Kristy is settled with Oscar and Charlie on either side of her. Oscar's arm lazily hangs around her chair, and Charlie is half sitting on her lap. They do make a sweet family.

I sit next to Zander and his brothers, surrounded by people who are slowly taking the role of my family.

Meanwhile, Clementine assured me several times that she'll be a wonderful housemate and is looking forward to living with me. Seeing her so excited is actually good. I'm starting to believe in Zander's words about me moving forward in life.

A clearing of a throat interrupts my thoughts, and I notice Zander standing and drawing everybody's attention to him. He's wearing the reputable cherry red tie today, looking handsome as always.

"*Rose*, my sweetheart. I know you hate surprises, but I'm hoping this will be a good one, for both of us." He swallows hard and takes a long pause, which only makes me more anxious.

Why can't he surprise me in private?

"You might be wondering why I'm doing this in public." As always, he reads me like an open book. "But I need to do this in front of people who care about us and our happiness."

I glance across and meet Kristy's wide smile. Her eyes widen, and I follow her gaze to find Zander on one knee.

W-what the hell is he doing?

My heart stops and then races as I latch on to his action.

"My sweet *Rose*. Since I met you, I've experienced so many emotions. I was curious about the girl dressed in a green flannel shirt and sleeping on the office couch—my couch girl. Your intelligence amazed me, Dr. Marlin. And your sweetness enamored me, my Rose."

Oh my god!

He's calling me Rose.

"These emotions grow stronger by the day. I know we've only known each other for a short time, but it feels like I've known you for a lifetime before. And I would like to spend each minute of my remaining life with you, knowing you more."

"Zander." I'm stunned by his declaration. There are others around us, but I can't pull my gaze away from this man before me.

Photographic memory can *go to hill*; even without it, I'll remember this moment forever. My eyes burn with happy tears as they race down my cheeks.

"I'm not asking you to marry me, or maybe I am," he says sheepishly and nervously. "But I'm in no hurry. I'm just asking you to accept this ring in front of our friends and promise to be mine. That's enough for me. We—"

"Yes, I promise to be yours. I'm yours." I crouch on the ground beside him and whisper only for him, "But no hurry, right?"

"Of course, Rose." He places the ring on my palm, and that's when I notice the rose made with small intricate red diamonds. My tears turn into full-blown sobs.

"I love it," I say as sunlight shines on the inscription on the inside of the band. I bring it closer to my face and read aloud. "U have Me, I have U. Forever."

"Are you sure?" I ask Zander as we watch the dancing reflection of stars on the lake, sitting under a cherry tree.

"More than anything, Rose." My heart trembles every time he's said my name since he proposed to me this morning, making today the most special day of my life.

I can't believe it.

I'm engaged. I twist my ring and remove it.

"You aren't supposed to take it off," he whispers in my ear, pulling me closer to his chest.

"I'm making sure it's real," I whisper back, grazing my fingers inside the band to feel the inscription. I can't read it in the dark, but I can still feel the letters and see the words in my mind.

"This is as real as it gets, Rose."

"Does it feel weird?" I turn around to face him. When he doesn't understand, I provide, "To call me by my name."

"No. It feels… right. I thought it would be difficult, but once I said it, I can't stop using it." He smiles.

"So, no bad memories?"

He shakes his head. "Only the best ones, my beautiful Rose."

SIX MONTHS LATER

37

ROSE

"How's my fiancée doing this morning?" Zander's raspy voice, half-drowsy with sleep, fills my ears.

"I'm very good," I whisper.

"That you are, my beautiful Rose."

My fingers tighten around the phone. Since the morning he proposed to me, Zander has taken it upon himself to call me by my name.

"What's your plan for today?" I ask, simply because I want to hear his voice more.

"Meetings, meetings, and some more meetings." Hearing his sigh, you'd think he hates all those meetings. "In your language, all *CEO stuff*."

My lips curl up, and my heart warms when he repeats my words from the past. They are subtle reassurances of Zander's love for me.

"How is the planning for your birthday weekend in Cherrywood progressing?"

I hear the rustling of covers as he settles onto his huge bed, where I have the pleasure of sleeping whenever I visit him in St. Peppers.

"You know Kristy. She makes a big deal of everything."

"She should. My girl deserves all the pampering." His voice is soft and husky. I close my eyes and bite back a smile. I am his—his girl.

A few years ago, when Kristy, and I came to Cherrywood for a job interview, I didn't know my life would change like this. Now, I have people who want to pamper me on my birthday, who want to celebrate a day which might not even be the actual day I was born.

"Will you be here?"

"No one could stop me. Are you honestly not going to tell me what to get you?"

I turn on my side, pulling the covers up to my neck. Zander's words, as always, fill me with a toasty, cozy feeling. "I need nothing. I have you and I have Kristy. That's all I need."

He groans. "You say all these sweet and cute things, and I want to pull you into my arms, but all I have is a fucking cold and empty bed around me."

"That's not true. You have four pairs of my lingerie that I know of. But looking at my diminishing underwear drawer, I suspect you have more than that."

"Maybe I'll buy you several pairs of your favorite Victoria's Secret panties. On your birthday, I'll make you wear each one of them, and then we'll spoil them, all ready for me to take back home."

His hot and breathy voice tickles my ear, and my heartbeat accelerates at his words. I'm sure no one would believe that Zander Teager, CEO of Elixir Inc., could be such a raunchy, dirty talker.

"What do you say, babe?"

"You are nuts," I mumble, hiding my face in the pillow, my body all hot and sweaty.

Every morning when he wakes me up with a phone call, I have no clue which Zander I'm getting. Some days, he's sweet and cute, making me emotional. But others, like today, he makes me delirious with need. On such days, I want to crawl inside the phone and just hide in his arms—or in his king-sized bed.

"Breathe slow. You're making me real crazy here," he groans in a voice I've become well acquainted with. It's a voice he uses when he whispers my name as he stands me in front of my big bathroom mirror and takes me from behind. It's the same voice he uses when he mumbles or curses while I'm lying on the bed and his head is buried between my legs.

"Crab," I murmur. My pulse quickens and his breathy groans from the other side are making me delirious. "What are you doing?"

"You know...very well." He continues to mumble my name and some expletives before releasing a heavy breath. "You like to unman me."

What did I do?

He's the one who did everything, while I'm a hot mess over here.

"Do you need something, Rose?" Zander drawls with his familiar teasing lilt.

"No," I reply fast. This crazy man.

"Are you sure?"

"I am." I squeeze my thighs together.

He chuckles, making me smile despite my...condition. "Don't worry, babe. You won't be left alone when I come to you next week."

"You are so bad," I whisper.

"That I am." I can hear the lightness in his voice. "As much as I want to continue this discussion with you, the business world is calling my name."

"Go. Do all the *CEO stuff*." I giggle before ending the call.

I spend some more sweaty and clammy minutes under the covers. My head and heart are light, as they always are after talking to Zander, but my mood instantly shifts when my gaze lands on the small gift box wrapped in soft pink paper sitting on my nightstand. It's from Sophia, Kristy's mom. She sent me my birthday gift—more than half a year in advance.

Like every year, her gift gives me bittersweet feelings. As much as it tingles my limbs with happiness, it also brings me down. It makes me realize that Sophia doesn't remember the right day, even after I've corrected her multiple times in the past.

When the distress hits me, I suck in a deep breath, following my therapist's advice. I continue to breathe heavily for a few more seconds before my gaze moves to Logan and Lucy as they chase each other. I get up from the bed and gently place my finger on the fish tank wall, where the two most beloved goldfish live.

Lucy joined Logan after my engagement.

Why? Because I wanted Logan to have a partner too.

"How are you, kiddos?" They both follow my finger as I slide it against the cold glass, and a smile pulls at my lips, my previous anxiety now forgotten.

Even unknowingly, Zander's gifts, his words, and just the thought of him have the power to slay the demons of my insecurities.

I amble into the living room and the adjoining open kitchen to prepare my morning coffee. My eyes involuntarily squint to escape the color blast. There are vibrant clothes strewn on the breakfast barstools and countertops, and smaller fabrics lying on the stove. I'm still iffy about how I like Clementine as a roommate.

A loud shriek leaves me when I sense something moving on the floor.

"Rose! You scared me."

My wide eyes fall to Clementine, who's crawling on the floor. She gets up and grabs a jade-colored thread spool from the counter before settling back on the kitchen floor. *On the floor.*

"I-I'm sorry." My hands clutch my pounding heart. "I didn't...see you there."

Why would she not sit on the couch or the recliner or the comfy ottomans?

"That's okay," Clem mutters, and she goes back to working on a teal fabric with a thin needle.

My legs shake a little as I reach the coffee machine. "I'm making coffee. Do you want some?" I check the water level before turning the machine on.

"I hate your coffee. What I wouldn't give for a cinnamon latte."

She lets out a loud sigh, but I don't understand what she's crying about. With just a press of a switch, I get amazing coffee, and I don't even have to talk to anyone to get it. I don't need to explain the size, type, or amount of milk, among other things. Plus, having coffee at home guarantees the absence of the long waiting line. I'm a huge fan of my cute red coffee machine.

"But I've been working on this pattern for the last four hours and can't walk away now, so I'll tolerate that crap you call coffee." Clementine shakes her head, as if the thought of drinking my coffee disturbs her largely.

This is another unusual thing about living with Clem. I'm not used to people being so direct with me. I'm used to people eating or drinking whatever I give them, regardless of how they find it.

After handing the first cup to my roommate, I grab my "I'm engaged!" coffee mug from the cupboard. My lips twitch at the sight of the picture of Zander and me wrapped around the white ceramic. I know it's cheesy, maybe even a little juvenile. Not something one would expect an almost twenty-seven-year-old woman to be in possession of, but...I love it.

I park my car in the parking lot of my office at Elixir Inc., before taking the elevator that brings me to my office floor. When I step out, my gaze lands on the picture of the Teager brothers on our company brand wall. Zander is in the middle, a small smile on his lips that creates a dimple on his left cheek.

How many times have I kissed that dimple now? I blush at my wayward thoughts.

Kristy steps out of the other elevator, carrying her coffee cup. "Why don't you take that poster to your office? The gawking will be easier that way."

I swiftly glance around to check if anyone heard my crazy friend. "Do you really have to say that out loud?" I mince toward my office, and Kristy follows.

"So, tell me. What are we doing for your birthday?" She flops onto a chair as I place my backpack on the table and check the water level on my bowstring hemp plant.

"What we've done all the previous years. Takeout and a movie." I perch next to her.

"Rosie, this year is different. Don't you see this?" She raises her hand, showing me her engagement ring and wedding band, and then grabs my hand. "And this?"

The elegant diamond ring with a rose flower that Zander placed on my finger six months back twinkles. It still feels like a dream. I twist and pull it off and read the inscription.

U have me. I have U. Forever.

These seven words have deep meaning for me. For the first time in my life, I have someone, and someone wants to have me. When you live with no family and no identity for as long as I have, it's only natural to believe that no one wants you. But Zander loves me so much that he gave me a ring with this inscription.

A ring with a pink rose and white diamonds around it.

Him buying it tells me everything I need to know about the depth of his love for me.

"Have you guys picked a date?" Kristy's voice breaks my musings.

My stomach roils, and my palms suddenly get ice cold, as they do every time someone asks me this question.

"We…want to wait." I hate lying to my best friend, but Zander did say there's no rush, and I'm counting on it.

38

ZANDER

"So, what do you think?" Zach cocks his head toward the paper he slid to me across the kitchen counter a few minutes ago. It's the list of potential locations for our upcoming third office.

I give another glance to the ten-line document before opening the bag of chocolate chips and throwing two handfuls into the pancake batter.

After wolfing down two full bowls of risotto, Zach declared that this dinner in my apartment, which he and Zane, invited themselves to, is incomplete without my unbeatable chocolate chip pancakes.

Yeah, Zach will say anything for food. And also, he doesn't care that I'm practically cooking a second meal this evening. I have full faith in his eating abilities and know he'll ask me to pack him a to-go container for his breakfast tomorrow.

"What's th-there to th-think about? It's Cherr-rywood," Zane says when I don't reply immediately.

"I thought you'd already be packing your bags and calling real estate agents." Zach steals some of the chocolate from the batter and then licks the mixing spoon before throwing it into the kitchen sink.

How he stays fit after eating sugar like a ten-year-old is still a mystery to me.

I place the skillet over the stove and turn on the heat. Then I throw a big dollop of butter onto the hot iron because my brother is not only a sugar addict but a grease fiend too.

I pour in the pancake batter, and Zach shoulder-bumps me.

"Why aren't you excited?"

Fuck. They won't drop it.

"Because moving to Cherrywood is a big deal. I need to talk to Rose."

"Then t-talk, what's-s the problem?"

"She might say no," I grunt before spreading the batter into a round shape, or I try to do so. This conversation feels like a grand test to my otherwise therapeutic cooking abilities.

"Why would she say no to the chance of living with you? You guys are engaged."

"Because we've been fucking engaged for six months, with no sign of a wedding date in the future." I throw the burnt pancake into the trash before turning to Zach. The black silicone spatula in my hand shakes between us.

He takes a step back.

"She needs t-time, Zander." Zane presses lightly on my shoulder, making me aware of my tensed muscles.

I switch off the flame and put a lid over the smoking pan before releasing a deep breath. I look away from the concerned gaze of my younger brothers.

"I thought six months would be enough time for her to fully believe in me and my love."

My stomach tightens, hating the vulnerability I feel. After my horrific childhood, I pledged that I wouldn't let myself feel vulnerable ever again. But since Rose came along, memories of my mother and all the nightmares my brothers and I suffered have been more and more recurring.

"You gotta ask her, Zander. How the heck will you know if she's ready or not?" Zach turns on the stove, placing the spatula back in my hand. "Just propose to her again with some flowers and maybe another piece of jewelry. I'm sure she's just waiting for you to ask again, bro." He grabs my shoulders and tries to turn me toward the stove. "Now make me some pancakes."

"How are you always hungry?" His actions distract me and pull my attention away from Rose.

"I work very hard." That bastard doesn't even smile as he blurts the stupid excuse.

Zane snickers. "Zach's r-right, you sh-should talk to her."

I nod, even though a nervous energy still courses through my body.

"Yeah, I'm driving to Cherrywood this weekend. I'll ask her then."

After my driver, Greg, parks the car, I saunter to the private elevator, which takes me to the top floor of my company building.

As I step out of the elevator, my executive assistant, Kelly, rushes to get up from her seat and wish me a good morning. I give her a smile and head into my office.

I power on my laptop and type in the name I've dreaded all my life but is slowly becoming the biggest comfort. The calendar app allows me to check if Rose is busy in a meeting. My staff, who use this app to book meetings, doesn't know their CEO has found an alternate usage in stalking his fiancée.

There's a knock on my door, and then Kelly pokes her head in. "May I come in, Mr. Teager?"

"Yeah." I minimize the window.

She places a cup of steaming coffee on my table. The warm liquid reminds me of my first meeting with Rose at the café. Her reaction to my coffee habits was one of the things that attracted me to her instantly.

"You have an eight-thirty meeting with the board, then a breakfast meeting at nine with your brothers." She swipes the screen of her tablet and then asks, "I also need to schedule your international business trip to Japan."

I relax back in my chair. "What are the client's preferred dates?"

"I don't have them, Mr. Teager. I asked if we could propose some tentative dates, and they could pick the most suitable one."

"Why? We usually do it the other way around." I look at the young woman in confusion.

"I thought… I mean…" Kelly shifts on her feet. Her nervousness reminds me of my girl, like every other thing these days.

"What is it?"

"I wasn't sure if there were any specific months or weeks you wouldn't want to be out of the country."

"I don't get it, Kelly."

"The wedding. I assume it'll be soon?" she stammers like she's trying to find the right words. "I mean, in the coming months?"

When I don't confirm or deny, Kelly says, "I'll ask the client's preferred dates, Mr. Teager."

She leaves, but this entire conversation has my stomach in knots.

My brothers' confidence, my assistant's assumption… It seems everyone in the world except my fiancée is excitedly waiting for the wedding. I maximize the calendar app and see that Rose is free for the next thirty minutes. I'll ask her outright why she isn't setting a date.

She asked for time, and I gave her time. Six fucking months' worth.

In the early days, whenever I broached the subject of our engagement, she froze. She fucking froze like she does whenever her panic attacks threaten to surface. Or whenever she's asked a question in the middle of a presentation. Or whenever she has to choose between two things she doesn't like.

I thought I was a definitive—a sure thing—but her reactions give life to my own insecurities.

Is she second-guessing her decision?

Is she waiting for someone else?

As these insane, nonsensical questions run through my mind, my gaze lands on the red cube she gifted me for my birthday. She traveled to St. Peppers and surprised me exactly at midnight. I play the MP3 file she played for me that day.

"I love you, Zander. Yours and only yours, Rose."

Her soft, breathy voice gives me chills.

My hand curls around the resin cube, and the titanium sound wave shines as her words ring out repeatedly.

She's mine. Only mine.

I close my eyes, the image of her face after I proposed to her forming in my mind. And then she thanked me for wanting her, for loving her.

I run my palms over my face, feeling like a moron.

How can I even think of her hurting me?

I click the call button next to her name on my computer, and she picks up immediately.

"Zander, you're late." Her beautiful face fills my computer screen. She's dressed in another of her red-and-black checkered shirts, buttoned all the way up to her neck.

I bite back a smile. "I didn't know we had a meeting."

"We don't. But you usually call me at eight ten after your assistant has given you a rundown of your morning. I've been waiting for the past ten minutes." She fixes her glasses over her knitted brows and squinted blue eyes.

She is going nowhere.

"Actually, Kelly took longer than usual. She is making travel plans for my Japan trip. She wanted to know if there are any dates I can't travel."

"Are there?" She's completely unaware of my misery.

"You tell me," I probe.

Her eyebrows furrow as she considers. "I don't think so. Do you?"

"No." I release a deep sigh. "How is Cherrywood?" I change the direction of our discussion because the current one is giving me a headache, and I'm not ready to approach this topic just yet.

"Cherrywood is waiting for you." Rose smiles, and once again, with one upward curl of her lip, she fills some of the cracks in my heart.

"I'm waiting too, couch girl."

39

ROSE

I open the drawer of my nightstand, and hidden under my USB sticks, blue sticky-note pad, and purple sleeping mask is my metal pill box. The small gold tin with pink and blue hand-painted roses and "Happy Pills" written on top was given to me by my therapist. When she placed it in my hands, I thought the writing was some kind of joke I didn't get, like many others she's made. But now this box has become a reminder that it's been over three years since I've last taken one of these green SSRIs, or antidepressant pills.

Every year on my birthday, I pull it out and remind myself how far I've come. But today, this moment feels less powerful. Maybe because I have something more potent to remind me of my journey.

A beautiful ring on my finger and the person who put it there.

My hand flattens on the small pill box, and there's a clink when the band of my ring touches the metal box. I graze my right hand over my left, feeling the diamonds digging into my skin.

My bedroom door flings open, and I quickly hide the box

under my pillow. Kristy prances in, holding a tray with three coffee mugs and cupcakes, each with a different-colored candle on top. She's followed by Clementine, who places a Happy Birthday headband over my head.

"What's going on?" I squeal before fixing my glasses.

"Birthday weekend, what else?" Kristy says as they both settle onto my bed.

"My birthday is tomorrow." I'm about to pick up a cupcake and remove the candle when Clementine shakes her head. She lights the candles, and only after I've blown them all does she allow me to pick one up. But my irritation soon dies. After all, the cupcakes are from Hawthorne Bakery, which is owned by Clem's grandmother and is a treasure in Cherrywood.

"We know that handsome hunk of yours will kidnap you tomorrow, so we are celebrating today." Clem always has crazy, though aptly fitting, nicknames for Zander.

The soft blueberry cupcake melts in my mouth and reminds me of Zander's amazing baking skills. These days, everything reminds me of him. "What's the plan?" I ask.

"We're going to hit the mall, followed by a lavish lunch at Giovanni's. Then we'll head to the spa, and our last stop will be the dance club." Clem even shimmies up and down, showing off her dance moves despite there not being any music.

I forget to chew, hearing her describe all the things which are *so* not me. I tug on the cuff of my shirt as my chest rises and falls in panic at imagining myself in a crowded mall or dance club.

"Hey, Rosie, relax." Kristy nudges Clem's feet. "You know Clem. She's kidding. We'll hang here and then order takeout from Giovanni's. Maybe watch some chick flick."

I nod. Anything is better than the mall-spa-club trio.

Clementine cocks her head at me while licking the white

frosting from her cupcake. "Did you see how fast this superhero junkie agreed to the chick flick?"

CLEMENTINE LEANS BACK on the couch. "God, I'm gonna miss Giovanni's when I finally get out of this stupid town."

"Why do you want to leave so bad?" I fold the empty pizza box as we sit on our living room vintage rug after lunch.

Cherrywood is one of those charming, postcard-perfect towns that instantly make you fall in love with it. In addition, all of her family is nearby.

"You have to ask? I've never been out of this town. Like *never*. If not for my brother and my gram, Mom would have homeschooled me." Her hands clench into fists, as they do every time she talks about her mother. Awful is a strong word, but there is no better adjective to describe the relationship between Clementine and her mother.

"It's not that fun, and aren't you living independently since you moved here?" I remind her.

"Yes. In a way, I am. But Mom's security is still outside twenty-four seven, monitoring me and anyone else who enters and leaves the house."

"Wh-what?" The iced tea glass in my hand suddenly feels ten times heavier, and my limbs freeze at the revelation.

Someone's watching me.

Twenty-four seven.

"It's no big deal, Rose." Kristy's voice is faint as she grabs my hands from mercilessly pulling on the cuff of my shirt. "They're all good people, and they just sit at the diner across the street."

When my tremors don't subside, she holds my face between her soft hands and forces me to look at her.

"Breathe." Her gaze is calm and patient as she waits for me to start my three-step breathing.

After a few seconds, I close my eyes and take deep breaths, filling my stomach, my lungs, and my throat, holding the air and then letting it all out.

Kristy's hands gradually move from my face to my shoulders. She presses lightly over my knotted muscles. "All's fine, Rose." Her words slowly bring me back.

"How do…you know about this?" I meet her gaze, but before Kristy can reply, Clementine jumps the gun.

"You have nothing to worry about, Rosie. Tony has been my head of security since I was seven."

"Y-you have a head of…what?" I don't wait for her to reply. "Head of security…who is watching you…me…our house?" My throat dries again, and the words barely come out.

My gaze shifts to Kristy, who gives Clem the stink eye.

"You know, the Hawthorne family is kind of a big name in Cherrywood. Security is part of the deal," Clementine murmurs.

"Why would…anyone hurt you?"

"I don't think anyone will, but having security gives my mother an opportunity to show that we're important people." Clementine's words provide no calm to my panic.

"Rosie, they will not enter the house unless it's an emergency," Kristy tries to reassure me. "They're also advised to keep a safe distance from you, and they're trained to be covert. See, you weren't even aware of them till now. I talked to Tony personally after Oscar told me they'd be sitting guard outside." Her concerned gaze meets mine.

It's on the tip of my tongue to ask why she didn't tell me all of this sooner, but I guess it's because she expected my freak-out. Given how I'm reacting now, she wasn't wrong.

I press my fingertips into my forehead, not liking this feeling of helplessness or being left out of something important.

"Are you feeling better?" Kristy asks softly. "I'm sorry for not telling you."

I nod. I know she means well.

I take another deep breath, my mind wandering to the men sitting outside, before I glance at my pillow and the pill box hidden underneath.

"Do you still want to go to the lake?" Clementine's hesitant voice breaks through my train of thought.

My gaze returns to the pillow before I reply. "I'll get ready."

AFTER SPENDING the rest of the day with Kristy and Clementine, I drive alone to my house. Kristy went back to her home, and Clementine's driver picked her up for dinner at her mother's estate.

I get out of my car, and my gaze drifts in the direction of the diner across the street. My car keys fall to the ground with a jiggle, and it takes me longer than usual to grab them with my shaky hands.

Just the thought that someone is watching me day and night sends a chill down my spine, and I shiver despite the balmy evening. I shake my head, trying to get rid of the dreadful memories threatening to surface. My excitement for tomorrow and seeing Zander has subsided, and I'm looking forward to spending the remainder of the evening locked inside my room, working on the new piece of code. I hope it'll distract my mind from the men sitting on watch outside my house.

I turn the key to the main door and take a step back instead of walking in. The living room lights are turned off, and the whole place is lit with candles. My natural reaction is to turn around and run back to my car. But before I can do that, I hear a familiar voice.

"Hello, dear fiancée. Planning to leave me already?"

With a burning candle in his hands, Zander emerges from the dark and walks in my direction. Placing the candleholder on the corner table, he stands before me.

"You scared me," I whisper. I can't believe he's here already. Wasn't he supposed to arrive tomorrow?

"I am sorry about that," he purrs, pulling me into his arms. His left dimple is on display, and so is his captivating smile. A smile that girls would die to have directed at them. A smile that, six months ago, was plastered on magazines alongside the words "sexiest bachelor."

I sometimes can't believe he chose me when he could be with anyone.

"You're here." I rub my hands on his fine-fitting suit, which does nothing to hide his muscular body.

"Yes, I am." He hugs me tight, and I fit well under his chin as his over-six-feet frame towers over my five feet three inches.

"How? Why didn't you tell me?" I whisper against his chest.

He smells of the same woodsy vanilla scent, and it reminds me of our first meeting in the conference room.

"I wanted to surprise my fiancée."

"You love that word." I smile as I always do when he uses it.

"I love *you*." He pulls back and tilts my face up with his finger under my chin. "Let me look at you. I've missed you, Rose."

"I missed you too." My voice gets wobbly. The wild revelations from earlier already have me on edge, and now seeing Zander in my living room…it's all too much for my tiny heart. With all the emotions bursting inside me, my eyes well with tears. "So bad."

He places a kiss on my forehead before wiping the stray tear that rolls down my cheek, even though I tried to hold it back. "It's been six months since I put this ring on your finger," he says. When he twists my ring, I wonder if the reality of being engaged is sometimes as mind-boggling for him as it is for me.

I've never felt this connection to anyone. I've never belonged to anyone, and if it were possible, I'd never be apart from him for a second. I know it almost sounds creepy, but that's how I feel.

My hands go around his neck when he pulls me closer, and then my lips are captured by his. He kisses me, soft and slow. Though I've got no one to compare it to, as Zander is my first boyfriend, I know he gives the best kisses. He never rushes but takes his time, like he's slowly exploring my lips. And then he pushes his tongue into my mouth and rolls it with mine, making me crazy.

It took me so long to realize that this feeling, which is a bit ticklish and a bit shaky and builds into a sensation that goes straight to my stomach and further down, is not fever but passion.

Without breaking our kiss, he moves us to the couch, then pulls me onto his lap. His hand wanders to my waist. I'm wearing my blue flannel shirt, which is, as usual, a size too big.

"Zander," I whisper when his lips leave mine.

He tries to nuzzle my neck, but I guess my buttoned-up shirt isn't to his liking. He opens two of the buttons, starting from the collar. He looks into my eyes, passion and emotion shining from his. My previous panic has left the building.

"I'm so happy to see you. Especially today," I tell him. He's become my talisman, my happy pill, which has all the power to make me feel safe.

"I got a call from your distressed friend." Zander's fingers run back and forth over my neck, his featherlight touch causing my insides to tremble as his gaze never leaves my face.

"And you came?"

"I told you, no one can keep me away from my girl."

"I love being your girl." My hand rests over his five o'clock shadow. My ring twinkles, reflecting the lights of the candles burning in the room.

"Me too, couch girl. You don't know how much."

40

ROSE

I look around my living room and notice for the first time that Zander has turned it into a cozy, romantic place I never could have imagined. He's lit candles on every surface, and I can count at least three bouquets of pink flowers.

He's the kind of boyfriend plucked out of every girl's favorite romance novel.

I'm still taking in my surroundings when he lifts me into his arms.

"Zander!" A squeal escapes me, and I hug him koala-style, which is kind of *our* style now. My hands go around his neck, my head resting on his shoulder while his hands are under my behind. He squeezes me and then heads confidently toward my bedroom.

When he places me down, I gasp at the sight of pink flower petals scattered on the floor, making a path from the door to my bed. The string lights hanging on the wall above my bed are on, illuminating the photographs clipped on them. Six months back, there were only two pictures of Kristy and me, but now the entire wall is filled with photographs of Zander and me that were taken on our numerous dates, some in Cherrywood and some in St. Peppers.

"Go in, babe." With his hand on my back, he gives me a gentle push, but I'm rooted to the spot. "It's all for you."

"I can't," I whisper.

"Why not?"

Our hushed voices, the lights, the flowers, the overall ambience—they all amplify the sensation of our surroundings.

"I'll ruin it and… I want to keep it like this for…" I want to say forever, but that would be stupid, so I add, "A long time." My voice breaks, and all the bottled feelings of the past few months strike me hard.

I've missed him so much. Every second.

"We can do it every day or as frequently as you like, couch girl." He turns me around to face him and squeezes my waist.

"We can't. You're not here every day." I know I sound childish, but these feelings are all foreign to me, and I don't know how to react.

Zander holds my face between his hands. He smiles, and the corners of his eyes crinkle. With his thumbs, he wipes my tears and then gently kisses my lips.

"Your lips are so soft," he says in a wistful tone. "They always are whenever you cry." He runs his thumb back and forth over my bottom lip. "I'm addicted to them."

"I can cry whenever you like," I state sincerely, and I know I'd do that, just for him.

"I would rather you not." He chuckles before hugging me tight.

When I turn my face toward my bed, I notice a wine bucket placed over my nightstand.

Crab.

Great, Rose! Your fiancé planned an amazing surprise, and you turned it into a sob party.

"I'm sorry for ruining the surprise." I try to pull away

from him, but he holds me captive, halting my movement and urging me to look at his handsome face.

"You ruined nothing. You don't know what it does to me, seeing you aching for me just as I do for you, couch girl. You crying for me and missing me like this makes me feel so loved and…cherished."

I rise on my toes and kiss his lips, pulling him down with my hands around his neck. "And I do. I love you so much."

Not wanting to further ruin his surprise with my sappy mood, I grab his hand, and we both make the brief journey from my door to bed, where more pink and red flower petals are scattered, which I now see are roses.

I turn to him, and his gaze is riveted on me.

To know this man would go to such lengths to make one evening special for me is beyond comprehension.

How did I get so fortunate?

His mere presence makes me believe that I was alone for so long because someone as caring and loving as Zander was meant to enter my life and take away all those years of pain.

"How did you do all this?" I point to the flowers.

I know Zander hasn't forgiven his mother. He hates anything that relates to her, her name, and the flower, as it stirs painful memories for him.

Do I blame him? Hell fishing no!

My cold blood starts to simmer, my own demons crawling from the dark, hating the people who didn't protect us.

"Hey, where did you go?" Zander's hands run up and down my arms, making me realize how tense my body is.

"I don't want you to remember any nightmares while doing anything for me."

"I didn't. I could bear thousands of crappy memories to see one smile on your face, but I only focused on your fondness for soft, pink things." Zander smiles, giving me his dimple that he knows I love so much.

He fell in love with me, a woman who not only holds his mother's name but also has her own positive association with the flower, which is, to say the least, ironic.

Zander picks the red wine from the wine bucket, his cherry-red tie wrapping around the dark-green merlot bottle.

The corners of my mouth quirk up at the reminder of our awkward dating days. It was the tie he wore when I met him for the first time. It was the tie he wore when he declared to a room full of Elixir Inc.'s staff that I was his girlfriend.

"You are the best," I tell him. "You remember everything. Every detail."

"I try. After all, I have to keep up with your photographic memory." He hands me a glass of wine before pouring a second for himself. "Thank you, Rose, for agreeing to be mine." He clinks his glass against mine.

"Thank you so much for wanting me."

41

ZANDER

I stare at my beautiful girl, her eyes closed as she lies next to me. Her soft breathing rhythmically causes her chest to rise and fall, and she has a hand tucked under her face. Covered in her baby-blue comforter, which I pulled over her once she fell asleep in my arms, she looks like an angel fallen from heaven and too good for this world.

My path has crossed with several attractive women, but no one has ever had this effect on me. One look at her gorgeous face and my body fucking revs up like a teenager's. She has a hypnotizing power over my mind and body, and the craziest thing is, she has no clue.

I run my fingers through her soft hair and tug on the flower petal hidden in the silky strands. Bringing it close to my face, I stare at the crimson leaf and wait for the familiar darkness to grip me.

I'm back in the dark, wet, and cold night. My back, legs, and arms are marked with bruises, my tears mixing with the rain. The pain in my limbs deepens, and my eyes blur as the rain falls harder.

Something red floats from somewhere, fluttering in the wind before me. I raise my aching hands and hold it between my fingers. The rose petal feels weird, and then everything changes. I'm no longer the weak boy, but I'm Zander Teager. I look down to the flower trapped in my fist. A gentle hand lies over mine, opening my grip, and there it is. The rose-shaped diamond I'm giving to the love of my life. I look up to the woman holding my hand, my loving Rose.

Something brushes against my lips, forcing me to open my eyes, and I come face-to-face with Rose. For a second, my groggy brain thinks this is part of my dream, but then I notice the pink walls behind her, the faint morning light filtering through the silk curtains.

Her eyes are closed as she kisses me softly, caressing my lips with hers. I stay motionless, doing nothing but basking in her love. When she opens her eyes, we stare at each other. Her lips are mere inches from mine. She tries to pull away, but I flip her under me. Her eyes widen in surprise.

"Happy birthday, beautiful. I like waking up beside you."

"Thank you. Me too," she says, running her hands over my face, grazing my stubble.

"You were kissing me." My voice comes out hoarse.

"I always do before leaving the bed." Her cheeks turn pink at the admission.

"I didn't know that." I nuzzle her neck, plastering wet kisses on her skin. Then I wait for her to squirm and moan. It'll take only two seconds. One, two…

"Zander."

My heart bursts with fucking joy watching how responsive she is. I know it's sickening to say, but I dig the fact that I was her first kiss, her first lover, her first orgasm, and all other future firsts.

With my face buried in her neck, my weight adjusted on my arms, I move one of my hands to her breast.

"So soft." I gently bite her neck, making sure I don't leave a mark. I'm not afraid of anyone seeing it, as my girl is usually clad in buttoned-up flannel shirts, but she has enough marks for a lifetime from her past.

She coos as I pinch her hard nipple through her thin cotton T-shirt.

"Stop squirming," I chastise as she moves her legs up and down in a futile attempt to get some relief.

"Please." She tries to free herself from my hold.

"What, baby?" I move from one nipple, which is now a stiff peak, to the other.

"Just…please."

"Say it and I'll give it to you." I look her in the eye. I know she's still shy with sex-talk, but God, what I wouldn't give to hear something dirty from her sweet-ass mouth.

"Please," she begs me.

"Say it, couch girl, and I'll do whatever you want."

I give her a long lick from the hollow of her neck to her chin, causing her to tremble in my arms.

Jesus. She looks so fucking hot when she peels my hand from her chest and places it over her sex, rubbing my fingers once over her cotton shorts.

"I'd love to hear from your sexy lips that you want me to rub your pussy and get you off."

Her breath hitches at my brazen words and then goes away as I rub her briskly.

She's like a wet dream come true when she twists in my arms, moaning and cooing.

"What an addict you have become, Rose." I gaze at her, feigning shock.

Hearing my words, her eyes open wide and her face and neck redden with embarrassment.

I smile and lift her chin up. "Sweetheart, I like you addicted. It fucking turns me on to see you like this." To prove my liking, I thrust into her stomach.

Her bright blue eyes sparkle, and then that shy smile is back. My nerdy siren.

Kissing her once more, I move lower, my lips trailing down her body.

"Where are you going?"

Before her sentence is complete, I'm tugging down her shorts. "Not far."

We lie on the bed, entangled in each other's arms, and I know I cannot dawdle any longer.

"Rose." I rub small circles over her arms.

"Hmm?" she hums in a drowsy voice.

"I need to talk to you about something. Something important."

She straightens up before turning around to face me. "Important good or important bad?"

"Important good, I hope." I try to hold on to a light smile at her expected question, but it's short-lived. My mouth dries, worried about her response to the news I'm about to dump on her. "You know Kristy and Zach were scouting a location for our third office."

She nods, her face emotionless and her hands already drifting toward the cuffs of her cotton tee.

"They've found a place. It's perfect. Until the office is up and running, I'll be spending most of my time there."

"And this is good news, how?" Her shoulders stiffen, and she crosses her arms, protecting herself from the looming blow. Her wacky brain is expecting the worst, as always.

"To decide that, you'll have to see the location." I grab my iPad from the nightstand and open the maps app. I point my finger after I've zoomed in on said location.

"But that's in…" Her gaze shifts from the screen to me.

"Cherrywood," I confirm.

"How?" Her crumbling face turns up, and she beams at me.

Thank heavens.

"Kristy found the best deal in Cherrywood. There was no reason for me to turn it down."

"So, you'll be staying in Cherrywood for some time?"

"That's the plan, baby." I caress her face, trying to distract her from thinking too hard. But my super smart fiancée can't be easily distracted.

"But what about your apartment in St. Peppers?"

"I haven't thought about it. Maybe I'll rent it out or… maybe sell it." I shrug as if it's not a big deal. And maybe it's not to some, but to Rose, it's a huge deal.

"Sell it?" She gasps and her hands shake as she scuttles a few inches away from me.

My enthusiasm plunges low at her reaction. "Yes. Maybe I'll…buy something here," I murmur, not wavering my gaze from her face for a second.

"Zander," she whispers. Her hand slowly flattens over the cuff of her shirt.

Fuck. This isn't what I wanted to do on her birthday. I haven't even had the chance to make her Sunday breakfast of granola and strawberry-blueberry-peach fruit mix.

"Couch girl, breathe." I slowly place one knee forward, trying to get close to her but also making sure she isn't startled. "Rose." I cup her face in my hands and mentally kick myself. I know, even though Rose has agreed to my proposal, that she isn't ready for the next step.

But why the fuck not?

I'm not having any second thoughts. Is she? I don't think so. I hate my fucking head for even considering it. She thanks me repeatedly for wanting her, for fuck's sake. If it were up to me, I'd drag her to the courthouse now and get that marriage license. I want to always keep her with me and never let her go.

Super cool, Zander. Maybe your impatience is scaring her away.

My hands clutching the bedsheets loosen their grip when I glance up. Her eyes are shut tight, but she breathes deeply through her nose. Her shoulders rise and fall as she tries to hold her breath. Being a witness of this action several times before, I know she's thinking of her happy moment, which is now our engagement day.

"Rose," I urge, and she opens her worried eyes.

"I haven't made a decision, couch girl. I just thought, if you would like, we could look at some properties…to stay at together. But you don't have to say yes. As I said, it's just a thought." When she thankfully doesn't flinch at my words, I continue. "I'd really like to come home to you in the evenings and spend my weekends with you, lazing on a couch with no hurry of being anywhere else."

"Zander!" My name falls from her lips as if she's scared to say anything more. Looking at her response, as always, I question our decision.

Did she accept my proposal in haste?

Did she need more time?

Why isn't she jumping up and down in excitement at the thought of us living together?

I pull her close to my chest. Her anxiety has made me anxious.

"Baby, like I said, it's just a thought. We can think about it, even do a trial run, and you always have the option to say no. You know that, right?"

She nods hesitantly against my chest.

I kiss her forehead and whisper, "Rose, the things you do to me are beyond words. If I could, I'd never let you go, even for a minute. But I also don't want to bulldoze you into doing something you're not comfortable with."

"You don't bulldoze me, Zander. You could never bulldoze me." She looks up from my chest, and I notice her misty eyes. "But what if…I fail to fulfill your expectations."

"There are no expectations, babe. When I met you, I had

no clue what was missing in my life. I just want you and your love. That's all I need."

Every time I think Rose's insecurities are subsiding, something like this happens. But I'll spend my lifetime reassuring her of my love.

She stays huddled in my arms, silent, and I worry. Despite everyone's efforts to bring Rose and me together, maybe her doubts about herself will win and we'll still be living miles apart.

But then she says, "This doesn't change anything, right? We'll not start looking at wedding dates or anything?"

"No, sweetheart. It's just a proposition from your fiancé to move in together." I hold my breath.

"I'd love to see some houses with you."

42

ROSE

As the elevator takes me to the floor of my office at the R&D department of Elixir Inc., my mind drifts back to yesterday. Zander and I spent the day surfing the internet for properties. I didn't know there were so many options—condo, penthouse, studio, service apartment, cottage, duplex, villa, and the list goes on. You say a letter and there's a house style beginning with it.

I grew up in Kindred Hearts Orphanage and later moved to the university dorm. When Kristy and I took jobs in Cherrywood, we found an ad from Mr. Hart in the supermarket. He was searching for tenants for the bottom unit of his two-story house, and I'm still living there. I'm so glad I didn't have more options back then because I'd be completely lost, just like I am now.

After dumping my laptop bag in my office, I leave to look for Kristy.

"Kristy." I enter her office, only to find her pressed at some weird angle on a wall holding company branding pics while Oscar ravishes her lips.

Instead of the enticing scene, my eyes rivet on a picture where Zander is receiving some award. Dressed in a classic business suit, he's just making his way down a ramp. And to think, this man wants to live with me. Why?

"Sorry, Rose," Oscar says mischievously as he pulls away from Kristy.

Shouldn't *I* be sorry for interrupting them?

Me walking in on them is becoming more and more frequent. Maybe I should knock now that they're regularly making out at the office.

"I'll see you later, wife." He winks at Kristy and exits after wishing me a good morning.

"Rosie, Rosie." Kristy hugs me excitedly. "I'm so happy."

I giggle at her excitement. As always, her presence calms me. "What's happening?"

"Zander is moving here. Isn't that enough good news?" She looks at me suspiciously. "You're not excited?"

"I am," I whisper and try to calm my quaking nerves.

But I guess I'm failing badly, as she asks, "But?"

How do you explain to someone that you're nervous about your beautiful and beyond-caring fiancé wanting to move in with you? Instead of imagining how wonderful it'll be, my crazy brain is focused on all that could go wrong.

"I…don't know. It's all going…too fast." I flop down onto a chair in order to avoid her prying gaze.

"What do you mean?" But she sits across from me, not letting it go.

I'm forced to give voice to my concerns.

"We've only been engaged for a few months, and we're already talking about moving in. It'll not be long before the discussions of marriage start. And then—"

"You don't want to marry Zander?" Kristy cuts in, looking at me incredulously.

"I do. Why wouldn't I? I love him. I love him so much." I hate my wobbly voice.

What's wrong with me? Why can't I just be happy?

"Rosie, what's the matter?" Grabbing my hands, Kristy

presses on them lightly. She knows light touches calm me. I'm so lucky to have a friend like her in my life. But there are hidden places in my mind where even I'm not allowed to enter. Some questions are better left unanswered.

I shake my head, trying to end this discussion. "Nothing. I'm just nervous. You know...how I get in such situations."

It's true—people make me nervous. I've no trouble solving a difficult problem or working on the most complicated piece of code, but it's people that get me all wound up. People are unpredictable, and I don't do well with surprises.

She nods and leads me out of her office. "Let's get rid of this sappy mood with a latte macchiato from Steamy Beans."

We quickly make our way to the café overlooking our office building. When we enter, I take a seat by the window, and soon, Kristy brings over a tray with two coffees and a piece of pecan pie.

"Zander is at the new office site?" she asks, taking a sip of her coffee.

I nod, slipping a piece of the heavenly pie into my mouth. Sweet sugar. It's really delicious.

"What did you guys do yesterday?"

"We were looking for houses," I say, adding sugar into my coffee.

"God, you guys are moving in together," she shrieks, and the sugar sachet falls from my hand into the hot coffee cup.

Using a spoon, I drag the wet paper out. "What's up with you today? You're excited about everything."

"I got married. You got engaged. You're moving in with your fiancé, who happens to be the CEO of our company. Is all this not enough to be excited about?"

When she says it like that...

"What's bothering you?"

I hang my head in resignation. "I don't know what house I like. Condo, house with a porch, without a porch, garden, no garden... I just don't know. It's all overwhelming." Even thinking about all those pictures right now clouds my brain.

She leans closer to me. "You can always talk to him, Rosie. That man worships the ground you walk on. Why are you so nervous? Just think about the house you see yourself living in with Zander. Imagine your dream house."

Dream house. Six months back, I never considered having a house of my own, let alone a dream house.

But how would it be if I had one? I close my eyes, imagining it. Something in Cherrywood, for sure. No other place has felt more like home than this town.

"Why aren't you ready to leave?" Zander walks into my office.

I look up from my PC, and my stomach does cartwheels at his slightly disheveled state. The top two buttons of his shirt are undone, and his tie rests loose around his neck. He takes off his jacket and drapes it over one of the chairs.

Goose bumps appear on my skin when he rolls up his sleeves, giving me a good view of those sinewy forearms. My breathing accelerates as my eyes follow his every movement until he stands still.

I look up to find him smiling.

Crab. His heated gaze brings those no-longer-foreign storms of flutters back to my stomach.

When he doesn't say a word or move but continues to stare at me, I squeak, "What?"

This man! How does he make me all mushy?

He bites his lower lip, barely hiding his breathtaking smile. "You can check me out as long as you like, couch girl."

"I wasn't…checking you out." My voice shivers when he bends until we're at eye level.

He kisses me briefly on my cheek before moving his head

further down to my neck. My collared shirt gives him only partial access.

Smelling deeply, he asks in a husky voice, "What is it today?"

I know he's asking about my body wash. For some inexplicable reason, Zander finds all my quirks adorable.

"Summer kiss," I whisper.

He takes one more whiff before pulling back, but not far. "Close your eyes, Rose."

I'm still getting used to hearing my name on his lips.

"Why?" I ask, but I do as he says.

Before my eyelids drop completely, he breathes over my lips. "I'm gonna give you a Zander kiss."

With that, he places his lips over mine. His tongue licks my lips, seeking permission, and I let him in as I always do.

We remain glued to each other until I hear sounds of doors opening and closing and people chatting from afar. I pull back, but Zander's hold on my face tightens, not letting me move.

"Zander, there are still people in the office." How I managed to form a sentence in my half-drowsy state is a surprise.

"I don't give a fuck." He leans in, but when we hear footsteps just outside my door, he pulls back with a suppressed groan.

"Zander, I was hoping to find you here." Kristy walks into my office, followed by Oscar. She gives me a knowing smile, and I narrow my eyes, asking her to shut up.

"How's the site coming?" Kristy asks before she sits on a chair and pulls Oscar onto the one next to her.

I have a hard time focusing on their conversation, and my gaze often lingers on Zander, distracting me from everything else. At this moment, in this office, he exudes a confidence, a power. While yesterday, in my home, he was my fiancé, vulnerable and totally in love with me.

I try to look past my doubts and fears. Him being here means I'm no longer alone. Since Kristy's wedding, my dinners are mostly takeout, which I eat at my desk. I leave work later than usual because I don't like going back to an empty house and eating alone. Clementine has some weird arrangement with her family where she has to be at Hawthorne Mansion every night.

Oh, how much I've hated it for the past month. After talking to Zander each night on the phone, I missed him more and more. But now, he's here. We don't have to pine for intimacy and curse the hundred miles between us.

Why the heck didn't I think about it sooner?

I jump in my seat when Kristy taps my Bluetooth mouse.

"What?" I try to hide my embarrassment when Zander chuckles and Oscar smiles at me.

"Nothing. We're off. You can gawk at your man all you want." She gets up from the chair and hangs her bag over her shoulder.

"I'm not gawking at anyone." I try to look anywhere but at the three faces staring back at me.

"If you say so." Thankfully, Kristy bounces out of my office with Oscar before embarrassing me further.

"You know, you can gawk at me all you want." Zander crosses his arms over his chest, tilting his head to the side like he's posing for a photograph.

"I said I wasn't."

Biting his lip, he takes a step forward, but his cell phone rings, stopping him. He takes it out from the inner pocket of his jacket.

"Fuck. It's a reminder for our dinner reservation at Giovanni's. You make me forget everything, couch girl."

"Wait. I've got something to show you." I quickly open the file and turn my PC monitor toward him.

He stares at the numerous images sprawled on the screen. "Is this for our new place?"

I nod. "I'm making our dream house."

"I don't understand." His gaze jumps rapidly from one picture to another before it glides my way. "You were so confused yesterday. What happened?"

"Um, there were too many options to choose from." I peer away as he continues to look at me in bafflement. Instead, I point to the cottage, photographed under moonlight. "I'd like a house in the woods."

"Okay." He takes a seat next to me as I show him various samples of the idea. When I minimize the photographs, he asks in surprise, "You did all this today?"

"Uh-huh. I was very busy."

"That, I can see." He leans forward, and his warm breath tickles my neck. Taking the mouse from me, he starts the slideshow. All the pics I saved to the folder titled DREAM HOUSE start to flash on my big monitor.

Zander pulls me closer to him as our gazes are glued to the screen.

If that's how my house will be, I can't wait to live in it.

"Did you spend the whole day researching this, or were you also able to get some work done?"

I push my chair back, forcing him to straighten. "Is this a question from my fiancé or my boss?" I have no clue how to act sexy, but I try to stand in a seductive pose, putting one hand on my waist. Zander's eyes follow my movements.

"I'm not your boss. Oscar is. I'm just a simple man smitten by your charms." He places a kiss on my lips and caresses my hand, still resting on my waist. "But I'm curious. How did you go from being so hesitant to…all this in less than twenty-four hours?"

Maybe it was Kristy's words about Zander's love for me. The reassurance I needed. But now I feel good about this.

I shrug. "I don't want to spend our lives in a house that we choose from some catalog. I want this to be our safe and happy place on Earth. Something we create for ourselves. I want to see the place grow and slowly fall in love with it. I want it to be...us." When he says nothing, I ask, "Does it make sense?"

"It makes perfect sense, couch girl. But is this dream home a temporary place or..." He leaves the end of his sentence hanging, as if it's nothing but wishful thinking. He keeps me in his arms, holding me close, noticing my every nuance.

How did I get so lucky to have such a patient man in my life?

"We are making our permanent dream house. But—"

"No pressure." He kisses me gently, making me tingle all over.

AFTER DINNER, we decide to go for a walk by Cherry Lake. "It's really beautiful," Zander says.

"Yes, it's like everything comes alive in spring with all the cherry blossoms painting the lake pink." I look at the row of pink trees dreamily. "I can't imagine being anywhere else."

"And now you don't have to." He puts his arms around me as we sit on some rocks by the lake. I settle closer to him until I'm sitting on his lap, my head resting under his chin. I like being surrounded by Zander, his woodsy vanilla scent keeping me safe and my anxieties away.

"Can I tell you something?" I ask and feel him nod behind me.

"I'd never given much thought to a future home. I just wanted to feel safe, and I felt it with Kristy in my current place. Slowly, I made it mine by adding my personal touches." I pull on his forearms, tightening his hold on me, and whisper, "I got nervous yesterday, first about the move and then about the house. I... I kind of worry that when we live together, you might think I'm too much."

He turns me around so fast that I almost get a head rush. I grab his jacket and look into his smoldering eyes.

"Rose, I love you for who you are. Don't you know that I'm in awe of everything about you? Your chic room, your supersmart mind, and your beautiful heart." His hand rests over my thumping chest. "I want our house to be the happiest and safest place for you." Caressing my cheeks with his fingers, he continues. "You've seen my condo in St. Peppers. It's huge and classy, but every moment I'm there, I itch to run back to you. I crave to spend my days and nights in this small town, in your pink room, in your small queen-sized bed. It's you I want. I don't care where we live."

"How did I get this lucky, Zander?" I whisper and close my eyes. I don't want to jinx my happiness. "You're all my dreams, seen and unseen, wrapped into one."

"And you are mine." He kisses me, taking away my fears and anxiety and replacing them with hopes and dreams.

Zander parked his car in front of my place thirty minutes ago, but I'm in no hurry to leave.

"Rose, are you coming in or having a sleepover with your handsome fiancé in his car?" Clementine shouts from the kitchen window.

I'm sure the entire neighborhood now knows about my handsome fiancé.

"I'll have to leave before all the neighbors are out hoping to get a glimpse of you," I say in between giggles.

He grabs my hand. "I don't like this." His rare, sulky pout is on display. "We should be spending every night together," he repeats for the hundredth time.

"I know, but I want to tell Clem about this."

"Do whatever you have to, babe, but tomorrow, I'm having you in my bed."

43

ROSE

Today I'm meeting Ashcroft Miller, aka Beast, as popularly called by the Teager men, in St. Peppers. Ashcroft adopted Zander and his brothers and raised them to be successful and independent. I already have so much respect for him, although thinking about him often reminds me of the time when I begged someone to adopt me. It was the day I learned the word adoption and thought my life was going to change forever. But nothing like that happened.

Zander is showing me around Beast's property when his brothers join us. I greet Zach and Zane with a hug. These men, who have accepted me wholeheartedly into their small family, have become so special to me in such a short time.

We all enter the beautiful European-style house. Everything from the heavy main door, the wooden staircase leading to the first floor, and the wine-colored carpets make it look like a set from some period drama. It fits the image of Beast I have in my mind.

Zander leads me to the living room. I'm about to sit on the ochre couch when someone walks in. Familiar yet foreign dark-brown eyes narrow on me, and I can't breathe.

"Roxy!" Zane leads his elder brothers as they welcome the

new woman.

They all hug her, while I'm glued to the couch. I close my eyes and focus on the memory of those brown eyes narrowing on me again and again.

I've seen them, but where? How could I forget? I never forget.

I have a photographic memory, daggit!

I only remember that those eyes spur bad memories. I wasn't able to breathe back then.

When was it? Was it in the hospital? Was she a nurse? Can she be someone from Kindred Hearts?

Why can't I remember?

"Rose. Rose. Couch girl!" My brain barely registers Zander's worried voice coming from afar.

I open my eyes to find him shaking my shoulders.

"What is it, baby?" He engulfs my trembling body in his arms, providing me with his warmth.

I can't believe I'm having a meltdown in Ashcroft's home. It's like a reality check for me, and maybe for Zander too. This is what it's like to be with me. I try to breathe, but all these thoughts are only making me nervous. I start to wheeze, and Zander hugs me tight.

"Rose. Baby, what is it?"

How can I tell him that it's nothing? It's just my sick mind.

"I… I…" My arid voice makes it hard to form words.

Zane hands me a glass of water, and I gulp quickly.

"Easy. Everything's okay." Zander continues to rub my back, his touch bringing my anxiety down. I try to refocus on my breathing. After a few minutes, my heart rate slows, and the trembling ceases.

"Are you feeling better?" Zach asks.

Everyone has a concerned expression on their face and I've no idea when *she* left. Probably when I was busy having a meltdown.

"I-I'm sorry. I didn't...mean to scare anyone." I cling to Zander, seeking more of his warmth.

"We don't scare that easy. Next time, try harder." Zach winks.

I don't want a next time, but I don't tell him that. I'm just glad they're all still here and aren't asking me to leave.

"W-what happened, R-Rose?" Zane asks in his raspy voice as he sits on the coffee table before me. "Th-there must have been a tr-rigger."

Should I tell them? But what would I even say?

"You can t-tell us." As always, it feels like Zane can read my mind. He leans slightly forward and holds my small hands in his bigger ones, squeezing them lightly.

"I've seen those brown eyes, but...I can't remember where? That's...never happened to me before."

Zander pulls me closer to his chest. "Brown eyes?"

"The woman who was here a few minutes ago." I point to the door through which she came.

"Roxanne?" Zach asks.

I nod.

"Her eyes ar-re a common sh-shade, Rose. Do you remember anyth-thing else?"

I shake my head.

"Is-s it pos-ssible you're anxious to meet Beas-st and probably w-weren't expecting anyone else?"

Zane's explanation makes sense.

I hadn't expected to meet a woman in Beast's house. When I was rehearsing this meeting in my head, there were only five of us.

And it's not news that I don't do well with surprises. Could it just be my nerves?

But what about those eyes? I know I've seen them somewhere.

Before I can think more, a tall—no, not tall, a giant—man walks in.

Zander and his brothers are tall. This man is huge. He has more than a foot over Zander's six-feet frame and is equally as broad. I now understand the nickname Beast.

"Good morning." Ashcroft's gaze meets mine, and his eyes widen for a second. Or is it just my brain tricking me again? "Rose, it's nice to finally meet you." The affectionate lilt in his voice takes me by surprise.

I get up from the couch, out of Zander's arms, to greet Ashcroft. He holds my hands before placing a chaste kiss on both my cheeks.

When we all take our seats, I stick to Zander like glue while Zane takes the other end of the couch. Beast and Zach sit across from us.

I close my eyes for a second, inhaling a deep breath and saying a silent prayer, hoping the rest of this meeting remains uneventful.

Proving that the day is still young, and my hope short-lived, Ashcroft asks, "Mind me asking about your parents?"

"I—I grew up in an orphanage for special children," I state flatly.

When he raises his eyebrow in surprise, I shift nervously in my seat.

Didn't Zander tell him about me?

"I've suffered from social anxiety disorder since a young age," I clarify, my mouth dry and my skin hot from embarrassment.

He nods, but just when I think we can move past this topic, he asks again, "So, your parents?"

I realize he's not interested in me and my experience.

"Rose didn't grow up with her birth parents like we did." Zander's arms tighten around me—as always, he's protecting me. My knight in shining armor.

I look up to see the angry glare he's giving Ashcroft.

"Yes, but you know about them."

Apparently, Ashcroft isn't going to let it go. "Someone

from an orphanage called Kindred Hearts found me when I was a baby. No one knows much about my parents." I hope this ends the discussion. I'm not prepared to go into all the gory details today.

Thankfully, my words seem to satisfy him. "I'm sorry, dear. It's just that…you remind me of someone." A sad smile pulls on his lips. "You have a rare shade of blue eyes. It's a genetic mutation. Did you know that?"

I nod. "It's a mutation of the OCA2 gene." Over the years, I've done extensive research on the gene. It's highly possible that I inherited it from one of my parents.

Ashcroft fixes his glassy, empty eyes on me. He's lost in another world, searching for something or someone in my face. I look at Zander for help, and he clears his throat loudly and suddenly, Ashcroft's trance breaks.

Without missing a beat, he springs out of his seat. "Let's have lunch. Roxanne has been cooking the whole morning. She misses these three." Ashcroft walks toward the door, and my mind once again zeroes in on the name Roxanne.

As if he can hear my heart thudding inside my chest, Zander whispers in my ear, "It's okay, couch girl. Beast likes you."

I can feel his smile as he kisses behind my ear, and I welcome the distraction he provides with his words and his kiss.

Minutes later, we're all seated around the table, and my trembling hands grab at the cloth napkin sitting on my lap. I ball the cotton as Roxanne places a salad bowl on the table. I avoid looking at her, but I can feel her gaze lingering on me.

What is it about her that's giving me chills in this warm, heated dining room?

After putting out the food, she leaves and thankfully doesn't show up again.

Ashcroft asks about my work at Elixir Inc. and my life in Cherrywood.

"Cherrywood is very pretty in the spring," I tell him. "You should definitely visit."

As soon as I say the words, I realize it's a first. The first time I have someone to invite to a place that feels like home.

"Thank you so much. I might take you up on that if you offer to be my guide," Ashcroft says, and something warms inside me at his approving tone.

"I'd love to, but I think you'd have a better time with someone who is more familiar with the town. Even Zander knows more about Cherrywood than me."

"Of course he does. He's a businessman. He's chasing three deals in that town; he has to know everything about it."

"Three deals?" I glance between Zander and Ashcroft.

Zach snickers and then raises his index finger. "Our third office site, one. Your new home"—he raises a second finger before waving his hand between Zander and me—"two. And you." Three fingers are up, and there's a huge grin on his face.

"Me?"

"You are the biggest deal of my life, Rose." Zander pulls my chair closer to him and puts his arm around me.

"Oh." I sit there in surprise. "I sound...important," I blurt, and of course, all four men chuckle.

"You are very important, Rose," Ashcroft says. "In this house, at this very moment, you are the most important person. After your wedding, this house will be as much yours as it is theirs."

My breathing halts for a second. My hands shake as I grab the edge of the table. Foreign emotions of gratitude hit me at his unexpectedly soft words.

"Th-thank you so much. It means a lot to me." More than he'll ever know.

"And I mean it."

I nod because I worry if I have to speak more, I'll turn into a sobbing mess.

44

ZANDER

After lunch, Beast asks for a few minutes of alone time with me while Zane offers to give Rose a tour of the house. Before closing the door to Beast's study, I notice Zane leading her to the sunroom.

"When is the wedding?" Beast asks before taking a seat behind his desk.

I linger close to the large bookshelf, hesitating for a moment, or maybe too long, as he raises an eyebrow at me.

"Is there a problem?"

I grab my neck in frustration. I don't even know what it is. "Nothing. Rose is just shy."

"And?" He lights his cigar, the smell of tobacco filling the space. This is the only room in the house he's allowed to smoke in, a rule enforced by Roxanne years back when the doctor first told him to cut down on smoking and drinking.

My mind wanders to Roxanne and Rose's reaction to her.

"She's having cold feet?" Beast asks.

"She has commitment issues. She didn't have a normal childhood."

"I know her background, Zander. Where she spent her childhood and all." He puffs curls of smoke before going on.

"You might be the CEO of Elixir, but did you think I wouldn't run a background check on your future wife?"

His words don't surprise me a bit. "Then why were you embarrassing her with all those questions about her parents?" His acute curiosity about her parents has come as a surprise to me, though. It seems he's more curious about Rose's parents than her.

"Because that's something my PI couldn't find." I read right through the questioning look he's giving me. He wants to know how much I know about Rose's past.

"Well, she has no clue about them. She grew up in a home, or something like a home."

"How did she land there?"

"Someone working in the orphanage found her, just as she told you." I try not to remember the state in which my girl was found.

Beast stares at me and takes another puff of his cigar. "Hmm."

"Why are you so interested in her parents?"

He doesn't reply immediately; instead, looks up to the ceiling. Then he pulls the Cuban close to his lips and exhales. "She reminds me of someone I was close with. Very close." He looks dreamily at the rising cigar smoke.

"Your wife?" I ask gingerly.

Beast has never spoken to us about his family. But years ago, Roxanne told us that his wife walked out of this home with their daughter. It's hard for me to comprehend why someone would leave Beast. Even now, when he's close to sixty, his presence turns the heads of both men and women alike.

"Her eyes," he says. "Exactly like my wife's. Exactly like Chloe's." Again, he's lost in his own world of memories.

"Your daughter?"

He nods, lighting another cigar. "You know, point one

percent of the population have the OCA2 or P protein mutation." A weak, sad smile pulls on his lips.

I've never seen Beast like this—lost—and I don't think I'd like a repeat of this rare moment.

"What are the chances?" He continues. "For a second, I thought she was Chloe."

"And?" I ask warily. Rose's early childhood is still in question.

Could she be Beast's daughter? My heart hammers in my chest.

"Chloe was blonde, and her features were more like mine—more German."

I release my breath silently. Rose and Beast have no similarity in their looks.

He opens his wallet and shows me a picture of a girl around three or four years old. Dressed in a red skirt and white blouse, she looks nothing like my couch girl. Rose has a small button nose, while this girl has a long, pointed nose like Beast. But the eyes...they're the exact same color.

"Yeah. She isn't Rose," I say in relief.

"Yep." His voice is clipped as he puts the photograph back into his wallet.

"Did Roxy ever work as a nurse or at a children's center?" I change the topic, trying to lighten the stressful environment.

"No, I don't think so. She worked at a restaurant before joining me. Why?"

"Rose had a minor episode when she saw Roxanne. She thought she had seen her somewhere before but couldn't remember. Zane thinks it's probably due to the stress of this meeting."

"Doesn't she have a photographic memory?" Beast's question resonates with the one in my mind.

I nod. "But before last year, Rose had never stepped foot in St. Peppers." I shake my head, trying not to make a big deal of something that's most likely just Rose's nerves. "Maybe Zane's right."

Beast nods. "Roxanne has never lived anywhere else." He picks up his cigar from the ashtray and takes a long drag. "Her whole family is based in St. Peppers, but I don't think anyone is alive anymore. She inherited some land close to your father's property."

My father's property. The only good memory of my childhood. It's the house we lived in before my father passed away. A few years ago, I bought the house, along with the land where my father grew his famous rose garden for my mother. Now, the entire place has been converted into a small B&B, run by one of Beast's ex-army friends and his wife.

Zach pokes his head through the door. "Are you two done?"

I nod as my brother struts into the room. He perches on the edge of Beast's study table and moves around the stone paperweight and wooden pen stand, which were hand painted by Roxanne.

Beast huffs and puffs in annoyance, but Zach pays no regard, plucking a cigar from the open wooden box and lighting it up.

I raise an eyebrow at my brother. "I thought you quit smoking."

"This isn't smoking. This is sampling the finest Cuban."

He winks at Beast, who covertly smiles, and if I'm not wrong, he looks proud of my little brother's knowledge.

Beast opens the top drawer of his desk and places an unopened pack of cigars on the table. Zach lifts it up, but the pack is immediately retrieved by Beast, and Zach receives a smack to his hand. "Not for you."

Zach shrugs, and my lips curl up at their playful banter until my brother's attention shifts to me. "You guys set a date yet?"

Jesus. It seems everyone except my bride is eager for the wedding.

"No. Maybe next year." My pulse shoots at the mere thought of it. "Maybe on my birthday." Now that's a load of baloney, but there's nothing wrong with being hopeful.

"You stupid prick." Zach slides from the desk and flicks my head. "You can't do that. Have you no understanding of the female brain?"

Fucker. I hit his hand away.

"Girls love to celebrate special days. Birthdays, proposals, engagements—all that shit." He counts off, raising his fingers up in the air. "You want to marry Rose on your birthday so she has one less day to celebrate?" He looks annoyed while stating the most ridiculous thing I've ever heard.

"Are you serious? What kind of fucked-up logic is that?"

"It's female logic."

"He spends the most time with ladies out of any of you, Zander. Listen to what your brother says." Beast chuckles, loving our stupidity.

"Okay," I concede. "I'm not marrying her on my birthday."

I hope it happens sooner than that.

We return to the foyer, and I find Rose with Zane, already waiting for us.

Beast pulls her in for a surprise hug. "It was a pleasure to meet you." He hands her his card and places a kiss on her forehead in something like fatherly affection. "Call me anytime."

"Thanks," she says. My heart fills with giddiness at his warm affection to my girl, and her cheeks turn rosy pink and her eyes gleam with excitement. "It was nice to meet you too."

"I hope to see you more," he says, patting her cheeks like she's his little girl.

After wishing goodbye to Beast and promising to meet Zane and Zach for dinner, we leave.

I'm walking on the clouds, my hand on Rose's back as I guide her to the car.

Beast approves of my girl. I guess this is what heaven feels like.

I settle into the driver's seat and pull her hands to my mouth to press open-mouthed kisses over them, making her giggle. "I'm so happy."

"Me too. I think Beast likes me." Her face has a hundred-watt smile.

"Of course he does. Why wouldn't he?"

I'm now seriously wondering why I even had a doubt about it.

She's too easy to fall in love with.

45

ZANDER

"What do you want for dinner?" I holler from the kitchenette of my hotel suite. We're back after a long day of work.

These past few days in Cherrywood have been...blissful.

Every evening, Rose and I leave the office together. Sometimes I show up at her building just to pick her up since my days are spent holed up the upcoming site. Sometimes I'm at her office for an afternoon meeting. Twice, she's paid me an unannounced visit with lunch at the new site, and I fucking loved it.

Rose asked Clementine if she's fine living in their house alone, and it seems Clem is more than happy about it. In fact, her excitement at having the house all to herself made me wonder if she ever wanted a roommate at all.

Life couldn't be better. Some days, like today, I make dinner for us in the kitchenette.

"I don't know." Rose enters the room, wrapped in a fluffy hotel robe. "What are you in the mood for?" she asks, drying her hair with a white towel.

I get up from the couch and stand behind her, taking the towel from her hands.

"You. I'm always in the mood for you."

She snickers and turns around in my arms. Her eyes are glazed, her cheeks a rosy pink. I'd wager a bit from the shower and a bit from me. "Um, I meant to eat."

"Me too, baby. I'm in the mood to eat you." I bite her earlobe.

"But I'm not on the menu." Her trembly voice is filled with that sexy lilt that calls to my body.

"No, you're not. You're prepared just for me, and I'm going to savor you bit by bit, piece by piece." I kiss behind her earlobe and descend lower to her neck. "You're tailored to my taste buds—a bit juicy, a bit fruity." I open her bathrobe and taste those beautiful rosy nipples. I get down on my knees, kissing her stomach. "A little mellow, a little lush."

"Zander! Did you...just call me lush...while kissing my stomach?" Her brows knit in confusion as she pulls back from me and closes her bathrobe. "You think I'm fat?" Her eyes widen, and her cheeks turn scarlet.

But I don't think it's because of me this time. Or maybe it is.

"Am I fat?" She runs to the mirror and turns side to side, looking at her flat stomach.

"No, couch girl. You're not fat. You know that." I stand behind her, rubbing my hands over her stomach through the robe. "You're perfect."

"Oh my God, you're patronizing me! You think I'm fat." Her eyes are as wide as saucers. "Isn't that the one thing you shouldn't say to your girlfriend? Even I know this." She stomps her feet in anger.

Fuck. How did this happen?

We were having fun. I was about to get her naked on the bed, and now she's leaving the room, marching toward the balcony.

"Rose. Baby, wait." I run after her. "You know I didn't

mean that. I got lost in the moment. And it just came out of my mouth."

"Then why didn't you say slim, fragile, or delicate? Why lush?" She shakes her head, her wet hair waving around.

Good question.

Think fast, Zander, if you want any chance at fixing this.

But holy hell, if only my brain would work.

Her anger is having an opposite effect on me.

Why are her simmering eyes and flailing hands such a turn-on?

"Don't be angry, couch girl. You know I find you perfect." I try to touch her, but she shifts away from me.

"Yes, now I know that you find my *lush* body very perfect." She storms back into the room before shutting the balcony glass doors on my face, leaving me outside.

I try to follow her, but the doors won't open. Did she just lock me out?

I can't help but fucking smile like a lunatic, even in this situation. She locked me outside. After a fight. If this isn't marriage, then I don't know what is.

I would certainly count this as progress.

I wait a few minutes, knowing she'll open the door eventually. She is my Rose, after all.

Minutes later, I'm still on the balcony, lying on the recliner, looking at the night sky filled with twinkling stars, when the glass door is pushed open. She walks to me, fidgeting from one foot to the other, seemingly confused about what to do. So, I decide for her.

I grab her hand and pull her into my arms. She falls on my chest and looks up with a worried gaze.

"I'm sorry," she says. "I—I don't know what got into me."

"I'm not sorry at all. I am ecstatic." I stroke her face gently and smile at her.

"You are? Why?" Her cute button nose wrinkles.

"This was our first fight. We're moving forward, couch girl. And, also, because I get to have make-up sex with you."

"You are incorrigible." She snorts, playfully hitting my chest.

"Only for you," I say, rubbing her ass through her soft pajama bottoms as she lies on top of me.

"Are we good?" She looks at me from under those bangs, which stay clipped back during the day.

"We are the fucking best." I kiss her hard, my heart in a perpetual state of high since I arrived in Cherrywood. "I need to make you mad more often."

"Why?" There's a squeak in her voice when my hand slips inside her pants, rubbing her silk panties.

"Because today I learned how hot you look when angry. With a scarlet face, red ears, and wild eyes, you're a siren calling out for every part of me." I take her hand and push it inside my track pants. "Feel what you do to me, couch girl."

She starts caressing me through my boxers before drawing them lower. Then her hands touch my bare skin, her fingers brushing against my pubic hair, firing all the neurons in my brain.

"Rose." A moan escapes me.

"Does this turn you on too?" she asks innocently. Too innocently, that tease.

Before I can reply, she starts pumping my dick—not lazily, not lightly, but solid, hard pumps like I showed her. Sometimes it's a fucking blessing that she has a photographic memory.

I push my own fingers inside her panties and start rubbing her clit.

"Ah, Zander," she moans.

I take her mouth in a kiss, damping our mewling noises. I push two of my fingers inside her, curling them, and at the same time, I rub her clit with my thumb.

We both work our hands in unison. Whenever the pleasure is too much and my hand slows down, she tightens her grip on me, reminding me that she wants the same pleasure.

Finally, she comes apart with a loud cry, pulling her mouth away from mine. I groan with pleasure and shoot my load in my boxers and all over her hands.

Minutes later, when our breathing has returned to normal, she asks, "Do you think someone heard?"

I shrug. Someone definitely heard. But I don't give a fucking damn.

46

ZANDER

"What do you think?" I ask Rose, although I already know her answer.

We're looking at the third property for our dream house. But this one, too, doesn't feel right.

"I don't know. It doesn't have that *thing*," Rose says apologetically. Her lips are pinched together as if it's her fault that we're not finding the right place.

I pull her closer to me. "I know. I feel it too." My gaze slides to the house and then to Rose, and it fucking twists my nerves to watch the excitement in her eyes dying.

We walk to where our car is parked and the realtor is waiting for us.

"This isn't it, Henry."

"Zander, you wanted a house with a view of the hills, in the woods, and close to the lake and city." Henry waves his hands around, showing me all those things. "This has everything. What's the problem? Is it the price?" He's been patient with us so far, and he's right. This property has everything, as per our wishes on paper, but it's still missing...that *thing*, as Rose said.

"No, the price is fine. It's just... It's missing something."

How do I explain that to him? "Do you have anything else around here? I like the area. What do you say, Rose?"

"Yeah, the location is good. Even though it's on the outskirts, it's well connected to the town. The commute to work is good. It's close to Kristy's place. It's just this property itself. It's not us." She tilts her head to the side and chews on her lip. Her chin dips into her chest, and my skin itches to bring a smile back to her face.

"Okay, okay. That's good." Henry scrolls on his iPad, regaining some of his lost excitement. "I have something. It's more into the woods, secluded from everything. We're advertising it as a hermit's paradise." He chuckles. "Maybe it speaks cozy and romantic to you."

We agree to see it, splitting off to our vehicles, and after getting into my car, we follow Henry's BMW.

"Wow, what's that?" Rose points to something in the distance as I slowly traverse my car on the rickety road. I follow her finger and see an unkempt, old cabin hidden behind the trees. I stop, and she dashes out of the car before I've even properly parked. With hurried steps, she walks toward the house, and I run to catch up with her. "Do you think someone lives here?" she asks as we stand outside the rustic, old place.

"I don't think so. It looks pretty cold and empty." I try to peek in through the glass windows. I hope no one's inside. I have no intention of being caught trespassing on someone's property.

"What do you think?" Rose points to the small house.

"Babe, we don't know if it's available. Heck, we don't even know if it's up for sale."

Before I can give her a hundred more reasons why this place might not be right for us, my phone rings.

"Zander, where are you guys? Weren't you following me?" Henry asks.

"Sorry, we got a bit sidetracked."

Rose shifts beside me. I place my free hand over her shoulders, and she looks at the cabin with deep longing. I can see in her eyes that this is it. This is what we're looking for.

"There's a wooden cabin some hundred meters away from the property we just saw," I tell Henry. "Do you know about it?"

"You mean the Jacobsens' cabin? Yeah, it's been sitting with us for fourteen months. We've had no bites on it."

"Does that mean we can see it?" My pulse speeds up, and Rose turns in my arms, her blue eyes gleaming with excitement.

"Um, you want to see that place? Isn't it too small for what you want? It's only got three bedrooms. It's more like a big summer cabin."

"Yeah, I see that, but Rose likes it. *We* like it. Can you show it to us?"

"Okay, give me ten minutes, and I'll join you guys. Meanwhile, feel free to look around." He pauses for a moment and then adds, "Zander, ask Rose to walk around the house. Maybe you guys have found what you're looking for." With a chuckle, Henry ends the call.

"What did he say?" Rose holds her breath, clutching my hand tight. Her smile is wide, her excited blue eyes focused on me. And I know this is her dream house.

Our safest place in the world.

"That we should walk around." I lead her to the back of the cabin.

"Holy shit!" The back view just sealed the deal.

Rose squeals, bouncing from foot to foot. "Is that a creek?"

There is indeed a wide creek flowing through the back of the house. I can picture us—me and Rose—huddled by the large window, just staring at the water and the woods.

"I love it. It's old and rusty, maybe a bit broken." I turn around, examining the house.

"But nothing that can't be healed with some love. Like us, Zander. It's us." She puts her arms around my waist and gazes lovingly at the house.

When we hear the growling of Henry's car engine, we join him in the front.

"So, lovebirds, you found your perfect place?" He has a triumphant smile on his face for the first time today.

I nod. "We definitely like it, even though it's smaller than what I had in mind." I wanted to have more open space around us.

I had some plans of my own to surprise my girl.

"Why don't you buy the next piece of land?" Henry puts on his sunglasses after waving them toward the open ground.

"It's available?"

He nods.

"That would be perfect. What do you say, Rose? Can you see us living here?"

"I love it." She beams at me, her blue eyes shining brighter than the fucking sun itself.

"You guys haven't even seen the inside." Henry chuckles. "And I'm not saying this to sell you the property, because I see you're already buying it," he says with a wide grin. "But the Jacobsens did a great job with the aesthetics. You can feel the soul of this place. At least that's what Mrs. Jacobsen told me on my first visit."

Henry turns the doorknob, and Rose and I walk hand in hand into our paradise.

This cabin does have a soul. The entrance opens into a huge sitting area. The tall windows overlook the forest and the creek from three directions. The rustic fireplace is hidden under a stone overlay. There's an open-style kitchen facing the living room. Henry leads us past everything and into the huge library.

Rose gasps in surprise. "Wow, it's an unusually large room for a library."

"Should be an easy remodel into whatever you'd like," Henry says. "Maybe an office space with a sitting nook." He's already started planning, throwing ideas around as we explore the house more. "This is the guest bedroom and the main bedroom is upstairs."

We climb up the wooden stairs, and Rose's hand glides over the smooth pine banister. She looks around the place and then at me. Watching the twinkling in her eyes, my heart bursts, ready to rip out of my fucking chest with joy.

I notice the rooms on either side of the landing as I stand behind Rose and Henry.

"This is the main bedroom, and this can be a kids' bedroom." Henry excitedly turns around.

But it's Rose's response that takes me by surprise. She stiffens in front of me.

She fucking stiffens.

Her hand drifts to the cuffs of her shirt as she starts tugging on it.

What the fuck happened in the last ten seconds? I thought she was swooned by the house, already imagining us living here, like I was. How did mention of a kids' room make her anxious?

"You don't like it?" Henry picks up on the shift in our mood.

"We like it. It's perfect actually," I reply while casually running my hands over Rose's tight shoulders in an attempt to calm her down. I don't want her to have a meltdown or for her first memory in this house to be of a panic attack. "We need two guest bedrooms for my brothers when they visit."

Henry's eyebrows crinkle in confusion. But he composes fast and nods in understanding. "You can remodel the house however you like."

Rose slowly loosens up, leaning against me as if a giant weight has been lifted off her.

Is she so wary about our wedding and future?

"Do you want to see the adjoining patch of land?" Henry asks.

I nod, even though my excitement has dampened.

Why is she so hesitant when I'm all in?

Once we're outside, Rose is excited again. She asks me if we can build a backyard patio facing the creek, if we can have a fountain, and all those other over-the-top ideas she has in her folder.

As the sun sets, we decide to go under contract. Henry leaves happy while we stay on the property for a little longer.

"You like it, right?" Rose looks over her shoulder at me from where we both are settled on the grass, looking at the reflection of stars dancing on the water.

"I love it. When I first saw this creek, I imagined us sitting here." I place a kiss on her hair and pull her closer as the excitement of the day finally calms down.

"Me too. Everything about this place is like a dream and more. I can't believe we found our perfect place, Zander." She peers behind me to the house. "I can see us hosting dinners for your brothers and Kristy. The living room space is perfect for a family gathering." Her eyes shine with excitement as she talks a mile a minute.

"You're looking forward to hosting parties?" I ask, surprised, and her wide gaze travels to me for a second before she looks away. "Couch girl?" I bring her attention back to me with my finger under her chin.

"Um, I don't know. Maybe." She shrugs. When I raise an eyebrow at her, she whispers, "Oscar's gram once invited us to their large family Christmas party, and I wondered how it would be to host a gathering of my own." She looks up at me from under her eyebrows. "Is it crazy?"

How could this be crazy?

Isn't this what I always wanted? My family all together.

"Why would it be crazy, babe? It's beautiful, like you. You making plans for the future, which includes my family and our friends, is the most wonderful thing. It means we're moving forward."

"Now your brothers are my family too. I'm no longer alone. I want to celebrate every moment with you in our home." Her twinkling gaze moves around.

"And that's the best thing I've ever heard." I hug her tight, her words washing away all the anxiety and insecurity from earlier. I've been worried about nothing.

47

ROSE

We have officially closed on the property. I can't believe Henry and Zander made this happen so fast. It still feels like a dream.

I once again swipe the hundreds—okay, not hundreds—of photographs on my phone, and each one is still there.

The rustic cottage with tall windows.

The flowing creek glimmering under the moonlight, making it appear like diamonds shining on a fairy's billowy skirt.

The cozy fireplace roaring in orange flames when Zander threw some wood in it on our last visit.

This is all perfect.

When I swipe one more time, my gaze stops on a photograph of Zander and me by the fire.

He'd placed the gray plush blankets on the floor and spread an extra over us.

My shoulders are bare, with the blanket tucked under my arms.

This girl doesn't look like me—that's my first thought.

Everything starting from my unruly hair, my dreamy blue

eyes, and the wide smile on my face, which has an orange glow because of the fire, is so unlike me.

How did this happen?

Because of him.

My gaze shifts to Zander.

Sweet sugar, he is beyond handsome. His side of the blanket sits pooled on his lap. His brawny arms and his chest and abs are on full display.

My breath catches at the sight of him.

It's like I'm transported back to that room, near that hot fireplace.

Crab, he's too hot. My whole body feels hot and…sweaty.

I glance back at myself, this time with less scrutiny.

I fit in this picture. I fit next to this handsome man. If some stranger sees this photograph, they would believe that I'm his and he's mine.

While I'm still drooling all over my bare-chested man, he makes an appearance out of my bathroom in nothing but my baby-blue towel wrapped around his waist.

When he leans forward, picking up the second towel from the bed next to me, ready to dry his wet hair, I get a good look at the tattoos on his shoulders—the angry, bare rose thorns drawn over his skin in black ink. Where the thorns end, blood is splattered in red ink.

My chest tightens, and all the warmth and heat evaporates as I'm suddenly surrounded by a feeling of cold.

They look so real. Every time I see them, I imagine the thorns pricking his skin and drawing blood. I flinch at my imagination.

"Hey, what's the matter?" Zander perches next to me on the bed.

I shake my head. My heart clenches just looking at his face.

"It's my back, isn't it?"

"No." I shake my head, but I guess it's not very convincing.

"Don't lie." His fingers run back and forth over my cheeks, making my throat scratchy.

I gulp down the pain, hating to see him this serious so early in the morning. "Does it hurt you too? To look at my back?" I grab his hands, which are resting on my face.

"Rose, your marks are different from mine. My art is self-inflicted. It's a reminder of my suffering. While your marks are a reminder of how far you've come. They show your strength." He squeezes my hand, trying to make me believe something I don't feel.

I haven't come that far.

I haven't gathered the courage to decide on a wedding date or to think of a future beyond getting engaged.

Sometimes I wonder if I'm doing the right thing with Zander, dragging him along in this hope that someday we'll get married.

Can I even do it? Marry him?

"Let's talk about something else," he says when he notices my hand gripping the cuff of my nightshirt. "What were you thinking before this?" Zander tilts his head toward his back before getting up and grabbing the glass of water on top of the nightstand. His neck bobs as he drinks.

"I was thinking you're too sexy."

The water he was drinking comes out of his mouth. "Holy fuck, couch girl," he chokes out. "I'd have never guessed those words could even come out of your mouth."

"Me neither." I look away from his burning gaze, suddenly feeling shy around him.

"No, don't you dare go back to being all cute and shy." He grabs my face and forces me to look at him. "Now that I know you have a naughty bone, I'd certainly like to see it more."

"I don't have a naughty bone." I shake my head, and his

hand drops from my face. "I have the exact same number of bones as any other woman in this world."

He flops down on the bed beside me. "Say something more." His shining eyes blink fast, causing a tingling in my chest.

"Zander—"

"Please." He wiggles his eyebrows, and my heart does a happy dance upon watching his amusement.

"I…" My hands twitch, pulling on the cuffs of my nightshirt, but this time for different reasons. "I want to do something." I look at him from under my lashes.

"What is that?" He grabs my hands, displaying a wide grin. His left dimple makes me all mushy and crazy.

"Something…you wanted."

"Oh, babe, you'll have to give me more than that. If you ever get to know what all I want from you, with you, to do to you, you might run for the hills." A low groan escapes his lips as his back hits the mattress and his arm covers his eyes.

My throat dries at the sight of him spread over my queen-sized bed, his broad bare chest on full display.

"Really?" I squeak. "I don't want you to hold back."

He removes his hand, and his steamy gaze meets mine. "Rose, I don't hold back. Your cuteness, your shyness, it just forces my brain to create all these fantasies. And most of those we live, like in front of your bathroom mirror or near the fireplace."

Before I can think about all the possible fantasies of his that we don't fulfill, he sits upright. "So what prize am I going to get for being sexy?"

"I'm gonna…blow you." I hold my breath, trying hard not to chicken out.

"Rose! Don't mess with me. This is not a thing to joke about." His face is suddenly serious, and I don't like his almost accusing tone.

"I'm not," I reply quickly. "But I need you to help me. I've done a lot of research, but still, theoretical knowledge can only take me so far. It's like I can read and watch all about driving, but it doesn't get real until I'm inside a car and my hands are on the steering wheel."

"Are you really comparing blow jobs to driving cars?" He's trying to act all calm like his CEO persona, but the excited lilt in his voice gives him away.

"Teach me. I want to do it." My body heats up, and my words shake, betraying the courageous front I'm trying to portray.

"Since when?" He grabs my hand, and his quickening pulse resonates with mine.

"Are you just going to ask questions? If you aren't interested, then it's okay." I have only so much courage. I push the covers down and get up from the bed. But before I can go far, Zander follows me and gathers me in his arms.

"I'm interested. I'm fucking beyond interested. You know I've been interested since the day you proposed to blow me in my office while wearing that black dress."

My heart rate skyrockets at his remark. "Then teach me."

"Are you sure?" His gaze doesn't leave my face, and I know he's checking for any of my nervous tics.

"I might be shy about these things, Zander, but I want to experience, or at least try, everything with you."

A playful smile plays on his lips at my words. "Everything. That's a big word, couch girl."

"Not as big as you," I murmur, rubbing myself against his hardening penis.

"Oh, Rose. You shouldn't have done that, babe." He leans forward and grabs my lavender pillow from the bed. Throwing it on the floor next to my feet, he says, "Get on your knees. Class starts now."

My hands move from where they were resting on his chest. Zander grabs them at the last moment and helps me get down.

"What should I do?" In this position, I'm eye level with the towel knot around his waist.

"Close your eyes."

I look at him in confusion. How can I do this with my eyes closed? I'm not even sure I can do it right with my eyes wide open. But when Zander simply stares down at me, waiting for me to follow his instruction, I comply.

"Do you really want to do this, couch girl?"

I smile despite the nerves. My heart swoons at his tenderness, and some of the nerves settle down.

He knows my heart.

I open my eyes and nod, determined to give him the fishing best blow job in the whole world.

"Then remove the towel. I'm all yours."

My hands tremble as I pull the end of the towel, and it pools at his feet before me.

Fish! He has strong legs.

How did I not realize this till now? Maybe because I've never been in this position. I've given him a hand job several times now, but I've never been face-to-face with his…penis.

Holy sugar!

I gulp and stare at his thick, long—

"You're killing me, Rose. Why are you staring at it like that?"

I bite my lip before looking up. "I just realized I've never seen it this close."

"You can't be all cute when you're down there." He groans, but there's an amusing smile on his lips. "Put your hands on me."

And I do. My hands cover his thick, and hard cock before I slowly move them up and down the length of him just like he showed me during our first time in my bathroom, not far from here.

His fingers gently push my bangs away from my forehead, and I glance up at him. His eyes are burning with fire, and his chest rises and falls. His expression, a perfect blend of being aroused, proud, and thankful, boosts my confidence.

My one hand stays on his hard cock, and the other curls around his muscular thigh. I open my mouth and swipe my tongue over the head of his cock. It tastes salty and…funny.

I look up and notice Zander watching me with deep concentration and hesitation. To prove to him that I do want this, I lower my mouth, and his smooth shaft slides in. I try to take it all in until…I gag.

Crab!

"Rose." He takes a step back and his shaft slides out of my mouth, leaving a trail of saliva down my lips and chin. "Babe, you don't have to take all of me in."

"But I want—"

"I know. I want it too, but more than that, I want this to be something fun for *both of us*. Take as much as you can in your mouth, and for the rest, use your hand."

When he steps forward this time, I do as he said. Curling my hands around his shaft, I then place the rest of his length inside my mouth.

"Just suck like you suck on my fingers before I put them inside you." His voice comes out hoarse, and his eyes close. His breathing frazzles, and when I suck him fast, his eyes open. They're blazing with fire. My own breath catches at the sight of this rare vulnerability on his face. He looks beyond hot.

My eyes widen as they meet his when he swells inside my mouth.

"You can…take me out…if you like," he whispers in a battered voice. When I don't do that, he curses loudly. Wetness gathers around my sex at his pleasure.

His face turns up to the ceiling as he clenches his fists at his sides. His thighs, his chest, his neck, all red and sweaty.

Then my mouth fills with his hot, thick, salty cum. I

swallow most of it, but still, some rolls down my chin when Zander pulls out. He bends forward a little, his eyes closed.

I sit on my heels, watching his every move when his eyes open. He looks at me with such intensity that it scares me to my bones.

I can't live without him.

And then he smiles, his left dimple making an appearance and calming my racing heart.

"As always, you blow my mind, couch girl."

"Apart from the other things I blew," I blurt, and his lips curl up.

"You're going to be the death of me." Zander lifts me off the floor before throwing me on the bed.

48

ZANDER

"Hello, boss." Kristy waves at me before sauntering into my recently furnished office.

"Hello, friend. What is my favorite employee doing at this time in this part of the town?"

"Hold on now." She narrows her eyes on me, hands resting on her waist. "What are you really asking here? Why am I roaming around town at this working hour or why am I here unannounced? Or are you just happy to see your favorite employee?" She bats her eyelashes flirtatiously while asking the last question, and I chuckle at her comic come-hither expression.

"How does Oscar handle you, drama queen?"

"It helps that it's not him who handles me but me who handles him." She snickers before glancing around my office. "I see you're settling in well here, and I hear the work on the new house is also going smoothly."

I rest back in my chair. "Yes, the construction is moving along well. Why don't you guys join us sometime? It's really a beautiful place."

"I'm sure it is because that's all Rose has been talking about these days." Kristy's eyes twinkle as she smiles before perching on a chair opposite of me and placing her handbag beside her.

"She is in love with it. She even asked me if we can live there while restoration is in progress. I had to think of twenty different reasons until I could fully convince her that living amongst the construction chaos is a bad idea."

"But why don't I see you in our office more often?" She arches an eyebrow at me, and my smile slips, causing her to sit straight. When I don't reply, she tries again. "You're mostly only there to pick up Rose. All okay?"

"I don't want to overwhelm her by breathing down her neck every minute of the day." My words are frustrated.

Kristy has become such a good friend over the past few months, and she helped me a great deal in convincing Rose to take a chance on us during our early dating days.

"Did she say something?" She raises her eyebrow in suspicion.

"Not in so many words." I grab the planner on my table just so I have something to keep my hands busy. "I think I'm reading too much into it. It's most likely nothing." I drop that stupid planner and grab my neck, looking up at the ceiling. "But when we were at the property with Henry and he showed us the kids' bedroom, she got…all cold and rock solid. You know, like when she's about to get a panic attack."

My gaze lands on Kristy, who stays uncharacteristically quiet, playing with the straps of her handbag.

"I'm reading too much into it, right?"

"Most likely. Rosie is still coming to terms with the idea of getting married. Maybe she just panicked hearing about kids." Kristy chews on her lower lip. "Do you…think about kids?"

"Isn't it a natural thing to think of?" Who am I kidding? Rose, kids, family…these things constantly run through my mind. She spent all her life alone. What I wouldn't give for her to experience the thrill, the excitement, of a little one.

But I guess that's one gift she doesn't want. "I definitely think about the idea of us having kids someday. Of course, not like tomorrow or even next year, especially after seeing how much it affects her." There's no hiding the bite in my voice.

"I'm sorry, Zander." Kristy gives me a sad smile, and I respond with my own.

"I knew there'd be speed bumps but having her in my life exactly as she is makes up for all the challenges that come our way." I focus on the memory of her excited face when we were in our house for the first time. The way her smile tugged on my heart. "And more importantly, we make progress every day." Never in my wildest dreams had I imagined her offering me a blow job. My throat dries as I remember how she looked on her knees, sucking—

"I'm so happy she found you," Kristy whispers, her misty eyes bringing me back from my wild imaginations.

"Okay." I clear my throat, pushing away the arousing images of my nerd from my head. "Enough with the sappy. Tell me why you're here unannounced. Not that I'm unhappy to see you."

She clears her throat, not responding as I'd hoped. "Actually, I have news. And before I share it with Rose, I wanted to share it with you. I don't know…how she'll react."

I nod, urging her to go on, but she hesitates. With uncertain blue eyes, she resembles Rose too much at this moment.

"But now, I don't know if this is the right time."

"What's happening? Everything all right?" I'm a mix of curious and concerned at seeing Kristy this nervous.

"It's just… I-I'm pregnant."

It takes my brain a second to register what she said. "Kristy! That's wonderful news." I get up from my chair and pull her into a hug. "Congratulations. I'm so happy for you and Oscar."

"Thank you so much." For the first time since she walked into my office, there's a joyous expression on her face.

"I'm sure you guys are going crazy with this news. I know I am. Look." I pull up my shirt sleeve and show her the goose bumps littering my skin. "I can't wait to see the look on Rose's face. She'll be beyond excited."

Kristy runs her hands over my textured skin, her eyes shining with pure joy. "We haven't told anyone else yet. But I want to share it with Rose so bad. I, too, think she'll be happy. It's eating me alive to keep this from her. We've never kept any secrets from each other, you know? Especially not this long."

"And how long has this been?"

"Since morrrning," Kristy drawls, as if her stretching of the word would make the time period longer, and I can't hold back my laugh at her theatrics. "Laughing at a pregnant woman?" She raises her hands up in the air in mock anger, which only amuses me more.

"It didn't take you long to play the pregnancy card." When I cock my eyebrow, she giggles.

"I never miss opportunities. I just wanted to give you a heads-up that I'll share the news with Rose this evening. Ask her to call me."

"Why can't you call her?"

Kristy fidgets, her fingers playing with her huge diamond ring.

"Kristy, what did you do?" I bite back a chuckle. There's never a dull moment with this girl.

"Okay, okay, I'll tell you. I promised Oscar…" she says in a cryptic voice. When I arch an eyebrow at her for further explanation, she huffs in annoyance before continuing. "I promised him that I wouldn't *call* anyone to share the news until he's back from St. Peppers tomorrow."

"And that's why you were so evasive in stating the exact reason for your surprise visit. So clever, Mrs. Hawthorne."

"Well, shame on Oscar for making me keep the biggest news of my life from my best friend. I'll do no such thing.

You better ask her to call me, or you'll find a surprise visitor in your hotel room tonight."

I have full faith that she'll drop by if Rose doesn't call her.

"We're staying at Rose's place tonight in case you decide to pay us an unannounced visit. But I'll ask your friend to call you in the evening."

She raises one finger over her lips.

"Yes, yes. I'll not say anything about your news to her." When she crosses her arms over her chest, I supply, "Or anyone else."

Finally, there's a wide smile on Kristy's face.

"Does Oscar know there's a loophole in his promise?"

"Of course he does."

"WHAT SMELLS SO GOOD?"

My hands folding the kitchen towel come to a halt at the sight of Rose standing by the kitchen door. She's freshly showered and now dressed in yellow shorts and a matching cotton T-shirt. Her toned, long legs get to me every fucking time.

"Zander, stop staring." She joins me next to the fridge and smacks my chest lightly.

I grab her hand and pepper kisses over her palm. "Then stop looking so pretty." Coming back to her every evening has been the highlight of my days since I moved to Cherrywood.

"Wow, that's too much food." Rose looks around at the table clad with salad, mashed potatoes, and chili as I take out the bread from the oven. "You baked bread?" Her gaze shifts from me to the pan in surprise.

"Don't tell me this is the first lucky bread prepared in this oven?" I stifle back my smile. "What do you guys use it for?"

"Pizza. But don't be surprised if you find some socks

inside. Clem is often finding new ways to use the oven." She giggles as I place the pan onto the table.

"Preparing pizza is more complicated than bread."

"Preparing?" She blinks rapidly before looking at me as if I've grown two heads, causing me to chuckle. Every moment with Rose brings joy into my life. "Do you honestly think I can prepare pizza at home? My association with this oven ends at heating an emergency frozen pizza." Her gaze then jumps to the table. "But seriously, this is amazing. I can't wait to come home to this every evening." She puts her arms around my neck and swings from side to side. "Is it wrong of me to say that?" She sounds unsure, and I grab her by her waist, all too eager to ease her worries.

"Not at all. You know I love to cook for you." I hold her close and place swift kisses on her neck. When she relaxes in my arms, I give her some more kisses before pulling away, which only causes her to make an annoyed sound.

"Couch girl, as much as I don't want to stop, I want you to eat. I've been working on this for an hour." I pull out a chair for her. "I also want you to call Kristy after we're done with dinner."

"Kristy? Why, is there a problem?" Rose asks as I fill her bowl with chili and place it before her.

"No. Since she was off work today, I thought you guys would like to catch up while I clean. But if you want to help me instead, that's perfectly okay with me."

She looks up at me with her eyebrows high, a spoon stuck in her mouth.

I try hard to bite back the laugh that's ready to burst out of me as an expression of genuine sadness pops up on her pretty face. But finally, I give in. "I'm just teasing. You don't have to be so sad, couch girl." I push her bangs off her forehead.

She pulls the spoon out and then looks at me under her

lashes. "I don't think I'm ever going to like cleaning up the kitchen, Zander."

"Hɪ, Kʀɪsᴛʏ," Rose says as I arrange the dishes in the dishwasher. I don't have to do all this household shit; I could easily hire someone. But I want to have a relationship with Rose where we experience life around us, every passing moment. Moments that will become our memories someday. My girl has already missed so much in life, and I don't want her to miss anything more.

Giving a final glance to the kitchen, I pick up my coffee and join her in the living room.

My steps halt at the door.

"Rose?" My legs fucking shake as I run to her.

Fuck. How long has she been sitting like this?

My gaze jumps from the front of her T-shirt to her shorts, both soaked in the hot coffee, before landing on her face. Her eyes are wide and emotionless as she stares at the wall.

"Rose." My hands tremble as I shake her, trying to bring her back from whatever mental hell she's in. But she screams at my touch.

My stomach roils at her response, and it scares the hell out of me.

She likes my touch. What the fuck happened in the last five minutes?

"Babe, come back to me." The sound of my rapid, terrified heartbeat thrashes in my ears as I plead.

I make another attempt to get to her by caressing her hair. This time, she doesn't protest. A jolt passes through my body at the flicker of life in her eyes.

Thank God!

"Rose, let me clean you up." I can already see her neck

turning red from the burn of hot coffee, but I also don't want to take off her clothes and catch her by surprise. I have no idea what triggered this—whatever the fuck *this* is.

She stares at me, her eyes haunted and pleading. Tears trickle down her cheeks, but otherwise, her face is impassive.

With trembling hands, I gather her in my arms. She doesn't move, doesn't flinch, doesn't react except for those silent tears now mixing with the brown coffee splatter on her neck.

I grit my teeth at the terrified expression in her eyes. She's begging for my help, but I don't know what to do.

I carry her inside the shower and turn on the water. Without taking off our clothes, I move us under the water, supporting her in my arms. I'm fucking scared to make a wrong move and worsen whatever the fuck is happening to her. My mind runs wild, not knowing what to do or whom to call. I feel so fucking helpless right now.

I turn off the water and leave her in the shower for a second after propping her up against the wall.

When I return with a towel, she's lying on the floor of the shower stall, curled up in the fetal position. My legs shake, and pain like never before rips through my chest and lungs at the sight of her.

She looks so fucking small, so broken. I can't help the tears that gather behind my eyes. Her body trembles as she weeps silent tears.

"Rose, stay with me," I whisper in a hoarse voice and wrap the towel around her. I bring her to her room, the floor getting wet and slippery as I walk, my wet clothes clinging to my body.

After pulling away the comforter, I place her on the bed, still wrapped in the towel. She hides her face in the pillow, and the bed shakes as she continues to tremble.

Giving her a pained glance, I quickly get out of my wet

clothes and put on a dry T-shirt and sweatpants. In record time, I'm back with her.

As I untangle her from the towel, she pulls away from me and dashes to the garbage bin next to her desk.

My hands freeze, and I'm rooted in place with a wet towel in hand.

What the hell just happened?

Did my touch nauseate her?

I can't breathe for a moment, but soon she retches, and I rush over to her.

I want to do so much—hold her, support her, rub her back—but I'm scared to do anything and make this worse.

Looking exhausted, she lies on the floor, and I get down on my knees, helplessly watching her and begging for a clue on what to do. And then she gives it to me.

She grabs my hand and mutters, "Please don't leave."

"I'll never leave you, baby." I pull her close to my chest. But when I try to get up, she protests, shaking her head.

We spend the night on the floor. She pukes a few more times, coming in and out of consciousness the whole night.

49

ROSE

"You're still here," I whisper in a croaky voice when I feel Zander near me. If it weren't for the cold tiled floor of my room against my forehead and cheek, I wouldn't even know where I am. His warm presence is the only thing keeping this room alive; otherwise, everything around me feels dead.

"How are you?" he asks as I try to sit up, supporting my back against the wall.

I peer up at him as he sits on his haunches in front of me, still not close. He continues to stare at me without so much as touching me or making a sound.

"Are you afraid of me?"

Hearing my words, he shakes his head. His eyes are bloodshot; I'm guessing due to lack of sleep. I'm sure he didn't shut his eyes for a minute the whole night. His hair is ruffled, and he looks years older than he did yesterday. Overall, he looks tired.

Tired of me.

"How are you still here?" I ask again, my parched throat making it difficult to speak.

Zander picks up a glass of water from the table and

passes it to me. I follow his movements, trying to understand what he's still doing here.

"Where else would I be?" His eyes are filled with so much sorrow that I can't even bear to look at him for long.

My mind says, *anywhere but here* in reply to his question.

I return the empty glass, and he places it back on the table, being careful not to touch me.

"You don't want to touch me?" I ask as he observes me with those sorrowful eyes from a distance.

"Rose, I'm afraid to do anything at this moment."

I nod. I understand. My chest, stomach, limbs, and most of all my heart, all ache knowing that it's over now. He won't be able to stay. But then he surprises me.

"I would do anything to hold you in my arms, to take away the pain, the…fear. But more than that, I don't want you to go back to whatever dark place you visited yesterday."

My eyes itch as fresh tears start flowing from them. I cry for myself, but also for him. How much pain have I caused him?

"You're killing me, baby." He looks up at the ceiling, and a single tear rolls down the corner of his eyes.

Oh my God! What did I do to him?

The pressed anguish bursts in my chest, and I forget to breathe. I jump into Zander's arms, and my action catches him off guard. It takes him a second to find his balance again.

He crushes me against his chest, as if this was something he's wanted to do for hours.

"I thought you'd leave," I say in between hiccups, my throat thickening every second.

"And go where?" he asks again, as if there's nowhere else in this world he'd rather be.

"Somewhere far. Someplace where I don't exist."

"That's the problem, couch girl. You're everywhere. In my every breath, in my every heartbeat. I'm never away from you, even when you're not around." When I sneeze in his arms, he says, "I knew you would catch a cold in those wet clothes, but I also didn't know what to do."

My heart cracks at hearing him so helpless. Zander likes to be in control. I can't imagine how he survived last night.

"Would it be okay to change now?" he asks.

I nod, and he gets up from the floor, bringing me with him. He places me gently on the bed as if I'm a breakable china doll and hands me my nightshirt.

"Why don't you change, and I'll make you some tea?"

I don't know if he really wants to make me tea or if he thinks I need some privacy. Before he can leave, I whisper, "I can change with you in the room."

Hearing my words, a weak smile pulls on his lips, which doesn't reach his eyes. "I'm very glad to hear that, couch girl. But I still want you to drink some tea. You were cold the whole night and your voice sounds croaky. I don't want you sick."

As I'm settling back on the bed, Zander walks into the room carrying a tray with a cup of coffee and a glass of hot water, along with a bag of lemon tea and honey. He places it on the nightstand, and I notice the time on the digital clock. It's already nine.

"Office?"

He shakes his head. "I called Oscar and let him know you're not well and we're taking a day off."

I don't complain. I'm in no shape to go, anyway. My head hurts so badly; it feels like a thousand hammers are banging it.

Zander slips my phone on the nightstand and says, "Kristy called earlier."

My hand, which was going for the cup of tea, halts and trembles.

He grabs and holds my cold hands in his warm ones. "No, Rose. Don't go there. Stay with me. I'm here, with you."

I look up at his warm eyes and try to calm my breathing. I

focus on his gentle hands, rubbing my palms softly before circling my wrists.

"What happened, couch girl?"

"Kristy is pregnant," I whisper, my mind running wild. We'll have to keep it a secret, even from the walls of my room. Don't they say walls have ears or something?

"You're not happy?" Zander asks, totally oblivious to the looming threat.

Happy? How can I be happy?

"She's in danger."

"Who, Kristy?" Zander grabs my shoulders, and I meet his surprised gaze.

"The girl...the baby." As I force the words out of my dry mouth, I can feel my insides crumbling.

He looks at me with a mix of worry and confusion. "Which baby, Rose? Kristy's?"

I nod. "There's a ninety-eight percent chance th-that the girl will inherit Kristy's eye color." My voice quivers with fear. My heartbeat races so fast that my chest hurts.

"Rose, what are you saying? Kristy doesn't even know if she's having a girl."

"But w-what if it's a girl?" I hug my knees and unconsciously rock back and forth. I don't even realize it until Zander grabs my shoulders, halting my movements.

"Look at me, Rose. What is it?" he asks slowly, but I just shake my head. "What if the baby is born with blue eyes, Rose?"

"They'll take her. They'll take her...away. We'll never find her," I say between hiccups as fresh, painful tears wet my cheeks, mouth, and neck.

He hugs me tight, hiding me in his broad chest, hiding me from this bad world.

"Like they took you? You remember something from your past?"

I don't need to reply.

He knows.

He knows I do.

"Something you haven't told anyone." He's talking to himself now, not questioning me, but his painful voice breaks my heart.

How much will I hurt this man with my baggage?

I HAVE no idea how much time has passed since I've been bundled in Zander's arms. At some point, he pulled a blanket over me to stop my shaking, covering us both. But it did nothing to calm my chilling insides.

I turn to my side and notice our tea and coffee have gone cold. My tears have stopped, but my headache has increased tenfold now.

"I want to sleep." Maybe when I get up, things will be back to normal.

He nods but whispers, "Why didn't you ever tell anyone?"

All my childhood and teenage life, I've trained my brain to suppress those haunted years. On my sixteenth birthday—the day that Kindred Hearts picked as my birthday—Sophia asked if I remembered anything, and I simply said no.

By that time, I'd repeated the same lie to my face every morning.

I was lost. No one knew where I was, and I don't remember anything.

Maybe the first two things weren't so much of a lie.

I even repeated the same answer to Zander when he first asked about my past. But how could I lie to him now?

We're going to start a new life together. I need to tell him why I can't give him the two-and-a-half-kids-white-picket-fence life.

I just can't bring a baby into this world, even if there is only a minuscule chance that it'll be a girl with my eyes.

Just thinking about another baby, alone and lost—

"Rose. Rose, stay with me." Zander pulls me back from his chest. "You're safe," he whispers as I clutch his cotton T-shirt, balling it in between my hands.

I lean in and smell his woodsy vanilla scent, which I now know is his Coach cologne in a steel flask. I think about the image of the horse carriage carved on the bottle. Any other thought to keep me grounded, to keep me in this moment.

"I know it's hard, but you need to tell me."

"I told you when I was found... I didn't speak for a very long time."

I feel him nod, his chin resting over my head.

"I was at the hospital and underwent grafting surgeries. During that time, police and social workers came in daily, blasting thousands of questions at me. When I gave no response, they all assumed I was mute. By the time I started speaking, everybody had forgotten. Like so many others, I was all but a case file gathering dust. No one cared enough to ask again." I feel nothing but a sense of emptiness remembering that time.

"I'm asking, Rose. I'm begging you to tell me everything, everything you remember." He stops rocking me just enough to say those words.

"Why? What's the point now?" My pulse goes wild, imagining those words finally coming out of my mouth.

"Because I fucking care. Because you're everything to me. Because it fucking matters to me."

I hold his face between my hands, and his smoldering gaze lands on me. His livid face softens, and he whispers, "Do this for me, sweetheart. Please."

I nod. I would do anything for him—walk on a bed of hot coals or relive the horrors that haunt me.

"I remember bits and pieces. I think if I didn't have a photographic memory, I might not even remember these instances. That's why I always curse this *gift*."

I take a deep breath before I break the promise I made to

my small self years ago. Before I open those bolted, chained doors that hide my worst fears and memories.

"I was heavily sedated most of the time. The doctors also confirmed huge amounts of drugs in my blood. But sometimes, in between, I remember"—I swallow hard—"a woman…and a man. The woman didn't hurt me. In fact, she'd apply something like a balm on my wounds. It felt cold, numbing, and nice. But the man…he'd put s-something hot on my back. I think I must've cried in the beginning, but when he increased the pain and burn, I—I became silent."

My back feels hot now, and the cotton of my T-shirt itches my skin. When I shift and twist, trying to get free, Zander's hands crawl inside under my T-shirt. He runs them all over my back, assuring me there is nothing there and it's just in my head.

"Anything else?" he asks gruffly, continuing the motion of his hands. When I don't reply immediately, Zander presses on my shoulders, his hands still buried under my T-shirt. "Tell me."

"He covered my face—most of it—with some fabric like cotton. It was breathable enough." I inhale deep, taking in clean air.

"But?"

"My eyes. They were open. He would sometimes force me to open my eyes when I was sleeping," I say. Zander's heart beats rapidly as my head rests against it. "That's all."

My chest feels tight and light at the same time. I fall back against Zander's arms and as always, he catches me.

I never imagined how this moment would be, when I'd finally let everything out in the open, giving it life. I never realized it'd feel so cathartic.

I DON'T REMEMBER when I closed my eyes.

But when I wake up, half a day has flown by. I get up groggily to find Zander sitting beside me, his face serious as he stares at the wall. I shift and his gaze falls on me.

"Got some sleep?" He kisses my forehead. When I nod, he adds, "We got company."

My body freezes at his words.

"Hey, Rose. It's okay. It's not Kristy. It's Zach." He caresses my hair. "Why don't you clean up and I'll get you something to eat?"

I nod and get up from the bed. Only after I've turned the water on, do I hear Zander's footsteps leaving the room outside the closed bathroom door.

I wash my face and pee before joining Zach and Zander in the living room. There's a takeout bag from Giovanni's in front of them.

Zach notices me and gets up from the couch. "Can we eat now?" He marches toward Zander, who is stirring my coffee mug next to the can of my new favorite chai latte. Zach shakes his head in annoyance. "You ask me to bring lunch, and then you don't let me eat it. You know I can't stay hungry."

His irritation pulls a surprise smile to my lips. Zander also notices it, and his lips curl up when he drags over a barstool for me and hands me my mug.

After placing a kiss on my lips, he grabs the cardboard takeout boxes and puts them in the microwave.

"It'll be a minute." Zander bats Zach's hand away when the younger Teager brother starts to open the microwave door almost immediately. When the food is done, Zander pulls it out of the microwave carefully and then puts the food into bowls.

"There, sweetheart." He places my favorite fettuccine before me.

Even though I'm melancholy, the warm pasta feels good against my sore throat.

We eat amid Zach's continuous bickering about how the restaurant didn't have his favorite calzone and he had to settle for lasagna instead. After we've finished, Zander removes the dishes from the table, and I notice he's dressed in one of his suits.

"Are you going somewhere?"

He nods. "I have to talk to Beast about something. Is it okay if I go? Zach will stay with you until I come back."

50

ZANDER

I reach Beast's house. As I park my car, there's another text from Kristy.

Kristy: How is she? It's killing me to stay away. Did she tell you what triggered the panic attack?

Me: She's better. I'll call you in a few hours. Please don't visit her until then.

Me: And don't stress too much.

I put my phone back inside my jacket. I know Kristy is worried, but I have more serious issues to deal with.

"Zander, what's the matter?" Beast asks in an exhausted voice as I enter his office. "What is so urgent that I had to miss my flight?"

"I need your help." I place the file Lukas gave Zach on the study table.

"What is this?" His gaze moves between the file and me.

"It's Rose's case file from back then." My body tenses at the thought of its contents.

"How did you get it?" Beast eyes me curiously, making no effort to pick it up from the desk.

"Lukas arranged it for me." I swallow back the anxiety. I just hope he didn't break any laws while doing so.

"You asked for Lukas's help?" Beast's eyebrows rise in surprise.

It's no secret that I'm not a fan of Lukas Spencer, Zane's friend. But these are desperate times. I'll do everything in my power, no matter how hard that may be, to get my girl out of the fear that has paralyzed her for her entire life.

After staring at me for another moment, Beast grabs the file. He sifts through the first few pages until his eyes and hands halt on one page.

"What is it?" I circle his table and find him staring at a grainy picture from police records. It shows the wounds on Rose's small back.

He runs his fingers over the picture, pausing in between as if he can feel them. "She has these?"

I hum around my pounding heart, my eyes fixed on the angry wounds. The current marks on my girl are just a whisper of these horrible, angry gashes and burns.

"Fuck!" Beast stands in a fury, forcing me to step back. All the papers fall down, littering the floor.

"You said she was found by someone. Where?" Beast suddenly grabs my shoulders. His grip is tight, filled with anxiety and eagerness, taking me by surprise. "Somewhere close?"

"No, not even close," I rush to answer. I wasn't expecting such an angry outburst from him. "She was found in another part of the country. She had never even stepped foot into this area before she took a job in Cherrywood."

"Are you sure?"

"Yeah. But why do you ask?" Watching his reaction, a flush of adrenaline tingles through my body.

"Because I've seen those exact same marks before." His wide, horrified eyes elevate my pulse. I've never seen Beast like this. He almost looks scared.

His hands shake as he opens the top drawer of his desk, withdrawing an envelope.

How many times have I seen it in his hands?

On several occasions, I've walked in on him with this yellow envelope on his table or the old sepia pages that reside inside it, close to his face. He'd carefully fold the papers, place them into the envelope, and then lock it away before looking up at me.

But today, he empties all its contents in a rush, not caring what lands where. He fumbles through the mess of pages until his hands find whatever he's looking for, and he plants a picture on the table.

It's a similar grainy shot of someone's back bearing the exact same wounds as Rose's. The only difference in this picture is it's the body of a woman, not a child.

"I don't understand. Who is she?" I hold the photograph to take a closer look.

"My wife." He slams his fists on the table.

His words take me by surprise, and the photo falls from my hand.

Beast lights a cigarette, walking back and forth anxiously. "Tell me everything you know."

I rehash the events Rose told me this morning and wait for Beast to say something. Finally, he does. A lot.

"My wife and I met by chance in a café. She was there on some kind of blind date, and I was dared by my friends to kiss a stranger. She slapped me at our first meeting. She hated me so much." His eyes are transfixed on the photograph as he takes back his seat.

"But I fell in love with her, there and then. I chased her, following her everywhere until she agreed to go on a date with me." A pained smile emerges on his face. I try to imagine a younger version of Beast roaming around the streets following a woman.

"Long story short, we fell in love and got married. When she got pregnant, we decided to make St. Peppers our home. My darling Chloe was born, and I was living a dream. A beautiful dream." He runs his hands over his face as if imagining those days. "But in all the happiness, I forgot that dreams break when the night is over, and so did mine."

Holding my breath, I wait for him to continue.

"My wife was a teacher, and one day, while she was returning from school, she was abducted on her way home. I moved heaven and earth to find her." He gets up from his chair and walks to the window, looking outside at nothing in particular. "I was devastated. I went through hell during that week."

"But you found her?" I can't stop myself from asking.

He looks at me over his shoulder. "Yes, but it wasn't me who found her. I tried everything to get to her. I spent days and nights holed up in my office or at the police station. I didn't sleep a minute those seven days. But I couldn't find her."

Beast slams his fist against the window sash. For a moment, I worry he'll break his wrist, but he continues before my mind wanders more.

"It was Roxanne. She found my wife. That day, I was put in a lifelong debt to her. I can never forget what she did for me, my family. She found my wife, heavily sedated and left to die on the highway, hands and feet tied together. Roxanne gave me back my life that day, or so I thought."

He gets back in his chair. "But she'd changed. Gone were her laughs that filled my house. Gone were her smiles that made my heart stop. She was lost and depressed. I got her the best doctors, and everybody told me it was the trauma, and it would go away with time. I just had to be patient."

He rests his head against the headrest, looking at the ceiling. I never thought there'd be a day when Beast would be so vulnerable. At this moment, he doesn't look like the giant, strong man from my childhood.

"She never spoke about what happened in those seven days, but she was shaken. She was terrified. And that's not how she was before." He looks me in the eye before slamming his hands on his desk, and the pens go flying around. "*My* girl made men cry at the shooting range. She fucking knew her place in the world, and she knew how to fight for it. But after that week, my brave girl was nowhere to be found. And there was always this lost expression on her face. I couldn't bear it."

My throat constricts, remembering how I found Rose in the shower stall last night and how fucking helpless I felt. I can undoubtedly feel Beast's pain.

"She wasn't sexually violated, thank God for that, but she had these burn marks on her back. That fucker possibly used a hot double hook to imprint her skin."

Sweat trickles down my spine as I imagine Rose being hurt in a similar way. "Rose said something about feeling hot on her back."

He nods. "I tracked the case, partly with the police and partly by myself, for several more months, but all our leads ran cold. I also had to focus on my wife. She was slipping away from me day by day. She started getting distant, not only from me but Chloe too."

Beast crushes his eyes with his palms as if trying to get rid of the bitter past images.

"It was a year after the kidnapping. We were invited to a friend's party out of town. I decided to take her, hoping it would be a good change, and it was. For the first time in a very long while, we had a normal evening. She smiled after almost a year. Gradually, my wife was coming back to me, and we found out she was pregnant again. I was walking on air as we rekindled our lost love. But then she went into premature labor, and our baby girl was born dead."

Beast's bloodshot eyes focus on me, and I suck in a breath. I never thought I'd see this man so helpless and lost. I always thought nothing in this world could shake him. But I guess when the storm of life hits, it doesn't matter how strong you are; it can still blow you away.

"I lost everything that day. A week later, my wife left me, leaving behind a fucking letter. She wrote that she couldn't bear the pain of living in a loveless marriage. Living with me reminded her of everything she'd suffered." He finds the letter among several other things that fell from the envelope and hands it to me. The white paper, now yellow with age, is wrinkled as though it's been folded and unfolded several times over the years.

While I'm busy reading the letter, Beast is staring at a photograph.

"Is it her?" I ask, and he turns it around. The ground beneath my feet slips away as a familiar face in black and white smiles back at me. "What did you say your wife's name was?" I try to keep my voice light, masking the tension that's surging through my veins.

"Sophia."

"Can I see the picture of Chloe again?"

Lost in sorrow, Beast mechanically draws out the photograph of his daughter from his wallet. I fix my eyes on the picture, and this time, I recognize the shapes and lines on the little girl's face, which has become very familiar to me in past months.

I return the photo and place Rose's file back on his table, rearranging all the papers. "I need to be somewhere, but I'm leaving this with you."

He nods, and before I'm out of his study, Beast calls out, "Zander, I have a feeling that your Rose is the key to my Sophia."

I nod without saying a word. I don't know if Rose is a key to finding his wife or if his wife is the key to the missing part of my Rose's life.

"I want to meet you. Now," I shout into my phone after parking my car on the secluded road. I pinch the bridge of my nose to hold on to the thin sliver of control I have left.

"Zander—"

"Don't even try to make an excuse or else I won't come alone, but with a fucking party of Rose, Kristy, and Ashcroft." I can hear her loud gasp through the speaker. "I need answers, Sophia, and I need them now. Give me your address."

"I can't give you my address, Zander."

There's an unusual quiver in her voice, but anger courses through my veins with one aim—to know the truth. "Are you fucking kidding me? You realize I know your secret, or whatever the fuck this is." Heat flushes through my body, and I grab the door handle, almost ripping it out.

"I'll meet you at a café in St. Peppers in an hour. I'll text you the address," Sophia says and ends the call before I can respond.

I can't fucking believe this coincidence.

Kristy is Beast's daughter. *She* is his Chloe.

Sophia is his wife.

Where does my Rose fit in all this?

This question haunts me throughout the entire ride.

Sophia sits across from me at the back table of this cozy café. I met her for first time at Kristy's wedding. I can't help but imagine her with Beast, trying to fit her into the story he told me.

"How did you get here so fast? From what I've heard, you live nowhere near."

She flinches at my words but then squares her shoulders, a hint of the woman Beast spoke about. The woman who takes shit from no one. But not today.

"So, this is another lie you've told your daughter."

Sophia purses her lips, and I know she doesn't like my tone.

"How do you know Ashcroft?" she asks me instead. Her voice trembles as she says his name.

"He adopted me and my brothers and raised us in his home."

If she's surprised by the coincidence, she doesn't show it. "How long have you known?"

"Since an hour ago. I took Rose's file to Beast. That's when he showed me pictures of your case and you."

A sad smile pulls on Sophia's lips. "You call him Beast."

But I don't entertain her distraction. "Does Kristy know?"

Sophia shakes her head before taking a deep breath. "I took her away in hopes to never return to this place. But fate plays out in strange ways. Of all the places in the world, Kristy took up a job offer in Cherrywood. I try to maintain my distance from her and Rose so that they are safe." Her confusing words and resigned voice don't help my restlessness.

Keep them safe? From whom?

My questions remain unspoken as the waiter appears and places two cups of coffee on the table.

Once he leaves, Sophia asks, "Why are you looking into Rose's case? It's been closed for years."

"She had a panic attack yesterday after learning about Kristy's pregnancy. She's petrified Kristy's girl will be born with the same blue eyes." My eyes narrow on her face. If Sophia and Rose suffered the same trauma, this piece of news would've affected her too.

And my thoughts turn out to be true when Sophia's hands tremble around the cup handle. "We don't even know if it's a girl." Her voice quivers.

"Is that fucking thought keeping you sane?" My anger and confusion meld together, and my words come out in a hiss.

"Otherwise, you too would be scared shitless of Kristy's pregnancy."

"I don't understand." She shifts in her chair nervously, avoiding any eye contact. Her chest rises and falls as she takes heavy breaths. Her hands clutch the cup tight, and I fear it will crack at any minute.

"Really? Rose told me there were two people who kidnapped her." I try to get something out of her—anything to learn if there's a connection between her and Rose.

"She remembered?" Sophia's mouth falls open, and her trembling fingers touch her parted lips.

"She never forgot. She has a photographic memory, for fuck's sake. But you know all of this, much better than me. You were kidnapped by the same people, weren't you?"

"I—I don't know, Zander. I don't know why you think I have answers to these questions, when even the police have no clue." Sophia grabs her purse on the table. I know she's ready to bolt out of here and go back to hiding from reality.

"Don't play games with me, Sophia. Just tell me if Rose is your daughter. Is she Beast's?" My fists clench under the table, imagining how many lives have been turned upside down. And I don't know who's to blame.

Tears roll down her cheeks, and in this moment, I feel sorry for her. She's lost so much, but isn't it her doing?

"How is that even fucking possible?" I ask.

"We never saw our second baby," Sophia whispers, averting her gaze from mine.

And that's when I remember the premature stillborn baby.

My Rose.

My heart jackknifes against my chest as Sophia continues. "When I met Rose at Kindred Hearts, I was struck by how much she looked like me. I called the hospital, and…they checked the records. There was no stillborn baby listed on the day of my delivery."

I can't believe it.

Innumerable questions run through my mind.

How is it such a small fucking world?

Is this fucking fate?

But out of all those, only one escapes my mouth. "You know her birthday?" The enormity of this doesn't go unnoticed by both of us as our eyes meet. "We have to tell everyone," I say with finality, getting up from my chair.

"Zander! No, we can't," she rushes out, grabbing my hand and halting my movements.

"Are you not seeing what this lie has done to your family? There is a man, whom I've never seen as broken as I did today, who carries the photo of his daughter, his Chloe, everywhere. He thinks it's his fault that you left him. He doesn't even know he has another daughter. Your daughters don't know they're sisters."

I can't believe how many lives will be stirred by this revelation.

"Why did you run away, Sophia? What's scaring you?"

She shakes her head, not saying anything, her face wet with tears. She reminds me so much of my girl.

No.

She and Rose just *look* the same. They are, otherwise, different.

My girl is fighting to be found, while Sophia is trying everything to stay lost.

"If you don't want to answer me, then don't. But tomorrow, I'm going to tell them your secret. This might be your only chance to get your life back, Sophia. To get your family back."

I place a card on the table next to her trembling hands.

"This is the address of a hotel in Cherrywood. I'll have a room reserved for you. I hope to see you tomorrow at Rose's place at nine. I'll have everyone there." Before leaving, I add, "I hope you make the right decision."

51

ROSE

Zander spent the whole day away. I know it had something to do with the information I dumped on him, but I tried not to think much about it. It was only possible by the welcome distraction Zach and Zane brought with them. After the panic episode, I had no desire for an eventful day and that's exactly what they gave me.

A few minutes after Zander left, Zane joined me and Zach, and we spent the day lazing on the couch watching movies. They bickered over movie selection, what to order for dessert, and which of them has more of a following among office girls.

I know most of their theatrics were for my account, especially when they came from Zane, but I enjoyed it regardless. I don't have much experience with siblings bickering, and I loved every bit of it.

I told them about our new house and that we'll have a room for both of them. They laughed at my face, telling me how they're never staying at our place, especially not so soon. They have no desire to see Zander's naked ass or hear his grunts and moans.

Their words, not mine!

My cheeks burned thinking about that perfect ass and those macho grunts. My reaction only made them laugh harder.

"How are you feeling?" Zander asks as we sit on the couch after dinner.

A documentary about empty villages in Europe is running in the background.

I smile. "Better than yesterday."

"I'm happy to hear it, couch girl." He sighs deeply, relaxing back and taking me along with him.

Whatever happiness he says he feels doesn't really reach his face.

"I love you, Rose. I want you to know that you can always talk to me about anything. For me, you and my brothers are the most important things in this world. Remember that." He brings my hands to his mouth and presses a kiss on them.

"I know. It kills me to see you like this." I know my truth has shaken him, but I hope we can return to some sort of normalcy soon.

He kisses me soft and slow, saying without words how much everything has rattled him. I kiss him back, telling him how much his concern means to me. His anxiety about something that happened to me in almost another life, when no one cared for me, fills my heart with so much warmth.

"Tell me something. Anything. Make me forget yesterday," I plead with him, my face hidden in his chest.

I thought he might resist and would insist we talk more about the incident. But he surprises me when he starts telling me a different story.

"When my dad was still alive, we didn't have a fireplace in the house. But I'd seen in movies that Santa comes through the chimney."

I glance up at him so that he can see my smile. He knows I love hearing about the happy part of his childhood. I crave those stories.

Zander smiles back and continues. "Zach was only four then, and he wanted a parrot so he could teach the bird all those bad words we weren't allowed to use."

I can so see a naughty toddler Zach concocting his devious plan.

"Now, I was young myself, okay? So don't judge me too much." Zander bites back his smile.

I giggle, itching to know where his story is going.

"So, the chimney wasn't possible. But a tunnel was." Zander makes an imaginary pathway with his curled fingers. "I dug out a tunnel from the main gate to the porch. Next day, I got a parrot from a neighbor lady. I told her it was a Christmas gift for my brother, and she gave it to me for whatever pocket money I'd saved. So, I kept the bird on the far end of the tunnel and closed both the holes with stones so that it didn't fly away."

"Oh my God." My hands clasp together, and I bring them closer to my chest.

Zander gives me a lopsided smile, the dimple on his left cheek on display as he blinks mischievously. "Now, come next morning, I took Zach to the porch and removed the stones I'd put on that side of the tunnel. I'd hoped to find the bird, but it wasn't there. I ran back to the other side, and I still couldn't find it."

"Fish! You killed it?"

"Yeah," he says, shrugging lightly.

I chuckle, watching him pull on the collar of his shirt in embarrassment.

"I told you I was a kid myself." A flush creeps across his cheeks, and I nod, biting back my shocked laugh. "So, I dug out the whole thing. The poor bird was a few inches into the tunnel, lying flat. I had to bury it again, before my parents found out about it. But Zach was happy anyway. Whenever he wanted to say a swear word, he'd run to the burial place and blurt everything. If my parents asked what he was doing, he'd say he was teaching the words to the bird."

I laugh out at the crazy story. "Zach was naughty all his childhood?"

"Till he couldn't be."

My smile drops at his words, my heart squeezing for Zach. I know Zander's brothers have their own scars. I might not see them, but they're there, a reminder of their mother's negligence.

"Thank you for sharing that with me." I kiss his cheek.

He rubs his nose on my naked shoulder, my loose T-shirt stooping low. "Do I just get a kiss in return?"

"What else do you want?"

"You. All of you."

"You have all of me, Zander. From the moment we laughed over that picture of Wolverine."

"And you me, couch girl."

"What's left?" Zach storms into the kitchen as Zander and I are just finishing our breakfast.

"How are you always hungry?" My eyes graze over Zach. He doesn't even have an ounce of fat on him, but he's in a perpetual state of food hunting.

He replies to my question with a grunt, scanning the kitchen to find anything to put in his mouth.

"We have some strawberry shake left." I point toward the blender when he starts looking inside every jar and pot, including the empty ceramic flower vase.

Without missing a beat, Zach opens my kitchen cabinet and pours the leftover shake into a glass that he'd just grabbed.

Thankfully, Clem is away for a week on an internship. I'm not sure how she'd feel about Zander and his brothers getting all domestic in our kitchen.

"Why ar-re we here?" Zane asks from where he's standing at the kitchen's entrance.

"Let everyone get here first," Zander replies, refilling his coffee mug.

Yesterday evening, he told me that we'd have a few guests over, including Ashcroft's family. I was surprised that Zander never mentioned Ashcroft's wife and daughter before. But I was more shocked by the fact that they're estranged.

Ash is a wonderful man. Why would someone leave him? And there's no way he would let his family slip away; he's so like Zander. Family means a lot to him.

My gaze wanders to Zander as he sips his coffee, leaning against the kitchen counter, and my breath hitches at the sight of him. Dressed in blue jeans and a white shirt with his sleeves rolled up to mid-forearm, he looks breathtaking.

When my gaze finally settles on his face, I notice his focus is on me.

Is he afraid I'm going to have another panic attack?

"I'm fine." I answer his unspoken question.

After a beat, he smiles and strides toward me. "I'm very pleased to hear that, couch girl."

My heart skips a beat when he bends down to place a kiss on my lips. If there was a silver lining to my panic attack, it was that it brought Zander and me closer. I didn't know this man could love me any more, but he surprised me yet again.

My hands go around his neck to hold him closer when he tries to pull away. I can feel his smile on my lips, and he kisses me again. This time, with more fervor, pushing his tongue into my mouth, and I follow his lead.

A throat clearing reminds me that we're not alone.

Crab!

"This is the reason we're not staying overnight in your

new house, at least not until the honeymoon phase is over."
Zach pretends to be irritated, or I think he pretends, because before leaving the kitchen, he winks at me.

THE FOUR OF us have moved into the living room when Beast arrives. He man-hugs the boys before moving to me.

"Rose, my dear, how are you?"

Instead of giving me a side hug like he did to the boys, Ash opens his arms for me to walk up to him, and I do.

"I'm well. How are you?" I ask after taking a step back.

"Can't complain." He affectionately pats my cheeks. His eyes, as always, are warm. Ash raises an eyebrow at Zander. "You said it was something urgent. What is it?"

"Not everyone is here."

As if on cue, the doorbell rings.

Zander opens the door, and the smile on my face disappears upon seeing Oscar and Kristy.

What are they doing here?

My gaze moves from her face to her flat stomach, and the familiar feeling of dread returns. Since my meltdown, I've tried to not think about her and her *news*.

My breathing quickens, and at once, Zander is beside me. He rubs my arms, providing me with his warmth and strength.

"Shh, babe. Just breathe," he whispers in my ear.

Kristy perches on the other end of the couch, while I'm bundled on Zander's lap. She keeps a distance between us, and tears fill her eyes to see me in panic. I hate myself for doing this to her, for making her feel that she's somehow responsible for what's happening to me.

"I'm sorry," I mouth to her, tears pooling in my own eyes as she shakes her head.

I try to keep my focus only on Zander's touch keeping me

safe. Slowly bringing me back from the world haunted by my fears.

When Zander introduces our new guests to Beast, Ash's gaze jumps between Kristy and me. I notice how his attention stays on Kristy for a minute longer before his head jerks back to me. People often mistake us as sisters due to our exact matching eye color.

"Why have you called us here, Zander?" Oscar's annoyed voice draws my attention to him. I can understand his lack of enthusiasm. He and Kristy would be celebrating the happy news if they weren't summoned here by my fiancé.

Zander straightens behind me, bringing his hand forward and looking at his favorite Patek Philippe watch. "I'm still waiting for someone."

Oh, yes. Beast's family.

When the doorbell rings the next time, Zane answers before he returns with Sophia.

What is she doing here?

I glance toward Kristy in question, but her frown tells me this is a surprise for her too.

"Mom? What—"

"Sophia?" Beast unexpectedly interrupts Kristy and gets up in a rush. His hands shake as he grabs the back of the couch to steady himself. All the color from his radiant face evaporates as if he's seen a ghost.

"Ash." Her voice is just a whisper as her chin and lips tremble.

"God! It is you, Sophia."

In one long stride, Beast reaches out to her, a myriad of emotions passing on his face—happy, sad, shocked. Then he does something surprising.

He pulls her into his arms.

And it's not a gentle hug like he gave to me and the Teager boys.

It's a suffocating, all-consuming hug. Like he's been

waiting to do this for all eternity. Like he thinks Sophia might disappear if he doesn't hold on to her tight.

"Is this a dream, Soph?" Their interaction is so intimate that I feel like a voyeur watching it while sitting on my couch.

"Mom! W-what's happening? How do you know Ashcroft Miller?"

Before Sophia can answer, Beast's head jerks to Kristy. His bloodshot eyes widen. "*Mom?* You are Chloe."

"Um… No, I'm Kristy." Her gaze moves around the room. "What's going on here?"

Zander interrupts Kristy before she can get hysterical. "Let's all calm down, and I'll tell you why we're here."

Everybody sits, but Sophia's soft words immediately jolt us all from our seats. "Ashcroft is my husband. We—"

"Husband?" Kristy shrieks in a shaky voice.

Sophia nods, avoiding eye contact with anyone. I notice that her hand is still in Beast's tight clasp. "We were married, yes. And when you were born, we named you Chloe. But when I…left, I changed it."

Kristy pulls away from Oscar's arms and stands before Sophia. "H-how is this possible? There's no mention of any Chloe on my birth certificate, and my father's name column is blank." Her tone is accusing as her gaze bores into her mother's face.

My stomach roils at the events playing before me. As much as I'm hurt to see Kristy's childhood secrets crashing before her, I dread something worse is yet to come.

"I asked someone to make new documents for us." Sophia hesitates, not meeting Kristy's eyes.

"You forged my birth certificate."

All the color drains from Kristy's face. My own body shivers, imagining what she might be going through at this moment.

"I had to. To keep you safe." Sophia's hand trembles as she

tries to place it on Kristy's shoulder. Remorse like I've never seen before dawns on her face.

"From whom? From him?" Kristy points toward Ashcroft, who is just as stunned as anyone else in the room.

"No, from o-other people...who did this to me." Sophia opens her purse and places some photographs on the table. Her teary gaze meets mine before she straightens up.

I glance at the table. The photographs she slid my way look old and gray. From where I'm perched, I don't have a clear view of them, and when I try to get up, Zander holds me in place. I look at him over my shoulder, but he just shakes his head. Confused, I follow his instruction and stay rooted close to him.

But Kristy is already sifting through the pictures, staring at them in horror.

"What the fuck, Mom? What the hell is this?"

Sophia's shoulders slump, and she takes a small step toward her daughter. "When you were two years old, I was kidnapped. The person who took me marred my back with a hot double hook, burning my flesh." After she finishes her sentence in one breath, her gaze lands on me. But I look away from her affectionate gaze and try to unclench my hardening stomach.

My own wounds itch and burn, making me nauseous. Sophia continues the story about her abduction, being back home, getting pregnant and her premature stillborn baby, and finally, leaving Ash.

At some point in between, Kristy flops onto the couch, her sobs filling the room. Tears race down Sophia's cheeks too. But I am just stuck in one place. My heart pounds fast against my rib cage. I can already feel that there's something more awful waiting to come out.

"Then I met you, Rose. You had my eyes, my looks. My heart called for you, and I couldn't believe that of all the people, you bonded with us, me and Kristy. After about a year, I couldn't rest and had to confirm if my suspicion was right." Her hand crawls up to her chest and neck, and she rubs her skin as if trying to calm the internal tornado of emotions.

"What suspicion?" Kristy rubs her forehead before looking between Sophia and me with wide eyes.

"I called the hospital in St. Peppers, where I delivered my second baby girl."

"Premature and stillborn?" I whisper, my numb fingers digging into the couch.

I know. I know.

"They had no record of a stillborn child on that date."

"What are you saying, Soph?" Ashcroft asks, his brows furrowed as he demands answers to his lifelong questions.

"We never saw the baby, Ash. We…we were so heartbroken, we didn't ask for our baby." She hides her face in her palms, and I can feel her every sob and every tear, which are in sync with my own sluggishly beating heart. "I had a maternity DNA test done for me and Rose." She looks at me with a contrite and hopeful expression.

But I close my eyes, shutting myself off from all this information. I don't need a family now. I don't *want* a family now. I'm making a new life with Zander. I want no reminders of my past, my lost identity, and my forgotten parents.

"No! Mom!"

I open my eyes again, hearing Kristy's cry as she turns around and hides her face in Oscar's arms.

"I did what I had to do to protect you both."

"I begged you to adopt Rose, didn't I? You said she was too much of a responsibility. Too much work. You could have made this right for all of us, Mom. If you didn't want Ashcroft to have us, you still could have kept your daughters together. Why didn't you?"

My heart aches. All my life, I thought I was unlovable, and

I was so right. My mom knew who I was, yet she couldn't love me.

"Chloe—Kristy, let your mother explain." Ashcroft attempts to placate Kristy, but his hands, which rose to grab Kristy's arms, drop immediately at her next words.

"Are you really going to forgive her? Forgive her for what Rose had to endure? For what you lost?" Her hands curl into fists at her side.

"I asked you to adopt me. I begged you to adopt me," I whisper through my thickening throat.

How many times have I tried to forget that day? I promised her I'd be the best daughter. My small self, clutching her hands, just wanting someone to love me, to accept me.

"Rose, I did everything to keep you safe. I couldn't let them get to you for a second time, my baby." Sophia takes a step in my direction, but I cower into Zander's chest, not wanting the affection she's offering.

"Who are they?" Beast bellows. With clenched fists and curled shoulders, he fits his name today. "It's about time you tell me who did this to us, Soph."

"Roxanne," Sophia whispers, and everything falls into place.

The brown eyes. The woman who looked at me in pity while I was lying hurt as she put salve on my burning back.

52

ZANDER

"Roxanne? What do you mean?" Beast runs his hand through his hair.

A sickening feeling develops in the pit of my stomach.

"She's in love with you, Ash. In some sick way, she thinks you are hers."

For the first time this morning, Sophia's eyes don't hold guilt but burn with rage. She recites the incidences that changed their lives forever in an almost mechanical tone, as if she has rehearsed this conversation with Beast several times in her head.

"Roxanne hired someone to abduct me, to hurt me. But when you were beyond consolation, she had to bring me back. She threatened me all those months in our house, Ash." When Sophia clutches Beast's tensed hands, his angry, pained gaze settles over her face.

"When I was pregnant, she kept her distance. I thought that whatever gross infatuation she had for you was finally over...until the day she told me about her sick plans. How she'd raise our baby with you. She wanted me to leave with Kristy or she would kill us. I was so scared that day, I went into premature labor. I couldn't take it anymore, Ash. I had to go away, to keep myself sane and Kristy safe."

Beast stares at Sophia with eyes filled with disbelief. As if of all the reasons he thought might have led to Sophia's departure, this wasn't even on his radar.

"Ash, say something."

"I'm gonna kill that woman." Beast's voice booms in the room as he gets up from the chair.

He marches out the door, and I'm torn between following him and being with Rose. I take a hesitant step toward the door and then look back at Rose.

"Go." Rose glances at me, tears shining in her eyes. "Beast —Ash," she fumbles, as if unsure what to call her father. "He's too angry."

"I'll be back soon."

"Don't worry, Zander. We're here." Oscar's gaze meets mine. I register his tight mouth. I don't blame the guy. I'm sure he hadn't planned on spending the day consoling his newly pregnant, sobbing wife.

After placing a soft kiss on Rose's lips, I motion for Zach to follow me.

A HEAVY SIGH leaves my body as we get out of the suffocating room.

"What the fuck was all that?" Zach asks as we stride toward his Porsche.

I slide into the passenger seat before searching for Beast's car, but it's long gone.

"I know only as much as you."

"Fuck! Fucking hell!" he shouts, honking at a delivery van parked on the wrong side of the road.

There's no time to think; it's time to act. I dial Lukas, and he picks up after two rings.

"Lukas, can you come to Beast's place immediately?"

"All fine?" he asks, but I can already hear him moving.

"We found out who hurt Beast's wife and Rose." I give him a short rundown of all the craziness I learned this morning. It felt like I was watching a movie when Sophia recited what led to her taking such drastic steps.

Roxanne. I can't fucking believe it!

"I'll be there." Lukas's response is clipped before he ends the call.

Zach eyes me, pulling his gaze away from the road for a moment.

"What?"

"Why Lukas?"

"Because we don't know what we're walking into. Roxanne hired someone to kidnap Sophia right under Beast's nose. Someone is fucking sick to torture a baby with a hot hook. I'm not walking in blind here." I run a hand through my hair as my mind jumps from Beast, to Rose, to Sophia.

WE PARK outside Beast's driveway, where Lukas is already waiting for us. When we reach the doorstep, the main door is wide open, and everything in the house is in total disarray. Beast has fucking ransacked the place.

"Beast!" I shout, but there's no answer. "Ash?" I try again. When I try to enter the kitchen, Lukas steps in with his gun drawn.

"Is that necessary?" I grimace.

"This is why you called me, Zander."

We follow Lukas into the kitchen, and it's empty. But the door that opens to the backyard is wide open. We find Beast in the greenhouse, causing havoc as he goes, emptying the plant pots as if they hold answers to his numerous questions.

"Ash!" Lukas shouts, grabbing his attention.

"She's not here." Beast's body shakes with anger. His wild gaze jumps around, scanning through his surroundings.

"Where could she go?" Lukas asks.

"I don't know. She never leaves the house except for groceries, but now her room is empty. She fucking left. I cannot let that woman slip away, Lukas. She has to pay for what she did to my family."

"Calm down, Ash. We'll find her. Tell me when you last saw her."

Beast pinches the bridge of his nose and releases a deep breath, taking a minute to straighten his thoughts. "This morning. I told her that Zander had asked me to visit him in Cherrywood."

"That's good. It hasn't been long. She couldn't have gone far." Lukas squeezes Beast's shoulder once before dialing someone. "I need you to locate Roxanne, Ashcroft Miller's housekeeper. She has our tracker on her phone."

A muffled voice sounds from Lukas's speaker, but I can't make out the exact words.

"She might have trashed it. Hold on," Lukas says to the person on the other side before turning his attention to Beast. "Doesn't she have some property on the outskirts of town?"

Beast scratches his chin, his gaze confused, before he replies slowly. "It's her brother's, I think."

"Give me the current location of the phone and look for the property owned by her brother."

Once the call ends, we walk back to the front of the house. Lukas and I jump into his Jeep, and Beast and Zach follow us.

I recognize the area as Lukas slows his Jeep close to my dad's property.

"Why are we stopping here?"

"Because that's the house." Lukas points to the broken-down cabin a few meters away from the place I lived as a child.

My insides twist as my gaze shifts between the cabin and my house.

Was Rose kept here?

Was there a time she and I lived close to each other?

Before my mind runs wild, fabricating fresh questions that each rip out a piece of my heart, Zach and Beast join us.

Zach points to my father's property. "What the fuck. Isn't that the house where we lived in with Dad?"

His words take me back to those happy memories.

"We don't have time for a meltdown, Zander." Lukas's sharp voice pulls me back to now, and my eyes slide to Beast, who's unlocking the safety on his gun.

"What the fuck are you doing with that?" My lips pinch together.

"I'd be stupid to go unarmed." He's already marching toward the rickety cabin.

"Fuck." Lukas shakes his head in disapproval and runs to catch up with Beast.

When we reach the unkempt porch, Lukas peers through the window before opening the door with his foot. "Roxy?"

A loud shattering noise comes from inside, and we all make a beeline toward the source.

My feet halt at the sight of Roxanne standing in the kitchen, a knife in her hands that's pointing toward us. I can't believe she's the same woman who cared for us all these years.

"Don't come closer." She waves the knife around. "You found her, didn't you, Ash?"

For the first time, I notice how she looks at Beast. The longing. The love simmering through her eyes.

"What lie did she tell you? Did you forget that she left you alone, taking your daughter with her? That fucking bitch!" Roxanne approaches Beast, who stares at her incredulously as if he doesn't understand what's happening. "How can you believe her? I stayed with you. I comforted you when you were alone. We raised the boys together. We are a family, Ash."

A sour taste fills my mouth.

She's fucking sick.

She places her hand on Beast's arm, and her touch seems to break his stupor. He grabs Roxy's throat, crushing it with his big hands.

"Ash!" We jump into action, grabbing him from behind, trying to pull him away from murdering this maniac.

"I'll kill you, you fucking psycho. You broke my family." Beast struggles to break free. Fuck, he's a strong man.

In all the commotion, the knife drops from Roxy's hand, and Lukas kicks it away. He pulls a zip tie from his pocket and ties Roxy's hands. After dragging her into the living room, he sits her on a chair and says, "Now you talk, Roxy."

"You kidnapped my daughter from the hospital!" Beast screams before she can say a word.

Roxy's face turns pale and sweat trickles down her forehead. "H-how do you know?" She gasps before her gaze shifts from Beast to me. For a brief second, her shoulders curl over her chest, and I catch a glimpse of remorse on her face, but it vanishes as fast as it appeared.

"I never meant to harm her. She was supposed to be *our* girl, Ash. Yours and mine. But my jackass brother spoiled everything. He got infatuated with your wife when he abducted her. He wanted to bring her back here again. But when I told him about Sophia's pregnancy, he grew quiet. I thought he'd no longer be a problem. I was wrong."

She rolls her eyes as if the story she's telling is nothing but a light neighborly gossip.

"He threatened a nurse and stole your baby from the NICU. I only found out when I came here to see him months later. He'd already inflicted wounds on the girl. I knew he'd gone crazy."

Beast barks a bitter laugh. "You're talking about crazy? This whole fucking thing is crazy. I thought you were a friend, but you...you destroyed every fucking thing in my life." He takes a step forward, toward Roxy, but Lukas intercepts him.

I tug on Beast's hand, urging him to listen to Lukas. We still don't know how Rose ended up at Kindred Hearts.

"I would visit the baby often, cleaning her and feeding her," Roxy continues. "I even tried to steal her, but my brother threatened me with a gun. That's when I knew things had gone too far with him. Finally, one day when I got a chance, I poisoned his stew. He was a worthless piece of a shit. No one paid any attention to the details of his death. Everyone was so happy that he was finally gone. But I had to do something about the baby. Over the years, I'd become attached to her, so I couldn't just kill her."

My heart lurches painfully, hearing her indifference and disregard for Rose's life. We could have lost her so easily.

"But I also couldn't leave her here. She had marks on her body. She had Sophia's eyes. I knew the case was still open with the police. It could very easily be traced back to me. Plus, the girl was weird. She never cried, never made a peep. So, I took her away with me across the country and found a school for slow kids."

"She is not fucking slow!" My pulse skyrockets, blood simmering through my veins. I can't believe what I'm hearing. Roxanne's words, as if Rose was nothing but a piece of garbage she had to dump someplace, makes my skin crawl.

Roxanne continues her horrendous story. "I left the girl in a house near that school. I was waiting for someone to notice her, and on the second day, a woman found her. I immediately returned, and for some time, I kept tabs on what was happening, but I realized they closed the case and all was fine."

"All was fine?" My entire body shakes with a wild mix of fear and anger. My insides boil as I think of what Rose had to go through. "You sick woman. Nothing you just spewed from your fucking mouth is fine. I can't believe I lived with you, cared for you when you were nothing but another disgusting person from my childhood."

I'm not shocked when Beast points his gun at her head. After hearing her words, I'd have done the same. "What you did to me, to my family, is beyond imaginable. There's no word in the dictionary you can say to make it right. I lost my wife, my daughters. Rose, my baby, suffered so much because of you." He chokes as he says the words, and I feel my throat tightening too. "My wife still lives in the shadows because of you. I cannot let you walk away from all this."

As Beast's finger glides toward the trigger, Lukas stands between him and Roxanne. "Ash, she's not worth it. You just got your girls. Take your fucking life back. Don't let a weak moment steal all that away from you. Once again."

Beast turns to Lukas, his eyes dropping to his hands as the gun is pulled from his tight grip.

"Go home, Ash. Go to your family. Your wife. I'll take care of Roxy. I'll make sure she's never a threat to anyone."

I give Zach a nod and mouth for him to take Beast home.

My brother grabs Beast's arms and leads him out.

I watch through the window as he opens his car door for Beast, and when they finally leave, I release a deep breath. But my mind stays unhinged, agitation coursing through my body.

Minutes pass by before Lukas comes to stand beside me. "I called the police. They should be here soon. I also recorded her confession in case she decides to change her statement." He cocks his head toward Roxy, who's tied to a chair.

I look away from the sick woman, her face reminding me of all the pain my girl suffered.

"You did well." I pat Lukas's shoulder awkwardly. When he doesn't respond to my praise, I add, "I meant with Ash. You said the right thing."

"It's okay, Zander. I know you're not a fan of me. But I'm also not as bad as you think." He smiles, trying to lighten the air. But it doesn't reach his eyes. "I understand how Ash is feeling at this very moment. He wants someone to pay for his lost time and his lost love. I was in the same situation, but the difference is, he has someone to go back to. He has someone to drag him away from this. I had neither."

It takes me a minute to form a response at his unconventional admission. "I never thought about it." I swallow the lump of embarrassment around my throat.

"It's okay." He shrugs, walking away.

"Rose likes you," I say after him.

He laughs in surprise. "And that's killing you."

I chuckle, the weight of the past two days slowly lifting from my shoulders. I know back in Cherrywood things are far from normal. But there's no more threat to Rose and Sophia. We can all move forward with our lives.

"Not exactly killing me, but I'm perplexed."

"Why someone likes me?" He raises an eyebrow at me.

"No, asshole. But what does she see in you that I don't?" I chuckle, hitting his back. He turns around, but there's something I've wanted to say to him for a long time. "Lukas." He looks at me over his shoulder. "Zach and Zane love you as if you're our missing fourth brother. My girl adores you as if you're a long-lost childhood friend. I think I'm blinded by irrelevant things to not see the good in you. I'd like to start afresh."

He whirls around in a flash, a shocked expression etched on his face. After a beat, he swallows hard and nods. Before we can talk more, the sound of an incoming police siren grabs our attention. Lukas walks out of the house while I stay inside and keep watch on Roxanne.

Minutes later, he treads into the cabin with two armed police officers.

"She needs to be taken in for the murder of her brother and the kidnapping and assault of Ashcroft Miller's wife and daughter. There are two cold cases that will need to be reopened."

The two officers nod to Lukas, and we finally leave the suffocating place as police carry on with their business.

I jump into the passenger seat of Lukas's Jeep, and he turns on the ignition. "Ready to go home?"

I give one last glance at my childhood house before saying, "Can we make a stop?"

We enter the bar Rendezvous. Although it's a bright, sunny day, it's dark inside the bar, with the blinds shut and sangria-colored walls allowing no light to reflect.

"What will you boys have?" a smiling bartender asks.

"Two Scotches neat," I reply, flopping down on one of the barstools.

"I thought you got your girl back?" She peers in my direction after placing the tumblers in front of us. It takes me a while to notice the tattoos on her wrists.

I was at this bar after Rose told me about her past. It was the day I first called her my girlfriend in front of everyone.

"You visiting this bar often?" Lukas cocks his eyebrow at me before grabbing his glass.

"Nah." I shake my head. "Just once."

"Yeah, dude got his girlfriend that day. I guess it was a happy-sad day for you, huh?" She plays with her tongue piercing. She's as talkative as I remember.

When she finally leaves us, attending to the two guys

sitting on the other side of the bar, Lukas asks, "Why are we here?"

"I don't know. I just want to breathe for a moment." My mouth dries as Roxy's words hit me again. "I can't wrap my head around all this…information. I can't unsee the image of Rose as a baby." My hands tremble against the Scotch glass. "If he wasn't dead, I'd have killed him myself," I whisper, my head hanging low.

There's a moment's pause before Lukas replies. "No, you wouldn't have. You have a lot to lose and nothing to gain."

"But the anger rolling through me… I'm worried I'll hurt someone. I'm scared I'll hurt myself, and I don't want Rose to see me like this—broken. I don't want her to be petrified again." My insides quiver just at the mere thought of her having another panic attack.

"I understand, Zander. I understand more than you want me to. But don't underestimate your love. You'll walk to hell and back before you let a scratch on her."

"I'm sorry, Lukas." I turn my head toward him. "I—"

"It's okay. My story is for another time. Today is a good day. Embrace it. Beast got his family back. Rose finally knows about her past. You guys can move forward toward a bright future free of past secrets. A future filled with love."

"I hope you get all that someday too."

He stiffens beside me and then, without saying a word, throws back the Scotch.

53

ROSE

This morning can't be real. I close my eyes, hoping that when I open them next, things will be different, but no luck.

Everything is the same.

I'm still sitting on the same couch. Sophia's intermittent sobs continue to turn the air in my living room icy cold.

"Rose." Kristy stretches her trembling hand toward me. "I'm so sorry."

I shake my head. What is she apologizing for? Sophia's lies have hurt her the same.

Whenever I secretly imagined this day, a day when someone would come searching for me, I always thought it'd be a bittersweet moment. My parents would have looked for me all these years, and now they wouldn't be able to wait to bring me home. They'd show me my room, a place they would have set up in hopes that they'd find me someday. They would have birthday presents stacked for all my lost years.

But the truth turned out totally opposite. My mother went above and beyond to hide my existence. My dad thought I was dead.

Kristy squeezes my hand from across the couch. "I always wanted you to be my sister."

Her words drag me to a childhood memory.

We were swinging in the courtyard of Kindred Hearts and Kristy said, "Why can't you come home with us? I don't like leaving you here. I wish you were my sister. Then we could always be together."

The next day, I learned the word adoption. I begged Sophia to take me home with her. I explained to her that I'd be the best girl. At some point, I even hugged her legs, begging her to show me what home really looked like.

My eyes swim with tears, remembering the small girl and how this event was another of those that had made her believe she was cursed to be unloved for life.

Fishing photographic memory!

Masking the humiliation brought by the bitter memory, I squeeze Kristy's hand in return.

"I'm so sorry, Rose." I glance at Sophia, hearing her guilt-laden words, but I quickly look away from her puffy, splotchy face.

I don't want to understand today.

All through my life, I thought it was somehow my fault that no one wants to be with me, but it wasn't.

"No, Mom." Kristy jumps from the couch and stands in front of her, *our* mother. "You don't get to say sorry. You just don't! You knew Rose wasn't happy there. You knew she missed us whenever we went for vacations. You knew everything and yet you didn't accept her."

"Krist-ty, I'm sure S-Sophia had her reasons," Zane interrupts, trying to pacify her.

"It doesn't matter, Zane, because we're all broken anyway."

"Calm down, Kris." Oscar pulls her in his arms.

"Can you believe it, Oscar? Can you believe what she did? You didn't introduce me to Charlie until you were sure about us. You are always protecting him, protecting me. But my mom…my own mom—" Kristy sobs into his arms before pulling back. "God, what kind of mother will I be?" Her hands rest on her flat stomach. "Oh God, Oscar, how can we be sure that I won't do something like this to our child?"

My heart achingly squeezes watching all this.

Sophia's sobs grow louder, and Kristy's crying heavier with every passing minute. All the noise and agitation become unbearable. I'm about to scream or have a meltdown when Zane perches beside me.

Putting his arms tentatively around my shoulders, he whispers, "Why d-don't you get some r-rest. Once Zander and Beas-st are back, there will be more dis-scussions, I'm sure."

I return to my bedroom and close the door, hoping the bolted door will keep the dreadful revelations outside. Under the covers, I'm alone with my thoughts, without the noise, the screaming, the sobbing.

For the first time since Sophia's admission, I contemplate. What does all this mean?

How will this affect my life?

I'M PULLED AWAY from some airy space. But I don't want to leave. I want to stay between the clouds for just a bit longer. I'm light-headed when I groggily open my eyes.

What was I dreaming about?

"Couch girl?" Zander coos in his gentle voice, his face inches away from mine.

"I—I don't want to get up." I twist and bury my face in the pillow. I just want to forget today.

"I know, baby, but you have to." He caresses my hair. "Everyone's waiting for you." Zander observes me carefully, as he always does whenever he thinks I'm about to fall apart.

I hold his gaze and notice how much of a toll everything has taken on him. My breakdown over Kristy's pregnancy, knowing Sophia's truth, and God knows what happened with Roxanne. My fingers lightly stroke his weary face, and he closes his eyes and falls into my touch.

When his probing eyes are no longer fixed on me, I get some courage to give voice to my emotions. "I don't know what to make of all this. For so long, I wanted to be part of a family, but today, I don't want this. I want to run away to a place where everything is back to how it was two days ago."

His eyes flutter open. "I know, babe. But now you do have a family. You cannot run away. You have to accept it." Before I can protest, he places a swift kiss on my lips. "Everyone is as confused as you, couch girl. But we can't just hide."

I shake my head, about to tell him that I'm a pro at hiding. That's what I've done all my life. But he places another kiss on my lips, this time taking it deeper.

"I told you last night, I'm here for you. Whatever happens outside, you're mine, Rose." He pulls me up and holds me close to his chest. "And you can choose who you want in our life. No one will force anything on you."

"You'll be next to me?" My eyelashes are sticky as fresh tears run down my cheeks.

"Always, couch girl."

Hand in hand, Zander and I walk into the living room, where everyone is sitting with a coffee mug in their hands, except Kristy. The gloomy feeling again settles in my chest. The air in this room has never felt so melancholy.

How is this a reunion? This isn't how we're supposed to feel after a good news.

I'm about to sit down on the couch when Ash walks up to me. "Rose, I'm so sorry, my baby girl."

His bloodshot eyes and grief-filled voice hit me with an onslaught of emotions, but it's his words that kill me. For so long, I've waited for someone to say sorry.

As before, he opens his arms for me and I step forward, trying to soak up the warmth of his love. But this time, he doesn't let go. Ash holds me close to him, and I can feel a shudder coursing through his huge frame. He radiates mixed emotions of happiness, grief, and surprise, which resonate with mine.

My father.

I never imagined or thought about a father.

But even if I did, Beast would never make an appearance in my wildest imagination. He's an honorable man. He'd never let his family slip away. He'd move heaven and earth before something bad could touch his family.

"I'm so sorry, my baby." His glossy eyes make the lump in my throat larger, and it's hard to swallow.

I hate to see him take the blame for something he didn't do. "I'm not angry at you. It wasn't your fault," I whisper as he slowly releases me from his tight hold.

Before I can walk away, Ash grabs my hands, pressing on them and forcing me to glance up at his face.

"I didn't even know you existed, honey. It's my fault through and through. I should have checked that day at the hospital. I shouldn't have taken the doctor's word for it." His head jerks from side to side as his grip on my hands tightens.

"I don't blame you." I try to take away some of the guilt he's harboring.

Sophia walks over to us. "Rose is right, Ash. It's not your fault."

I try to take a step back at her arrival, and Beast's gaze falls to me. But he doesn't let me go far, tightening his grip on my hands.

"I'm to blame for everything," Sophia says in a throaty and brittle voice. "I was weak and scared. I didn't care about anything except myself. Even when I found out Rose was ours, I got terrified of what would happen to her, to me, if they found us again."

As much as I hate it, my heart squeezes at Sophia's words. There's no one in this room who'd understand her fears better than me.

"Later, I was petrified of the day when Kristy and Rose would eventually find out what I'd done. I was terrified of today." Her chin trembles, and she wipes her cheeks, but more tears run down.

Beast places an arm around Sophia and pulls her close. I suddenly realize I've never seen Sophia with any man.

My heart mumbles, *She was alone too.*

Kristy stands beside me, and I glance at her tearstained, sad face before replying to her bittersweet smile with my own, until realization sets in.

This is my family.

Everybody's gaze is locked on me. I can feel the hope floating around, and I have to look away.

"I can't forget." I somehow get the words out through the heavy block around my throat.

Immediately, Zander is behind me, and I lean into his familiar touch.

When Ash lets go of my hand, I turn around into Zander's arms.

"I don't know if I can forgive," I mumble "At least not so soon."

AFTER EVERYONE LEAVES, Zander and I return to his hotel suite, and we promptly decided on a bath.

"How are you feeling?" He gently strokes my calf underwater. I rest my head on his shoulder and notice the intricate details on the ceiling above the bathtub.

"I remember the times when I wished Sophia was my mother. I'd imagine the day she would take me home with her." When he places a featherlight kiss on my forehead, my eyes shut involuntarily. I'm so thankful for his love today. It's the only constant thing in my life, keeping me sane while everything else has been turned upside down. "But I never imagined feeling this *lost*. I don't know what to...think." I lean forward and puncture some of the bubbles in the bathwater. "What do you think will happen next?"

Zander's fingers start massaging my shoulders, and I try to relax the tight muscles under his gentle touch. "Most likely, Beast will bring Sophia home. They've lost a lot."

I nod. They did. They lost each other and their life together.

"Is h-he really gone? Are they both gone?" I whisper, still not completely believing that my worst nightmare is over.

Zander's body goes taut behind me. I feel his curt nod as he places his chin on my shoulder.

I close my eyes, trying to fill my lungs, my heart, with fresh relief.

I can live now.

My brain struggles to think freely, but it's so hard. I don't know what I can and cannot do. Living in fear is the only way I know.

I close my eyes, trying hard as Zander caresses my back.

He knows what I'm feeling.

He knows me.

My eyes open, and a small smile pulls on my lips as a stray tear runs down my chin.

I know what I want.

I turn around, sloshing some water on the floor before throwing my arms around his neck. "Will you marry me?" I blurt.

He freezes and his wide eyes simply stare at me for some moments before he speaks. "You—" His voice comes out as a squeak. Clearing his throat, he starts again. "You want to marry me?"

"I always wanted to marry you." Did he change his mind?

A fearful fluttering develops in my stomach. "Why are you so surprised?"

He doesn't answer my question, but instead asks me, "When do you want to get married?"

I can feel the giddiness in his eyes and happiness radiating from his body.

"Soon," I whisper and pull his face closer to mine.

"Tomorrow?" He breathes the word over my lips.

I shake my head. "I want to get married in our new house. I want to start our life there, with the happiest day of my life."

"Thank fucking God," Zander whispers before capturing my lips.

54

ZANDER

I ravish her lips with mine, pouring everything into this kiss. The exhaustion of the past few days, the fear of losing her, the anger over her suffering. Everything.

When I suck her dry lips, a whimper escapes out of her. For the first time since I found her in the middle of a panic attack in her living room, she's so relaxed in my arms. However hard I try, I can't throw that image of her out of my mind.

My hands tighten around her back, bringing her closer to me. I wish there was a way I could pull her inside me and lock her in my heart, where I can protect her and keep her away from all the bad in this world.

She mewls like a kitten, rubbing her body against me. I cup her behind and drag my hand closer to her sex. The soapy bathwater has warmed her skin, and my two fingers slip easily inside her. I thrust them in and out, slowly for as long as I can, because I know, soon, she'll eagerly ask for fast.

I'm not disappointed when she starts thrusting her bottom against my fingers, demanding what belongs to her.

"Zander!"

I give in to her demands and increase my speed. My

thumb finds her clit, and within minutes, she falls apart in my arms. Before she can come down from the high, I hoist her up and place her on my cock.

I've been rock hard since we started kissing, and I can't wait any longer. Lost in her orgasm, she slowly rides on my cock, but that's not enough. Not right now.

I put my arms under her legs and haul her up and down on my dick. Her throaty moans and my hoarse groans echo in the bathroom. Her head falls back, and I drag my mouth to her pointed pink nipples, going back and forth from one to the other. I bite on them, followed by deep sucking. In response, her sex tightens and crushes my dick, and I know she's close.

"Come with me, Rose."

And she does. She falls apart with a loud cry in my arms, and at the same time, I find my release inside her.

Her body trembles with aftershocks as she clings to me.

Thank God she started taking the pill. I don't think I'd have had the courage to leave her in the bathtub and go hunting for a condom at this moment.

I push away the wet hair sticking to her forehead and place kisses all over her face. She sighs deeply.

"You really want to marry soon?" I can't fucking believe it.

She opens her eyes unhurriedly, and the way they shine fuels my desire. Her blue eyes widen as I get harder, still inside her.

"Don't look at me like that." My face and neck feel hot with a hint of embarrassment. "You like unmanning me with your eyes."

She giggles in response and pokes her tongue out at me. I try to pluck it, but she shies away. In all our jerky movements, I slip out of her, and we both groan at the same time, feeling bereft, which is followed by a hearty laugh.

"What are you laughing at, couch girl?"

"I don't know," she says in between laughs.

I hold her in my arms and get up from the bathtub. After placing her on her feet, I hand her a towel before grabbing one for myself from the heating rack. We dry ourselves before stepping into the small closet. While we continue to steal glances at each other, she grabs one of my T-shirts and then puts on her red boy shorts with white stars.

Her in nothing but her underwear and my T-shirt is always such a fucking turn-on. Before I get distracted by the smothering mix of her sexiness and cuteness, I pull on my track pants and T-shirt, dragging her out of the closet, which is too small to think straight.

She sits on the couch, and I turn on the fireplace. I can't count how many evenings we've spent huddled together in this exact spot, talking about work, Elixir, our love, my brothers, but always avoiding the most relevant thing—our future.

But tonight is different.

I sit beside her as she continues to look at the fire, mesmerized by the flames. I noticed the first day we sat here that Rose is in love with this fireplace. This is the reason, even when we started to make improvements to the property, I knew we need to keep the traditional fireplace in the living room intact. I can already imagine our family and friends sitting around it or Rose hanging Christmas stockings on the mantel.

"Why did you agree to marry so soon? I thought you wanted to wait." I try to keep my cool, even though I'm anything but cool inside. My pulse is running wild with a heady mix of emotions. I'm exhilarated that she agreed but nervous that she didn't agree on tomorrow.

"I was nervous that once we got married, everyone, including you, would expect a baby." Her eyes remained focused on the flames.

My heart stops beating. "And now?" I try hard to bury the hope behind my words.

"I'm not scared." She turns slightly, looking at me from the corner of her eyes. Her face glows under the orange flames. "Do you want to have a baby…someday?"

My heart leaps into my throat. It's as if I'm in a dream. Isn't she saying everything I've wanted since I met her?

"I'd love to have a baby or two with you, Rose. I would love to have some mini-Roses running around."

"What about mini-Zanders?" Her eyes twinkle with happiness.

"Them too." My throat clogs, imagining our kids running around our new house in little white diapers.

Rose and I both were unlucky receptors of a crappy childhood, but I swear I'll give my kids all the happiness possible in this world and beyond.

"Me too. I would love to have them. But someday, right?" The nervous, shy girl who turned my world upside down with her smile and words makes an appearance.

I pull her into my arms and squeeze her against my chest. Doesn't she know I'll do anything for her? "Yes, someday. I want you to be exclusively mine for some more time, couch girl."

55

ROSE

"Hello, sis." Kristy strolls into my office.

It's been more than a month since our lives were turned upside down by Sophia's revelations. We're all slowly finding our way and making peace with it. At least as much as we can.

The best thing that came out of all this mess was that Kristy is my sister. The heartfelt connection I've always felt with her now goes beyond a matching eye color. It's made of blood and flesh.

She perches on a chair, playing with the red tassels of her blouse. At three months pregnant, Kristy isn't showing much. But she has already given up on her huge collection of fitted formal dresses. At present, she has a strong infatuation for custom-made bohemian tops and peasant shirts designed by Clementine.

With time, I've accepted her pregnancy, maybe with a tad too much enthusiasm. Whenever Zander and I are in the mall, by some miracle, we end up in the kids' section. I don't know what'll happen when we have our own kids.

But we have time for that.

Last week, I bought her a journal where she can mark all

her special moments with the baby, as well as things she'll want to share with him or her.

Yeah, that's another thing. We don't know if it's a boy or a girl.

Kristy and Oscar have decided to keep the sex of the baby a surprise, which is quite stupid in my opinion. Why would you want to intentionally not know something?

The crazier thing is, everyone is taking a bet on the baby's gender.

That's something I don't understand at all…

Kristy slouches back in her seat. "What are you thinking about?"

"The stupid bet."

She giggles at my agitation.

It's really driving me crazy.

I turn on the hot water kettle that now sits on the windowsill. Since Kristy's pregnancy, our ritual of going to Steamy Beans for coffee has been put to a halt. Instead, she joins me in my office every morning for a cup of hot tea.

"So, you're fine with tonight?"

I shrug. My feelings are all over the place about this evening. Zander asked me yesterday if I would like to accompany him to Beast's house for dinner. I didn't realize what he meant exactly, until he told me Ash wants to celebrate Sophia's return in his life, Kristy's pregnancy, and all of us finding each other.

To say I'm conflicted would be an understatement.

Only after Zander assured me that he'll bring me home the minute I don't feel good did I agree. He repeated the exact words to Ash while I was sitting in his arms by the fireplace.

"But you are coming, right?" Kristy's question breaks my reverie.

I nod.

"Is this some kind of practice mute protest to avoid

talking tonight?" She smiles with mischief shining on her face.

I know she's trying to lighten the mood, urging me to talk to her.

"No. No mute protest." I show her a box of mango-peach tea and she nods. "I'll be there. But if I don't feel good, Zander and I will most likely leave."

She nods and continues to watch me carefully as I squeeze honey into our mugs before dipping the tea bags in hot water.

Tonight is going to be an emotional evening for her too, maybe even more than me. She spent some of her early childhood in that house with Sophia and Ash.

"How do you feel? Do you remember anything yet?" I ask, passing her the mug.

"Not much. I've been trying to remember for some time now. I think of a purple room and...some elephant posters on a wall. I don't know." Her eyebrows furrow, and I can see how much this is affecting her. "It could just have been a dream or some TV show," she says with a grim expression I don't like at all.

Over the weeks, I've transformed into some sort of pregnancy podcast junkie, making notes on what to do and what not to do when someone you know is pregnant. Making her unhappy is a topper on the list of not-to-do things.

"I got you something." I open the top drawer of my desk and pull out a plastic box.

She immediately recognizes it, and her eyes twinkle as the corners of her mouth quirk up in a huge smile.

Another effect of pregnancy? Mood swings.

"Zander baked for us?" she asks, already opening the lid of the box.

Zander didn't just bake, but he baked her favorite.

"Lemon bars!" Kristy squeals. "Rosie, you hit the jackpot with that man."

I sure did.

"Remember, if you feel uncomfortable, just say the word and we'll leave. No one is gonna think anything," Zander tells me for the umpteenth time this evening.

We walk hand in hand to the porch, and Zander rings the bell. My heart pounds against my chest as I stand in front of the door for the second time. But today it looks different.

"Did something change?"

"Yes. Beast renovated the house. The exterior was gray before."

Now it's painted ivory; that's why it feels warm.

Ash opens the door. He hugs and pats Zander on the back before engulfing me in one of his bear hugs.

I'm at once startled, and my body stiffens involuntarily. He quickly realizes his mistake, but before he can draw back, I return his hug.

When we pull apart, he has a wide smile on his face.

"Come in." He ushers us from the living room to the backyard.

Wow!

My heart skips a beat, and my steps halt at the sight of everyone seated under the huge magnolia tree, lanterns hanging from its branches. There's a fire pit roaring on the side. If not for the tense and hesitant faces, this scene would look as if it were plucked out of a family magazine.

After Zander and I have taken the two empty seats around the circular table, Kristy, who's sitting beside me, gives my hand a light squeeze.

An awkward silence stretches for several moments, until Ash clears his throat. "We made some changes to the house. You girls can look around, um—only if you like."

When Kristy nods and I mimic her response, Ash's face lights up, and he gives us that wide, happy smile again. "Soph and I really hope you girls like it." His gaze shifts from us to Sophia, who's sitting next to him.

Tonight, she's wearing a red dress. I don't remember ever seeing her in any other color than white, gray, or black. But next to Beast, in this gorgeous house and beautiful backyard, with burning candles and daisies on the table along with polished cutlery, she fits in well.

She belongs here.

Upon seeing her happily getting back on with her life, an ache develops in some corner of my heart.

Will it ever get better?

Kristy nods again to Beast's question, and some of the sparkle disappears from his eyes when I don't mirror everyone's enthusiasm. But I don't know how to suddenly play house with people who always kept me at arm's length.

"I told you, Zane, Beast most likely ripped our rooms apart and turned them into some pink or purple shit," Zach jabbers, breaking some of the tension.

"I sure wanted to, bugger. You never kept your room clean anyway. I'd love to fix up that monstrosity you left behind. Heck! There are still posters of half-naked girls on the walls. I don't even want to step inside that shithole." Ash squeezes his eyes closed as if he can still see all those posters.

Their playful banter reduces the stress. My clenched chest relaxes a little.

"But Sophia didn't let me touch your haven." Ash shakes his head in mock defeat.

"That's good. I'd like to spend some nights here, you know." Zach pays no regard to Ash's words.

"Have I not tolerated you enough? Is that lavish hotel of yours lacking rooms for you to stay in?"

"No, and no. But what I don't have there is you. How can I annoy you if we aren't together?"

"You piece of shit."

I jump in my seat as, out of the blue, Ash throws his cloth napkin at Zach's face.

Their encounter earns a laugh from Charlie, and this time, I can't hide my smile.

For the first time in the evening, we all look like that perfect family portrait, and I like it.

"Girls, will you join me?" Ash asks Kristy and me as we sip our coffee after a hearty dinner. The guys have already moved to the patio pool table. But I don't miss Zander intermittently looking our way.

I give Kristy a subtle nod when she glances in my direction for confirmation. Ash leads us into the house while Sophia stays back, playing with Charlie. I don't know if she's nervous or just wants to give us some alone time with…our father.

Kristy has made it very clear to Sophia that she isn't going to forgive her anytime soon. I, on the other hand, have done nothing but avoid her since that morning.

Ash leads us to the left wing on the first floor. "The right wing is where the boys' rooms are."

I remember when Zane gave me a small tour of that part of the house. But everything looks different today.

"This left wing used to be for guest rooms, but this last month, your mom and I renovated it. Take a look." He opens a door, and I hesitantly step in after Kristy.

The room is painted purple. One of the walls is lined with cute pictures of a baby girl elephant. There's a throw pillow with a similar picture and *Kristy* written on it.

Kristy gasps next to me. "Oh my God."

"I don't know if you remember, but the ground floor is where we had the main bedroom and your room." Ash's gaze moves from Kristy to the purple-painted walls as he grabs the back of his neck.

It feels weird that a man as big as him is walking on eggshells around us.

"I wanted to set up rooms for both of you in case you ever wanted to come home. I mean…here. I was going for a more sophisticated, grown-up setup, but your mom suggested you girls would like a piece of your missed childhood."

A painful expression dawns on his face, and I realize it's not only us who lost that part of our lives, but he also missed out.

With a sad smile, he continues. "So, I asked the designers to get all the decorations from the ground floor to recreate your rooms. But other than that, the furniture is new and sturdy." He grips the frame of the queen-sized bed. I notice that even though the décor is childish, the furniture is all adult, including a vanity and a larger dresser.

Kristy picks up the pillow with her name written on it and looks at Ash questioningly.

"You don't remember?" He perches beside her on the bed and takes the pillow from her hand. "We went to the zoo, and there was a newborn baby elephant named Kristy. You were so enamored by her that you wanted to bring her home."

Kristy giggles, and my lips curl up in a smile. If anyone could take home an elephant from the zoo, it would definitely be my sister.

"You even made me talk to the mahout, and he was able to convince you that she was still a baby and couldn't live without her mother. But when we were back in the car, you started wailing and thrashing. The next day, I got you this pillow and the posters, and we decorated your room. You wouldn't go to sleep without it." He clears his throat. "Sophia told me that she…named you Kristy so you still had some part of your early childhood."

Hearing Sophia's name, Kristy's face turns murderous.

"I know you're angry with your mother. I'm not happy either. I had two beautiful, amazing girls, and I missed... everything in their lives. But I also understand why she did what she did. I don't like it, but I get it. What could she do when she wasn't safe? When you weren't even safe in your own house?" He releases a harsh breath of anger, but I don't think it's directed at Sophia. "But today I want to tell you, if you ever need a place of your own for a while or just a change in scenery, this is your room. You, Oscar, Charlie, and my soon-to-be grandchild are welcome anytime. This is your home, Kristy."

My heart clenches as the onslaught of emotions hits me hard. Tears roll from Kristy's eyes, and she hugs her father—our father—whispering something in his ear.

A pang of jealously hits me in my chest.

There's nothing for me here. No elephant stories, no purple walls. My hand slips into my pocket, where my cell phone is resting. I know one text to Zander and I'll be back in the hotel room in no time.

"Rose, my sweet girl, would you like to see your room?" Ash asks before I can take my phone out.

Kristy's eyes shine with tears as her head rests on Ash's chest. They look so similar. Kristy not only inherited Ash's sharp features but also his confidence. They already share a bond, a memory, whereas I'm as alien as before. As much as that thought hurts me, in some hidden corner of my heart, I don't want to be an alien. I also want to share something with him. So, I nod.

"But first, I want to show you something else." He leads us to a small pantry-sized room and flips on the switch.

It's a small nursery.

"This is everything your mother and I got when we were expecting you, my baby girl."

There's a small crib in blush pink, and a blanket in the same color.

"Your mother was obsessed with pink things during her pregnancy with you."

"I'm still obsessed with pink," I whisper, and his wide gaze shoots at me. If he's surprised I even responded, that makes two of us.

I'm not sure how to feel. I hate seeing my unused crib in a storage room. I love that my parents got me a pink crib and blanket.

"Then maybe you'll like your room." He leads us away from the small space, but I want to stay for a little longer. Or maybe much longer. My unlived childhood resides in this small storage space.

I reluctantly follow Kristy and Ash to the next room.

Three walls are painted sweet pink, while the fourth is covered with wallpaper of pink and white roses. My gaze lands on a picture frame resting on the nightstand. On a blue craft paper are three handprints, and on top of them, in a child's broken writing, are words that shake my core.

MY DEAR SIS,
COME SOON. WE ARE WAITING.

Kristy sobs as my own tears threaten to fall.

They were waiting for me.

Kristy hugs me, and soon, Ash joins us, hiding us in his huge arms. An unexpected sense of safety falls over me when he kisses my hair and whispers, "My girls, you are safe."

After several moments of golden silence, we all pull back.

"There's one more thing I want you to have." Ash opens the drawer of a computer desk, and that's when I notice the latest high-power programming laptop.

"You got me a computer?"

"I want my daughters to have everything."

Before I can soak in his affection, he places a journal in my hands.

"Take this. Your—" He stops and clears his throat. "Sophia wants you to have it. This was her journal during her pregnancy with you. In it, she talked to you."

He grabs my hands, causing me to grip the journal so tight that the leather spine bites my fingers. But I want nothing more than his intense love.

"I know you didn't have a proper childhood, but it wasn't because we loved you any less, sweetheart. We were robbed of the sweet memories of your every milestone. Your first roll, your first word, your first step… Everything was stolen from us. But that doesn't change the fact that we didn't save you, my Rose girl. I'll never forgive myself for it." He holds my face between his hands, looking at me, searching for his lost baby girl.

"All okay?" Zander asks, standing by the door, hands in his pockets and his eyes focused on me.

"Yes, yes. All's well." Ash turns away and quickly wipes his eyes, not letting Zander see his emotion.

"Zach and Zane are leaving. Charlie is about to fall asleep." He informs us that it's time to go.

Ash nods. "Come back anytime, girls. This is your home. Call me whenever you need anything or…if you just want to talk."

I squeeze his hand. "Give me time," I whisper, only for his ears.

I want to embrace this fatherly affection he's offering so badly, and I hate the prickle of doubt that doesn't allow me to do so.

"Take all the time you need. You deserve all of it."

I kiss him on the cheek, possibly surprising everyone, including myself, before I join Zander.

Sophia is nowhere to be found by the time we're ready to leave. Maybe she's just as overwhelmed as everyone else. This family gathering has been a long time coming for her too.

56

ROSE

"What's that?" Zander cocks his head toward the journal resting before me on the bed.

My gaze follows him as he plugs his phone into the charger, and then it skims to his back and his tapered waist. When he sees my attention wandering, he smirks and flexes his arm, giving me a better view. My heart races, and a weird giggle escapes me when he puts his hands at the back of his head, flaunting those muscular arms and back. He looks at me over his shoulder with a twinkle in his eyes.

Woof, he is hot! And by some miracle, he's all mine. I do a happy squeal and he chuckles.

My smile and giddiness fall when I spot the rose thorns digging into his skin and drawing blood. I try to focus on the other images, but as always, my gaze slides back to his shoulder.

"Rose, I'm different now." He perches next to me on the bed and caresses my face with his long fingers.

I know he no longer feels that abhorrence of the flower. But I can't help wondering if I'm hurting him in some way... just by existing.

"You being in my life has healed me in a way I never

thought was possible." As always, he reads my heart and says the perfect thing.

"Me too. You did more than heal me. You breathed life into me, Zander."

When he kisses my face, starting at my forehead, moving to the tip of my nose, and finally reaching my lips, my toes curl. My fingers clutching the bedsheet meet something hard, and I look down to find the journal

Zander smiles and places it back onto my lap. "Tell me, what is this?"

I graze the golden spine with my fingertips. "Ash gave it to me. It's Sophia's. From when she was pregnant."

"With you?" His eyebrows rise in surprise. When I nod, he asks, "You planning on reading it?"

"I want to. This is my first connection to my…mother, my family. But I'm also scared." My heartbeat races against my chest as I whisper, "What if there's something I don't like? What if Sophia…never wanted me?" I hate the words coming out of my mouth, but I also can't get rid of these insecurities, however hard I try. I've struggled with the feeling of being unwanted for so long that I don't know how to escape it.

"I don't think that's possible, couch girl. Beast would have never given you this otherwise." He holds the journal in his hands, turning it around. "Doesn't it look familiar?"

"What do you mean?"

"It looks similar to the one you got for Kristy."

I take stock of the leather-bound book in his hand.

Sweet sugar! He's right.

This is so similar to my own purchase. On one hand, I can't believe it, but on the other, I'm not surprised. Sophia and I always had similar tastes. I run my hand over the cover, which has *Made with Love* embossed in gold.

Instead of opening the first page, I flip to a random one. There's a date over it, and my grip on the book tightens. These dead pages hold so much of my lost life. I shift my gaze lower, reading Sophia's curly, bouncy writing. I can imagine her making those hearts over the i's and twirling the flowing r's.

My darling,

Today it was CLIMATE. That's the word with which your dad and sister beat me in Scrabble. I'm eagerly waiting for you to come out and join my team so that we can give them a taste of their own medicine.

Let me tell you a secret. Promise to not share it with anyone?

I've always envied the bond your sister and dad share. I always feel left out.

But now, I know. It's because you were coming for me. A part of me, my heart, my soul.

I'll bring you into this world, but in a way, YOU have given me a new life. You don't know how much happiness you've brought into our lives, especially when everything was just slipping away.

Sleep, my dear child. We'll meet soon.

Waiting for you,
Mom.

I CLUTCH my chest while my eyes fixate on the last word. I can see Sophia stroking her stomach, taking her baby to a dreamland where everything is well and they both are safe.

Zander wipes a tear that's leaking from my eye. "All okay?"

I give him a teary smile and curl beside him. "Did Beast ever play Scrabble with you?"

"Scrabble? No. Why do you ask?"

"No reason."

"You've started reading it?" Kristy points to the journal sitting on my office table.

I nod. I now carry it with me everywhere. Even though I'd never admit it out loud, it's my most precious possession these days.

"How do you feel?" she asks, removing the tea bag from her tea and placing it on the empty dish.

"Confused. Conflicted." I release a sigh. "When I read the journal, I see my—our—mother. I feel this connection to her. She has written so much about you and Dad. But then I see Sophia, and I can't shake away the image of her being so—"

"Coldhearted?"

My lips twist. I hate thinking of my mother from the journal as a coldhearted person.

"The woman in these pages is so emotional. She's waiting for me to come into this world. She loves me so much, even before knowing me." My throat tightens every time I think about the entries I've read. "I love that woman, and I yearn for her. But that's not Sophia. At least not the one I know."

"I'm so angry with Mom, Rose." Kristy grits her teeth, and my ribs squeeze tight, envying her for her capability to be angry.

If only I could be angry instead of sorry and broken.

On my lunch break, I close my eyes and open the journal, letting it take me to whichever page it likes.

There's a small treble sign at the top of my page.

My baby girl,

What's the matter? You are very quiet today.

I composed a piece.

It's nothing great, but I'm happy I could finish it. I told you, right, how I always wanted to be a composer?

That was my destiny, or so I thought.

But then I met your dad, and he became my destiny.

I forgot everything else.

Life with him is larger than any dream I ever had. But some days, like today, I imagine how things would have been if I hadn't met him at that café. In any case, I cannot see myself being as happy as I am with him.

I'll keep the piece here, if someday you want to play it with me.

Mom.

ON THE NEXT PAGE, I find a small white paper pasted in the journal. There are only eight measures, and as I read them, I imagine my fingers over the piano keys.

I can hear the music. It's beautiful, but sad.

I imagine Sophia sitting at her piano, writing this music.

Was she thinking about her kidnapping? Was she scared? So far, she hasn't said anything about those incidents.

ZANDER LIES PEACEFULLY on the yellow picnic mat, his aviators hiding his eyes. His fingers skim my ankle before he grabs my foot and places a kiss on my instep.

"Zander. There are kids in the park."

Before him, I didn't know kisses on places like my instep and toes could be so arousing.

He just smiles and places my feet back on his chest.

I peep once more at his handsome face before opening the journal.

Today, it opens on the first page.

My baby,

I don't know what to say, but there is so much I want to.

I just took the test last week, and when the doctor confirmed I was pregnant, your dad got me this journal.

He thinks I might like talking to you, as I'm not talking to him much these days.

You don't know what you have given us. You came at a time when I was close to thinking my life was over.

Yesterday, in the kitchen, I looked at the knife and thought of...

But then I thought of you. I couldn't do that to you.

And later, I resented myself for even thinking about something like this.

What would happen to your sister?

It would kill your dad.

You saved me, my girl.

I'm sorry for sounding depressed. But that's my state since...

She didn't sign the letter.

The ink has been smeared in several places, and the yellow page is rough and dried, as if her tears were falling down while she was writing.

My mother was depressed.

She didn't even complete the sentence.

My captivity affected me, but I only have a faint recollection of that time. It was the abandonment that shaped my insecurities. But my mom, on the other hand, remembered everything. Even after coming back home, there was Roxanne, a constant reminder of her suffering.

"Baby?" Zander gets up and wipes my tears before righting my glasses. "You okay?"

I nod and hide my face in his chest as I sob for my mom and her pain.

57

ZANDER

Today's the day. Our house is ready, and by some miracle, I've managed to keep Rose away till now. The place has been remodeled to include several features we discussed and some I know she'll love. And then there's the surprise.

Not only for her, but for me too, in some sense.

"Are you sure about it?" Rose asks Clementine, who's packing her own stuff.

Packing might not be the most appropriate word. Clementine throws a half-open candy packet in with her shoes. I've also seen some magazines being dumped in the same box.

"Rose, it's cool. My driver should be here any minute now. Don't you worry." Clementine perches next to Rose, who's folding some of her roommate's clothes that are spread out on the bed.

After our move, unfortunately, Clementine has to return to the Hawthorne Mansion.

If she's too upset, she's not showing it. She's still her same perky self.

"What's this?" Rose picks up something wrapped in silver crepe paper, hidden under one of Clem's blouses.

"It's a housewarming gift for you guys. I think you'll love it." Clementine excitedly bounces on her feet, her hands folded before her. She's like a kid in a candy store.

"You didn't have to do that." Rose turns the packaged gift in her hands. "I know you want to save for your own place."

Clementine rolls her eyes at that, making me chuckle as I take a few steps closer to my girl.

"I want to save, but I have no clue how to. Plus, this cost nothing except some sleepless nights."

Rose unwraps the square box, and there's a small picture frame. "Clem!"

Jesus. I fucking love it.

"How did…you…do this? I never take off my ring. This is like…exactly the same." Rose strokes the design of her ring through the glass. It's like she's trying to feel the grooves and ridges of her ring on the shiny flat surface.

"This isn't designed from your ring, but your ring is designed from this." Clem clutches her fists to her chest, barely holding her excitement.

A tingling warmth speeds along my limbs at Clementine's thoughtful gesture. Her gift just made our day more memorable and gave me a chance to share a memory with my girl.

And don't I know how much she loves listening to my crazy stories.

My pulse beats in my throat when Rose's big blue eyes gleam behind her red glasses, and she looks between the gift and me. "I don't get it."

"You remember the day we were at the carnival?" I pull her close and look at the beautiful sketch.

"Yes. I could never forget that day." Her face heats up.

Of course she can't. I can't either.

It was the day she lost her virginity, after all. One of the best fucking days of my life.

"I purchased something from Clementine," I say before the memories of that day distract me too much.

From my wallet, I take out the small sterling silver ring I now carry with me everywhere.

Rose's mouth falls open, and her hands fly to her chest.

"Though I hadn't come to terms with us, your name, or my past, I couldn't resist buying it. But it was so early in our relationship." The ring, wrapped in a paper bag, had felt so heavy in my pocket.

"It was only the next day that you agreed to be my girlfriend, couch girl. I knew you would run for the hills if you saw me buying a ring." I kiss her forehead.

Sometimes I can hardly fucking believe she finally agreed to me mine. My wife.

"Maybe I would have," she whispers.

"No maybe, baby." I peck her nose. "Anyway, I kept the original ring with me, and then when I was planning my proposal, Clementine made some adjustments to the design and worked with the jeweler."

"This was the final design Zander agreed to." Clem points toward the picture frame. "He has a copyright for this. Your ring is one of a kind, Rose."

A tear from Rose's eyes drops onto the shining glass. "I don't know what to say, Clem. This is exceptional. Thank you so much." She gives the picture another look before throwing her arms around her roommate.

Clementine's eyes widen, then she returns the hug and smiles widely. "Rose, I don't know what has happened, but over the past few weeks, you have changed. Maybe it's the effect of your hunk..." She wiggles her eyebrows at me suggestively, making me chuckle. "But you look so happy."

And she's right.

Rose is not only happy but also more confident. Her anxiety attacks are almost nonexistent. She is opening up more. But I can't take the full responsibility for this change.

I would say it's Sophia's journal. Every night, Rose reads it. I've noticed how she closes her eyes and picks a random page. She smells the book, her fingers gliding over the letters. She takes almost an hour to read one entry.

That's saying something, considering my girl can speed read. But she savors the words written by her mother like they're the last slice of a birthday cake.

Every night after reading the journal, she cuddles next to me. Sometimes there are tears in her eyes; sometimes she is just giddy with joy. Sometimes she is thoughtful, and sometimes she hits me with random questions. I never ask what she read. That journal and its contents are meant for Rose and Sophia and no one else. I just hope the written words will somehow ease the tension between them.

Rose has just about accepted Beast. His frequent dinner invitations have helped him to get close to his daughters. I often find him showing Kristy and Rose some hidden crook of his house that holds a meaning to only them.

I can't even imagine how many emotions are trapped in his heart, fluttering to come out. The same is true for Rose. She holds on to his every word, grabbing random pieces of her lost childhood. Last week, I even heard her calling him Dad.

But to Sophia, she is distant. I don't understand why. When Rose thinks no one is watching, I often find her staring at Sophia with anticipation. But of what? It seems as if she's waiting for her mother to do something. Give her a hint. And I think the same is true for Sophia. I hope they don't spend too much time just *waiting*.

An hour later, Clementine's driver, Scott, arrives. I must praise the patience of that man. He didn't even release a sigh of exasperation while hauling Clementine's heavy bags and boxes into the car. Only two of those ten boxes made the journey from the house to the car trunk without toppling over. But that man picked up everything and even cracked a joke about Clementine's cat lamp.

After handing the keys to Rose's landlord, Mr. Hart, we get into my car to start the next, and hopefully the most amazing, chapter of our lives.

I slow the car as we get off the highway and take the narrow lane. It has been paved with concrete but not widened. I wanted to preserve the charm of the location.

"Zander, this looks so magical." Rose points toward the blinking lights.

A few meters beyond the highway, there are solar lights on either side of the road. This was one of those things we discussed.

I take a turn, and as before, hidden behind some trees, is our house. There are several other cars parked outside.

"We have company?" Rose's brow furrows as her gaze shifts from the open parking space to me.

"It's a small housewarming party." I give her a smile, hoping she'll smile back.

"I thought we…were celebrating alone." Watching her shift in her seat, my insides soar. My nerd craves for me as much as I do for her.

"Oh, we'll celebrate alone all right, couch girl." I raise my eyebrow as her face becomes scarlet. I turn off the ignition, and holding her hands in between mine, I place a kiss on her palm. "But everyone is too excited to see the house we've been raving about for months."

"I guess that makes sense." She giggles before opening her door.

I lead her to our front door. Before she can turn the knob, I hold her hand.

"What is it?" She looks up at me in confusion.

"Ring the bell."

"Isn't it open already?" Rose cocks her head to the side but rings the bell regardless. The sounds of chirping birds and smooth piano music greet us. "Wow!"

This is one of those surprises I thought she'd like.

I open the door, but before she can walk in, I grab her by the waist, lift her into the air, and enter the house.

"What are you doing?"

"Crossing the threshold with you." I kiss the tip of her nose. I can't believe this is my life. In such a short time, this girl has changed everything. I'm looking forward to a future I never even dreamed for myself.

All because of her.

My fiancée. My couch girl. My soon-to-be wife.

"Isn't that something we're supposed to do after we get married?" She peeks at me shyly.

"For me, we're already there. God, I want to carry you to our bedroom. To hell with the family," I say before capturing her lips with mine.

"Come on, guys. Let's get this party started!" Zach's holler interrupts us. He's probably starving already.

"Let's go before he burns down the place."

Rose chuckles, then she grabs my hand as we join the others in our living room.

58

ROSE

"Rose."

Dad joins me, sitting down on the gray upholstered armchair by our beautiful fireplace. Zander didn't even tell me about this—like so many other additions he implemented in our place.

"Congratulations, my Rose girl! You've built an amazing place."

My heart does that happy dance whenever he calls me his Rose girl.

"Thanks. But I can't take all the credit."

He grabs my hand, forcing me to look at his beaming face.

"We got you something." He clears his throat before adding, "Your mom and me. It means a lot to us. Especially her."

I hate the heaviness seeping into his voice. I don't know why, but Sophia and I are drifting apart instead of getting closer, and I know this growing distance between us is killing Dad. Every time I look at her, I try to find my mom, the one from the journal, but all I see is Sophia from my childhood, rejecting me, keeping me at arm's length. Even though I know now she was doing all this to keep us safe, the hurt doesn't go away overnight.

"I would love to see it, Dad." I try to dwindle his sadness with my words, and thank God it works. A small smile graces his lips.

He leads me to the back of the house. I still need to see the entire property. Zander gave me a quick tour when we arrived, as everyone was eagerly waiting for lunch. But now I notice that under the giant window overlooking the woods sits a grand piano. Walking closer, I realize it's not new.

Maybe a vintage.

As I place my finger on C major, the brassy sound echoes in the room.

"It's your mom's," Dad says. My hand on the keys trembles at the knowledge, but he continues. "This was my wedding gift to her. We have spent countless nights sitting at this piano. It's where your mom taught me how to play." I sit on the stool as he reminisces, and my fingers play a melody on autopilot.

"Rose!" Sophia whispers from the corner, where she's hiding behind a wall.

Only then do I realize I've played the notes she tucked into the yellow pages of the journal. Her heavy voice draws my attention to her. Tears are rolling down her face, mirroring my own.

"I found it in your journal," I explain, suddenly feeling nervous. "W-what's it called?"

She looks at me in surprise.

"I know you don't like notes without a title." My heart clenches at the admission. As much as I don't like to admit it, Sophia isn't a stranger. She has been in my life since I can remember, or since my life mattered.

"*Lost Love*," she whispers as more tears race down her cheeks.

For the first time, she doesn't look like the strong, confident woman I know her to be, but a mom grieving for her lost but cherished child. My mom.

Her teary eyes widen, and I realize I've spoken the last words out loud.

"M-mom," I say, consciously this time. The word doesn't come out easily.

"Rose," she whispers my name as if saying a silent prayer. "I'm so sorry. I am so, so sorry." She breaks into heavy sobs and runs toward me. Throwing her arms around me, she hugs me tight.

"I am…sorry too," I whisper into her welcoming warmth.

"Don't you say that, my baby."

"I'm sorry for taking so long, Mom." I hide my face in her neck and breathe my mother's flowery smell.

"You could have taken an eternity, and it would still be justified. There is no forgiveness for my sins. I'm so sorry."

She continues to apologize for all the things she did and did not do.

Her tears, her words, slowly heal the long, deep wounds etched onto my heart. Several moments pass by. I don't know how long, but Dad walks over and engulfs us in a huge hug.

"Today is the happiest day of my life. I got all my girls back."

"How are you?" Zander asks as we wave the last of our guests, Zane and Lukas, goodbye.

"Good. I'm tired," I correct myself when he raises his eyebrow at me. He pulls me into his arms, and I inhale the calming woodsy smell. "It was a good housewarming party."

"A good memory?" He kisses my forehead.

"Definitely." My eyes close as I try to relax myself after an emotionally tiring day.

"Shall we try to make it better?"

"Somebody is eager to go to bed." I smile, proud of my ability to find an apt, playful reply.

"I'm always eager to go to bed with you, babe." He laughs. "But I didn't mean that."

"Oh," I mutter and my disappointed, drooping shoulders only make him chuckle.

"Now I'm second-guessing, couch girl. Should I take you to bed or show you your surprise?"

I squeal in his arms. "My surprise? There's more?"

He nods. "I hope you like it."

The hint of nervousness in his voice piques my interest. I used to hate surprises until Zander, but over the last year, he has given me some of the best memories, and now I'm no longer scared of the unfamiliar.

"Show me."

Taking my hand, Zander leads me to the back of our house. It's not the same barren land anymore, but there's a fence bordering our wide property. Zander and I walk further in, and I suck in a quick breath. On the other side of the flowing creek sits a gazebo.

Oh my God!

A real gazebo plucked out from some postcard or painting, with a turquoise roof and shining white pillars. There's a white wooden bridge that connects the gazebo to a garden, which is filled with roses of different colors. It's a rose garden.

"Zander." His name falls as a whisper from my lips as my heart races against my chest.

"How is the surprise?"

"I... I don't know what to say." My legs shake as I'm hit by overwhelming emotions. "How? I...didn't even know so... many colors existed." I caress a soft rose petal between my fingers. It has pink insides and deep red edges. So pretty.

"I learned to graft from my father. I made this in his

memory, for you." Zander pulls on his tie, looking around nervously before his gaze finally settles on me.

I suck in a breath. "You made this? On your own?" Is he for real? Do guys do things like this? Gifts, I understand. But making someone a garden?

"With some help."

"But when?" When did he even have time for all this?

"I might have played hooky a few times over the past few months. Don't tell anyone. It doesn't make a good impression when employees learn that their CEO is gardening during office hours." He winks playfully, but his nervous voice isn't fooling me. "You want to look around?" He holds my hand after placing a gentle kiss on my forehead.

We walk hand in hand through our garden and finally through the heavenly footbridge to the gazebo. My heart skips a beat at the sight of a couch and a coffee table, where there's an ice bucket with champagne and two flutes.

How did I get so lucky?

My throat chokes with emotions, but I tap them down. I want to smile and laugh today, not cry.

Zander opens the champagne bottle and fills the glasses with the bubbly pink liquid. But before handing me the drink, he bends down and grabs an envelope from under the table.

"Congratulations on our new house, couch girl."

"What's this?" I look at the envelope he just placed in my hands.

"Open it," he mouths, and I pull out a few A4-sized papers, which look like legal documents. My eyes quickly scan the words, and my stomach ties in knots as I realize what I'm reading.

He named our home. *My house*.

The Rose House.

His over-the-top, beyond-thoughtful gift feels like a hundred-ton weight has been put on my shoulders.

"What's this?" The so-familiar-but-recently-forgotten feeling of loneliness surrounds me. My throat thickens, signaling an onset of silent tears.

"I—I thought you would like it." Zander quickly places the champagne bottle on the coffee table before looking at me carefully, already aware that I'm no fan of this surprise.

"I don't like it at all." My voice breaks. "Why do *I* own the house?"

"Rose, because it's ours?"

"Then why do I own it alone?" I sniff into my shirt cuffs. "Haven't I done enough alone already?"

"Oh, couch girl, I didn't think—" He rakes his fingers through his hair. "I thought it would be reassuring for you, for our future." His voice thickens, and he pulls me into his arms.

As always, I go willingly.

"You are all the assurance I need. Don't make me own anything alone," I plead. "I want to share everything with you —our home, our life, our future. I just don't want to be alone anymore."

He hugs me tight and flops onto the couch, taking me with him. "I'm so sorry, babe. I didn't think this through." Pressing gentle kisses on my forehead, he says, "When Henry asked whose name to make the deed out in, your name slipped off my tongue." Pulling me away from where I'm hiding in his chest, he holds my face with his hands. "I want to give you the world, Rose, and all the happiness that exists."

I hold his gaze with my blurry eyes. "And you do by just being you."

He lifts my chin up and kisses me softly, sighing deeply.

"I promise to share everything with you. I'll ask Henry to include both our names on the deed."

"Thank you." I return his promise with a kiss. "I love you."

"And I you."

I lie peacefully in his arms until I remember something.

"I also have something for you," I whisper and pull out a check from the back pocket of my jeans.

"What is this?" His body tenses beneath me, and it's his turn to be the recipient of an unwanted and unhappy gift.

"M-my contribution," I stammer as his narrowed eyes bore into me. I have never seen him look at me with so much —is it anger? "Toward the...house?" I ask because suddenly I'm not sure. Zander never talked about the cost.

Isn't it natural for me to pay for some part of it?

"This is too much," he says, and in this very moment, his voice sounds unfamiliar to me. This is the voice he uses at work. For the first time, he doesn't feel like my fiancé or boyfriend or friend. He sounds like my boss.

"It's...all my savings."

"And you're giving it to me?" His voice and face remain impassive.

"Zander." My scalp prickles with unease. I don't like this side of him one bit.

He sighs loudly, as if he doesn't know what to do with me.

"Rose," he finally says in a voice that he reserves exclusively for me.

Thank God.

"I don't want this. It's the same as you not wanting to own the house alone. I want to make a place for you and our family. I want to do this for you. I have to do this for you."

"Okay," I acquiesce. When he says it like that, how could I not agree?

"Thank you. I can't take any more emotional discussions for today." He strokes my cheek with his fingers. "I would just like to enjoy some time with my girl here and later make love to her in our new bedroom and christen our bed. Do you have any objection to that?" He raises an eyebrow at me playfully.

I giggle. "None."

"Good." And just like that, my smiling, affectionate fiancé is back.

"How long will the flowers bloom?" I ask, looking at the colorful blossoms.

He grazes his long fingers over my arms, and the simple act gets me going. I can't help but think about all the things those fingers can do. I release a sigh, and Zander chuckles. His hands rest over my wrists, where I'm sure he can feel my rising pulse.

"Are you ready to go to bed?" he whispers in my ear.

I press myself closer to his chest. "Not yet." My voice is hoarse, causing him to laugh again. I hit his chest, hiding my smile from him. Remembering what I just asked him, I repeat my question.

"Unfortunately, not much longer. Summer will be over soon, so they'll only be here for a few more weeks."

"Oh."

I can feel the smile in his voice. "Don't be so sad, couch girl. Next year, from spring until fall, we'll have an amazing view."

"I would love to have this background in our wedding photographs," I whisper wistfully.

His body jerks as he sits upright, taking me with him. "This"—he cocks his head forward—"isn't large enough to hold a big gathering."

"You want a big celebration?" My voice quivers at the thought of hundreds of people staring at me.

"I want what you want, Rose. Like I said, I want to give you the world."

My insides tingle at his words. "I want us to get married here. Just family and friends."

"Family and friends sounds right. When?" His heart thumps under my hand, mimicking my own.

"What do you think about next week?"

"Next week!" he shrieks before clearing his throat. "You don't need more time?"

"No. Do you?"

"I don't. But won't you…need a dress or two and everything else?" He sweeps his hands around as his gaze excitedly jumps from my face to the garden.

I laugh nervously, my pulse skyrocketing. Are we really doing this? Getting married in less than seven days? "I'm sure Clementine can get me a dress tomorrow."

"Next week," he repeats. "You sure?" His eyes sparkle with excitement.

I nod, and without missing a beat, Zander pulls his phone from his pocket. He keeps me tucked into his side while dialing someone.

"Zach. Shut up, you fucker." He cuts through whatever his brother was saying, and I can't help my giggle as I imagine Zach's pout. The middle Teager brother is really growing on me. Zander smiles, looking down at me before he asks Zach to wait. "Let me pull in Zane." After a pause, he says to his brothers, "I'm getting married next week."

"No, we haven't decided on an exact day yet, but I need you both here tomorrow. We need all the help with the arrangements." I hear his brothers' muffled voices before Zander replies. "No. It'll be just family and friends."

After his call is over, I open my hand to him. "Phone, please. I left mine inside." I flutter my eyelashes in a cute way. At least I think it's cute, by the way he smiles back.

Kristy picks up my call in two rings. "Shouldn't you be curled up around your fiancée in your beautiful home?"

My cheeks turn hot. "It's me."

"Shouldn't you be curled up around your fiancé in your beautiful home?" she smartly repeats.

"I am curled up around my fiancé." Immediately, Zander tightens his arms around me. "But I need to tell you something." I take a deep breath. "We are getting married next week."

She squeals into the phone, and Zander's body shakes with suppressed laughter.

"Can you believe it, Kris? I'm getting married." She squeals again, and this time, I join her.

"Congratulations, Rosie. I'm so happy for you. We need to celebrate. I'm gonna throw you the most amazing bridal shower." Excited words rush out of her mouth.

"I get a bridal shower?" I literally jump onto Zander's lap, pumped by her excitement.

"Of course! You get everything."

"But first, I need a dress. A wedding dress!"

My sister jumps into problem-solving mode. "Don't you worry about that. We'll meet Clementine tomorrow. I'm gonna talk to her tonight."

"Thank you, Kris. See you tomorrow."

We both squeal again before ending the call.

"That's done. Who else?" I hang my arms around Zander's neck, sifting through his hair with my fingers.

"Beast? Shit! He's your dad. Do I need to ask his permission or something?"

I chuckle, watching him panic. "We're already engaged." I show him the beautiful ring sitting on my finger.

"Um, yeah, good point. But let's call them." He puts the phone on speaker as he hits Beast's contact info.

"Hello." My dad's throaty voice resonates in our gazebo.

Zander nods, giving me the opportunity to speak. "Dad?"

"My Rose girl." I can hear the shift in his tone as it gets laced with affection. "All okay?"

"Yes. We have news. Is Soph—I mean, is Mom with you?"

"Yeah. Let me put you on speaker." After a second, he says, "Go on, honey, your mom's listening."

"Mom, Dad, we've decided to get married next week."

"Oh, my baby! That's lovely news." Mom's voice trembles as she congratulates us. "Have you guys decided on a day?"

"Not yet. We're still thinking." My heart bounces against my chest in giddiness. I don't think I've ever been so happy in my whole life.

It takes my elated brain a second to register the silence. I worry we've lost connection. "Hello?"

"Yeah, we're here," Dad replies after a beat. "We wanted to share something with you next week." He pauses again. His hesitation forces Zander and me to sit upright. "How does Wednesday sound? For the wedding?"

Before I can reply, he adds, "Of course, if it makes sense to you guys."

"Is there a reason for such a specific day, Beast?" Zander asks while I'm lost for words.

"It's…it's Rose's birthday."

Everything goes dead silent for a minute as Zander stiffens beside me. My ears can't even hear the chirping of birds anymore as the words hit home.

My birthday.

"Are you sure?" I hear Zander's voice coming from afar.

"Sophia and I went to the hospital last month to collect whatever information they had from that day." He pauses again. "We weren't hiding it from you, my Rose girl. We were planning to tell you next week. Hoping to make this day special for all of us."

"My birthday?" I whisper.

I hear Mom's sniffles as Dad hums in agreement.

"But nothing could be more special than your wedding day. A day when you're starting a new life in so many ways." Mom's croaky voice makes my heart and head hurt.

I thought the mystery of my life was solved, but it appears not. For so long, I wondered if I'd ever learn what my real birthday is. But I never imagined how I'd feel if that day came.

I guess confused and conflicted is the answer to that question.

"We'll think about it and let you know," Zander tells my parents when I can't seem to find the right words. His grip around me hasn't loosened a bit.

"Yes. Of course." Mom's wobbly voice reaches my ears, and I hate to hear her this heartbroken.

"Mom, I'm meeting Kristy and Clem tomorrow to go wedding dress shopping. Would you like to join us?"

"I would love to." She sniffs into the phone.

"Oh, Mom, please don't cry. I'll text you the details."

Zander ends the call.

Our earlier excitement to head inside and christen the bed gets lost in the new information.

I slouch back, resting against Zander and thinking about a wedding in this beautiful garden.

Can that be next Wednesday?

59

ROSE

"How about this one?" Clementine shows me the last of the ten dresses she dragged from the back of her small store.

I bite my lip nervously. "I'm so sorry." I didn't know selecting a dress would be such a difficult task. An empty, nervous feeling develops in the pit of my stomach. If I can't even make up my mind about a dress, how am I going to make all the important decisions in our marriage? Self-doubt rears its ugly head again.

Is this too fast?

"Don't overthink, Rose," Mom whispers. "A wedding dress is a decision that every girl struggles with. You're not alone."

"There's nothing to be sorry about." Clementine perches on her stool. "Tell me if you liked any of the dresses we've seen so far. This way, I'll know where to look."

"Um, I like this one, especially the lace."

She smiles—maybe for the first time since I started rejecting her beautiful dresses. "It's handmade."

"But the bodice...is too revealing," I whisper nervously. "I would like something with a full back." Mom's grip on my hand tightens.

"Okay." Clem writes something on her notepad. "What else?"

"I don't know. These veils are very long." I pause. "Also, there's lots of frill." I grimace as my gaze flicks at all the fabric hanging around the skirt of the gowns.

Clem bursts into laughter. "Ballgown style is so in these days. Believe me, Zander will go crazy."

Only if I make it to the altar without breaking my neck.

"What about a sheath style?" Mom asks her.

When I look around in confusion, Kristy rushes to show me a picture on her phone. "It has less flare."

My ears perk up. This style is definitely better for me and my balance.

Clem gnaws at her lips thoughtfully. "Unfortunately, I have nothing in that style. The wedding is next Wednesday, right?"

I nod.

Last night, after Zander and I returned to our new bedroom, we talked. A lot. Finally, we agreed that next Wednesday is definitely a day we don't want to forget. But I can't simply swap it with a day I've known as my birthday all my life. As meager as they are, that day has some memories, especially this year with Zander.

Clementine's mumbling pulls me from my thoughts.

"To start something from scratch, hmm... I'll have to order some new fabric." She talks to herself, making notes as her eyebrows draw together in worry.

I'm about to tell her that I can wear my flannel and jeans when Mom asks, "Is it easier if you have something to start with?"

Clem nods absentmindedly while making long strokes on her notepad with a pencil.

"I'll be right back." Mom rushes out of the room, leaving me and Kristy in confusion.

But a minute later, she's back with a huge box. Kristy and I jump to help her while Clem continues with her scribbling.

"What's that?" Finally, we have Clem's attention, and she looks up from her notepad.

Mom opens the box and scrapes away the tissue paper to reveal a wedding dress.

We all gasp, and after a beat, Clementine expertly draws the dress out of the box and holds it up.

It's an elegant silk dress without overflowing yards and yards of fabric.

Clem hangs the dress on the mannequin and starts inspecting the different layers, adding some pins here and there.

"It's my wedding dress," Mom says. "We found it while we were cleaning the attic during the renovation. Your dad put it in the trunk of my car today, in case…you'd like to try it on." She fidgets, rubbing her hands over her pants.

Sparing me not even a second to overcome the emotions coursing through my heart, Clem claps loudly and throws her arms around Mom.

I'm surprised by the flash of anger that hits me. I don't like when she leaves me on the sideline and gets all chummy with *my mom*.

But then she springs to me and pulls me into a hug. "I'm going to transform this dress into your dream, Rose." Pulling back abruptly as if she remembered something, she turns to Mom. "I can modify the dress, right? Um, like major changes?"

Mom chuckles and waves her hand toward the gown. "Yes, feel free to use your magic, but only if Rose wants it."

"I'd love it, Mom." I speak through the ball of emotions welled up in my throat.

Kristy squeals with a wide dazzling smile on her face. "This can be your something old!"

Her words cause a foreign tingling in my chest. I never thought I'd have a wedding, let alone all the cheesy traditions. "My...something old?"

"Yes. One of your four somethings. As your matron of honor, it's my responsibility to make sure you have all of them."

"You're my... matron of honor?" My pulse races in surprise. How much my life has changed in the past year. I have my mom's wedding dress, a sister putting together my bachelorette party, and a fiancé at home taking care of wedding arrangements with my dad.

Everything feels like I'm in a dream, and I plan to never wake up.

"Get up, Mrs. Teager." Zander strokes my face, and I open one eye ruefully.

He smiles and my heart does a little jump. Spread out next to me, sun kissing his beautiful face, he makes me wonder, once again, how I got so lucky.

This man, this handsome man, is going to be my husband.

As he tucks a stray hair behind my ear, I whisper, "It's too early."

"It is. But it's only two days until our wedding. I can't wait for Wednesday to come, Mrs. Teager." His wistful voice drifts my sleep away.

"I love how it sounds." My fingers glide over his short stubble. Zander knows how much I like it overgrown, and he's seen that it grows to my liking.

"Mrs. Teager," he repeats with a heartwarming smile.

I nod and pull a little on the spiked five o'clock shadow,

making him groan. His eyes transition from dreamy to lustful in a fraction of a second.

"What do you do to me, Rose?" he whispers, closing his wild eyes as my fingers drift to his hair. I tug on it with more force.

Without any preamble, he lifts me up and places my body over his. I'm naked underneath the duvet, and my sex rests on his strong, muscular thigh. His hands skim over my shoulders and further lower to my sides until they stop at my waist. He then drags me further up, making me sit on his crotch.

"Zander," I whisper, feeling him hard beneath me.

Without a word, he pulls my face down and kisses me mercilessly, taking my breath away. His one hand moves from my face to my neck, gliding across my back until he reaches my behind. He squeezes my butt, and it's my turn to groan. His hand slides lower, from between my ass cheeks—ew—to my sex—ohhh...

My heartbeat picks up as he moves his fingers over my sex. In no hurry, as always. Just giving me all the pleasure. But I want to return the favor.

"Not so fast," he protests half-heartedly as I take him inside me. "Babe, slow...down."

I listen to him and move slowly up and down. He gazes into my eyes with so much love and affection that my throat chokes. Even in such an exposed position, I don't feel shy or nervous, but cherished.

That's how he's changed me.

I'm no longer unlovable.

He loves me, my soon-to-be husband.

I pick up speed, chasing that amazing release. My gaze is fixed on his face as several expressions blend in. Adoration, excitement, and passion.

My hair falls over my face and shoulders, and for a moment, my view of his handsome face is blocked. But then

Zander leans forward and captures my nipple between his teeth, making me insane and effectively forcing me to shut my eyes. I arch my back, unable to hold back. Sensing I'm close, Zander starts thrusting into me, matching my movements.

"Ah, Zander," I cry.

"Let go." He bites my earlobe, and that's my undoing. I combust around him, and he follows me with a loud groan.

As we come back down to planet earth, my phone rings.

"Hello." My out-of-breath voice sounds wheezy.

"Did I disturb you?" Kristy asks in an overly honeyed singsong voice.

"No." I'm sure my face is scarlet. Zander smirks at me before pulling on his sweats. My gaze follows his movements as he grabs a glass of water from his nightstand and brings it closer to his mouth. There's something erotic in the way his neck muscles move as he swallows.

I must have made a sound, because Kristy whispers, "I'm guessing you weren't done."

Her words startle me, and I reply without much thought. "No, we were done."

"Then it looks like you can go for round two." She mimics my throaty voice.

"Kristy!"

"Sorry, Rosie. Unfortunately, we don't have much time to satisfy your carnal needs." She snickers, too proud of herself.

I don't respond, knowing that whatever I say, she will twist it into something to tease me.

"We're going for the first fitting of your wedding dress. I'm so excited to see what Clem has done."

Her contagious excitement gets to me. I, too, can't wait to see Clementine's magic on Mom's dress.

"You have twenty minutes to get ready before Mom and I pick you up. So, say bye-bye to your carnal needs for today."

Wedding dress versus carnal needs…

I didn't know this was such a tough decision. While my brain is still making a list of pros and cons, Zander strolls out of our closet dressed in a navy striped suit.

Wedding dress, then.

I pick up my robe from the couch and put it over me. On my way to the bathroom, he snags my arm and pulls me closer.

Kissing my neck, he unties my robe, and his fingers graze my stomach, causing goose bumps to rise on my skin. With him fully dressed in front of me, I feel more naked than before.

When he kisses behind my ear, my phone pings in my hand. I look down and see it's a text message from Kristy.

Sis: Idea of round 2 was a joke.

Fish! She's good.

Before my carnal needs make me change my decision, I get out of Zander's arms. "Kristy and Mom will be here soon. I need to get ready." I rush to the bathroom without looking at his gorgeous face, which will tempt me to do something stupid, like jump back into bed with him.

Once freshly showered and dressed, I walk down the stairs of our new house and find Zander in the kitchen drinking coffee and reading something, most likely business news, on his tablet.

"Is it wrong that I find you hot in the kitchen?" I whisper after placing my keys and cell phone on the breakfast bar.

He looks up and gives me his wide, sexy dimpled smile, which makes my heart race.

"No. I love that you find me hot." Pulling me closer, he kisses my forehead and then my lips. Releasing a heavy breath close to my ear, making me shiver, Zander whispers, "Eat your breakfast before I get distracted."

"I like you distracted."

"I know, my bewitching Rose."

Wow! Today, I'm bewitching.

60

ROSE

"Time to go." Kristy enters the bedroom where I've been waiting since the makeup artist left after she was done dolling me up. The bouquet of pink and white roses that my hair stylist gave me—a nice lady with rainbow hair—feels heavy in my hands.

"Kris, thank God you're here." I get up and turn around. "There's something wrong with my dress. It's itchy." I put the bouquet on the chair and show her my red palms. "Who made this bouquet? It weighs too much! And this veil is so tight." I'm about to rip the pinned veil out of my overly tight bun when Kristy grabs my hands.

"Rosie!" Bringing my arms to my sides, she says, "You look lovely."

Hearing her words, my tense shoulders drop slightly.

"Just breathe." She squeezes my lace-covered forearms, and I close my eyes before releasing a heavy breath, taking comfort in her familiar touch.

"Nothing is wrong with the dress and veil." She turns me around to look in the floor-length mirror. The pink roses embroidered on the skirt of my dress shuffle as I shift on my feet. "You're getting married, Rose." Her teary eyes meet mine in the mirror as she rests her chin on my shoulder. "Zander is a lucky bastard to have you."

My eyes meet her watery gaze in the mirror. "You look so pretty." Dressed in a blush gown with her heavily pregnant belly sticking out, she looks amazing.

"Thank you. But today, no one holds a candle to you." She adjusts my sapphire earrings, which are a gift from her—also my something blue and something new. Opening her clutch, she takes out Zander's cherry-red tie.

Any remaining anxiety in my heart ebbs at the sight of it. It's a tie Zander wore when we first met in the closet, when he declared to a room full of people that I was his girlfriend, and even that morning when he proposed to me.

Wow! How far we've come.

"I have your final something—something borrowed. Your fiancé gave it to me."

A smile breaks on my face, my mood already better. "As much as I love it, I think Clem will kill me if I wear a tie with this dress."

"She sure will. You and me both." Kris laughs as she picks up my bouquet and wraps the tie around the stems. She hands it to me and whispers, "The flowers won't feel heavy anymore."

We walk down the stairs to find Mom and Dad waiting. Mom has been teary all day. It's like all her emotions that were bottled up over the years are finally finding an escape.

"You look lovely, my Rose girl." Dad kisses my cheek and then Kristy's. "You both do."

"I'm so happy. I never thought I'd see this day." Mom removes some invisible lint from the lace covering my shoulder, trying hard to hide her wet eyes.

"Mom—" My throat closes with emotion, but Kristy pulls us away.

"Okay! We're all happy." My sister tries to patronize us, but by the way her misty eyes shine, she's not fooling anyone.

"Come on, Mom, it's time. Don't ruin your makeup, or Rose's." She leads Mom to the backyard where the wedding ceremony will take place.

Minutes later, beautiful piano notes flow, and that's our cue. Dad puts my hand over his arm. "I'm so proud of you, my baby."

My throat constricts at his words. I never imagined my wedding day would be filled with this much love—a doting mom, a dependable sister, and an affectionate father. And the man waiting for me beyond these doors.

A teardrop rolls down my cheek, and Dad quickly takes his handkerchief out. "Time for tears is over. There are only smiles from now on."

He leads me to the backyard, where Zander is waiting for me under the gazebo. On his left stand Zach and Zane, his two best men. On my side is Kristy, smiling and holding a bouquet of blue and lavender roses from our garden.

My mom sits at the piano, playing the song that was played at her own wedding. Tears run down her cheeks, but she doesn't miss a note. Dad's strong but trembling hand guides me through our guests—Lukas, Oscar, and Clementine, with other members of the Hawthorne family; my previous landlord, Mr. Hart, and his wife; and a few of Zander's acquaintances.

Everyone greets us with smiles as we reach the altar.

Reverend Marsh says something, but I only have eyes for my groom. Warmth spreads from my heart through every part of my body at the sight of the most handsome man. My man.

Zander blinks rapidly as if he can't believe it's me. That makes two of us.

His hand rises, and he brings it closer to his heart. But as soon as he realizes we aren't alone but in front of guests who are eagerly looking at us, his demeanor changes. He stands tall before fixing his cherry-colored bowtie. Tilting his head to the side, he grins at me and whispers, "I love you, Mrs. Teager."

"Yes, Mr. Teager, we are all very aware of that fact. Let's get you and *Ms. Marlin-Miller* married so that she can officially hold that title."

Loud chuckles fill the space after hearing Reverend Marsh's words.

In a daze, we say our "I do's," as we already decided to forego vows. Zander has promised and done so much for me since we met, that today, on our wedding day, I don't want any new vows. We have a lifetime to say and fulfill our promises. I don't need the presence of a reverend to know that Zander will hold on to his every word.

"How are you feeling, Mrs. Teager?" Zander whispers in my ear as he sways me in his arms.

"Amazing!" My head rests over his chest, and I look around the dance floor. Most of the guests are gone, and we're left with just family.

Kristy is trying hard to dance with Charlie, but it's a struggle due to their height difference and her swollen belly.

Mom's head rests on Dad's chest as they sway to the music like us. She blows me a kiss, and I smile.

In the center of the dance floor, Zach and Zane exhibit a perfect waltz. My lips pull up, and my insides shake as I suppress my growing laughter. But they dance effortlessly, their stoic gazes never leaving each other's faces.

"I'm just waiting for them to crack." Zander chuckles, watching his brothers' theatrics.

"I don't know. They look pretty serious to me." I clamp my lips tight, swallowing my laugh.

Zander's hands stroke my arms, pulling me closer. "I love your dress."

I look down at the perfection Clementine made for me. Pink embroidered roses adorn my mom's wedding dress, altered to fit me and my taste.

"Shall we go inside?" Zander whispers in my ear.

"But we still have company!"

"They'll all understand. Come on." He pulls me toward the house, and when I look back, Kristy waves at me before giving me a thumbs-up.

Zander grabs my waist, halting my steps from walking inside through the back door of the house. Before I can ask him why, he throws me over his shoulder. "Time to officially walk my bride over the threshold."

"Yeah, you don't sound like a caveman at all!" I giggle as he passes by our living room and takes the stairs with me still over his shoulder.

Throwing me on the bed, Zander smirks. "I'm one hundred percent okay being a caveman, Mrs. Teager."

I shake my head. This man will never get tired of calling me that.

"I have a gift for you," he says, placing his tux jacket on the couch before removing his cufflinks.

Immediately, I sit upright, my perpetual smile dropping. "Zander, we said no gifts except these." I hold up my hand, showing him my pretty wedding band.

"It's something else, couch girl." He's already pulling his shirt out of his pants.

I don't understand. His actions and words make no sense. Except for last night, when Kristy dragged me to her place, we've spent all of our nights together this past week. I mean, I do believe Zander is a gift in bed, but I already have that.

"It's not sex, my lovely wife." He smirks before yanking the shirt from his body.

Holy crab! My husband is hot.

I'm still drooling over his broad chest when he turns around. My gaze instantly slides to the shiny transparent bandage over his shoulders. It takes me a second to realize what's different.

I suck in a deep breath at the sight of the small red roses on his tattoo where there used to be blood drops. There are even some small leaves drawn in black ink.

My hands skim over my wrists, hunting for some fabric to tug, but unfortunately, my wedding dress doesn't have cuffs.

Zander looks at me over his shoulder. When he finds me scratching my wrists, he settles next to me and grabs my hands, halting my movements.

"What did you do?" My voice trembles, and it's a task to force the words out around my constricting throat.

"A rose is now the most beautiful part of my life." Zander opens my fists, and his fingers lightly graze my palms, effectively distracting me.

"When did you do this?" I nod toward his back, my pulse still wild.

"Yesterday morning when you were out with your mom and Kristy." He caresses my cheek with the back of his thumb, and I can't stop the tear that rolls down my face.

"I'm so scared, Zander." My chest tightens with fear, and suddenly I'm ice cold. Zander presses kisses over my palms, silently urging me to continue. "I can't believe there's so much happiness and love in my life. I fear that this is a dream."

"This is as real as it gets, couch girl." He presses his lips to mine, savoring me.

I hold on to him like *always and forever* is now.

A YEAR LATER

61

ROSE

"Maybe we should have taken Dad's offer and stayed the night in St. Peppers," I whisper as we drive through the heavy rain.

"We'll be fine, couch girl. It's only for a few miles." Zander's grip tightens around the steering wheel.

We're returning from a family dinner at my parents' house. My dad likes us to visit as often as we can whenever he and Mom aren't traveling. So today, at seven sharp, Zander and I; Kristy with her family, including my new niece, Chloe; and Zander's brothers showed up at my parents' doorstep.

As always, it was wonderful, with lots of good food, laughter, and music. Mom and I were joined by Dad on the piano. It was magical. It was family time. It was everything I've ever craved.

As for our own family, Zander and I talk about it a lot these days.

But there's something stopping me from ditching my pills. It's not the fear of danger that haunted my whole life, but it's something inside me.

How can I give a perfect life to someone when this family stuff is still new to me?

"Fuck." Zander brakes the car sharply before bringing it to a screeching halt.

"What? What happened?"

"There's someone on the bench," he says, looking through the rear window.

I turn around to see something yellow through the rainy haze. It looks like a plastic bag. "Are you sure it's a person? It's very small. Maybe someone left their luggage."

"No, I saw it when we passed through. It's a boy... I think." Zander grits his teeth before his hand rakes through his hair.

"Oh God. Where are his parents?" I look back again, my eyes falling to the small bundle on the bench.

Zander curses before putting the car in reverse. The incessant rain continues to come down harder than before.

We stop in front of the bench, and I look through the blurry window.

It's a boy with a yellow plastic raincoat.

My chest clenches at the sight of the forgotten child.

Zander brings his window down and calls out. "Hey, buddy."

But the kid stays still, leaning forward with his shoulders folded over his chest.

Only after Zander calls out for the fifth or sixth time does the kid gingerly look up, and then immediately, his head drops down. In fact, he tightens his arms a bit more around himself.

"Hey, where are your parents? Are you lost?"

When he doesn't reply to Zander, I look around the secluded stretch of road. There's just forest behind him; no houses, no buildings. The next gas station is about ten miles away. We don't even know how long he's been sitting there.

"He'll get sick in the rain." Zander looks between the kid

and me, his expression grim. I know his protectiveness is kicking in.

But more than that, watching a young boy soaking in the rain, all alone... I can't even imagine what it's doing to my husband's heart. I grab the two umbrellas from the back seat and hand one to Zander. We both step out and approach the scared kid.

"Hey, buddy!" Zander's words elicit no reaction out of the small stranger.

I notice the red backpack on the ground, soaking in a puddle of water. Wet hair peeks out from under the torn plastic cap of his raincoat.

I hold my breath when Zander glances at me before he takes a step closer to the boy. When he places his hand over the boy's shoulder, shaking him gently, the kid collapses, falling on the wet bench.

"Oh God." I take the umbrella from Zander as he tries to sit the kid up and lightly pats his face.

"How is he?" Words barely come out of my mouth as I try to protect Zander and the unconscious kid from the rain.

"He's burning with fever. We need to take him to the hospital, Rose." My husband's pained gaze shoots to me, and I nod immediately.

"Yes. Yes." I dart to open the back door of the car as he gathers the boy in his arms.

"There's a towel in my workout bag." Zander nods toward the car trunk while placing the small kid in the back seat.

After getting in from the other side, I towel dry the boy's hair as Zander jumps in the driver's seat.

"Why isn't he getting up?" I ask as I clean his face gently, wiping away the grime and dirt. He looks like he's been on his own for a while. I notice Zander brought the muddy red backpack and has placed it on the floorboard. That's good. We don't know what important things are stacked inside.

"He might be unconscious due to high fever. Will you be

okay in the back seat, or would you like to drive?" Zander turns around, his arm resting behind the passenger seat. His gaze shifts from the kid, his head resting on my lap, to me.

The offer is tempting. He can clean and take care of the boy better, but I'm also not confident driving through this weather.

"I'm fine here," I reply, giving him a confident smile so that he has one less thing to worry about.

I try to warm the kid's small blue hands, rubbing them between my palms as Zander takes us to the hospital.

When we arrive, the kid is immediately rushed into the emergency room, and Zander and I are asked to stay in the waiting area.

"How old do you think he is?" I whisper.

"Don't know. Maybe nine or ten." Zander's mouth twists as he pulls on his tie.

He and I have both lived through our harrowing childhoods, which have highly influenced our adult lives, and we also understand abandonment and loneliness like no kid should ever have to. I close my eyes, saying a silent prayer, hoping this boy doesn't have a horrible backstory that will tarnish his future.

"Mr. and Mrs. Teager?" A middle-aged woman dressed in scrubs approaches us. "I wanted to inform you that we've called the police. Can you please wait until they arrive? They might have some questions for you about where you found the boy."

"Of course." Zander nods before motioning toward the door from which she walked in. "How is he doing?"

"He has a high fever. The doctor also found some infection in his lungs, mostly due to the cold. We're giving him an IV. He's too weak. Poor kid. We hope we can find his parents soon." Her lips twist into a sad smile before she leaves us alone in the sterile-smelling waiting room.

Zander and I settle back on the plastic chairs. There's no

one except us in this room, but through the open door, we can hear the usual activity at the nurses' station.

I hide myself in Zander's arms, the hospital smell taking me back to my own childhood days.

Half an hour later, a police officer knocks on the door of the waiting room. "Mr. and Mrs. Teager?"

We nod before getting up.

"I'm Gabriel Cole from Cherrywood Police Department." He shakes hands with us. "Thank you for bringing the boy here. Would you mind if I ask you a few questions?"

He sits on the couch while we take our seats.

"Where did you find him?"

We tell him all about how and where we found the boy. It feels strange to call him "the boy" during the whole conversation. I wish we knew his name.

"Were you able to ID him?" I ask.

"Actually, Mrs. Teager, I was hoping you'd be able to help me there. Did you find anything on him?"

"Yes. He had a backpack." Zander grabs the small backpack from under his chair.

Officer Cole opens the main zipper and takes out an empty plastic water bottle. After placing it on the wooden table, he pulls out two frayed and faded cotton T-shirts and two pairs of pants. The last items are a notebook and a small pencil box. Everything is wet and isn't of much help in identifying the owner.

The police officer puts everything back and opens the smaller compartment. After inspecting the picture frame he just retrieved, he hands it to me. It's a photograph taken at some amusement park—a happy couple with a small boy, maybe five or six years old. I wonder if that's him.

Officer Cole finally opens the smallest pocket on the top of the bag and retrieves a plastic card.

He reads it and then shows it to us. It's an ID card from a group home for kids with no family.

"It's an address from Cherrywood, but I can't see the kid's name." I struggle to form the words as my heart gallops inside my chest. There's a room and bed number, but no name.

"How did he reach the highway?" Zander grabs his neck, and I can feel the frustration seeping out of him.

"I'm wondering the same." Officer Cole puts the bag back on the ground, except for the ID card, which he tucks into his shirt pocket.

I'm about to ask him what will happen next when a nurse enters the waiting room. "The boy is awake."

The police officer nods to her before turning our way. "Thank you so much, Mr. and Mrs. Teager. I'll speak to the boy and try to find out how he landed on the highway." When we make no move to get up and leave the hospital, as he most likely expected, he adds, "Thank you for bringing him in."

I notice from the side that Zander's grip has tightened on the arm of the chair. Unease settles inside me, watching him so shaken.

"Will it be okay if we wait? We'd like to see him."

Zander's grasp loosens, and he pulls me closer to him as we wait for an answer.

"Um, wouldn't you like to leave? It's already ten thirty." Officer Cole jerks his head toward the large clock on the wall.

"If it doesn't bother you, we'd like to wait," Zander replies quickly. I can feel his speeding pulse under my hand.

"Not a problem for me. I'll update you once I have more information."

After the officer leaves with the nurse, Zander and I sit silently in wait, and I'm sure his thoughts are drifting to his own childhood, same as mine.

We stay in the waiting room for another half hour before Officer Cole returns.

"The boy's name is Alexander." My heartbeat escalates, and I grab Zander's cold hand. "I just ended a call with the headmistress of the group home. He got there eleven months ago after his parents' death in a car accident. He's up for adoption, but it seems nine-year-olds aren't in high demand." Officer Cole's lips flatten in annoyance.

I stay tongue-tied, not sure what to say next.

Zander clears his throat twice before speaking in a low voice. "Something must have happened recently for him to run away like that."

"It seems the boy was rejected twice before a third refusal two days back. The whole incident, not to mention the recent loss of his parents, must have led to the decision."

"And the home didn't report the missing kid to the police?" My husband's voice rises as his fists curl. He so rarely loses his calm, but this situation must be driving him crazy, especially now that we know the boy's name.

Officer Cole once again seems taken aback by our reaction. I don't know how he feels about Zander asking him all these questions. But after a beat, he replies. "It seems it's not unusual for the kids to hide in the compound after such a refusal. They saw him last night, so he's been missing since morning. My guess is that he escaped last night after dinner."

My shoulders slump back in light relief. He wasn't on his own for very long.

"What happens next?" Zander asks, tension dripping from his voice.

"Kid's fever is down. The doctors gave him an IV, and in about an hour, he should be ready to leave. But as the weather isn't so good, I've asked the headmistress to pick him up tomorrow. So, for tonight, I'll take him to the station with me."

"Police station?" My hands tighten around the cuffs of my shirt, and Officer Cole shrugs helplessly. "Can we take him for the night?" The question leaves my mouth before I've fully thought it through.

I look at Zander, who is equally surprised.

"You want to take him with you?" Officer Cole does a double take.

"We know it's an unusual request," Zander says, and his hand rests over my shoulder as we wait for the officer's response.

"I don't know what to say, Mr. Teager." Officer Cole's brow creases as he looks at us incredulously. When we continue to stare at him with a hopeful expression, he says, "I understand you're feeling bad for the kid, Mrs. Teager, but I need to talk to the caseworker at the hospital to see if that's even possible. I'd also need some sort of ID and your background information."

Zander takes out his business card and his driver's license from his wallet.

"You're the CEO of Elixir?" Officer Cole sounds impressed, and I pray the small smile that pulls on his lips when he returns the cards means he's in our favor. "I thought you looked familiar. I was reading your interview on improving the local economy with technology."

"So, do you think there's any possibility for us to take the boy?" Zander asks.

Officer Cole's smile wavers, and his lips press together, making my heart race. "Like I said, Mr. Teager, I need to talk to the caseworker and then to the headmistress of the group home. Most importantly, I need to talk to Alex. If anyone thinks for any reason that it might not be healthy for him, I would have to, unfortunately, decline."

Zander nods. "My lawyer can also draw up a document confirming my character, and maybe I can have something signed from the local judge. We'll also make sure to give you updates every two hours, or anything else to keep you posted that he's doing well."

Officer Cole rubs the back of his neck under his collared uniform shirt before glancing up at my husband. "You understand why I'm surprised by your concern for a stranger, Mr. Teager? Even family doesn't go to such lengths sometimes."

Zander looks down at me, and the cautious police officer follows his move. "Rose and I didn't have a normal childhood. My wife was raised in an orphanage before she was reunited with her parents not too long ago. I lost my parents at a young age myself and was raised by a man who took me and my brothers in." He speaks in a steady, low-pitched voice. "We understand what the kid is going through."

The suspicion in Officer Cole's eyes is replaced with…a hint of awe, if I'm not wrong. "Let me talk to some people and see what we can do." He ambles toward the exit, and at the last moment, looks over his shoulder. "I really appreciate what you guys are doing here. I just have to follow the process."

When he leaves, Zander calls his lawyer, Grayson, and explains the situation. I only hear half of what he's saying as my mind wanders to Alex, who's alone somewhere in this big hospital.

Once Zander's call is finished, we wait impatiently in the meeting room. I don't know why, but this feels like a big moment for us.

"Are we doing the right thing?" I ask softly, afraid of my own words.

He turns around and grabs my hand. "We're doing the right thing, couch girl. No one understands better than us how it feels to be cold, scared, and alone in the dark night."

"Zander." I knew he was visiting his dark memories, but his words hit my chest hard. My throat constricts, and my eyes pool with tears.

"His name is Alexander, Rose. The name my father gave me. The name inscribed on my back." Zander's hand reaches behind his shoulder, where hidden under his jacket and shirt is a tattoo of that name. A reminder of his past, like many others.

I hold his face, looking into his eyes. He's back in those dark nights, left outside his house in the rain. When he places his forehead against mine, tears run down my cheeks. Very seldom does Zander remember his past. But when he does, it all comes crashing down, and my man, who is my rock, is in his most vulnerable state. I hate to see him like this.

A throat clears, and Zander and I part as Officer Cole walks from the door to us. "I tried speaking to the boy, but he isn't talking much. However, the headmistress of the group home thinks if you're still open to the idea of taking him with you tonight, it might be good for him. Of course, the letter from your lawyer and the judge's recommendation helped things with the caseworker."

"Really?" My heart races as my mind drifts to all the possible things that we must do or have in our house so that Alex's stay tonight is comfortable.

"Yeah, the headmistress thinks it might do him good if he stays in an environment that he obviously misses so much, even if it's just for a night."

My gaze skids to Zander's serious face before I give more than a few nods to Officer Cole. "We want to help in any way we can."

62

ZANDER

My heart has been pounding against my chest since I heard his name. Alexander.

The image of my father calling my name swims before my eyes, a memory of a time when my life was still normal.

My gaze skids to the back seat of the car. Alex's head hangs low, his chin almost hitting his chest. Since the hospital released him, he hasn't spoken a word. Thankfully, he lightly nodded when Rose asked him if he'd prefer to come with us instead of going to the police station.

My hands on the steering wheel tighten.

Are we doing the right thing?

Rose asked me the same question, but after having met the kid, I wonder if I'm healed enough to take care of someone named Alexander, even for a night.

He doesn't move or lift his gaze to look at us. There's no protest or anything, and my chest clenches in sadness. He's too young to have lost his spirit. Sitting in the back seat, he reminds me of myself and my brothers in different phases of our broken childhood.

How is he handling everything alone? We had Beast, but it seems like he's got no one.

I park the car outside our house. Rose joins me as I open the door on Alex's side, but he makes no attempt to get out and remains seated on the back seat, clutching the red backpack close to his heart.

"Alex." I call his name softly, but he doesn't budge. "Buddy, come out." My heart clenches as I watch him trying to make himself smaller. My grip on the door tightens to a degree that I can feel the metal digging into my palm.

Rose places her hand tentatively on my arm, silently urging me to relax. I'm sure she can read the pain in my eyes. She bends forward a little and says, "Alex, if you step out of the car, we can go inside the house. Out of the cold. We have a fireplace. Would you like something warm to drink? Maybe a hot chocolate?" Her words are so soft and filled with nothing but care and love.

I'm so fucking proud of my couch girl. I know caring for a child is unfamiliar territory for her, but she's doing so well. So well, in fact, that Alex looks up at us through his lashes.

"Marshmallows too?" His whispered words are only heard because it's dead silent at this dark midnight hour.

Rose's hand clutches mine as she excitedly replies. "Yes, of course! Zander makes the most amazing hot chocolate in the world. Would you like to try it?"

He nods and finally steps out of the car, the wet red rucksack held tight to his chest.

Rose leads Alex to the fireplace in our living room while I march toward the kitchen. I can see my sweet wife guiding our guest to a chair before she bends down to start the fire.

I take my phone out after giving them a final glance. The hospital told us not to give Alex any solid food tonight, but to be safe, I shoot a text to his nurse, Erica, and confirm that a hot chocolate would be okay.

Her reply with a yes is immediate.

After I add some milk into the melted chocolate heating in a saucepan, my gaze drifts back to Rose and Alex, now sitting close to the fire burning in our living room. They're not speaking, but Alex is no longer clutching his bag close to his chest, and I even see him look around our house a bit.

I fill the three cups, topping one with two giant marshmallows, and amble toward the sitting area.

Even though Alex hasn't spoken a word, there's no sign of impatience on Rose's warm face as it glows under the orange light of the fire.

I place the tray on the center table and take a seat in a chair between them as they sit across from each other.

"There you go, buddy. If you'd like more marshmallows, just let me know."

When I hand him the cup, his gaze skids from my hand to my chest—or precisely, to the apron tied around me.

"That's Wolverine!" His words are a little stronger than before.

I smile. "Yeah. He's our favorite." The tension eases off my chest as his excited gaze flies between Rose and me.

"You like superheroes?" For the first time tonight, an emotion of surprise ghosts his face.

"We do. I have a huge Wolverine comic collection." Rose's eyes gleam, mirroring Alex's excitement.

After another glance at Rose's face, Alex's bright gaze drops to the table. "You're lying. Grown-ups don't like superheroes. Also, grown-ups lie."

Fuck. Rejection over the past few months has for sure messed up this kid's head.

What do I say to him? Because he's right, grown-ups lie and do things for their own convenience.

"I'm not lying, Alex."

Rose's words have no effect on him. He's again silent, and much like before, he's gone back to hiding in his shell. His marshmallow-topped hot chocolate sits untouched before him.

"I can even lend you one for tonight," my sweet wife prods further.

Alex's head jerks up, but his lips are pressed together in a mix of surprise and doubt. His untrusting gaze stabs my heart, urging me to make a decision. To show him that not all grown-ups lie. I place the mugs back on the tray and get up from my chair.

"Why don't we check them out?"

I stride toward our study and briefly glance over my shoulder to find Rose and Alex following me.

I place the tray on the coffee table next to the small couch as Alex steps into the room, which is a library-slash-office for me and my couch girl.

His gaze jumps from my austere desk, where there's a lone laptop, to Rose's side on the other end of the room. Her desk is topped with two shiny silver monitors, her laptop, and an iPad. There are string lights on the wall, through which hang photographs of us and our family. Not to forget her superhero poster sitting proudly in the middle of the room.

"Wow, this looks like a time machine." My chest warms as Alex's voice fills with amazement.

I chuckle. "Rose does a lot of superhero stuff here."

"You do?" His gaze on my wife is almost reverent, making me bite back my smile, which slips upon hearing his next words. "Does that mean you can go back in time and bring my mom and dad back to me?"

Rose's breath hitches as her pained gaze shoots to me.

"I don't have any superpowers, Alex. I'm so sorry." She gets down on her knees and hesitantly holds Alex's hands. I know in her heart she's cursing herself for not being a superhero and being able to take away Alex's pain. That's how my girl is.

"Rose and I, we both grew up without our parents. We understand what you're going through, kid." I lightly stroke his hair, trying to tell him that we understand.

Alex looks up at me. "So, your mom and dad also died?"

"Mine did. But Rose got lost as a baby, and she found her parents only recently."

"You mean I can also find my mom and dad once I grow up?"

His hope-laced, innocent questions hurt my heart. I don't know how to reply to him, but thank God Rose has better answers for him.

"You'll find new parents who will love you so much."

"Everyone in the home says that, but no one wants me. I'm broken." He hitches up one leg of his pants, and there's a scar running from above his socks and hiding under his raised pant.

He must have been in the car with his parents.

Rose's eyes shine with tears as she tugs Alex's hand away, letting his pants fall down.

"You're not broken, Alex. Someday, you'll meet people who'll love you so much that you'll forget these painful months."

He doesn't look convinced, not even a tiny bit. Most likely because he's been told the same thing multiple times over the months.

A determined look crosses Rose's face. She gives me a last glance and then turns around. Hitching up her shirt just a tiny bit so that the scars on her waist are visible, she looks over her shoulder.

Confusion etches on Alex's face until he realizes what's in front of his eyes. He gasps. "You're broken too."

My fists clench, and my heart fucking tears out at the sight of Rose's scars as she shows Alex he isn't alone and forgotten. There are others too.

"I'm not broken, Alex, and neither are you."

When she turns to face him again, he throws his arms around her. "I don't want to be broken."

My eyes fucking well up, and my heart beats wild as hiccups tear through Alex's body. Maybe he doesn't need someone perfect but someone like us—a little broken like him.

"You're not, and you won't be." Rose's misty gaze meets mine, and I smile at my wife. My chest is filled with nothing but pride for her. As she wipes Alex's tears, I grab two Wolverine comics from her stash and place them in his hand.

A spark lights in his teary eyes. "These are really yours?" His gaze jumps between Rose and me. When Rose nods with a huge smile on her face, his hold on the books tightens. "Can I read them?"

"Only if you drink your hot chocolate first." I motion toward the coffee table, and Alex nods furiously before walking to the couch.

My gaze follows him as he places the comic books beside him and then grabs his mug before sipping the hot drink.

"He looks comfy," Rose whispers in my ear, her hand brushing against mine before she clutches it tight.

"You don't know how to cook?" Alex's raised eyebrows reach to the middle of his forehead. His stunned gaze skips from Rose to me as I beat the eggs for today's breakfast. "And *you* cook?" When I nod, he asks, "But you're also her boss, like the biggest boss in the office?" He repeats the words Rose just used to describe our work relationship.

I bite back my smile at his bewildered state.

Last night, after drinking hot chocolate and finishing one comic book, we brought him to the guest bedroom adjacent to ours. He hesitated, but when Rose told him that he could come to us anytime in the night, he finally got under the covers.

I left the light in the corridor on and also rechecked the motion sensors around the property. I hoped it wouldn't come to that, but I still didn't want a repeat of the previous night—Alex running around the streets of Cherrywood.

And thank fuck it didn't happen. He slept soundly. I checked multiple times, as sleep didn't come easy to Rose and me. We stayed up almost the whole night, hiding in each other's arms and remembering our own childhoods.

We were sipping coffee when Alex walked down the stairs this morning. His worried face relaxed when he found us, and it fucking warmed my heart knowing we built some trust with him in one night.

"Zander!" Rose's voice brings me back to now. "Your phone is ringing." Her confused face confirms this isn't the first time she's called my name.

"Sorry." I place the bowl of over-beaten eggs on the counter before grabbing a kitchen towel. Wiping my hands, I stride toward the sitting area. As soon as I pick up my phone, the ringing stops.

It was Officer Cole.

My heart leaps in my throat seeing his name.

I glance toward our open kitchen, where Rose and Alex are softly talking. Most likely, Rose is telling him more stories of our friends and family.

"I'll be back in a sec," I holler, and when Rose looks at me, I covertly tilt my head in Alex's direction before marching into our office.

I shut the door slowly and hit the dial button. "Good morning, Officer Cole. Sorry I missed your call."

"Good morning, Mr. Teager. I just wanted to inform you that in about an hour, I'll arrive with the headmistress to pick up Alex. Hope that's fine with you and your wife," he says. I hesitate for a second, and the good officer speaks up. "Mr. Teager, are you there?"

"Yeah. Yeah, I'm here."

"We'll see you soon."

My heart sinks as soon as the call is over. I suddenly feel a heaviness settling on my shoulders as I clomp toward the kitchen. But my feet halt halfway at the sight before me.

Rose has turned off the stove, and she and Alex are nibbling grapes from a bowl. Rose is saying something when her hand brushes Alex's hair off his forehead. Their discussion continues without either of them missing a beat, as if this is something they've done all their lives.

I know that after seeing Rose's scars, Alex has bonded with her. Maybe deeper than any other bond he could possibly form right now.

I'm about to tell them about our soon-arriving guests when they both turn toward me.

"Zander, we're hungry. Aren't we, Alex?"

A smile lights Alex's face as he nods. I can't fucking believe he's the same kid from yesterday. The words that are ready to slip out of my mouth stop in my throat. I want him to have this happiness for a little longer before I rob him of it.

AFTER WE POLISH off our breakfast, I know I can't hold off anymore. We'll soon have the headmistress at our doorstep, along with the police officer.

"Alex, do you remember Officer Cole?"

Upon hearing my question, the wide smile that was etched on his face slips. His hands slide from where they were playing with the fork, and he tucks them behind his elbows.

My fists tighten around the counter as Rose's hand slides toward the cuff of her shirt.

We all knew this was just for a night, Zander. Don't overthink.

"Officer Cole is coming with the headmistress from your home. She'll be here to pick you up soon. Why don't you get ready?" I blurt it out in a rush as helplessness courses through my body. I haven't felt like this in a long time, but my jaw clenches to a point of hurt as Alex mechanically gets up from the breakfast bar and heads up the staircase.

"Zander, he isn't happy there," Rose whispers as soon as he's out of earshot.

"We can't do much, couch girl. We're lucky Officer Cole let him come with us last night." I look away from her face, but she grabs my hand, and her serious gaze meets mine, stopping me in my tracks.

"But he likes it here." She stresses each word.

Before I can think more about what she's trying to tell me, the doorbell rings. I get up from my chair and press a kiss on Rose's forehead before going to open the door.

Officer Cole greets me with an older-looking woman who's wearing a simple floral-printed skirt, a white blouse, and a black cardigan. She fixes her glasses before her astute gaze meets mine.

"Mr. Teager, meet Ms. Dorothy Day. She's the headmistress at Alex's group home."

"I'm so thankful to you and your wife for bringing the boy to the hospital and taking him in for the night." Ms. Day shakes my hand before I lead them into the living room.

"It was no problem at all. We're happy we could help," I say when Rose joins us, and we all take our seats.

"He's a very sad and lonely child." The headmistress's words don't help the helplessness growing within me. "Did he give you any trouble?"

"No, not at all," Rose quickly responds. "We had lots of fun with him until—"

"He spoke to you?" Ms. Day interrupts as her eyebrows rise in surprise.

I nod, but before we can explain more, our conversation halts as Alex's soft feet hit the landing on the stairs. He stops at the last step and then stays there.

"Alexander. Why don't you join us and thank Mr. and Mrs. Teager for last night?" Ms. Day says.

Alex doesn't move, but his gaze shoots at us—Rose and me. It's as if someone just stabbed me with a thousand knives. He has transformed into the same shy, lonely kid from last night. The spark in his eyes from this morning is long gone.

Rose's hand clutches mine. Her fingernails dig into my skin as we watch her new friend slipping away.

I clear my throat before asking, "What happens next?"

"We have some more applications for foster parents. We'll try our best to find a happy home for Alex." Her smile doesn't reach her eyes.

I'm sure the accident and the subsequent injury must have brought their own set of problems for Alex. I don't know how many new parents are willing to look past that.

My heartbeat accelerates, knowing Alex might have no choice in picking his happy home.

"We should leave." Ms. Day gets up from the L-shaped couch.

Is it my imagination or did Alex take a step back? His hands clutch his backpack, which Rose dried last night after carefully slipping his things into a plastic bag with his help.

My wife walks to him, and his grip on the bag loosens.

"I have a small gift for you." She places the two comics in his hands, and Alex immediately hugs her legs. My heart clenches at the sight and then more when my wife looks at me over her shoulder. She's pleading with me for something, and I don't know how to give it to her.

"He isn't interacting with us at all, but it looks like your wife won him over." Ms. Day's words have more guilt rising inside me. She doesn't know there might be no one who'll understand Alex as well as Rose.

"Don't let me go." His words cut through my heart, and Ms. Day gasps. My gaze shifts to Officer Cole as his mouth falls open in shock.

Ms. Day recovers fast from her surprised state. "Alexander, please come here."

I walk toward Alex and Rose, just in time to hear him whisper to my wife. "Please, I don't like it there. I want to live with you."

"We shouldn't have let him go." Rose's finger digs into my wrist as we watch the police cruiser leave our property.

"Rose, we can't keep a kid at our place."

"Why the hell not?" Her gaze meets mine. I've never seen Rose challenge me or anyone else, and it takes me a while to let go of the shock.

"What are you asking, couch girl?" I pull her into my arms, not liking the distance between us. I also don't want to look into her blazing eyes. They accuse me of not doing the right thing.

"Zander, you know what I'm asking." Her body goes lax against mine. "Why can't we adopt him? Why can't he stay with us?" Her questions, her sobs on this gloomy, cloudy day as we stand on our porch, kill me.

"Calm down, Rose." I rub her back gently, urging her to take a deep breath. "We can't decide this on a whim, couch girl. It's an important decision, and it affects Alex's whole life."

"He thinks he's broken, Zander." Tears run down her cheeks as she looks up at me. "He thinks he's unlovable. He thinks no one's gonna love him." Her every sob, her every hiccup, hits me hard. "We can't leave him there, Zander. We can't, especially after knowing he was in an accident."

"Shh, babe. I'll talk to the headmistress. I'll do everything to make this right." I hold her in my arms, making a promise to her that Alex won't be a kid left alone and forgotten like us.

63

ALEX

Ms. Day walks into my room and explains to me that someone is coming to meet me tomorrow.

"I have a very good feeling you're finally going to go home." She holds my face before placing a kiss on my forehead and leaves.

This isn't the first time she's said that, so I know it's a lie. I never leave. I'll never find a home like the other boys here.

I look at the empty bed next to mine. Nick came here a month ago. His parents died like mine. But yesterday, he found new parents. They brought gifts for everyone.

I open my drawer and count the items inside it. There are five storybooks, three small cars, and two baseballs. All gifts I got when each of my friends found new parents.

I don't know how many more I'll get. Maybe I should ask Ms. Day for a bigger desk, because I know I'll never leave this place. No one can love me.

No one except Rose and Zander.

They're like me—broken. And they're also superhero fans.

I take out the comic books Rose gave me. She even wrote

my name on the inside in orange marker because I told her orange is my favorite color. She remembered.

I try to read, but I can't focus as I remember the taste of the hot chocolate Zander made. When I told him it's the most tasty hot chocolate I ever had, he said he didn't make it from "package shit."

I smile, remembering how Rose scolded him for using the s word. I laugh at the thought, like I laughed then when Zander held his ears and promised to never repeat the word.

THE NEXT MORNING, I brush my teeth, moving the toothbrush up and down, then front and back, just like my mom showed me. My mom also told me that we get bacteria that eat our teeth if we don't brush them properly. I don't want my teeth to be gone, because then I could only drink soup, and I hate soup.

I shower before taking out my yellow T-shirt. Ms. Day says I look very handsome in it. Maybe the new parents won't know I'm broken if they find me handsome. After combing my hair like Mom used to do, I smile in the mirror. Ms. Day says a smile wins the heart, so I should smile first and then shake hands before telling my name to the new parents.

"Ready, Alex?" Ms. Greta walks inside the room. "You look very handsome. Are you excited about meeting these people?"

I give her a nod. I don't know if I'm excited or not, but I don't want a bigger dresser drawer to store more gifts in. I want to leave this place with five storybooks, three small cars, and two baseballs.

Ms. Greta and I walk inside Ms. Day's office. The new people have their back to me, but I know the shirt. It's red and black, and hidden under it are scars like mine.

"Rose?" I whisper. "Zander?"

They both get up before turning around to face me. "Alex!" they say, almost in unison.

"What are you doing here?"

"We want to take you home," Rose whispers, her eyes shining with tears.

"*Your* home?" I hold my breath. *Please say yes!*

"And yours too." She opens her arms, beckoning me to her like my mom used to do.

I try to run, but my leg doesn't allow me to, and I fall down.

My heart falls to my stomach. *They know, Alex. They know you're broken.*

Rose rushes to me and then holds me in her arms. "Are you hurt?"

Tears run down my cheeks as I shake my head. "I can't run. I'm broken."

I hide my face from them.

They won't take me now.

They won't make me their boy.

But Zander puts his finger under my chin, making me look up at him. "You can't run *now*, but someday you'll win a race. I promise."

"Really?"

He nods and I believe him. Zander can do anything. He is a big boss, but he can also cook. That's his superpower—to do anything.

"You'll take me?" I ask him, and he nods. "And I'll never come back here?"

"Never. Unless you want to visit your friends," Rose replies, then her lips turn up in a smile.

"All my friends are gone. I never want to return."

"Oh, but I got some gifts for them." Rose shows me a big bag, opening it so I can take a peek. Inside are chocolates and toys.

"No!" I grab her hands in mine. "Please don't give this to anyone. Please." Tears race down my cheeks.

Her eyes widen for a second, and my heart beats fast. Like it used to when I could still run.

What did you do, Alex?

You have to smile. New parents don't like crying kids. Ms. Day told you this.

But this is Rose. She holds my face between her soft hands. Her fingers are cold like mine when they lightly touch my face. "I won't. I'll never do something you don't like, Alex," she promises me, and I know she isn't lying. Rose doesn't lie.

"I'll never do something you don't like, Rose," I whisper and Zander holds me in his arms.

"Then let's go to your new home."

I laugh, I cry, I smile when he throws me up in the air before placing me back in his arms.

I finally found my happy home.

THE END

NEXT BOOK - MARRYING HOPE

ZACH

Curious to know who steals Zach Teager's heart? I can tell you already it's five year old kid who calls our billionaire *Your Highness* and his single-mom, Hope, who takes care of Zach's sugary *needs* (wink wink).

She's a baker, ladies.

Read Marrying Hope, for free in Kindle Unlimited or buy a paperback on Amazon.

Check out the blurb below.

I fall in love with my husband and that's one thing he didn't promise me in our marriage vows.

A sinfully rich and wickedly hot businessman like *Zach Teager* has no business in my bland, rickety world.
Yet, he barges in like a storm, leaving everyone mesmerized by his charms.

Every evening I find him at my doorstep in the pretense of a silly promise he's made to my son.

And let's not talk about my boy, Ray who believes Zach is some sort of a Prince and maybe he is.
But not of my story.

Until events lead me to accept Zach's insane proposal of a contract marriage.
He promises me everything. Care for my mom. A better future for my son. A loving group of family and friends.
Except one thing. Love.

And that's okay.
I have full faith, I can never fall for someone as spontaneous and impulsive as him.
Yet, I do. Another stupid mistake to add in my long running list.
I fall for his stupid jokes, his crazy habits and most of all for him.

ALSO BY VIKKI JAY

Elixir Billionaires
Beautiful Rose (Zander & Rose)
Chasing Sophia (Asher & Sophia) novella
Marrying Hope (Zach & Hope)
Saving Vienna (Zane & Vienna)

The Kings World
Second True Love (Keith & Clementine)
Promised Love (Lukas & Autumn)
Protected Love (Gavin & Minnie)
Forever Love (Carter & Merida)

ACKNOWLEDGMENTS

This book would never have seen the light of the day if not for my best friend and husband. He has been extensively patient and beyond motivating while I smiled, laughed, growled, cried and threw several fits. Thanks, babe!

So many people have helped me in bringing this book to a state where I was confident enough to hit publish.

I cannot thank enough my editing team: Susan Barnes, Amy Briggs, Amanda Cuff (Word of Advice), Brandi Zelenka (My notes in the margin). A great thanks to my beta readers Amy and Kirsten. I'm very grateful for your valuable advice and feedback.

My amazing cover designer, Najla Qamber and her team has been god-send to me.

I also want to thank all the authors who have knowingly and sometimes unknowingly helped, inspired, motivated and guided me as I embark on my author journey.

And finally a huge Thanks to you, my amazing reader, for taking chance on a newbie author and my debut book.

Lots of Love,
Vikki.

ABOUT ME

In those early morning hours when I'm alone, my imaginations run wild and I pen down the life of people living in my head. All my life, I have lived in small towns in different parts of the world. The friendships, the camaraderie that people share around me inspired me to create Cherrywood and St. Peppers, the two towns where all my stories take place.

I write about beautiful coincidences, finding love in unexpected places and times, and fighting hard to get that happily ever after.

I reject to read, see, write anything that does not promise a HEA. My characters are sexy yet shy, strong yet reserved...

I am married to a man whom I fell in love at an age of 15, proposed him at an age of 23 and married at an age of 30. He has no clue what I write or do when he is snoring quietly in the next room.

You can find me on the different social media websites:

Facebook
Instagram
Bookbub
Goodreads

Printed in Great Britain
by Amazon